STAR WARS

AFTERMATH

LIFE DEBT

STAR WARS

AFTERMATH
LIFE DEBT

CHUCK WENDIG

BOOK TWO OF THE AFTERMATH TRILOGY

DEL REY

NEW YORK

Copyright © 2016 by Lucasfilm Ltd. & ® or ™ where indicated.
All rights reserved.

Published in the United States by Del Rey, an imprint of Random House, a division of Penguin Random House LLC, New York.

Del Rey and the House colophon are registered trademarks of Penguin Random House LLC.

ISBN 978-1-101-96693-8
ebook ISBN 978-1-101-96694-5

Printed in the United States of America on acid-free paper

randomhousebooks.com

2   4   6   8   9   7   5   3   1

First Edition

Book design by Christopher M. Zucker

To everyone whose heart
goes a-flutter every time
Han Solo steps onto the screen
or onto the page . . .

THE DEL REY

STAR WARS™

TIMELINE

I) THE PHANTOM MENACE

II) ATTACK OF THE CLONES
THE CLONE WARS (TV SERIES)
DARK DISCIPLE

III) REVENGE OF THE SITH
LORDS OF THE SITH
TARKIN
A NEW DAWN
REBELS (TV SERIES)
CATALYST: A ROGUE ONE STORY

ROGUE ONE

IV) A NEW HOPE
HEIR TO THE JEDI
BATTLEFRONT: TWILIGHT COMPANY

V) THE EMPIRE STRIKES BACK

VI) RETURN OF THE JEDI
AFTERMATH
AFTERMATH: LIFE DEBT
AFTERMATH: EMPIRE'S END
BLOODLINE
THE PERFECT WEAPON (EBOOK ORIGINAL)

VII) THE FORCE AWAKENS

A long time ago in a galaxy far, far away. . . .

STAR WARS™

AFTERMATH

LIFE DEBT

The Empire is in chaos. As the old order crumbles, the fledgling New Republic seeks a swift end to the galactic conflict. Many Imperial leaders have fled from their posts, hoping to escape justice in the farthest corners of known space.

Pursuing these Imperial deserters are Norra Wexley and her team of unlikely allies. As more and more officers are arrested, planets once crushed beneath the Empire's heel now have hope for the future. And no hope is greater than that of the Wookiees of Kashyyyk. Heroes of the Rebellion Han Solo and Chewbacca have gathered a team of smugglers and scoundrels to free Kashyyyk from its Imperial slavers once and for all.

Meanwhile, the remnants of the Empire—now under the control of Grand Admiral Rae Sloane and her powerful, secret adviser—prepare to unleash a terrifying counterstrike. If successful, the New Republic may never recover, and anarchy will be loosed upon the galaxy in its greatest time of need . . .

PRELUDE

JAKKU, THREE DECADES AGO

The boy runs. His footsteps echo across the hard, unforgiving ground. His feet have no shoes—they are wrapped in ratty bindings, the same bindings Mersa Topol uses to mend the wounds of those miners and scavengers who come to the anchorite nurse for succor. As such, the ground is rough beneath him. It bites through the thin cloth. It abrades. But he does not bleed, because his feet are tough even if many think him weak.

Clouds of dust kick up with every step. Scree hisses across rock.

The boy is chasing something: a pair of streaking contrails bisecting the dead sky. It comes from a ship that flew overhead, a strange ship like he had never seen. It gleamed black. Clean like shined, polished glass. He was out scrubbing solar arrays when he saw it pass overhead. One of the other orphan boys, Brev, said, "Look at the pretty ship, Galli."

Narawal, the girl with one dead eye, drew back her cracked and bleeding lips, responding with: "It won't stay pretty for long. Nothing stays pretty here." That, she says with some authority.

The boy had to see. He had to see the pretty ship before Jakku ruined it. Before the stone winds scoured its hull, before the sun baked off its color. Anchorite Kolob told him to stay behind, finish his chores, but the boy would have none of that. He was compelled, as if by destiny.

He ran. For one klick, then another, until his legs ached so hard they felt like clumps of cured, dried meat hanging from his hips. But now here he is, atop the Plaintive Hand plateau—an outcropping of bent, flat rock that the anchorites say is a holy place, a place the Consecrated Eremite considered home thousands of years before, when Jakku was supposedly a verdant, living place.

Out there, down in the valley, he spies the ship. Sun trapped in its perfect steel, the bright and blinding bands stark even in the light of day.

He thinks: *I could stop here.* In fact, he *should* stop here. The boy knows he should turn tail and go home, back to the habit house, back to his work and his contemplations and to the other orphans.

And yet he remains compelled. As if something invisible is tugging him along—an unseen thread bound to his throat, leading him like a leash-and-collar. *I will get a little closer. I won't be missed.*

The boy creeps down the narrow switchback path leading into the valley. At the bottom, all that separates him from the ship are dozens of rocky outcroppings: spires of crooked red stone jutting up out of the sand like broken, bloodied teeth. He moves from stone to stone, hiding behind each. Trying to stay silent, silent like the skittermice that cross the desert when night falls and the ground cools.

The ship roams into view. This is a ship that does not belong here. A dark mirror, long and lean, with swept-back wings and crimson windows. It sits, as silent and as patient as a perching raptor—like the vicious vworkka, the birds that swoop and eat the little skittermice.

The boy scurries from stone to stone until he is close. Close enough to smell the ozone coming off it. Close enough to feel the warmth of the sun radiating from its hull. A heat haze rises above it, warping the air.

Nothing moves. No sound comes from inside.

I have seen enough. I should go.

The boy remains rooted despite this thought.

Finally, a shudder and a hiss. A ramp descends from the ship's smooth underbelly. Vapor gases off into the heated air.

A figure eases down the ramp. The boy almost laughs—this someone must certainly be lost given the way that he is dressed. A long purple cloak drags behind him. A tall hat sits poised upon the man's head. Then the boy thinks: Some of the anchorites wear heavy robes like this, don't they? They say it tests them. It is sacred to learn how to withstand the heat. It is *necessary,* they say, to shun pain and learn to live beyond its margins.

Maybe this man is an anchorite. Though the anchorites avoid pretty, precious things, don't they? *No material entanglements,* they say. This ship, the boy believes, certainly qualifies as a material entanglement.

As do the droids that follow swiftly thereafter. Six of them. Each upright on legs shining like black, sun-blasted glass. Antennas rise from insectile heads, and the man in the purple robe waves them on without a word. Mouthpieces vocalize a series of tones and clicks just before they step out onto the hard, sand-scoured rock. The boy watches as they place down black boxes—boxes that connect to one another with beams of green light, beams bright enough to see even in the day, beams that connect to one another and form a kind of frame.

The man eases slowly down the ramp, his cloak whispering against the metal like sand blown across sheets of tin. "This is it. This is the space. Mark it and begin excavation. I will return."

One of the droids says, "Yes, Adviser Tashu."

There is a moment when the boy realizes that an opportunity has presented itself. He hates this world. He does not belong here. As the man in the purple robe returns up the ramp, he thinks: *This is my chance. My chance to leave this place and never return.* For a moment, he is frozen. Paralyzed by indecision. Affixed by the fear of uncertainty—he has no idea where this ship will go, or who that man is, or what they will do if they find him.

But he knows this place is dead.

The ramp begins to rise.

And the boy, Galli, thinks: *I must hurry.* And hurry he does. Fast and quiet like the skittermice. He bounds across the sand in his bare feet and catches the lip of the ramp as it closes. Galli tucks his body up and in, crawling into the dark moments before the ship begins to take off.

PART ONE

PART ONE

CHAPTER ONE

Leia paces.

The Chandrilan sun burns a bright line around her drawn shades. In the center of the room sits a blue glass holoplatform—it remains quiet. She comes here every day at the same time waiting for a transmission. She should've heard from Han by now. He's days past their scheduled talk and—

The platform flickers to life.

"Leia," says a shimmering hologram as it resolves from erratic voxels into the form of her husband.

"Han," she says, stepping close into transmission range. "I miss you."

"I miss you, too."

The way he says it, though—something's wrong. There's a dark edge to his voice. In it she senses desperation. No, not just that. Anger lurks there, too. The anger isn't pointed at her. Even from here her feelings reach out and find him, and she senses an anger turning inward, like a knife twisted toward one's own belly. *He's mad at himself.*

She knows what he's about to tell her.

"I still haven't found him," Han says. Chewbacca is missing. Two months back, Han told her that he had a shot to do what the New Republic wouldn't: liberate Chewie's home planet of Kashyyyk from the chains of the Empire. She told him to wait, to think about it, but he said the time was now and that an old smuggler had info—a woman named Imra whom Leia told him not to trust.

Turns out, she was right.

"You still in the Outer Rim?" Leia asks.

"Edges of Wild Space. I have a few leads, but it's not looking good."

She pleads with him: "Come home, Han. I'm working on the Senate. If we can get them to vote, we can push on Kashyyyk—and maybe find Chewbacca and the others in the process. Testimony from a general like yourself will help to sway them—"

"It didn't sway them before."

"So we try again."

The hologram shakes its head. "That's not who I am. I'm not a general. I'm just some pirate."

"Don't say that. Everyone here knows how you led the Alliance team on Endor. They know you as a general, not as a—"

"Leia, I resigned my commission."

"*What?*"

"I have to do this my way. This is on *me*, Leia. I have my job to do and you have yours. You take care of the Republic. I'll find Chewie."

"No, no, no, don't you do this. I'll come to you. Tell me where you are. Tell me what you need."

A slow, sad smile spreads across the face of his flickering transmission. "Leia, they need you there. *I* need you there, too. I'll be all right. I'll find Chewie. And then I'll come home."

"You promise?"

"I pro—"

But the hologram suddenly shakes—Han turns his head sharply, as if surprised. "Han!" she calls.

"Son of a—" he starts to say, but the image flickers again. "Under att—" But the words break up, and then the image dissolves and he's gone.

She feels her middle clench up. *No.* Again Leia paces, hoping he'll come back, hoping that the interrupted transmission returns again and he tells her it was all a false alarm. She waits for minutes, then for hours, and then until night falls. The holoplatform remains dead.

Her husband is out there. She doesn't know where.

And he's in trouble.

She has to find him. Good thing is, she knows just who to ask.

CHAPTER TWO

The grav-raft slides through the mist. Alongside stand massive stone spires, black as night and straight as spears. Vigilant sentinels, their tips are carved to look like howling faces. Below, far below, glow rivers of swimmy green light—the glowing fungus of Vorlag's cavernous interior.

Jom Barell reaches out, grabbing a chain and pulling the raft along, hand-over-hand. These chains sit moored to octagonal eyebolts jutting out of each spire, connecting each of those dark sentinels to the next. The raft has no engines of its own, and so its motion through the mist is nearly silent except for the faint throb of its hoverpanels.

"I don't like this," Jom says, his voice low.

"What's to like?" Sinjir Rath Velus asks, lying back across the flat of the raft, his arms crossed in front of him. "The mist is cold. The day is terrible. I'm sober as a protocol droid." He sits up suddenly. "Did you know the Death Star had a bar? Ugly, austere little place—really like all Imperial architecture, ugh—and the selection of spirits was hardly commendable. But if you knew Pilkey, the drink-slinger, he would give you some of his 'special batch'—"

Norra Wexley interrupts him. "Everything is fine. Everything is going according to plan." The essence of the plan is the same as it always is: Sneak in, capture their Imperial prey, bring him to justice on Chandrila. Of course, normally they're not sneaking into the mountaintop fortress of a galactic slaver to do it . . .

"Oh, yes," Jom answers in a sarcastic growl. "It's the idiot's array right here, isn't it? Our girl in there better be doing her job."

"She's not *our girl*," Sinjir says, snapping back. "She's not even *a* girl, Barell. Jas is her own woman, and the kind who would gladly kick your tail off this raft for sprinkling your . . . *mustache* dander everywhere."

"What she *is* is a bounty hunter." Jom grunts as he pulls the raft forward to the next stone pillar. "And I don't trust bounty hunters." Unconsciously his hand moves to his bushy mustache, which he quickly smooths down over his scowling mouth.

"Yes, we know. We also know that you don't trust ex-Imperials. We know that because you tell us. Constantly."

Jom turns his shoulder and sneers. "Should I? Trust you?"

"After all this time? You could start."

"Maybe you don't understand what the Empire meant to people like me, and why the Rebellion—"

Norra again cuts them off. "We get it, Jom. We're all on this boat together. In this case, literally. Look." She points.

To their starboard, a massive shape emerges from the mist above them—a black, mountainous shadow. The contours of a palace: spiraling towers and bulbous parapets. If they keep following the chain bolted to the rocks, they'll begin to lift as they pull—up, up, up, to the front gates of this massive compound carved out of the top of a dormant volcano. It's the home of Slussen Canker, aka Canker the Red, aka His Venomous Grace, Keeper of Men and Killer of Foes, the Prince and First Son of Vorlag, Master Scion Slussen Urla-fir Kal Kethin-wa Canker.

Murderer. Slaver. Scumfroth.

He's not their target.

Their target is an ex-Imperial vice admiral. A man named Perwin Gedde. He fled the Empire, absconding with a considerable bucket of credits—enough to keep him fat and happy and firmly ensconced with a crime lord like Slussen Canker. High on spice. Serviced by slaves. Living the good life. Living the *protected* life here in a well-defended volcano-top fortress. So well defended that marching right up to the front gate would be highly inadvisable. The front gate is protected by two slavering hroth-beasts. And two phase-turrets. And a pair of hroth-keeper guards. *And* a portcullis made of crisscrossing lasers—

It doesn't matter, because they're not going that way, are they?

They're not taking the high road. They're going low.

As Jom eases the raft down two more stone pillars, he reaches back with his hand and shows his open palm—a silent request that Norra refuses to fulfill. Instead she says, "I can handle this. You don't have to do everything, you know."

She pulls the grappling spike and screws it into the tip of the concussive pistol. Jom watches her with narrow eyes as she takes aim at the massive rock. "Give the signal," she says.

Sinjir holds up an emergency beacon—the one that came with their ship, the *Halo,* for use in case it ever crashes—and he gives it three quick pulses. Red light flashes in quick succession.

Moments pass. Then, through the mist—

Three more red flashes in return. These come from the base of the rock mountain underneath the fortress. "Jas, you glorious spiky-headed freak," Sinjir says, cackling and clapping his hands.

Norra shushes him and fires the grappling spike toward the space where the three flashes lit up the mist. The gun is quiet enough. It barks out a *paff!* sound as it goes off. The cable looped under the raft whizzes and spins as the spike zips through the air.

In the distance: *clink.* Pay dirt.

Jom grabs the cable and pulls the raft now in a new direction—not toward the gates of the fortress but to its underbelly. Out there should be a breach in the mountain, which their intel marks as Slussen Can-ker's hroth-beast feeding room. The awful things have wings and like to hunt in the air a few times a day—and that is their staging point. The mountain breach is open to the air, with a ledge beneath it, and the hroth-beasts are kept inside by another crackling laser portcullis. Except, right now, that portcullis is down thanks to Jas, who came here several days ago. The signal pulsing through the darkness is clear: *The way is open.*

"Told you she'd do us right," Sinjir whispers in Jom's ear.

Jom's only reply is a dubious grunt.

The raft eases through the mist. Ahead, the way into the mountain comes more clearly into view: It's like a yawping mouth with stalactite and stalagmite fangs waiting to swallow them up. No red glow, though. The gate is down. The way is truly clear. Jom pulls the raft over, cinches the cable up, and loops it around one of the rocks. One by one they step off the raft and into the cavernous space.

The smell hits them hard. Along the wall are metal bins heaped high with dead things: birds plucked of feathers and missing their heads, gobbets of rotten meat from who-knows-what-animal, hoofed legs, quivering offal. Clouds of hungry gnats swarm in the air in the space above. *This must be food for the hroth-beasts,* Norra thinks. Given the red splatters along the dry rocky ground, she surmises that someone stands here and throws the meat out into the air—and the beasts go flying to catch it.

Sinjir says, "I am quite seriously considering throwing up."

"That smell," Jom says, making a face. "It'd knock a monkey-lizard sideways." He frowns. "Where's Jas?"

"She must be farther in," Norra says. "Come on."

The plan is simple enough: Jas Emari snuck in here days before under the auspices of being a bounty hunter looking for work. Which is true enough, and her reputation surely has preceded her by this point. Crime lords attract bounty hunters the same way these piles of carcass-meat attract flies: Hunters are hungry for work and crime bosses are quick to supply it.

She opened the gate for them. And now the work begins. They already have a layout of the fortress, thanks to the holo-cron supplied by (well, stolen from) Surat Nuat, the Akivan boss who had been keeping tabs on the connections between Imperials and the criminal underworld in case he one day needed the leverage. They've been mining that data cube for information—it served, in fact, as a springboard to launch their little team.

Once they leave the feeding room (an exit that cannot be quick enough for Norra's nasal passages), it should be a short skip down a long tunnel to a lava tube that runs up the length of the fortress. Of course, the tube also leads down into the belly of this slow-simmering volcano, which means they should be careful not to fall. Climb up to the south tower, wait for Gedde to emerge from or head to his chambers—then bag him, tag him, and drag him. The goal is to get him onto the raft and out of the palace before anybody even notices. Then they'll serve him up to the Republic Tribunal. Justice comes to the Empire. One war criminal at a time.

Then Temmin will bring in the ship and hopefully they exit the atmosphere before anyone even knows Gedde is gone.

Temmin. Her thoughts turn to her son. Poor, fatherless boy. He's part of this team and not a day goes by without her fearing he shouldn't be. *He's too young,* she tells herself, even though he proves himself every day. *He's too precious,* she thinks, which is more true than the other thing—now that she and her son are reunited, she is reminded how vulnerable he is. How vulnerable *all* of them are. Dragging him along for the ride seems entirely irresponsible of her as a parent, and yet a greedy, selfish part of her offers the cold reminder that the only other option would be to once more discard him. Leaving Temmin behind again would kill her. But what other choice would she have? Retire? Give up this life?

Why is that not an option for you? she asks herself.

Now is not the time to ponder it. They have work to do.

She heads toward the tunnel, Jom and Sinjir following close behind—

A lightning crackle rises behind them. Followed by a red glow.

The portcullis is back. A mesh of lasers, crackling against one another. The searing red cuts through the cable mooring the raft to the rock, and it suddenly drifts into the mist. "No!" Jom cries out.

Ahead of them, the scuff of heels.

Figures and forms fill their escape. The fortress guards—thugs of varying size and breed, heads hidden behind rusted faceplates. Four of them stand there, blasters pointed. Jom draws. So does Sinjir. Norra's about to reach for the pistol at her own hip—

A loud throat-clearing comes from behind the guards.

A Vorlaggn steps out. Skin like the cracked char on a piece of fire-cooked meat. Clear fluid suppurating from between those fissures, fluid he dabs at with a filthy brown rag. He blinks his three hollow-set eyes.

Slussen Canker.

His tongue clicks and clucks and when he speaks, his voice is wet and rheumy, as if the words must push their way past some kind of bubbling clot. "I see you thought to intrude upon the peace established by His Venomous Grace, Slussen Canker. Slussen does not like you here. Slussen finds your trespass very rude, in fact."

Norra thinks for a moment that this *isn't* Slussen, then, but something Jas said pings the radar of her memory: The Vorlaggn speak in the third person, don't they? Strange habit.

Jom keeps his pistol up. "We're not here for you."

"We're here for Gedde," Sinjir says. "Just toss him our way and we'll stop intruding upon this *lovely* ordure pile you call a palace. Hm?"

The Vorlaggn gurgles. "Slussen will give you nothing. Gedde?"

From around the corner, their target emerges. The vice admiral himself. A man also said to have been in charge of one of the Empire's more brutal biological weapons programs. Testing various *ancient diseases* on captive worlds, raining sickness from the battleships above.

He is thin everywhere but for the pale belly pooching out from his unbuttoned—and filthy—gray shirt. His skin is the sallow and pitted flesh of a spice addict. A man lost to his addiction.

Gedde is not alone.

He yanks someone hard toward him—

It's Jas. He has her by the back of the neck, a pistol held to her temple. She wrenches her head away, but he wrenches it right back.

"Slussen has captured your bounty hunter. If you do not drop your weapons, Slussen will have your bounty hunter's head perforated by blasterfire, and her brains will go to feed the hroth-beasts."

Sinjir sighs. "Blast it." His pistol clatters to the floor.

Norra gently unsnaps her holster and lets it fall.

Jom keeps his pistol up. "I don't surrender my weapon. In Spec-Forces, we learn that our weapon is who we are. I can no more surrender it than I can surrender my own arm or my—"

The hand moves fast—Sinjir grabs the gun from the top and wrenches it out of Jom's hand, flinging it against the wall. "They've got Jas, you oaf."

The guards creep into the room and fetch the weapons.

Gedde licks his lips and grins. "You rebel fools. We'll sell you to the Empire and I'll buy myself a full pardon—"

Irritated, Jas pulls away from him and bats the gun from her head. "I think you can stop pointing that at my skull now."

At first, Norra thinks: *Here's our chance.* Jas is free. But her freedom came easy. *Too* easy. No fight at all except the irritation on her face. The realization hits her like a wall of wake turbulence: Jas betrayed them.

Jas steps away from Perwin Gedde, her hands tucked casually in her pockets. "Sorry, team," she says, that last word spoken with a special kind of sarcasm. "Can't change my horns, can't change my ink, can't change who I am." She shrugs. "They offered a better bounty. In fact, this deal is a pretty good one—" She pulls out a datapad and tosses it to Norra.

Norra catches it.

With trembling fingers she lights the screen:

On it, she spies a bounty.

It's *their* bounty. She sees their faces. Her *son's* face among them.

"You conniving little bilge-bug," Barell seethes. "I trusted you."

"No, you didn't," Jas says. "And you shouldn't have. I'm going to do very well with this. Not only is Gedde paying me for alerting him to the attempt to capture him, the Vorlaggn here is going to pay me a twenty percent finder's fee—"

"Slussen said fifteen."

"Well. A girl can try. A *fifteen* percent finder's fee for your bounty."

"Jas, don't do this," Norra pleads.

Sadness crosses Jas Emari's face. "I'm sorry. But I have bills to pay. Bills that are coming due, and the Republic just isn't keeping me flush." Then she gives a flip little salute and says: "It was fun while it lasted."

Jas exits the room.

Gedde laughs. "Let's get you into some cages, shall we?"

Sinjir is not fond of cages. Especially ones that dangle over an open precipice, regardless of whether it's here on Vorlag or back on Akiva in Surat Nuat's dungeon. These cages are boxy things like caskets stood on their end, hanging from black rock outcroppings not far from the gateway to the hroth-beast feeding room. Mist gathers. Fungal light crosses beneath them in sharp, bright lines.

"Still feeling good about your friend?" Jom calls. His cage hangs from another overhang about ten meters away. "Still think I should trust her?"

"I do," Sinjir says, thrusting his chin out defiantly.

And that surprises him more than a little.

He doesn't trust *anyone*. And yet here he is, certain as the stars that this is all part of some *secret plan,* one the others just don't see.

A little voice tells him it's because he's so very good at reading body language. It's his job to dissect people with but a glance, cutting them down to all their treacherous little atoms. And another competing voice warns him that maybe, just maybe, he missed something about Jas Emari.

But that doubt is drowned in a washtub of his own confidence, and he feels oddly *sure* about her. So he says as much to them: "She'll get us out of this yet, wait and see."

Jom grunts. "Keep dreaming, Imperial."

"Whether she's playing us or playing them, we can't count on her to save us," Norra says. Her cage hangs on the other side of Sinjir's and she wraps her fingers around the iron. "We have to get out of here ourselves. They're going to sell us to the Empire. We can't let that happen."

"I think we already let that happen," Jom grouses. Then he leans forward against the cage, staring out. "What even *is* the Empire anymore? Who controls it? Who will pay for us?"

That is a question Sinjir has been asking himself. At first, it surprised him how swiftly the Imperial forces crumbled. Though over time it puzzled him less and less. The unity of the Empire existed because all its chains and threads were held fast in a singular grip: the hand of the Emperor. With the Emperor gone, who was to hold it all together? Rumor said Vader had been taken out, too. So who then? The admirals? The moffs? They were always rats kept in line by the cats, and now there are no cats.

No clear chain of succession was evident. Palpatine had no family of which to speak, at least as far as anyone knew. Vader didn't have family, either (and for all Sinjir knows, wasn't even human anymore). And with two Death Stars gone, a significant portion of the Empire's best and brightest were snuffed out, too. The New Republic seized that opportunity. The Rebellion was gone, and a new government grew swiftly—if clumsily—in its place.

That left the Empire scrambling in survival mode. No clear leadership because, most likely, they were fighting over it. And day by day, the Imperial forces peel away—defeated, destroyed, abandoned, or stolen.

Sinjir imagines that the Empire as a whole was not all that different from how he himself was on the forest moon of Endor that fateful day—dizzied, bloodied, surrounded by bodies. Unsure of where to go next or what to do or what by all the stars even to *believe in* anymore.

A crisis of faith and purpose. That's what it is.

Sinjir still suffers his crisis. The New Republic has not been an answer. This team has been an answer, somewhat, though now with his friend's betrayal he feels back on the edge of things. The question of faith and purpose is left hanging. And no answer is easily seen.

The Empire will need its answer, too—and if it doesn't find one in time, it will be destroyed. Deservedly, he decides.

I need a drink, he also decides.

Not far away, the familiar buzz of the laser gate suddenly goes silent—leaving everything eerily quiet. But only for a few moments.

Soon a new sound arises: chuffing snorts and moist gibbers. Out of the yawning mountainside opening, gobbets of meat launch out into the mist.

Hroth-beasts follow fast. Red, leathery creatures with long wings and a dozen legs leap into the void, chasing the falling offal. Ducking and diving. Their faces are hardly faces at all: just squirming, eyeless piles of polyps and tubules. A fleshy mass that looks more like fungus and less like anything you'd find attached to an animal. Out there, a trio of the things swoop and roll, catching meat thrown to them. And then soon, the meat stops.

But nobody brings the beasts back inside.

The hroth-beasts soar higher. Still hungry, maybe.

Or worse, Sinjir thinks: *They're bored.*

And we may make very good playthings.

As if on cue, one swoops down right toward Sinjir's cage—and *wham,* it slams into it with the weight of a flung vaporator. The beast clings to the side of the cage, pressing its tentacular mess through the grate. Sinjir has just enough room to stab out with his foot—and the tendrils grab his boot and suck it right off his foot. The beast makes greedy nursing noises as it tries to . . . eat the boot? Disgruntled, the creature mewls and gurgles, flinging its head to the side. The boot sails into the vapor.

Jom yells through cupped hands: "Don't let it touch you. Those things on its face are full of stingers. You'll go numb."

Blast. Sinjir presses himself against the back of the cage as the thing probes and bangs its head and fore-claws against the metal.

As its teeming masses of tendrils push through the grates like worms, Sinjir spies something shiny under its neck. Something hanging there by a chain. It looks like—

A key. A dark metal octagonal key. Just like the one used to lock them in here in the first place.

Well, that's curious.

Suddenly the creature flies away, sailing once more into the mist.

No, no, no!

That key—

Certainly Slussen's men didn't put it there, did they? They don't seem smart enough for such cruel games. Which means the key is secret, but intentional. Which means the key is from someone who wants them free.

"Jas," Sinjir whispers under his breath, suddenly giddy. It's just like in Surat Nuat's dungeon—him trapped and her acting as the one to free him yet again. An oddly comforting pattern, that. A classic move! Sinjir moves to the front of the cage and presses his hands through the tight spaces—his arms will fit through up to the elbow, and he waves his appendages around like an animal in distress. "Hey! *Hey!* You flying sacks of slime! Here, here! Don't I look delicious? *Mmm.* Don't I look like a tasty—"

Whonnnng. The same one swoops up from below, unseen. Tubules gather around his left arm, and it's like being electrocuted—the limb tingles at first and then suddenly feels like a thousand little pins are pricking it all at once. Sinjir screams, but maintains. With his free hand, he darts out and snatches the key from around the thing's neck with pinching fingers, then wrenches his hand out of that writhing mass of tentacles.

Whining through gritted teeth, he quickly peels back the now ragged tatters of his sleeve—the arm is red, blistering, swelling up.

And, as Jom predicted, totally numb. He shakes it, trying to urge feeling back into the limb.

Sinjir resists the desire to immediately unlock the cage and—

Well, then what, exactly?

Leap into the void?

Jump onto one of these things and try to ride it?

Those sound like very good ways to die. And Sinjir is all about not dying. He's not entirely sure what he's living for, not yet, but *not dying* is a very fine start. He whispers to himself: "Patience, old boy. *Patience.*"

He waits. The beasts harass Norra and Jom, too, slamming into the cages, the metal banging against the mountainside behind them. Sinjir wants to yell to the others to check for keys—but Slussen's guards, the beast-keepers, could be listening. Eventually, the hroth-beasts tire of trying to eat the wriggling meat inside the unyielding metal exoskeletons, and soon the beast-keepers offer a shrill whistle. The beasts leap and swoop back into the cave from whence they came.

And then the familiar buzz of the laser gate returns.

Now is the time.

Sinjir thrusts his one good arm outside the cage, the key held firm in his grip. It takes a bit of fumbling, but he manages to spin the key around and get it in the lock—a quick turn and the door springs open.

Its hinges squeak as the cage hangs in open air. Now what?

"Uhh," he says, clearing his throat. "Some help here?"

Jom and Norra both turn, mouths agape.

"Is your cage open?" Jom asks.

"*Obviously,* it is," Sinjir snarks. "It's not exactly a hallucination." Under his breath he adds: "I hope."

"How?" Norra asks.

"A key. Jas left me a key. Wound around the neck of one of those . . . awful flying things. It, uhh, it was helpful, but . . ." He leans out of the cage, holding on with his one good arm. The other remains without any feeling at all—that limb hangs at his side like a broken branch still dangling from its tree. "Well, let's just say my next steps are a bit up in the air."

"We don't know it was her," Jom barks. "Coulda been one of the slaves. They have a vested interest in getting free."

Yes, Sinjir thinks, *but that's not precisely our task here, is it?* Perhaps it should be, but it's not.

Plucking the key from the lock, he places it between his teeth and bites down hard. Then Sinjir reaches up and grabs the top of the cage. He uses the bands of the metal cage like ladder steps and clambers to the top. The cage swings beneath him and he almost loses his footing—but he reaches up and balances himself against the rock from which the cage dangles. Up above that rock is a ledge just narrow enough for one. That ledge is how they got down here in the first place: Two of Slussen's guards shimmied the cage along, hooked it to the chain, then dropped it down—a plunging fall that for Sinjir at least resulted in the feeling of his teeth cracking together and his innards launching up into his throat.

Breathe in, breathe out.

Imperial fitness mandates kept him in pretty good shape. But after going AWOL, he . . . admittedly let himself go a bit. Got a bit thinner, let his muscles go slack. And it's not like the New Republic demands much—they've no regimen in place. They don't have much in place, yet.

"You can do it," Norra says. Ever the cheerleader. Ever the group's collective mother. Funny thing is: It works. He believes her.

I can do this.

He reaches up to the rock above and palms around until he finds a viable handhold. There. He swings his dead arm up just in case it somehow stirs the damn thing to life—but it's for naught. Upside: Feeling is coming back into that arm. Downside: That feeling is a fiery, prickling pain.

He must do it with the one arm then. Sinjir pulls himself up, feet scrambling fruitlessly against the chain . . . already his arm aches—it burns at the socket, feeling like the whole thing is gonna rip out. Like he's a doll being played with by an overenthusiastic child.

And then half his torso is up. He shimmies his way up. Panting.

The ledge isn't far—it only requires a step up. Easy enough for one with long limbs such as he.

"C'mon, c'mon," Jom growls.

If Sinjir weren't gasping for air with a key locked between his teeth, he'd say: *Sass me again, you gruff thug, and I'll leave you here for the Empire.* Instead he manages to offer up a three-fingered gesture that he has been *assured* is offensive on many Outer Rim worlds. Something about one's mother and a gravity well.

To spite Jom—and because it's sensible—he goes to free Norra first. Sinjir creeps along and reaches down, letting the key dangle in his hand.

Norra reaches up and grabs it.

In a few minutes, she's got her cage open and she's up on the ledge with Sinjir. Then it's Jom's turn—and soon Sinjir's least favorite person in all the galaxy is *also* free, joining them on the ledge.

"Now what?" Sinjir asks, idly poking at his less numb, now hurting arm. "If I recall, there is a crisscrossing laser portcullis that is quite likely to turn us all into bloody cubes."

Jom thinks. "Look, c'mere, look." He gets to the edge of the ledge, which takes them right up to the border of the crackling gate. "Usually these things are a closed-loop system. The beams emerge from these emitters—" He points at the rusted emitters bolted to the dark mountainside. They look like the tips of blasters, almost. "I need a rock."

Norra searches around, finds one by her feet. "Here."

Jom palms it, reaches out, and bashes it against the emitter. Nothing happens. He hits it again, and again, and then really seems to put his all into it, roaring as he slams the rock down—and then the rock rebounds out of his hand and plummets into nowhere.

It seems like he's failed. Sinjir sighs and both he and Norra start looking around for another rock, finding none . . . but then the emitter suddenly sparks and swings loose, hanging by one bolt.

The laser gate fizzles and goes dead.

And like that, the way is clear.

One by one, they make their way back into the only room of the fortress they've managed to see—the hroth-beast feeding room. The stink again assaults them. Sinjir tries very hard not to heave.

"So now what?" he says, his voice nasal as he smashes his own nose flat with the back of his good hand. "Do we have a plan? Jas is still here, somewhere, and that means—"

"It means nothing," Jom says. "We don't know it was her. So we do what the plan always entailed: We go up the lava tube, get Gedde, and—"

"I can't go up that tube. My arm is dead. I'm tired."

"You need to be in better shape, Rath Velus."

"I'm sorry, do we or do we not live in a universe where I just saved your brutish mug? Because—oh, I'm sorry, I assumed you would be kissing my one uncovered foot right now, and yet here you are, giving me grief."

Norra steps in between them. "Sinjir, you hunt around for a comm. They took ours, so we don't have any way to call Temmin or Jas or— well, anybody. We'll come back this way and—"

From outside the room, voices and footsteps. Jom says: "We got incoming. And we don't have any weapons—"

With the voices comes another familiar sound:

Grunts, barks, gibbers.

Hroth-beasts. *Damn.*

The animals are followed by Slussen's guards—drawn here presumably by the noise. Or maybe they somehow learned the gate was down. Either way, they come hard-charging in, blasters up, hroth-beasts on long leather leashes. Their tendrils search the air.

But Norra thinks fast—and *moves* fast, too. She's already over by the bins of rotting meat, and Sinjir watches in awe (and disgust) as she starts throwing it. One by one she pelts the guards with rotten meat, their blasterfire going astray as rancid flesh hits them in the face, chest, and arms.

The stink of the meat is too tantalizing to resist.

Brilliant, Sinjir thinks as the beasts turn on their owners. The monsters attack, slathering their screaming keepers with their wet tendrils in a desperate search for gobbets of rank meat.

"Move!" Jom calls, and they hurry past the scene of carnage.

The lava tube is tight, but not so tight they don't have a little room to move. The tube itself is ridged and scalloped, giving them handholds and toeholds as they climb. Norra and Jom easily brace themselves and shimmy up the long channel. Slowly but surely.

Below them, far down, glows a pinprick of bright-orange light.

Don't fall, don't fall, don't fall, she repeats to herself like a mantra. That fall would not be a pleasant one. A slide down the porous volcanic stone would scrape half her skin off just in time for her to plunge into a searing-hot magma bath. Cooking her raw. Scorching her dead.

These tubes are how Slussen heats his fortress, it seems—the air coming up is like hot breath from a hellish monster. Sometimes they find adjacent tubes branching off at perpendicular angles. And when they pass, they hear the sounds of distress going through Slussen Canker's palace—voices raised, an alarm called. *We don't have long.*

Up, up, up. Her arms and legs aching. Jom telling her to keep moving—she wants to tell him, *I'm not cut out for this,* but she has to be. It's too late to be anything else, and so she pushes, and when her hands finally reach the lip of the last branching tube—it feels like forever has passed. She pulls herself up and slides out, stone abrading her stomach as she lands in a lavish (and hideous) room, panting.

Norra looks up. Black walls are decorated with gaudy golds and borzite mirrors. A statue of Slussen stands in the corner, carved out of fire-red kwarz crystal. The bed is octagonal, like the key that unlocked their cages—and it's piled with animal skins and pillows of red leather. Such wealth is alien to Norra. And in a place like this, it has clearly gone to waste.

"Good, you're here."

Norra's heart about hops out of her throat as she hears Jas's voice from the corner of the room, out of sight. She turns and sees the bounty hunter sitting there in a high-back chair, legs crossed, arms crossed, and one Imperial vice admiral lying at her feet. Gedde's hands are bound behind him with wire. His mouth is gagged with what looks to be a pillowcase, wadded and rolled and knotted behind his head.

From the lava tube, Jom emerges. He instantly sees the Zabrak and, once on his feet, marches toward her, growling in rage.

"You almost got us killed—"

"I got us all saved *and* paid *and* I'm getting the job done. We can talk about this later—" She grabs the comm at her belt and speaks into it. "Temmin, we need an extraction. Still in the tower. You'll know the sign." When she puts the comm back on her hip, she asks: "Where's Sinjir?"

"Downstairs looking for a comm," Norra says.

Jas makes a face like that personally wounds her. "That . . . is a complication. I'll go find him and meet you at the feeding room."

From outside the room, the rumble of footsteps. The door to this chamber is a round, gilded portal sealed with an electrical panel— a panel that has been torn out, its wires dangling and still sparking. Someone pounds on the door. From the other side, a muffled voice:

"Slussen wants to know: Is Gedde in there?"

Gedde doesn't even seem to hear. His eyes are bloodshot. The pupils are big and fat and he doesn't even blink. From behind his gag, the Imperial makes faint cooing and gurgling noises. Norra realizes: He's high. Nearby sits a small tin—once again, octagonal in shape—of dark spice.

From the other side of the door: "Slussen commands this door to open." The whine of a drill rises. *They're going to take the door off.*

"How are we getting out of here?" Norra asks. "The tube?"

"That's the way I'm going," Jas says. "But the two of you are going out that way." When she says *that way,* she points to the massive bow window at the far side of the room.

Norra is about to protest but to her surprise, Barell says:

"I like that. Let's get it open."

Jas says, "The *Halo* should be incoming. See you soon." And without further word, she slips back down the lava tube.

Barell and Norra head to the window. Jom feels along, looking for hinges, a latch, something, anything. Norra tells him she can't find any and he agrees—and then goes to pick up the chair Jas had been sitting in only moments before. Without further comment, he flings it through the window.

Kssh!

The chair punches a hole through the glass, then is gone.

He kicks out the rest of the glass, framing it with his boot.

Out there, above the fog and near the peaks of other dark mountains, Norra spies a ship—an SS-54 gunship. The *Halo*.

Temmin.

"Tell Vice Admiral Gedde his ride has arrived," Norra says. Then she makes the mistake of looking down. Vertigo assails her. "And tell him I hope he's not afraid of heights."

The *Halo* bangs and rattles as it skips across the mists of Vorlag. The ion engines on each side are spun horizontal, screaming loud as the gunship—classified by its manufacturer, Botajef Shipyards, as a light freighter in order to avoid regulations—punches forward. Ahead, the volcanic fortress of Slussen Canker rises out of the fog, its bent and twisting towers like charred fingers reaching for the heavens as if to pull them down.

Temmin sits at the controls, the flight sticks pushed all the way forward. This ship isn't as fast as an X-wing, but it has *power*— especially given the modifications that Temmin made to the engines. The thing moves with weight and purpose, and it has his blood pounding in his temples like Akivan drums. He cracks his knuckles and snaps his fingers: a nervous habit picked up from his father.

"You ready?" he asks his copilot.

"ROGER-ROGER," chimes the B1 battle droid, Mister Bones: a bodyguard and pal who has seen more than a few "special modifications" all his own. The droid, painted in red and black, has the cut of a human skeleton topped with the skull of a rock-vulture—and Temmin has only worked to make the droid more intimidating as time has gone on. Jagged metal cut out of the front to look like teeth. Hands sharpened into claws. His frame now features half a dozen extra joints to allow the droid a degree of contortion unseen in the already collapsible B1s. Gone are the little bones that decorated him—their mission these days necessitates stealth, and Jas said the wind-chime rattle of those bits would be a problem. Temmin was reluctant, but he listened. He likes Jas. He trusts her. If she said stealth matters—

Then stealth matters.

Of course, right now, stealth is about ten klicks back, isn't it?

"I AM EAGER TO ERADICATE OUR ADVERSARIES," Bones says, his voice warped and warbling. "I HOPE TO TURN THEM INTO A FINE RED MIST. JUST SAY THE WORD, MASTER TEMMIN." The droid has his claws wrapped around the gun controls. The *Halo* packs a wallop: twin-mounted ZX7 laser cannons hanging below the well-armored front cockpit, and at the top, a quad cannon railthrower mounted to a jury-rigged turret. Right now, though, the mission is extraction, not chewing the landscape apart with weapons fire, so Temmin tells his pal to cool down.

Bones nods and hums to himself, skull moving in time with the tune.

"Here we go," Temmin says, and he eases the engines, then pivots them vertical, letting the *Halo* hover. There he spies the second-tallest tower in the fortress—its window busted open.

His mother—looking nervous and agitated—waves him forward.

He gives an okay and then slides the gunship sideways so that the access ramp is pointed toward the tower. "Bones, go help. I'll keep us steady." The droid springs up, does a handspring over the seat, and then whirls out of the cockpit and into the belly of the *Halo*.

Temmin flips the screen to the access cam, and he extends the ramp—the side of the ship peels away and becomes an entry hatch.

Bones helps Norra carry their prisoner on board. Jom takes his own running leap and clears the space easily.

But then something hits the side of the ship, rocking it.

What the—?

He glances at the cam again and sees chaos: a shape scrambling against the access ramp. Some kind of creature. Its face is just a sloppy pile of something that looks like soft, searching fingers. Bones pirouettes, his claw snapping back as the concealed vibroblade along the long metal bone of his forearm springs forward. He slices it upward, cutting through the tangle of tendrils before punting the thing out of the ship.

Two more appear where the first one fell.

And then the *Halo*'s scanner beeps as something pings it.

Four red blips. Coming in from aft.

He checks the signatures—one Imperial shuttle and a trio of TIEs. He yells back: "Who invited the Empire to the party?"

His mother answers as she sidles into the cockpit: "Slussen Canker did. And Gedde, hoping to buy his way out of whatever punishment awaits an AWOL vice admiral." Then she explains to him where Jas and Sinjir are. "We need to go pick them up."

"And if they're not there?"

"Then we wait."

Suddenly there's Jom's head through the door—and he's scowling and sneering and Temmin knows what he's going to say. He's going to say, *We leave them behind, they aren't the mission,* because that's how he is. Everything is the mission. And he sure doesn't like Jas and Sinjir, does he?

So that's why it's a surprise when he says: "No one left behind."

Temmin grins. "Not even an Imperial and a bounty hunter?"

"Not when it's *our* Imperial and *our* bounty hunter. Let's go."

Temmin banks the ship away from the fortress. The scanner shows the shuttle and TIEs incoming fast on his tail.

He has an idea. He boosts the ship forward, giving it a hard kick from the engines before putting it back to hover again. His mother protests: "Temmin, don't stop. Keep this ship moving!"

"I know what I'm doing," he says, spinning the *Halo* around 180 degrees.

"Temmin. *Temmin!*"

Ahead, the TIE fighters shriek forward, cutting the air like razors—they start to swoop in low toward Slussen's fortress. Already the air is peppered with laserfire, and the blasts pock the front of the *Halo*.

Now, Temmin thinks.

He takes control of the guns with a flip of a switch, then turns the rail-throwers forward and up—his fingers squeeze the triggers. Thin, nanofiber rail-tubes rattle off, the cannon firing them at hundreds of rounds per second. They chew through the black rock tower. Stone coughs up in chips and splinters.

The tower, like a notched tree, begins to fall.

And it falls right onto two of the TIE fighters. It takes one out clean—crushing it in midair, leaving nothing but a burning streak across Temmin's vision. The other catches debris against its wing panel, and suddenly the thing spirals downward like a bird with its wing sliced off.

Jom claps the boy on the shoulder. "Quick thinking, kid. Let's go get our people and get the hell out of here."

What has my son become?

That question sticks in Norra's belly like a knife. Her thoughts, her awareness, sit separate from her actions—almost like she's two different people. Like one of her is the internal version, this sudden bundle of fear and worry. The other is Norra the soldier, Norra the pilot, Norra who retakes control of the weapons system and peppers the fortress with laserfire.

Inside, she's a tumult of feelings, all of them fighting for supremacy like whole planetary systems desperate to dominate one another. Her son is doing exactly what he's supposed to do. He's fighting for the New Republic. The Empire is their enemy. What he did was smart, sharp, and demonstrative of his capability—meaning that now *he* is both soldier and pilot, too.

Is that what she wanted for him?

He's young. He's only fifteen. (Though she's reminded: His birthday is coming up soon. Time moves fast, and it only gets faster when you have children.) He just took out two TIE fighters. No—he *killed* two pilots. Two lives, snuffed out. The problem isn't whether they deserved their fates; those pilots signed up for war and knew what came with it. The problem is what that makes Temmin. It haunts her, suddenly. Will it haunt him? Is he too young to even understand what's happening? Will one day he awaken to ghosts in his head, or will he toughen to it too quickly—will it kill the kindness inside him and make him mean like Jom Barell?

These thoughts tear her apart inside even as she does her duty: Norra operates the guns and fires. Even as Temmin brings the ship alongside the feeding room entrance, even as she lays down suppressing fire and cuts apart the masked guards who rush up to defend Canker's empire.

"*There,*" Jom says, placing a hand on her forearm. His voice seems distant. Everything seems distant. Her pulse kicks in her chest, in her neck, in her wrists. Adrenaline eats her up the way those rail-throwers gnawed apart the palace tower. She blinks and pushes past all that—

In the feeding room, two guards rush up to the edge, but before they can do anything both of them shudder and pitch face-forward into the fog. Bodies plunging. Coming up behind them are Jas and Sinjir. The former has a blaster out and is using her free hand to help support the latter—Sinjir hobbles along, his arm hanging limp at his side.

One of the TIEs swoops in from above, and Norra quickly turns the rail-throwers toward it as Temmin slides the *Halo* up to the entryway. A quick burst sends the TIE pivoting back into the sky, momentarily dissuaded.

With Jas and Sinjir back on board, Jom says to the boy: "Punch it."

And Norra's blood goes from her brain to her feet as the *Halo* accelerates fast through the atmosphere above Vorlag, the TIE fighter hopping on their trail and following close behind.

CHAPTER THREE

Sloane stands in the center of a glowing blue circle and speaks to the galaxy.

"This is Grand Admiral Rae Sloane, commander of the Imperial Navy and de facto leader of the Galactic Empire. The Empire remains vigilant in combating the anarchist criminal government calling itself the New Republic. The dream of a safe, sane, and unified galaxy did not die with the glorious Emperor Palpatine. The Galactic Empire continues to march forward, tirelessly diligent in its quest to return order and stability where none before existed. Meanwhile, the New Republic continues its own mission to destroy what we have built together. Crime has returned to the galaxy tenfold as the underworld dynasties have regained dominance over worlds once kept free of their toxic influences by the Empire. Supply lines have been cut, and many worlds are now starving without adequate food. The corrosive influence of the New Republic has caused a seemingly insurmountable loss of jobs, income, and even lives."

This is the moment, she thinks. Sloane puts steel in her spine and—what was it her new "adviser" said to her? *Bronze in your voice.*

She continues:

"But fear not. The Empire remains, as sure as a mountain, as certain as the stars across all the systems. We will defeat the insurgency. We will make this false government pay for its crimes against you. Even now we are building new ships, new bases, and founding new technologies to keep you safe. The Empire is coming. We will deliver you from harm. And we will strike back against our enemies. Remain calm. Remain loyal. With true hearts, victory for us—and for the whole galaxy—will soon be at hand."

She gives a curt nod, and the blue glow around her dissipates. The circle goes dark and for a moment, she's left alone in the lightless room, listening to the murmuring sounds and shuffling feet. It is a moment of peace, rare and precious, and she clings to it like a child holding a doll.

Then the lights come back on and once again, her new life resumes.

This room is the Office of Imperial Promotion, Galactic Truth, and Fact Correction. Most just call it the OIP. It grew out of the ashes of COMPNOR to countermand the influence of the New Republic across systems and sectors.

Sloane is here a lot, much to her chagrin.

Over walks Ferric Obdur with his assistant—a pretty thing with skin so pale Sloane can see the dark veins beneath her skin—and they help Sloane down off the projection platform. Obdur is older than she is, an irascible cad with sharp tufts of silver hair coming off his cheeks, jowls, and chin. He's something of a relic of the old days: Obdur was a young man in the army during the tumultuous shift from the Republic to the Empire. He helped design the informational assault that soothed the galaxy in its transition. Which is why Ferric Obdur is now the chief informational officer—a role Sloane assigned to him, but not by her own choice. Rather, it was assigned *through* her.

Obdur is smiling, always smiling. A glint in his eyes like he thinks he knows more than everyone else in the room. "Grand Admiral Sloane, a fine job. If a bit . . . stiff."

"I was told to put steel in my spine, so I did."

"Of course, of course. You did fine, just fine. Here, over this way, I have some images I need you to look at." He directs her to a long metal table against the far wall—a table inlaid with lights that he flicks on. He opens a folder and lets a series of translucent pages slide out; the light beneath them makes their colors and inks pop. "These are posters, as you can see. We'll hang them on worlds both safe and contested."

One poster depicts two stormtroopers handing out a basket of fruits to a human family in need. Another shows a small battalion of New Republic troops—portrayed as dirty, unshaven slobs in ill-fitting helmets—pointing flamethrower streams at the front gates of an Imperial academy. In that image, children are seen at the windows, screaming against the glass. A third image shows another series of scowling Republic soldiers, these with the shadow of a Hutt slug behind them.

Obdur pulls that one toward him. "I don't much care for this. Too subtle. The goal is, of course, to infer the connection between the rebels and criminal organizations. But we need to do *more* than infer. We need that connection to be clear, concise: a hard slap to the face. Dose of reality."

Reality, Sloane thinks. What grave irony. None of this is real. And she says as much: "Why are we resorting to these . . . exaggerations when truth will out? We have facts on our side. The Empire *is* stability. The galaxy is too big to be left to its own devices, and the New Republic would let them govern themselves, which sounds fine in theory—"

"Your weapons in this war are ships, and blasters, and armor. My weapon in this war is words. And even more important than words are *images.* Pictures depicting an *artistic representation* of reality. Facts are flexible, and these graphics point to the truth of which you speak even if they do not *precisely* portray them." Obdur lays a steadying hand on her forearm. He may mean it to comfort, but it does no such thing. She wrenches her arm away, and then catches his wrist and gives it a hard twist.

"I am Grand Admiral Sloane. I am not some girlish assistant for you to paw or comfort or cajole. Touch me again, and I will have the offending limb removed, and all the nerves of the stump obliterated so that no robotic hand will ever respond to your commands."

His face goes ashen, though to his credit his smile never fades. Instead, Obdur offers a few gruff chuckles: "An error on my part, Admiral. You are right. A thousand apologies." He licks his lips. "Do we have your approval of these images? Or do we need to revise?"

Sloane hesitates. Acid backs up in her throat like venom. It kills her, but finally she concedes: "Let them go as-is. You have approval."

It hits her, then—clear as a blaster bolt to the center of her forehead.

I'm no longer an admiral.

I'm a politician.

The chill that grapples up her spine will not be suppressed. The only rescue she has from this is her own assistant, Adea Rite. A bright young woman. Strong and determined. Not to mention provably loyal. Sloane thought the girl was lost to her, but the reach of the Fleet Admiral Gallius Rax is quite far, indeed. He has people on the inside of the New Republic, and getting her away from Chandrila—before she was ever put in a prison cell—was a favor he paid to Sloane. One for which she is truly thankful, because the Empire needs more Adea Rites and fewer Ferric Obdurs.

"Admiral," Adea says.

"You should be the one doing this," Sloane says under her breath. "It should be you in charge of our propaganda efforts."

"I'm sure they're doing their best, and I do my best at your side."

At that, Sloane finds a rare smile. "What's next in my day?"

"A new entry in your schedule."

"Oh?"

"He requests your presence."

"Oh." Him. Gallius Rax. Her "adviser." "When?"

"Now, Admiral."

With steel in her spine and bronze in her voice, she says: "Shall we?"

What Rae Sloane knows about Fleet Admiral Gallius Rax amounts to very little. What she *does* know is this:

He appears in the naval roster two decades ago. Rax's debut at the age of twenty was at an abnormally high ranking for someone with little to no history: He joined up and immediately was assigned to the NIA—the Naval Intelligence Agency—and given the rank of commander. His reports bypassed his superiors, skipping even the offices of Vice Admirals Rancit and Screed. Instead his reports were *eyes only* for Wullf Yularen, who perished on the first Death Star during the strike force assault by rebel terrorists.

Once Yularen perished, Rax's reports went right to the top: to Emperor Palpatine himself.

Worst of all, most of those reports remain 90 percent redacted. And *that* means they remain almost entirely incomprehensible. She has the dates of his service in the NIA under Yularen and then under Palpatine, and that is all the usable information Adea was able to pilfer from the records.

Examining the nonredacted portions of his reports did little to complete the picture. From it she surmised that most of his operations were kept to the Outer Rim—but she was out there, too, and had never even *heard* of him until the last few years.

After that? The information about him is distressingly thin. He is considered a Hero of the Galactic Empire, and has collected a host of medals: the Nova Star, the Medal of Service, the Galactic War on Insurgency medal, the Gilded Sun, and the vaunted (if ambiguous) Emperor's Will medal. And yet, information on how he gained these or when he was even *awarded* them remains unlisted.

Rax is a specter—once just a name, but suddenly summoned and made manifest. That is how she feels whenever she meets him, as if she is meeting the hologram of a dead man made to pass as real.

That feeling is no different even now.

She steps into his chamber. He has taken to meeting her here, in his quarters, rather than on the bridge. ("That is your territory," he told her. "I do not control this fleet. You do." She filled in the rest of his statement inside her own head: *But I control you, "Grand Admiral" Sloane.*)

His chamber is far less austere than the expected Imperial aesthetic. He has punctuated the grays and blacks with punches of color: a strange red tapestry on the wall whose labyrinthine intricacy is maddening if you stare at it too long; a cylindrical tank of diaphanous water creatures flitting about, their organs glowing different colors; a golden chain connecting two sickle-shaped vibroblades, the weapon hanging in its own blast-glass case with a light on it to reveal the ornate scrollwork etched into it.

At present, a new color fills the room: the blue glow of a galactic map. Sloane can see the territorial divisions, and it makes it easy to identify as the present state of political unrest. The galaxy has been butchered and stitched back together into an ugly quilt. Some systems have gone over to the New Republic, with just as many separating into their own fiefdoms. The portions of the galaxy that the Empire controls dwindle. The New Republic has had a deleterious effect; their assault has been ceaseless and effective. Even just looking at this map suddenly overwhelms her. Anxiety crawls inside her.

But Rax seems unfazed by that anxiety, which she believes should be comforting but instead only serves to make her feel all the more alone.

There he stands, no longer garbed in an admiral's uniform but rather in a floor-length robe. Red as blood, that robe. When he meets with others, he tends to wear the raiment of a fleet admiral—his formal role while serving as her so-called adviser—but here, in his chambers, he is often garbed more comfortably. He turns toward her with that confident, feral sneer fixed to his face. One eyebrow arches and he spreads his arms. "Admiral Sloane. Thank you for coming."

As if I had any choice. When the puppeteer works the strings . . .

"Of course" is all she says in response.

"How is our Empire doing?" That, said with no small irony. The sarcasm there is applied with such a thin layer, it would be undetectable to most. But Rae hears it. She recalls his words one night, months ago: *That is no longer our galaxy.* He explained to her then that they had lost. That the Empire she served was—what were his words? Inelegant. *Crude.*

Steel in my spine. Bronze in my voice.

"We are focusing overmuch on the battles of propaganda—hearts and minds will be swayed by military victories over the New Republic, not posters shellacking cantina walls."

He *hmm*s, then walks through the floating ghosts of the galactic map with a dramatic step and a showy gesticulation of his hand. "You raise a good point. Military action is not yet in our stars, but tell Obdur to find some footage of us routing the Republic traitors. Battle footage. Violent, but not *too* violent. We must look like the hero-conquerors, not thugs. Would that assuage your worries, Admiral Sloane?"

No, she thinks. But instead she nods, stiffly. "It's a start. But I am uncomfortable, *increasingly* uncomfortable, with all this artifice—"

He stops her there. "Rae, do you know much about opera?"

"What?"

"Opera. The Nonagon Cycle? *The Esdrit and the Tholothian*? *The Masterwork of Illure Beelthrak*? Even the Hutts had their own opera: a rather . . . *disgusting* narrative of betrayal and breeding. The *Lah'chispa Kah Soh-na*." He makes a sour face. "The galaxy should be spared singing from such worms."

"I know opera, though I am not an enthusiast."

He clasps his hands together. "Become one. It will make our partnership more rewarding for you. Opera moves me. And yet none of it is real. Therein lies the crux of what you need to understand: Something does not need to be real for it to have an effect. The instruments and song, the drama and melodrama, the pathos and tragedy. It's a lie. A *fiction*. And yet what happens on the stage speaks a kind of truth just the same. Facts and truth are separate things. I am more interested in truth than I am fact. I am comfortable with artifice when it suits our needs. And here, it does."

"But—"

He seems suddenly impatient. His nostrils flare and his hands tighten into fists. "We agree that the New Republic is dangerous, do we not?"

"We do. Of course."

"We can see that because we are *elevated minds*. But most? They're fools. I know you agree with me on that. And so, as long as you and I know the reality, I see nothing wrong with pushing weak minds to a conclusion we have already reached. They need that kind of drama and melodrama to get them to an understanding that was easy for you and me. We came to it naturally. Others must be nudged, even pushed. Is that more clear?"

Sloane swallows hard. Though his voice is calm and measured, the anger is plain on his face. He crackles with a kind of quiet intensity. Once, a lifetime ago, she was refueling her battleship—the *Dreadstar*—at a floating depot on the Sea of Carawak on the ninth moon of Tilth. A storm was incoming and the sea took on this *look*. The waves turned gunmetal gray, and though those waves stayed low, they churned and frothed. When the storm finally hit—the sea became like a monster.

Rax reminds her of that.

When will the sea become a storm? Will he become a monster?

Perhaps she is too paranoid.

"It is clear," she says, finally. "What is less clear is our goal."

He grins. "Our goal is the resurgence of the Empire. A stronger, leaner Empire."

"Yes, but how? We have made no overtures to Mas Amedda, who remains entrenched on Coruscant. Will we elect another Emperor? Though our meeting on Akiva was . . ." *A dangerous and callow deception,* she thinks but does not say. ". . . a necessary ruse, it does not eliminate the need for unity. We have moffs rebelling and claiming Palpatine is alive, we have Grand General Loring dug in on Malastare, we have—"

"Have faith in me, Rae. Faith will light our path. Let me worry about all these problems. Those are future concerns. In the present, I have tasks for you. One for the moment, but more to come after."

Tasks. Like she's an errand girl tackling a to-do list. That feeling is an odd one for her. Is it because she controls the Empire in name, but not in reality? Is it because she has no idea who Rax really is, or if he is deserving of the honor required to command her?

Is it because she simply doesn't trust him?

He begins to pace around the room, his hands clasped stiffly behind his back. "I need you to fetch someone for me."

Fetch. Another demeaning term. As if she is just a pet chasing after a flung stick or kicked ball. "Who is it?"

"Brendol Hux."

That name—she knows it, doesn't she? Hux, Hux, Hux . . .

"Commandant Hux?" she asks, suddenly. "At the Arkanis Academy." Again, a strange and unnamable fear ripples through her. Hux trains children. The best and brightest the Empire has to offer.

"The very same."

"Arkanis is under siege by New Republic forces as we speak." *We are, in fact, losing that system.*

"Yes, and I want you to rescue him personally."

"Rescue? Truly rescue? Or are you again speaking in metaphor?"

It would not be the first time Sloane had been tasked with eradicating those in the Empire whom Gallius Rax considered inept or a competitor. The events on Akiva were only the beginning in that regard, and the list of the missing and dead at his hands has grown considerably since. Rax refers to the winnowing down of the Empire as the sharpening of a blade, but even still she finds the idea troublesome. Sickening, even.

He shows his teeth in a grin. "For now, rescue. Hopefully, he will appreciate our efforts and in *good faith* he'll join us. He has a child— a bastard boy, as I understand. Not born of his wife, Maratelle, but of some . . . *kitchen* woman. Don't worry about the mother or the wife, but a child is a child and blood is blood, so make sure the boy finds rescue, as well."

"Is it wise to devote resources to rescue his boy?"

"The Empire must be fertile and young. Children are crucial to our success. Many of our officers are old. We need that kind of vitality. That brand of *energy* you get with the young. The Empire needs children."

The Empire needs children.

That sentence repeats in her mind again and again.

Each time, it grows more terrifying.

And yet, he's not wrong, is he? The New Republic is driven by the young. Though it may be naïve, its rebels are believers. They are vibrant and, though not always capable, driven.

She adds: "We can reinstate some of the breeding programs from the earlier days of the Empire. To encourage our people to start or grow their families. We can reward them for it."

His hands clap together. He beams. "Yes. I knew we made a good team, Rae. When we are done with the galaxy, there will be no worlds left to conquer. They will all be ours. Thank you."

She offers a reticent nod. "Of course."

"Once all this messiness is complete, and Hux is with us, I believe we may have our Shadow Council and the future of the Empire will be clear."

Shadow Council? She doesn't even have to ask. The look on her face is enough to prompt Admiral Rax's response:

"I'm sorry, I didn't tell you? I'm forming a Shadow Council to govern the Empire from behind the scenes. Only the finest of our kind:

the first and highest order of Imperial minds. Once Hux is on board, we will have our inaugural meeting—you are, of course, a member. But more on this when you return. Safe travels, Admiral Sloane. May the stars speed your success."

Now go fetch, she expects him to say. But all he does is turn around and step once more into the blue glow of the star map.

Gallius Rax's words cling to her like a bad smell. *Faith will light our path. The Empire needs children. I'm forming a Shadow Council . . .*

This is not how you rule an Empire. The man wants a cult, not a government. The rumors about Palpatine always ranged from the strange to the sinister: dark fairy tales of him sacrificing creatures or hunting children, stories of him disappearing for months on end, fears that the old man was eternal and had lived not one life but many. No matter how true or how false those stories were, one fact remained true, which was that Palpatine never let the Empire fall into instability. He ruled as more than a politician and more than some hooded theocrat. Imperial worlds never went hungry. They never fell to lawlessness. Though the galaxy was held fast and firm in the Empire's carbon-jacketed gauntlet, that was for the good for the galaxy—a galaxy too big to be left to its own devices, too mad and too scattered to survive without strong governance and clear vision to unify it. If Palpatine knew one thing it was to put people in place to run the machine. He trusted them. He let them do their jobs. The Emperor knew when to delegate.

Rax keeps too much, too close. His hands on all the controls.

Sloane does not know what the endgame is here. That troubles her. Gallius Rax is so in love with artifice. So what, then, is he hiding?

Ahead, toward the turbolift, Adea stands and waits. The girl's back is straight, and her eyes are flinty and clear: *That* is the pride of the Empire. Adea Rite is the type of person they should be striving to elevate—an administrator, loyal and true. In love with data. Logistics. Cause and effect, truth and consequence. She is a much better Imperial than someone like Brendol Hux—a slithering thing who views people as tools and props. (*No wonder,* she thinks, *that Rax wants him kept alive.*)

For a moment, Sloane's mind drifts to a fantasy where Adea Rite is more than just her assistant—Adea would make a fine daughter. Sloane never chose that path, of course, never thought to raise a family lest it be yet another excuse for the men in power here to keep her from rising in the ranks, but now she wonders what her life would have been had she gone that route. A family. A husband. A daughter like Adea . . .

As Sloane steps into the turbolift, Adea follows after and hands over a datapad with an adjusted schedule on it. The door closes behind them, just as it closes on Sloane's fantasy of having a family. That dream is one that has come too late, she decides.

Sloane takes the datapad but doesn't look at it. Instead, her eyes stare off at an unfixed point a thousand kilos away.

"Is something wrong?" Adea asks.

The turbolift begins to move, taking them down into the lower levels of the *Ravager,* the Empire's last Super Star Destroyer. But therein a question suddenly persists: Is it? She has taken it on as fact, but Rax said that *fact and truth are separate things.* Sloane reminds herself that it is time for a new accounting of all the naval ships. In fact—

She stops the turbolift.

"Adea," she says. "I need your help."

The young woman looks around, confused. "Why are we—?"

"Because this is a sensitive conversation and I can't have anyone listening in whom I can't trust." *And the list of who I trust is shorter than I would prefer.* "I . . . admire Admiral Rax, but he is a cipher. I am not sure I trust his hand to be steady in ruling the Empire, yet."

Adea is one of those who is well aware that Sloane's power in the Empire is secondary to Rax's. Many of the officers on this ship know it, which means ultimately many in the Empire will know it soon enough. But Sloane can't concern herself with that right now.

"I will launch another search into his history," Adea says.

"No. I'll handle that this time. Not because I don't trust you but because I need you on other things. First, get me a proper accounting of all the ships that were in Imperial service when Palpatine still lived. Second, I need you to put me in touch with the bounty hunter again. Find Mercurial Swift and arrange a meeting. Oh, and I'll also need a draft of a new breeding program initiative. For every child an Imperial has, they get a reward: credits, perhaps, or a boost to paid leave. Can you do these things for me?"

"I can."

Those two words: precious and perfect.

I can.

No argument. No question. Just the affirmative.

"Good."

"What are you going to do, Admiral?"

"Everything is bound up in a knot right now, Adea, a knot I can't quite untie. You know the best way to undo that kind of knot?" She smirks. "You cut right through it."

INTERLUDE

VELUSIA

The atoll of Kolo-ha: the mouth of an extinct undersea volcano pushed up out of the water and given new life as an island. This island is a claw-shaped thing, its soil rich and black like powdered soot. The plants that grow up out of its small jungle are twisted together, with bright flowers whose petals snap at the air as buzzing insects pass. Beyond the island is a ring of shimmering sediment beneath the sea—an aggregate of crystalline matter that, as it turns out, is actually composed of the fossilized corpses of gelatinous chomong, drifting sea creatures that look like diaphanous blobs of glowing flesh.

The local Velusians eat them, Mon Mothma had said before adding: *Raw.*

Leia shudders at that thought. Her time as princess, ambassador, and general has led her through an unholy host of culinary trials and tribulations—pickled coodler-roe on Goliath Mal (the texture alone was enough to haunt her), half-rancid durang fruit (which tasted not unlike how death smells), skewered mandlertok over an open fire (she admits that those little lizards were actually quite good once you got past how they *popped* when you bit into them). Curiously, the worst of all remains the protein paste they sometimes had to eat in the early days of the Alliance. Looked and tasted like hull caulk. Actually, it might've *been* hull caulk for all she knew.

Eating strange things is what you do with galactic citizens that are not you, she reminds herself. It is a welcome honor, if an occasionally uncomfortable one. Thankfully, that will not be her task today. The native Velusians do not occupy the island of Kolo-ha. No one does.

She stands on the deck of a floating cruiser—what once was a luxury swiftwing pleasure-liner, though it has seen better days. Much of what the New Republic possesses for equipment remains dinged, dented, blast-scarred, or just plain *old*. That is changing slowly, as they ramp up their own political machine and oust the Empire system by system. But for now, this old thing—which transitions well enough from sea to sky to the stars—will have to suffice.

As she stands there, a woman in white joins her—with her, that flash of fire-red hair that belies the woman's calm, placating smile. Mon Mothma has that effect. She is serene, even when she is worried or when she is angry.

Mon says, "You seem uncertain."

"This is all more than a little deranged," Leia says. "What are we doing out here? This surely can't be a real plea."

"Maybe it isn't. It seems earnest enough. And it's not as if we're unprotected." The chancellor's eyes drift heavenward—there, beyond the atmosphere, is a fleet of New Republic ships. And ahead of them, on the atoll, their own soldiers—the most elite, the most *capable*—wait for what may come. "They've already combed the island. Relax, Leia. We are safe."

"It could be a trap."

"You sound paranoid."

"As I should," Leia says. "Every good thing in this galaxy seems to twist and turn in our grip like a serpent—just as you think you've got it by the tail, it whips its head around and takes a bite."

"Where's that idealist I met on Alderaan?" A rare smile tugs at Mon's mouth. "We don't see enough of each other, Leia. I miss you. How's your husband?"

"He's good," Leia lies. She adds another lie to the heap, because once you've set one down as the foundation, why not build a house and live there? "His mission goes well. He's a changed man."

Mon watches her. Is that suspicion glinting in her eyes, or just more paranoia on Leia's part? "I gather it must be hard being married through all of this. But I promise that the transition will be over soon enough. And peace, prosperity—and stars help us, a little *normalcy*—will return soon enough." Again her eyes tilt skyward. Leia sees it, too: a ship entering atmosphere. A nondescript mine craft: a Kinro 9747. Even from here Leia can see the plasma scarring and the pockmarks from debris.

From behind them, the voice of Staff Sergeant Hern Kaveen—a bearded Pantoran who works on the protective detail around the chancellor. (Leia has been told she needs a protective detail as well, but she has told them that she will be her *own* protective detail, thank you very much.)

"He's here, Chancellor," Kaveen says. Behind the mining ship fly two flanking Y-wings—weapons ready, just in case.

"He's alone?" Leia asks.

"It's just one ship, and only one bio-sig aboard."

On the atoll, a space has been reserved upon the beach for landing—and the Kinro 9747 hovers over the makeshift pad, its exhaust blowing a hissing wave of sand into the sea before finally settling down.

A passel of New Republic soldiers, their weapons raised, surround the ship. As soon as the landing ramp descends, the soldiers storm inside.

Despite the warm, balmy sea air, Leia suddenly feels cold. She knows what could come next: The ship suddenly detonating, killing those men. Or maybe it would be filled with something worse: a biological agent, a chemical weapon, *some starving creature* like a cybernetically enhanced rancor monster . . . at this point, nothing would shock her short of the black, gleaming visage of Vader himself stepping off that ship and into the sand.

But then Kaveen confers with the soldiers on the comm.

He relays their response: "Chancellor: They've given the all-clear."

Mon nods.

And that's all it takes.

The soldiers escort the pilot of the mining ship off and onto the beach.

Mas Amedda is an imposing figure. His Chagrian skin is the blue-gray of troubled waters (failing to match the bright aquamarine of the ocean here on Velusia), and his long, horn-tipped tentacles give him the cut of something sharp and poisonous. Which, Leia supposes, is not entirely inaccurate: There stands the man who was once Emperor Sheev Palpatine's chief administrator and has now become the proxy Emperor, at least in name and in politics.

He watches them from the beach. His gaze remains fixed upon them, in fact, even as the soldiers bind his hands behind him and help him step onto the seaspeeder. The craft pivots in the water and flies toward the old pleasure-liner, twin trails of sea-spray cast in its wake.

"Here we go," Leia says.

As they approach, she sees that the imposing figure is less so, now. He looks *old*. Weathered and worn. The tentacles topping his head seem wilted. His stare is hollow and, dare Leia say it, hopeless.

The seaspeeder slows to a halt below the deck of the pleasure-liner.

Leia and Mon step to the edge, looking down at him.

"May I come up?" he asks. He offers a lifeless smile.

"No," Mon says. "You will speak to us from where you stand."

He wastes no time. "I offer myself to you as prisoner. I, Grand Vizier Mas Amedda, head of the Imperial Ruling Council, turn myself in to Chancellor Mon Mothma and Princess Leia Organa of the *New Republic*. Take me away."

It's Leia's turn to say it:

"No."

Tectonic shock crosses his face. "Wh . . . what?"

"We do not accept your 'surrender.'"

He turns suddenly toward the soldiers, panicked. "Will you kill me? Here and now? It's not in you. It's not *like* you. This . . . this isn't—"

Mon calls down: "Calm yourself, Mas. We do not execute our prisoners—or those trying to be our prisoners."

"We simply don't accept you *as* a prisoner," Leia adds.

"B-but," he stammers, "I am the *head* of the Galactic Empire. I am its *pinnacle*. No target is greater than me. I am a prize!"

"You're a figurehead," Mon says.

"I know things! Names. Details. I can help you. I . . . I came all this way, I fled the throneworld." His voice booms, but the desperation in it is keenly felt. "I will not be denied my surrender. It is against the Galactic Accord of Systems established in the fiftieth year of—"

"The Empire has long ignored the accord. It is considered obliterated thanks to your efforts. And the names and details you know are, I suspect, far less impressive these days than you'd have us believe, Mas."

Leia smiles. "But there is a deal to be struck here if you're willing to make it, Grand Vizier."

"Anything. Anything at all."

"Sign a treaty of surrender."

He laughs at first, and then the laugh dies in his mouth. "You . . . you're serious. You want me to surrender . . . the entire Galactic Empire?"

"That's right."

"I don't . . ." But again he swallows the sound.

Leia suspects what he was going to say, and she helps him finish his statement: "You don't have the power, do you?"

"I . . ."

"So, get it back. And then bring a treaty to our door."

"*That*," the chancellor says, "is the only deal we will make, and the only deal that earns you a life beyond this existence. Anything less than that will be met with a charge of war crimes and a brutal trial to follow—if your own people don't jettison you from an air lock first."

"How do I accomplish this?"

Mon shrugs. "You're an administrator. So *administrate*." Then, with a curt nod, the soldiers turn him back around, facing the island. The seaspeeder's engines thrum to life, and it returns to the atoll. All the way, Mas Amedda protests and pleads until his voice is swallowed by the sound of the sea. In the distance, they watch as they shove him off the speeder and onto the sand. They cut his bonds. He's left standing, gaping, shocked.

"It was our only play," Mon says.

"I know. For a big fish, he's surprisingly little. Still, I worry we just made a terrible mistake. It could've been a coup. We could've spun it as a victory for the New Republic."

"Mm. True. But you don't strike me as the type to want to spin any-thing. Unless war has changed you?"

Leia sighs. "It has not. I'd rather play the long game and secure a real victory, not a ceremonial one."

"Good. Now let's get back to Chandrila. The war goes on."

CHAPTER FOUR

They expect a fight, but the TIE following after the *Halo* turns back before breaking atmosphere and returns to the surface of Vorlag. Considering how those things are usually like burrs stuck to your back, Norra half wonders if there's something they don't know—maybe they're flying into a trap, or out into some random asteroid field that the TIE would never survive. (And even then, wouldn't it continue to follow?)

But the Imperial fighter turns and goes, lobbing off a few lazy shots before peeling away and disappearing.

Temmin sits at the controls and says, "That was weird."

"It was." Though she starts to round on a theory. "Maybe the Empire is hurting that bad. Maybe they can't stand to lose even a single TIE. Or maybe they just don't care anymore."

"You mean . . . maybe we're winning?" Temmin asks.

"Maybe we are, Tem. Maybe we are."

The burst of confidence and comfort in her heart doesn't last long—

outside the cockpit, in the belly of the *Halo*, loud voices rise in a clamor.

Uh-oh.

"Stay here and start setting hyperspace coordinates," she tells her son, then gets up and heads into the gunship's belly. The *Halo* isn't big—the cockpit is cramped, the main hold can barely contain them all at once. Behind that is the head and the two-person brig, and then two bunkrooms. All the way aft is the engineering room (and it's not a room so much as it is a crawl space you have to shimmy up into in order to get anything done). This is a ship for quick trips, not long-haul flying. There isn't much privacy to be found. Arguments in this ship go big. They refuse to be *contained.*

In the main hold, Jas is crouched down next to Sinjir, whose arm is swollen up like a bloodsucking bloatworm—he winces, his brow damp, as she dabs at it with some sort of goopy, tacky unguent found in a half-empty medkit up front. Bones stands nearby, beaked droid head swiveling from person to person to watch the exchange. Above her stands Jom Barell, angrily berating her and punctuating every word with an air-stab of his thick, callused finger.

"You don't just . . . *change the plan* without giving us some kind of signal. We could've been killed, Emari. We could've—"

The bounty hunter stands up fast, like she's ready to strike. But instead, all she does is smile and pat his cheek like he's a child and she's his mother. "I didn't change the plan, Barell. That was the plan all along."

His face is dumbstruck. Jom looks to Norra and wordlessly asks an obvious question: *What is she talking about?*

But Norra doesn't know. So she asks. "Jas, what do you mean?"

"I *mean*," Jas says, opening up bins and pulling out drawers as if she's looking for something. "That I always planned it that way."

"You didn't tell *us* that, did you?" Jom grabs her and wheels her around, but Emari breaks his hold fast and shoves him back, hard. "Hey!"

"Don't," she warns.

"You planned to double-cross us all along, didn't you?" Jom asks.

She shakes her head. "*Triple*-cross. I swear, Barell, you are as daft as that tatty carpet of yark fur you wear on your face."

"Why?" Norra asks. "Why would you do that?"

Jas bares her teeth. "Did you see the bounty poster? We're *all* on it. My face included. I'm a bounty hunter with a bounty on her head. I have been compromised. There exists *no* way that Slussen and Gedde were going to just let me waltz in there and scurry around his dung pile of a palace like some little don't-pay-attention-to-me spider. I had a play and I went with it. I sold you out. Then, when they were distracted with you, I snuck my way into Gedde's room and waited for him. I paid one of the stable slaves to put keys around the hrothbeasts' necks. Then I waited." A twinkle shines in her eye. "Besides," she says, patting her pockets. They jingle. "That means I got paid twice, which is never a bad thing, right? I really do have bills."

"You should've *told* us," Norra seethes.

"You don't get it, do you? This is what I do, but it's not what *you* do." Jas Emari's finger draws an invisible perimeter in the air, containing both Norra and Jom. "You're a pair of bright-eyed rebel saps in the bag for the good of the galaxy. You're not bounty hunters. You're not one of the *bad guys*. I am. I can fake it. I can lie and cheat and swindle and smile the whole time. That's not who you are. I can't trust you not to blow it."

Sinjir woozily lifts his blister-red arm. "Uh. Hello? I was told I might get a bacta shot? Anybody? No?"

"Did *he* know?" Jom snarls, pointing at the ex-Imperial. Then, accusing Sinjir directly: "Did you?"

"I did not," Sinjir answers, a bit testily.

"I did."

They all turn. There stands Temmin, beaming.

"What?" he asks, showing his palms defensively. Norra sees a glimmer of his father in the boy's eyes, just then: a playful, puckish gleam. "Jas trusted me and said it was the right thing to do. She said I had to be ready."

Norra gapes. Her son lied to her. (*Again,* she reminds herself.) She does her level best to tamp down the sudden flux of anger rising inside, but she feels suddenly, woefully out of control. Like things are slipping out of her hands and spiraling away. Her son. This team. This mission.

So when Jom points to her and says, "Control your boy," he is the unwitting recipient of her fury, lashing out like a crackling vibro-whip.

"I'm the leader of this team," she says, her words hissing through clenched teeth. "Not you. I'll handle him how I choose."

"Maybe you shouldn't be leader," he says with a half shrug that somehow manages to be aggressive.

"Well, she *is* our leader," Jas says, shoving past him. "You don't like it, go find another starship to hitch your grav-raft to. I'm sure Spec-Forces would be glad to have you back, stinking up their air with your ego. Now get out of my way, Barell. I need to get that bacta shot and some gauze for Mister Calamari-Arm over there."

At that, Sinjir pouts. "That hurts my feelings. More than a little."

Norra wheels on her son and pokes him in the chest. "You," she says under her breath. "You and I will have a conversation about this."

"Uh-oh," he says.

"Uh-oh is right."

She's hoping for now the fight is done, but it's far from over. Even as Jas excuses herself to search the bunkroom for another medkit ("Preferably one with a bacta shot"), Barell follows after, still barking mad.

"Wait right here," Norra tells her son, then goes to break up the fight once and for all.

"I knew I should never have trusted you," he says, standing in the doorway as Jas roots around in one of the underbunks. "Bringing some bounty hunter on board? Antilles must've had his head knocked around real good while caught in the Empire's clutches—"

Jas laughs, finally finding a capped bacta shot. "You've got it spun around, Barell. This team needs someone like me. They don't need some thick-skulled law-bound brute who has all the imagination of an overturned mine cart. We need *moral flexibility.*"

"I'm flexible. I've got imagination." He storms into the room, fists at his side. "I'm not just one of your marks. I can handle myself."

Whap. Jas slaps him hard with an open palm.

"Can you? Really?"

He reels for a moment, rubbing his face. His jaw crackles and pops as he moves it left and right. That moment is over fast.

"Why you little—" He growls and steps into a fighting stance. Two fists up in front of his face, legs placed apart. Jas begins to pace the half circle in front of him, her limbs down and loose. He bats at her, but she blocks it. She kicks out with a leg and he turns inward, taking the hit on the outside of his knee. The two of them move around each other like a pair of wild-eyed creatures shoved together in the same cage.

Norra shouts: "Quit it. Both of you. You're not a couple of mating murra, locking horns—"

The SpecForces officer slaps at Jas with a wide paw, but she bows her back, handily letting it catch open air. The bounty hunter moves fast, hooking her leg around his and wheeling herself onto his back. Her arms tuck under his pits and her fingers lace behind his neck.

Jom roars. He tilts back, his boot jabbing out and connecting with the door controls—and the bunkroom portal slams shut.

When Norra tries to open it, she finds it locked.

Inside, the clamor rises. Something falls, *bang.* A rattle. Grunting.

Suddenly the space outside the door is crowded. Temmin to her left, Sinjir to her right. The droid, Bones, humming some mad song behind.

"Can either of you get this door open?" she asks. She tries the button again but the door won't budge.

"Man, they're really fighting," Temmin says.

Sinjir tilts his ear toward the door. His eyes narrow. "Well. They *were* fighting."

"Still sounds like they . . ." But the boy's eyes go big as moons. *"Oh."*

Even Bones whistles—a warbling, discordant note.

Which means that Norra is officially the last one to figure out what's going on. They're not in there fighting at all, are they? Beyond the door, something bangs, then rattles, then falls. Jom growls. Jas laughs.

Kissing sounds.

Those are kissing sounds.

"I choose to ignore all of this for now," Norra says, taking a deep breath. "Tem, go plot for hyperspace and get us back to Chandrila. And take . . . him with you." By "him," she means Bones. The boy and the droid wander off, leaving Norra and Sinjir standing in front of the door.

"I never got my bacta shot," Sinjir says.

"I think you're going to have to wait."

"If I wait much longer I fear the arm might pop like a bladder-bug. It really hurts." He pouts. "It's really gross."

Norra sighs. "Fine. Come on. Let's go see if there's another medkit in the second bunkroom."

In a singsongy voice, he answers: "Thank you, Mom."

"Don't call me that."

"You're no fun."

"That is becoming abundantly clear, Sinjir."

The *Halo* drops out of hyperspace.

There, looming into view, is Chandrila—a small, blue-green planet, now the home of the nascent New Republic. Nearly idyllic, Norra thinks, with its calm seas and rolling hills. The weather is mild. The seasons are present, but never dramatic. The people are peaceful—if a bit haughty and pedantic and over-invested in every political maneuver and measure that proceeds through the Galactic Senate.

This would be a good place to call home, she thinks, then looks over at her son. "Are you good?" she asks.

He cocks an eyebrow. "I'm golden."

She doesn't think he's lying, but her skill at reading people fails to match that of Sinjir, who can cut you into your constituent parts with a half-second glance.

"I need you to trust me," she tells him.

"I do." He narrows his eyes. "This is about the Jas thing, isn't it? Mom, it's like she told you—"

"Life is a series of moments—" Norra suddenly stops talking, then pinches the bridge of her nose and sighs loudly. "Gods, I'm about to give you one of *those* talks, aren't I? I hated when my mother gave me these talks and usually I went out and did the opposite of what she told me to do, and that's what *you're* going to do because you're *my* son. So stupid."

"Fine." He rolls his eyes. "It's not stupid. Go on. Give it to me. I promise I won't, like, barf into my hands or anything."

Norra hesitates. "It's just . . . I just want you to be good. To be good with yourself and to know where you belong. Not where you think other people want you to belong, but where you really belong. In here." She puts her hand on his chest and he makes a goofy face because this is really very mawkish and sentimental and they both know it. "You sticking with Jas—you're not a bounty hunter. You don't have to be like her. You can be a soldier but—" Again she bites her tongue and growls past it. "You know what? You don't have to be a soldier, either. I just want *you* to be *you* and not worry about what the rest of the galaxy thinks you should be."

"I think the galaxy wants me to be a crazy-rich droid manufacturer living in a palace out on the Outer Rim."

There again, his father's playful twinkle flickering in his eye.

"Then go be that," she says, laughing.

He cups his hand to his ear. "Or maybe the galaxy is saying to become a lounge singer in a backwater space station cantina. I can belt 'em out."

"Now, I don't know about *that*."

"Oh! Oh wait! I think I'm going to be a Jedi."

"Now I know your brain is busted." She gestures toward the viewscreen. "Take us down to Hanna City. Gently, this time? Or Wedge will have your head and maybe mine."

The arm looks, well, *better*. But not much. The angry redness has cooled down to a somewhat aggravated *pink*. The blisters have faded, but have been replaced with craters of dry, puckered skin. Sinjir's arm looks like old meat left to hang too long on a butcher's hook.

At least it has all its feeling back. He wiggles his fingers. The skin feels uncomfortably tight. Blessedly, Norra found some painkillers.

"Hello, hand," he tells his hand.

"Hello, Sinjir," he makes his hand tell him back.

From around the corner of the main hold comes the sound of a door hissing open. And who should waltz out but Jom Barell.

"Your hair is a bit of a mess," Sinjir says.

"Hm?" Jom's gaze rolls up, where his hair is sticking out. "Oh."

"Here. Let me help you." Sinjir stands, and fast as a spark is standing right in front of Jom. He gently begins to move the man's hair back in place.

"Well, isn't this romantic."

"Ah. Yes. Speaking of romance—I'm really glad you brought it up, Jomby—did you have a nice fight with our resident bounty hunter?"

"She knows how to, ah, fight."

"Oh, I'm sure she does." As Sinjir continues to adjust the man's hair one strand at a time—and by now Jom is starting to look more than a little uncomfortable—he lets a vicious foxlike grin stretch across his face. "Curious bit of trivia: As you know, when I served at the pleasure of the Empire, I served as a loyalty officer, and sometimes extracting loyalty from my fellows took a bit of *doing*. I learned that the human body has four hundred thirty-four trigger points of pain. I know it lacks humility to say, but I actually discovered another three all by myself, although amending an Imperial training manual is like trying to move a boulder with a spoon, you know? All this is a very long road to a very simple destination: I am *excellent* at causing pain."

Jom pulls his head away from Sinjir's grooming efforts. "Are you threatening me, Rath Velus? It sure sounds that way."

"I am, and for good reason. I want you to know that if you hurt Jas Emari in any way—emotionally, physically, I mean, even if you accidentally step on her foot—then I will personally make sure to find all four hundred thirty-four, oh, sorry, I mean *four hundred thirty-seven* trigger points on your body. Are we clear?"

A strange calm settles over Jom—which Sinjir finds rather unexpected. He suspected that his little speech would goad the man into fighting. Barell seems hotheaded, after all. But that's not what's happening here, is it? Instead, Jom crosses his arms and nods.

"Your loyalty to her is commendable," the commando says. "I'll take your, uhh, *words of wisdom* under advisement. Though if I'm being honest, I suspect if anybody will get hurt in this arrangement, it'll be me."

"Likely."

"And that wouldn't bother you at all?"

Sinjir gives a half shrug.

"All right. Fine. Lemme ask, though: What's your deal with her? I was led to believe you and she would not be . . . romantically compatible?"

"This isn't about that. I value her tremendously. I feel connected to her. I think she's a 'friend,' or the closest thing to." He says that word *friend* like it's a foreign word in an alien tongue whose full contextual meaning he has not yet grasped.

"For a time I thought maybe you had your eye on me." Jom is just goading him, but he decides to play along.

"I did. It's the facial hair. But I'm spoken for now."

Jom smirks. "Really?"

"Really."

"Good for you, mate."

Sinjir puts one more stray hair on the commando's head back in place. "Have fun with Jas. And remember the number: four hundred thirty-seven." The *Halo* starts to shudder—the walls are shielded, but still the sudden warmth bleeding off them is telling even as the ship bucks along clouds like a stone skipped across a pond. "Sounds like we're down. Better secure the prisoner, Jomby."

Landing Platform OB-99. In one direction are the rolling hills and sweeping meadows of Chandrila: the soft balmgrass and spiky orcanthus are already turning from red to green with the coming of spring, and the sun and clouds cast shifting, shimmering shadows over the land. In the other direction is the Silver Sea, its placid waters as calm and gray as slate. Out over the water, bands of dark clouds roll, spitting rain and pulsing lightning. Another symptom of the seasons shifting from winter into spring.

Standing off to the side and leaning against a stack of crates is Wedge Antilles. Temmin is first off the ramp, and he runs over to Antilles—the two of them clasp hands and embrace.

"Hey, Snap," Wedge says—a nickname he's given Temmin because of the boy's finger-snapping habit.

Bones trots after, his skeletal arms going wide. "I TOO WILL SHARE AN EMBRACE WITH MASTER ANTILLES TO SIMULATE JOY." Wedge leans away from the "hug" as the droid wraps his many-jointed arms around the captain, looking less like a human sharing camaraderie and more like an insect trying to eat the face of its mate. "OKAY," the droid says, apparently satisfied. It lets go and begins dancing around the landing platform in dramatic swoops, pliés, and pirouettes.

"Sorry," Temmin says, shrugging. "He's trying to learn how to be more . . . human? And less . . ."

"Singing, dancing murder-bot?" Wedge asks.

"Yeah." Bones has been Temmin's bodyguard and friend now for a while—and once he rebuilt his pal from spare parts (thankfully rescuing the data-brain from the New Republic soldiers who secured the Akivan palace), he was surprised when the droid declared a desire to fit in better with the crew. (Apparently it was something Sinjir said to the droid about how he creeped them all out.) Temmin fears that the droid's attempts have only made him *more* creepy, but uh, yay for effort? "Oh, man, Wedge, you should've seen me out there. I was piloting the *Halo,* right? And we were swooping along the edge of Slussen Canker's mountaintop fortress and—"

"All right, Snap," Wedge says, laughing. "Ease off the throttle a minute. I need to talk to your mom. You can tell me more from the seat of my X-wing tomorrow morning. Deal?"

"Whoa, yeah, yes. *Deal.*" Wedge has been giving Temmin time in the X-wing. He said Temmin has a natural gift for piloting a fighter, like his mother (though Norra wasn't exactly *happy* about her son following in her steps as a pilot). Wedge lets the boy run training exercises out over the Silver Sea. Last time he said to the kid, "I'm cooking up a little something called Phantom Squadron. Maybe by the time you're spaceworthy, you'd be interested in joining up." Temmin hasn't told his mother about *that* yet.

He's not even sure that's what he wants, either. Sometimes Temmin's mind drifts and fantasies play out—okay, no, he doesn't really want to be a lounge singer in some crummy cantina, but the bounty hunter life sounds pretty great. Go where you want, track down the bad guys, get paid to do it. But being a pilot gives him a thrill like no other: Cutting clouds with the scissor-foils of Wedge's old X-wing is the scariest and most amazing thing. And then again, he still misses his black-market dealings on Akiva—the danger of the deal, the joy of the sale, the buzz from peddling illicit weapons, parts, and droids to thugs and criminals who might kill you for looking at them wrong. Temmin doesn't know what he wants to be.

He mentioned it to Sinjir a few weeks back and the ex-Imperial shrugged (he was a bit sauced at the time on Corellian sap-wine) and said: "Nobody knows who they are or what they want, and most people just wait for everyone to tell them. Then they line up and do what they're told. My only advice to you, boy—" He burped, then, and never got around to giving the advice because he passed out. Maybe one day.

For now, Temmin only knows that he's so excited to get back in the cockpit he's almost jumping out of his own skin.

"Captain Antilles."

"Lieutenant Wexley."

A cool breeze kicks up over the landing platform as the rain clouds drift closer. Temmin circles his droid, kicking the metal skeleton in the hindquarters with his boot and then waiting for Bones to chase after. Which the droid does, like an eager friend.

Wedge smiles, then grabs his cane and moves toward Norra, embracing her as they meet.

"Much nicer than when that droid did it," he says, giving her one last lingering squeeze before letting her go.

"Bones?" She laughs. "Oh, he's harmless. Well. Not *harmless* . . ."

"I get it, I get it. How'd the mission go?"

"We bagged Gedde," she says, looking over her shoulder. Nobody's emerged with the prisoner, yet, though here comes Sinjir down the plank. Chin up, lips puckered like he's proud of himself about something.

"Off to get a pint of . . . something," he calls, and then heads right for the stairway. "Toodles."

She thinks to call after him with some motherly admonishment, but she stays her tongue and gives Wedge a slightly embarrassed look. "It's a rough crew, but they work. How's your treatment?"

"Physical therapy is good, and they're giving me serolin injections now. They say I might be in a cockpit again by the end of the year. But it's fine. I like this. I like . . . commanding, too." She doesn't have to possess Sinjir's gift with body language to suss out Wedge's lie. He'd do anything to get back behind the flight stick. His whole body seems to hunger for it. "Never mind that, Norra, there's someone who wants to—"

"We've got a problem!"

There, standing on the ramp, is Jom Barell. Norra gives him a shrugging, half-irritated look like, *Well, go ahead, get on with it.*

"It's Gedde," he says. "He's dead."

———————

The Imperial vice admiral's body lies there on the table in the main hold of the *Halo*. His lips are slick with spit froth. His skin's already gone pale and gray. Dark striations mark the brow and draw shadowy lines around the mouth and wide-open eyes. Norra is reminded how something seems truly gone when someone dies—it's not just about the little micro-movements of the body or a chest no longer rising and falling. It's something deeper. Something less tangible, less substantial. She has little cause these days to think overlong about the nature of a soul, but . . .

Maybe the Force really exists.

And if it does—it is gone from this body, sure as anything. It's like nothing connects it to the world anymore. It's just meat on the slab.

"Simple," Barell says, solving the mystery. "He was a spicehead. He'd just taken a pinch before we took him. Wouldn't be the first addict to take too much and go sucking void, would he?"

"Jas," Norra says. "How hard did you knock him out?"

"Please. I'm a professional. I don't make mistakes like that."

Wedge scratches his head. "We'll have to do an inquiry. I'll call down and get a couple of droids to take the body to Doctor Slikartha—he'll give the body the once-over and rule out any malfeasance—"

"You can take the body to whoever you want, but I assure you, this man was murdered." Jas stoops down and gets her face near to the corpse's. Cupping her hands, she scoops air near his mouth and takes a long deep sniff. "That smell. Bitter citrine. Like a too-ripe kakadu fruit. And see the fluid in the mouth?" She peels back his lip, already gone stiff. Saliva there has pooled, but it's neither white nor clear: It's bruise-dark. "He was poisoned. Kytrogorgia. Aka cerulean slime mold. It goes dry, then you powder it, and then—well, if I had a guess, someone sprinkled it in his spice tin, ensuring that he'd blissfully off himself without a clue in the world."

Wedge and Norra share a look. He says, "I'll tell the doc. Thanks."

"At least we don't need to waste time or money on a trial," Jom says.

"This guy killed a whole lot of people. Sometimes poisoning whole worlds. Whoever did him in has a good sense of irony, you ask me."

Outside the ship, Norra tells Wedge: "I'm sorry, Wedge. It's our job to bring these guys in alive, not dead. I assure you, it wasn't one of us—I know I said we're a rough crew, but we're not that rough—"

"It's okay. I know. Whatever this was—it wasn't that."

"Okay. Good." But he's still on the cusp of something. "What?"

"Someone wants to meet you."

"Us? The team?"

"Just you."

"Who? And . . . when?"

"Princess Leia. And she wants to meet right now."

CHAPTER FIVE

"My husband, Han Solo, is missing."

Norra blinks. *Husband?* Her lips move to form words, but no sound actually manifests. All she can do is stand there, gaping, *gawking* at the woman who singularly represents the voice of the New Republic across the galaxy. Leia Organa is a princess and a general and, most important, a figure of inspiration that few can deny. She stands there wearing loose-fitting white robes—somewhat traditional in the style here—with her hands clasped in front of her. The woman offered no introduction. Norra simply stepped into Leia's expansive office— which overlooks the coast of the Silver Sea—and tried to control the quivering in her voice as she announced herself: "Lieutenant Norra Wexley. You asked to see me?"

All Leia said in response was that one thing:

My husband, Han Solo, is missing.

"I'm . . . sorry?" Norra asks. "I don't understand. If General Solo—"

"He is no longer a general. He resigned his military commission."

"Oh. I . . ."

Leia lifts her chin, closes her eyes, and takes a deep breath. The Chandrilan air must agree with her—her skin shines. She's like a precious stone, flawless and glowing. After a slow exhale, Leia says: "My brother taught me to center myself. To be mindful of what I'm feeling—a cup to be filled up, he says." She winces. "And I'm just now realizing that this is likely quite sudden for you and I'm being very rude. Hello, Lieutenant Wexley, I am Leia Organa."

She hesitates when she answers: "I'm Norra. It's a great pleasure to meet you, Your Highness. All you've done for us . . ."

It's a strange thing to watch, but Leia has this façade, this *veneer*—it's not haughty, not exactly. A bit icy. Certainly confident—a confidence, in fact, that borders on arrogance. It's not as if she's looking down on you, but it is very much as if she is in *command* of you. It's a command that is as natural as the elliptical orbit of a world around its star, as obvious and as eternal as the flow of time itself or the presence of gravity.

But Norra watches that ice crack. The veneer crumbles. The tension goes out of Leia's shoulders as she leans against her desk. "Please, Norra. Don't call me 'Highness.' I have too many people who can't seem to break that habit."

"I just . . . feel weird calling you Leia."

"I can order you to call me Leia, if that helps."

". . . it *actually* would."

Leia again stands more stiffly, as if to invoke a special formality. "Lieutenant Norra Wexley, I command you by the power invested in me as the Last Princess of Alderaan and the Supreme High Something-or-Other of New Republic forces—" And here Leia moves her hands about in impatient gesticulations. "And so on and so forth, I demand that you call me Leia."

Norra gives a small bow. "Thank you. Uh. Leia."

"I summoned you here because I have heard good things about your team. You get results. In just a few short months you've already found half a dozen notable Imperial criminals—"

"We brought in number seven today. Vice Admiral Gedde. But something . . . happened. Regrettably, he didn't survive the trip."

"I heard about it. I'm sure that mystery will provide answers soon enough." Leia reaches over and takes Norra's hand. "Your work is important. It tells a fractured galaxy that the New Republic is capable of delivering its own brand of law and order. And it helps us understand how all of this happened. Once we know that, we can work together to ensure that history does not repeat itself."

"Thank you. But I don't understand what this has to do with General, ah, *Captain* Solo—"

Leia pauses. Her face is like a wave about to break. There in her eyes is a war for control, as if she knows it is her job to be calm and measured, but what she really wants is to let it all loose. All the pent-up feelings, all the frustrations of running a government, all her fears and desires.

She says the words slowly, carefully:

"Han went missing. I need him found. And your team finds people."

"You want . . . *us* to find him?"

"You don't need to go out of your way." Leia seems suddenly rattled. "To speak frankly, none of this is precisely aboveboard. And you can in turn tell me no. This isn't me commanding you. This is me asking for your help." She proceeds to explain what she knows. "Han and Chewbacca, his copilot, went on some half-cocked mission to free the Wookiee planet of Kashyyyk. But it was a ploy by the Empire. They captured Chewie, and Han barely escaped. Now he's out there alone and his last transmission ended abruptly and I haven't heard from him since. I fear he's in danger . . ."

Leia pauses. Her face tightens with sorrow. But again she pauses, takes a deep breath, and seems to swallow her grief.

Norra says: "I didn't realize you two were married."

"It was right there on the Endor moon after everything. We had a small ceremony, just those we trust. We don't keep it secret, but we didn't make it public, either."

"It must be hard, then, having him gone."

"It is. You know something about that, don't you?"

She means Brentin. Even just thinking about him brings the memory to bear like the bloom of heat from a crashing ship. Stormtroopers kicking down their door. The Imperial officer with a writ of arrest. Them dragging her husband out into the night. Her comforting Temmin into morning, assuring the boy that they'd bring Brentin back in the morning, that it was all just a mistake, that everything would be fine. That was years ago. They haven't seen Brentin since. Norra has grown woefully comfortable with the idea that her husband and Temmin's father is most likely dead.

"I understand, yes," Norra says, forcing a small smile. "Do you have any information on where Captain Solo is?"

"He was searching the Outer Rim and he said he was close to Wild Space. I can send you a map of the *Falcon*'s movements—he's far enough out there our sensors can no longer reliably track that hunk of wonderful junk he calls a freighter. I'll forward the map to your quarters."

"You can send them directly to the ship. Docking Plat OB-99." Norra pauses, then adds, "We'll find him." It's a promise she feels ill equipped to make, and as soon as she makes it the burden of the task at hand puts a tremendous weight on her—a crushing weight, in fact. But what can she say? What can she do? It's out there now. Her promise is a living thing.

Leia smiles—warmly, *truly* warmly, as all the ice has melted—and nods. "I believe you. Thank you, Norra Wexley. May the Force be your guide."

CHAPTER SIX

It is not easy to sneak away from your own command.

It took a bit of doing, in fact. She considered faking an illness, but these days, with all eyes on her as the identified leader of the Galactic Empire, the barest sniffle will have her swarming in nursedroids and health technicians. Instead, Rae Sloane's ruse went like this: She used her already overburdened schedule as an advantage. She told Ferric Obdur that she had to take time to talk about fleet movements with Vice Admiral Gaelan—which was true enough. Gaelan's been asking for a meeting to discuss just that for days—no, weeks—now.

She sent word ahead to Gaelan's office that she couldn't meet today because she had a meeting with General deVores to discuss *troop* movements. (That would incite the ire of Gaelan, but the man would take it in stride. He would swallow his impatience and toe the line as he always had.)

To deVores she sent word that she wanted a meeting but had to take time out to meet with Ferric Obdur in propaganda . . .

And so, the triangle of deception was arranged. Three points, one leading to the other. Unless someone was truly diligent about checking her whereabouts, it would seem from each to each that she had to move one meeting in favor of another. Few would seek to disturb her, lest they incite *her* ire—and Sloane was known for *not* taking that in stride. She did not toe any line. These days, she *was* the line, and none dared cross her.

(None except their mysterious fleet admiral, of course.)

The next step of her ruse required Adea's help. Sloane couldn't just hop into a craft and take off for regions unknown; she ran a tight ship. Accountability was king. A single ship gone missing was a breach of bureaucratic structure. And bureaucracy, vile as many considered it, was the foundation on which the entire galaxy was built. Bureaucracy would save them all. Violating that bureaucracy would upset the checks and balances . . .

. . . unless, of course, Sloane had Adea change the designation and destination of a small supply ship. And so an Imperial *Lambda*-class shuttle scheduled for Questal got rerouted instead to bring a load of naamite batteries and transponder arrays to the throneworld of Coruscant. The pilot: a young recruit named Dasha Bowen. Or so the registry says—really it's just a watertight identity also put together by Adea.

"Imperial shuttle CS-831," Sloane says into the comm. "This is transport pilot Dasha Bowen. Transmitting clearance code and credentials now."

Ahead, Coruscant glows brightly. A massive world carved with lines of light, the geometric patterns of its planet-encompassing ecunemopolis giving it the look of being on the edge of breaking apart. As if a frozen moment in time captures it seconds before it glows, swells, and detonates.

That may be truer than I care to admit, she thinks. The throneworld of the Empire is in the midst of being pulled apart—not so dramatically as having its mantle shattered, no, but its populace *is* undergoing that kind of tectonic shift. The citizens in some sectors have risen up against the Empire. While others have instead fought against their insurgent neighbors—a veritable civil war. One whose flames are stoked nicely by the New Republic resistance fighters entrenched on the surface. They sow distrust. Chaos is the result.

All around her little cargo ship, a defensive armada forms a protective shield around the planet. These are ISB ships—Imperial Security Bureau. Not the navy. Admiral Rax was very clear on that point. He said that they were not to commit resources protecting the throneworld. The ISB is controlling this world—and the navy doesn't want any part of it. It shows the fractures in the Empire: all the broken pieces drifting apart.

"It is a symbol," he told her, "of our indolence and torpidity. It is the moldering core of our overripe fruit, and I wish to cut away such rot so as to preserve our sweet remains. And, of course, the seeds within."

She argued that saving Coruscant would be a better symbol.

He answered with: "It is of far greater consequence to show how much we are willing to lose to preserve the strength of our Empire." It was then that he echoed the words of Count Vidian: *"Forget the old way."* Was this echo deliberate? How would he know what Vidian told her? "We must discard the obvious choices, Admiral Sloane. We must forge our own path through the stars if we are to survive."

And with that, the argument was done.

Now she hovers above the world, a world they have willfully forgotten. One left to the ISB under the command of Palpatine's old administrator, Grand Vizier Mas Amedda.

She wonders idly what it would take to retake the planet. The New Republic could fairly easily wipe out the ISB's defensive blockade. It would take time, but reports arrive daily of the Republic's growing military might. Still, the Empire's presence here on the surface is deeply dug in. An aerial campaign wouldn't be enough—

Finally, her comm crackles and a response returns:

"Code checks out. Cleared for landing, CS-831."

Of course it does, she thinks. Adea knows what she's doing. "Dasha Bowen" sets the ship for a landing trajectory.

Sloane leaves the cargo ship behind on the landing platform—droids move to unload the very real technical parts from inside its hold. While they are occupied, she pulls her visor low. The visor both hides her face and, with the tap of a button on the side of the helmet, pulls up a heads-up display glowing on the plastoglass shield. In this case, it's a map of Coruscant.

Her destination is a pulsing red star on the map:

The old Hall of Imperial Register building.

Less affectionately known as: "The Pit."

It is a storehouse of deeds, records, and data dumps.

It is to most a worthless aggregation of the Empire's bureaucracy—as records pile up in ships and transports and nav computers, across offices and academies and depots, those records must occasionally be off-loaded to backup. And so they are dumped here, offsite (often via droid). Few care to come here, for combing through the information is an act not unlike trying to find one particular grain of sand on a windswept beach. Worse, the information is often quite valueless. Trajectory calculations, inventory lists, personnel records all fill the massive warehouse of data.

But it's that last bit she's looking for: personnel records.

If there's anything about Gallius Rax, it will be here. That is, *if* she can find it.

Thankfully, Sloane is quite adept at navigating this place. To others, it is a Pit. To her, it is a *temple*.

The Pit sits at the margins of the Verity District—a well-fortified Imperial part of Coruscant. Home to the Hall of Adjudication, the Institute to Preserve Imperial History, and the ISB Academy and Offices. The streets here are usually clean, well kept, and busy. But now, not so much. She passes a pair of stormtroopers sitting against a steel barricade, helmets off their heads and held between their legs—the two men are sweaty, tired, and staring off at nothing. Ahead, the street is scarred with starburst streaks of char—the plastocrete shattered and cracked, as if by thermal detonator.

It's quiet, too. Usually, she'd hear the thrumming, vibrant traffic of the city above her—speeders and grav-bikes whipping past in criss-crossing lines like little myrmidants serving their colony. Now, though, the sky above is dead. Not a single speeder. No droids, no birds, nothing. The airspace is closed, isn't it? She'd heard reports of citizens loading up their speeders with explosives and driving them into Imperial buildings.

Then, as if on cue, the ground shudders. Somewhere off in the distance, just such an explosion: She can feel it vibrate up through her heels, all the way into her *teeth*. Sloane can't see anything, but it isn't long before she sees the trail of red smoke climbing into the sky like a crawling serpent.

Klaxons go off. A pair of ISB speeders streak overhead.

What a horror show, she thinks. But Rae has no time to dwell on this. Her time here is limited, and she has to move.

The Pit is ahead. From the surface, it looks like nothing but a single-story fortified bunker. It has a single door and a shuttered window.

As Sloane approaches, the shutter slides up with a rattle-bang. There stands the top half of an administrative droid, its capsule-shaped head leaning forward. From its mouthpiece comes a tinny, mechanized voice:

"HOLD STILL FOR OCULAR SCAN."

Sloane can't hide from this. No matter how well crafted the persona of Dasha Bowen, Adea's efforts do not carry as far as creating a whole new pair of eyeballs. This one will not be faked, and so she lifts her visor.

From the droid's own eye comes a shimmering red beam.

She blinks and winces as it passes over her face.

"GRAND ADMIRAL RAE SLOANE," the droid says. "IT IS GOOD TO SEE YOU. WELCOME TO THE HALL OF IMPERIAL REGIS-TER. PLEASE WATCH YOUR STEP. THE FALL IS *QUITE* STEEP."

The droid is right. The Pit is fifty floors. Not straight up, but rather, straight *down*. Plunged into the exomantle of Coruscant like a pneumatic bolt. The shape of it is circular, and it spirals ineluctably downward, giving Sloane the sense that she is swirling down the drain. At the bottom, she half expects that the Hall of Imperial Register gobbles you right up like a mouth: a sarlacc nesting at the nadir, digesting wayward data-miners.

She will not be digested, not today.

She will, however, go mad if she doesn't get moving. Inertia is a curse and Sloane's whole life and career have been about combating it. So she sets up shop in a little alcove. Hours pass. The droid attendants—more administrative droids, these fixed to the railings so that they can zip past the shelves of records both hard copy and digital—bring her old data cartridges. She told them that she needed a proper accounting of all the ships of the Imperial Navy in play as of the destruction of the second Death Star. She's on her eighth and final cartridge.

She starts with the Dreadnoughts—the Super Star Destroyers.

Thirteen were in service before the revivified Death Star was destroyed above Endor. One of those is the *Ravager,* the SSD from which Sloane rules the Empire (and which, strictly speaking, is now Gaelan's command). One of those is the *Executor,* Vader's command ship. The *Executor* was lost that day, plunging into the surface of the Death Star. Taking hundreds of thousands of the best Imperials with it.

Sloane shudders as she thinks of it.

That leaves eleven others.

Three are now in the hands of the New Republic. Two of those were from admirals willingly surrendering the ship and its people. One was taken forcibly by New Republic forces while it underwent repairs over Kuat.

Five were destroyed outright in battles across the galaxy with the New Republic—the ships were understaffed, underprotected, and on the run. (The Dreadnoughts are home to massive batteries of fleet-killing weapons, yes, but are also slow, unwieldy beasts—they hang there in the sky like bricks, and without adequate protection it is an inevitability that enemy forces could erode the ships until obliteration ensues.)

One was taken by pirates: the *Annihilator*. Tagge's old ship. But who controls the *Annihilator* now? The reports don't say.

Another, the *Arbitrator*, made a bad hyperspace calculation to escape pursuing NR ships. It evaporated when it was sucked into a gravity well.

That leaves Palpatine's own command ship:

The *Eclipse*.

Records show that it, too, was destroyed by a fleet of New Republic vessels—Ackbar's own frigate, *Home One*, firing the ship-killing shot.

Ah, but there's the catch, and it's why Sloane is *here:* The ships dumped data across the stars, transmitting pulses of information to this location. That provides a black-box recording of information so one could discern what exactly happened before a ship was destroyed, captured, or surrendered. All the other tracking data adds up to the known fates of each SSD. Their stories match the data for all of them— except one.

For the *Eclipse*, the data ends a full day-cycle before the ship was reportedly destroyed. It shows no siege by New Republic forces. It simply . . . drops off the star map. Gone. Vanished.

Sloane concedes that it's possible the ship stopped reporting due to a malfunction in its data recorder. Though redundant systems were supposed to alert command if that had happened—again, bureaucracy and reiterative mechanisms should have saved the day here.

And yet they didn't.

Is it possible that the *Eclipse* is still out there? Could the *Ravager* not be the last Super Star Destroyer in the naval arsenal?

The inventory of the Star Destroyers is similar, but on a far grander scale. Seventy-five percent of the Star Destroyers in service before Endor can capably be tracked to similar fates: destroyed, captured, lost in confirmable if curious ways. But a full quarter of those ships cannot be accounted for. Records show fateful ends that contradict their black-box recordings.

Does the Empire have more ships than she knows? Ghost fleets out there somewhere? Are they operating independently? Have they been captured or abandoned? Something else may be going on.

Does Rax know? Or is he in the dark, too?

Speaking of Gallius Rax . . .

Picking through the data to find anything on the erstwhile fleet admiral will be an act of finding a precious gem in a box of broken glass—it will be a slow and miserable retrieval. But it's why she's really here, so she summons a droid and sets it to work.

"I WILL SEE WHAT DATA I CAN EXCAVATE," the droid says, then gives a small nod before its servomotors whir and carry it away.

Excavate, she thinks. A perfect word. And from a droid, no less.

Flip, flip, flip. Page after page on the cartridge reader—she palms the control orb and swipes it left again and again, scrolling through endless administrative pages. Here, as with the naval archives, the presence of Rax is naught but a vapor trail. She's chasing shadows.

And so she's down to searching the records of those who associated with him: Yularen, Rancit, Screed, and Palpatine himself. She cross-references personnel reports, genealogical records, inventory lists, anything, everything. Hours pass. Her eyes are bleary. She feels alone and overwhelmed, and the only sound that accompanies her frustration and her anxiety is the sound of droids clicking and clacking and rattling about.

She stands up. The search is over.

Rax barely exists.

Trying to figure out who he is or who he *was* is an act of grabbing at fog—it dissipates in your hand while still obscuring everything beyond it.

It's time to go, so she packs up her notes and tucks them in a side satchel before slinging it over her shoulder.

Suddenly movement behind her—

She wheels on it. Reaching for her blaster.

It's the droid. Of *course* it is. It wouldn't be anyone else, and yet—well, she has to excuse her own shock. *I'm tired and angry.*

The droid buzzes: "AN IMAGE CRYSTAL." It extends a telescoping arm. In it, a small smoke-gray crystal. The Empire doesn't use these anymore, as they're somewhat antiquated, but decades before, single-serving image crystals were still in use. Now the Empire has the ability to archive visual and textual information across cartridges or data-cards.

She's about to hand it back. What could one image matter?

Still. The reader is right here. She unslings the bag and, without sitting, places the crystal in the smooth portal on the alcove desk, then hits the button beneath it so it lights up.

A three-dimensional image emerges in the space before her.

It looks like somewhere in an Imperial docking bay. In the background, a *Lambda*-class shuttle sits. At the margins of the holo, white-armored stormtroopers and a pair of red-armored Imperial Royal Guardsmen.

There, in the middle of the photo:

Wullf Yularen, Dodd Rancit, Terrinald Screed, plus three others: Grand Vizier Mas Amedda, Emperor Palpatine, and . . .

A boy.

Or, rather, a boy on the cusp of being a young man.

The boy looks like a dirt-cheeked rube shoved into an ill-fitting academy uniform. His hair is dark, his skin is pale. Those eyes, though. A familiar arrogance shines there. Each a black hole swallowing the light.

One thing stands out: One of the boy's hands is facing outward, and Sloane sees something across his palm. A marking of some kind. A tattoo?

Or a brand?

This holographic image by itself does nothing to illuminate who Rax is. And yet it stirs in her a strange kind of hope: In this act of "excavation" she has found a rather curious fossil, hasn't she? If this is him, *if* this is Gallius Rax, then the mystery of his presence becomes one she can solve. He becomes a beast she can kill.

(Not literally, of course. Or so she hopes.)

What next, then, for this mystery? She has a bit of thread in her hands—how shall she pull it? Four of the men in the image glowing before her are dead. Palpatine is gone. Yularen died on the Death Star, Rancit perished in a Rebel attack (though she's heard rumors that Vader executed him for treason), and Screed was killed by pirates off the Iktari Circle.

Which leaves one left alive.

It is time, she thinks, *to pay Mas Amedda a visit.*

INTERLUDE

CORONET CITY, CORELLIA

Erno watches the kid do it. The little dum-dum doesn't even *know* he's being watched. Kid creeps up to the wall like a scuttling spider under the cover of night, then takes the stencil to the pale brick and pulls out the light painter—he shakes it a few times and gives it a hit, and then it pulses an image onto the side of the P&S (Peace & Security) station.

An iconic image of a bad, bad man.

Maybe not even a man. Maybe a *machine.*

VADER LIVES, it says. That, stenciled underneath the all-too-familiar artist rendering of the helmeted thug.

The kid turns, grinning like he got away with it. He didn't.

Erno steps into the halo of light from the street-orb overhead, and he clears his throat so the kid in the dark hood and cloak looks up. Another one of these Acolyte idiots. Erno whistles. "Nice art. A real original."

The kid doesn't say anything. He stands there, quaking in his bare feet. He's young, dumb, scared. Erno sighs and levels his blaster.

"C'mon, you little roach-rat, turn around, turn around. Let's get these binders on."

Pouting, the boy turns and Erno slaps on a pair of binders, then hauls him around front and in through the doors of the station.

The new hire at the front desk, a pretty Pantoran named Kiza, says, "Hey, Detective," and he gives her a wink and a nod even though she'd probably never have anything to do with a scruffy thick-neck like him. Erno drags the kid through the station and past the desks and the holoscreens and the peace officers and into one of the back rooms. He gives the kid a light shove and the boy lands hard in a chair.

The boy hisses something at him. It isn't in a language he understands, and he doesn't care to ask about it.

"Uh-huh, sure, sure. Whatever, kid." Erno sits down across from the boy, and pops a cut square of rubber-root in his mouth, giving it a good chew. It tastes like the underside of a boot but gives his mouth something to do, and better this than the stimsticks he used to smoke.

He gets the boy's measure fast. Human punk, maybe fourteen, maybe fifteen. Pale like the others (they pretend they're nocturnal). Black hood, black cloak. This one doesn't have a mask, though. A lot of these Acolyte freaks, they put together these masks—hammering together plastoid, metal, wood, goggles, ventilators, whatever—and wear them as they harangue the locals. It's all pathetic, paltry stuff. Vandalism, mostly.

"Vader lives," Erno says, chewing on the rubber-root. "Vader lives, you say. Last I heard, he went up with the Death Star. *Whoom.* He's dead. If he was ever even alive. Empire's falling apart, and it wouldn't be if he were still around, don't you think?"

"Death isn't the end."

"Last I checked, it's pretty much the final stop, kid."

The boy grins. His teeth are white, too white. His tongue snakes along them, and for a moment Erno feels his guts clench. His instincts are telling him something's wrong here, but he doesn't know what.

No, this kid's just getting to you. It's late. You been on duty for too long now. Get this moron booked, then head home.

"What's your name?"

"Oblivion."

He snorts with derisive laughter. "Oh. That's a nice name. That a family name?" The loser doesn't say anything, he just sits there, chest rising and falling like a cornered, feral animal. "Look, kid. I got you for vandalism. You can spend a couple nights down in the hole. But I'm feeling friendly. I'm feeling *generous.* You roll over on a couple of your Acolyte buddies—you *are* an Acolyte of the Beyond, right?—and I'll get you out of here with a stern finger-wagging and not much else. Hm?"

Still the boy says nothing.

Erno sighs.

"What's the deal with you pouty little thugs, anyway? You're, what, a buncha suck-ups for the Empire?"

"Not the Empire. Something *greater* than the Empire."

"Vader."

The boy grins.

"Not Palpatine?"

Again the boy says nothing. That grin only widens.

Makes sense, Erno figures. Who would think that old withered twig was worth a measure of twisted hero worship? Vader at least looked like a tough guy. Imposing, dangerous, a real bad bag of tricks.

"You don't have a mask?" Erno asks.

"I don't."

"Why not? The mask is more of the Vader thing, huh? Trying to look like him? You know he was a bad guy, right?"

"Are you a decent man?" the boy asks. "A 'good guy'?"

Hardly, Erno thinks. His wife has left him for a pair of artists in the Teeno Village district. His neighbors think he's a slob. Even the fish in his fishtank give him a dubious look every morning when he leaves for work.

"I asked about your mask."

The boy shifts in his seat. "You have to earn your mask."

"*Oh.* Ho ho. You haven't earned it yet?"

The kid looks up at the ceiling, then around the room at the bare walls. "This building is very old."

"Yeah. So?"

"I know what's downstairs."

What's downstairs . . . ? The museum next door uses the shared basement with the P&S building. The detectives keep evidence locked up down there, and the museum uses the same lockup to keep a bunch of old musty, dusty artifacts and the like.

Erno's about to pick this apart because really, why does this snot-dribbling punk care? Maybe it's a clue. Maybe the kid's parents work for the museum. Could be a—

But then someone comes in the room.

It's a security officer, Spob Rydel, hat in hand. "Erno, you oughta see this."

Ennnhhh, I'm busy, Rydel, he thinks, but fine, fine, if one of the security ops guys wants him to see something, so be it. He takes the kid's wrists and brings them to the tabletop before slapping a button underneath the surface—the table goes magnetic, and the kid's binder cuffs *thud* hard to the tabletop as the magnetic field pulls them down.

Then he's up and back through the station, and the holoscreens are turning to CCI—the Coronet City Info channel—one by one.

It takes Erno a second to gauge what he's even seeing. Holofeeds from various areas around the city all show similar scenes: Downtown, in Diadem Square, a horde of hooded and cloaked figures are mobbing storefronts and leaping on top of the air-tuks to pull the speeders down to the ground; on the 1-line of the mag-lev subway, they swarm aboard as soon as the train stops at the Juni Street Station; down by the casinos, they rush those coming out and going in, dark cloaks fluttering in the night.

They carry sticks.

Sticks painted red.

They have *masks*.

Some kind of concerted attack. A riot. Or worse.

Already the officers here are mobilizing—streaming out the door or heading up the stairs to the speeder pad on the roof.

"It's the kriffin' *Acolytes,*" Rydel says. "Ain't you got one in the back room there? Bring his narrow can out here. Let's kick it around a little."

Yeah. *Yeah,* Erno thinks. He stomps to the back room he was in, throws the door wide and—

The kid is gone.

Just then: The lights flicker once, then twice, then go out.

Erno is in darkness. Thankfully, a few seconds later the emergency lights come up—they line the floor and the ceiling, casting everything in a red glow. He curses under his breath and heads back out into the main room, and already most of the building has cleared out. It's him, Rydel, a couple of other detectives like Shreen and Mursey, and—

Wait, wasn't Kiza here? Where the hell'd she go?

He's about to say something to Rydel, but then a blaster shot threads the air, clipping the officer square in the forehead. Rydel falls backward. Two more blasts and Shreen and Mursey fall—Shreen flips backward over her desk, and Mursey just slumps forward against a hydro-cooler.

Erno fumbles at his back for his own blaster—

But he's too slow.

There's Kiza. *Kiza,* of all the people. She has a standard sec-issued blaster pointed up and at him. The kid in black is nowhere to be seen.

"Kiza, I don't . . . I don't get what's happening here, doll."

"I'm not your doll." Her voice trembles as she speaks.

"What . . . what is this?"

She slowly crosses the space between them. Winding her way through the sea of desks, through the red-lit half dark. "This is a revolution. This is the revenge of the darkness. This is oblivion."

"Borkin' hell," Erno says. "You're . . . you're one of *them.*"

He figures, she's not trained. She's scared—he can hear that much in her voice. So he goes for his blaster anyway. He's old, but she's not a cop. His hand finds his blaster and his arm extends—

The air lights up next to him. The world thrums as a red beam of light whisks upward through open space—

A searing line of pain across his wrist.

And then, the hand that held the blaster is gone. It thumps against one of the desks, still clutching the blaster. He watches it fall and tumble away. It's an absurd thing to see, your own hand coming off like that.

Next to him, it's the kid in the cloak.

He has a red-bladed lightsaber in his hand.

"I told you I knew what was in the basement," he seethes.

"That's the blade we've been looking for?" Kiza asks him.

The Acolyte gives an over-eager nod.

Then—*wham.*

Kiza clubs Erno in the side of the head. The world spins away from him as he tumbles to the floor. She bends down and whispers in his ear: "Vader lives. And so do you. Tell everyone the Acolytes are coming, *doll.*"

CHAPTER SEVEN

The bar is a little seaside joint off Junari Point—a few klicks outside Hanna City proper. It's not much to look at: a round bar of dark wood under a wind-ruffled tent. Bulabirds strut about the pebbles-and-sand, their star-tipped beaks overturning rocks to look for their next meal to come skittering out. The ocean slides in and out with less of the crash-and-clamor of proper waves, and more the hiss-and-whisper of a calm lake lapping at its shore. The night is cool. The spitting rain is done, leaving behind a breeze.

Sinjir sits, staring into a white mug of black liquid. Steam rising around him, warming his chin.

Tonight the bar has a few other patrons. Other Chandrilans—over there, an angler with a firm chin staring down at her pint of fizzing something-or-other. On the other side, a young man in a fancy, breezy shirt glaring at his holoscreen with grave disinterest. The bartender—a tall woman with her white-blond hair pulled back in a complex braid that loops around her neck like a collar—eases past, asking: "Everything good?"

He gives a small nod. As she passes, he sees her gaze turn up. She spies someone coming. Someone behind Sinjir. He's about to tense up—

And then, half a second later, an arm slides around his neck on the right side—and on his left, a scruffy and familiar head appears on his shoulder. Sandy beard scratching his collarbone.

"Well, hello," Sinjir says, arching an eyebrow.

The man's free hand snakes over Sinjir's right shoulder and grabs the mug, then pulls it to his head so he can sniff it.

"This is *caf*," the man says with a frown.

"*What?*" Sinjir says, feigning shock. "Caf? Well, I didn't order this. I must burn this place down in protest. It is the only recourse."

The man—Conder Kyl—rolls his eyes. "You're very dramatic. I'm just surprised you're drinking *this* and not, say, Kowakian rum or, I don't know, *hull stripper*."

"I'm trying to stay awake to see you. Hence, the caf." He holds up the mug and leers over its lip. "Oh, and I'll have you know that Hull Stripper was my nickname at the Imperial officers' academy."

"I don't doubt that." Conder leans in to kiss Sinjir's cheek.

Alarm bells go off inside his head. Reflexively, he pulls his face to the side. He scoots his stool a few centimeters away from the man.

"That can't be good," Conder says. "You done with me so soon?"

"Now who's being dramatic?"

"So what is it, then?"

"I *told* you. I don't like . . . this."

"This?"

"This! *This*. The . . . *public* thing."

Conder hip-bumps a stool closer to Sinjir, then plops down on it. His elbow plants on the bar and he leans against his hand, his face twisting into a dubious, bemused mask. "You do know where you are, right? You're safe here, Rath Velus. *We're* safe here. Chandrila is . . . pretty open."

Conder exists on that perfect line between *pretty* and *manly*. He's got a barrel chest and big arms, a laser-shorn scalp, and that patchy, spiky beard of his. But he's also got long, theatrical lashes and pouty lips. And skin as smooth and tan as a statue carved of Nimarian korabaster. Even his voice: It's gravelly, but it has a lilt to it, too. It is rough but beautiful music.

He's also one of the best slicers the New Republic has on deck. Not many systems Kyl can't cut to ribbons if he sets his mind to it. That's how he and Sinjir met—two jobs back, hunting Moff Gorgon, the crew needed someone to break into an interrogator droid's head, and Temmin wasn't up to the task. They brought in Conder Kyl.

Conder, whom Sinjir just publicly rebuked.

"It's not that," Sinjir says. "Not exactly. The Empire . . ." Well, he's explained this all before, hasn't he? Conder knows the deal. The Empire cared little about any sexual or romantic entanglements, *provided* they didn't have to see it. No matter what your peccadilloes, the manual of decorum made it clear that you kept all of that behind closed doors. (Especially if it violated any of the Empire's family initiatives— they wanted breeders above all else.) Worse, Sinjir knew all too well that *affection* was a weakness. Relationships were a rope to tie around your throat—a rope all too easy to tug and choke. First thing he did when investigating one of his own for disloyalty was find out whom they were bedding. It was always a vital weak spot—as vital and as weak as stabbing a thumb into a person's windpipe or pumping a fist into his kidneys. Knowing who loved whom was a path to exploitation and control. "Affection exposes us. I don't want us exposed. And look, people are staring."

The angler continues to stare down into her drink. The young man in his fancy shirt keeps gazing at his datapad. The bartender stands off to the side, polishing glasses.

"Oh, yeah," Conder says. "I feel completely *dissected*."

"Well, what do *you* know?" Sinjir sips his caf loudly.

From behind them, footsteps against the pebbles. Bulabirds chatter and hop as two other customers step up to the bar. Sinjir has seen them here before: Both are pilots for the New Republic. The first is a long-nosed Chandrilan with a faint scar across his brow. The other a slump-shouldered woman with pocked cheeks and a permanent scowl screwed to her ugly mug.

Mister Browscar steps up to the other side of Sinjir, raps his knuckles on the bar, and calls to the bartender: "A balmgruyt. Now."

"Two," Miss Scowlface says, slapping the bar.

As the bartender fetches their drinks, Browscar looks over and glowers long and hard at Sinjir. "I don't like your kind," he says.

Sinjir applauds. "Thank you, sir. Thank you very much for proving my point. See, Conder? These pilots do not approve of our lifestyle."

Scowlface pokes her head up over Browscar's shoulder and her eyes narrow. She sticks her chin out. "We don't like *Imperials* around here."

So disappointing.

"*That's* your problem?" Sinjir blusters.

"He's not an Imperial," Conder says, standing up. "He's on our side."

"Well," Sinjir corrects, "let's not go *that* far—"

"He's a kriffing Imp is what he is." Browscar leans forward, baring his teeth. Sinjir can smell the spirits on his breath; the man's already lit up like a laser battery. "A blackarmor, corner-turning cur who'll cut our throats if we let him. We don't like his kind. We don't care for Imp-lovers, either."

"I get it," Sinjir says, faking a sip from his mug of caf, a mug he fully intends to break over this man's fool head. "I do. For a long time, the Galactic Empire has run roughshod over every system and station—from the warm gooey center of the Core to the coldest fringes of the Outer Rim. But the Empire is breaking apart and now all us *bad guys* are showing up at your door with a shrug and a smile and asking to be forgiven. And we probably don't deserve it, yet here we are. That presents a problem for you because now the question is: Will you prove that you're truly the champions of the galaxy? Are you the good guys who can forgive, or are you just as bad as—"

Bam. Sinjir's head snaps back from the hit. It's got power behind it, but it's as inelegant and imprecise as a stampeding nerf—his brain rattles, but he doesn't taste blood. He licks his lips to be sure. Nope.

His hand curls around the mug. The caf is still hot.

It'll leave a lovely burn across the man's scalp.

But then Conder's hand finds his, and steadies it. "We can just go," the slicer says in his ear. A breathy whisper. Not scared. Simply confident.

The pilot stands. Browscar's hands are squeezed into fists and he's ready for the fight. The man is just *itching* for it. Sinjir echoes that itch—it crawls inside him like wires in his blood, hot and electric.

All Sinjir does, though, is nod. "Good night, gents."

Browscar and Scowlface seem taken aback as Sinjir and Conder lock arms and leave. The caf mug still on the bar, steaming.

Morning. Same beach, same sea, same bar.

Sinjir had gone, but now he's back. He left Conder and a warm bed behind. *A proper bookend to the night,* he thought at the time—that before he drank more and passed out right there.

The smeary light of sunrise melts across Sinjir's shut eyes. He smacks his lips and peels himself off the bar top. It makes a noticeable sound, like unwrapping a bandage from a sticky wound.

His mouth tastes of—

What is that? Ah. Yes. Tsiraki. A liquor born of fermented salakberry and pickling spices. Sour and sweet and totally terrible and also amazing.

He blinks sleep from his eyes. His head still feels wobbly. Which is good, because that means the hangover has not yet gotten its claws into him. A little *hair of the garral* then to keep him going and—

Ugh, but where *oh where* has that pesky bartender gone?

That's grumpy-making.

It's then, though, that he realizes someone is sitting next to him.

"Hello, you," he says.

"You brined yourself quite effectively," Jas Emari says. She's on the stool next to him, picking her teeth with a narrow-bladed knife.

"Hm? Yes. Tsiraki."

She makes a face.

"Don't judge until you've partaken," he mumbles.

"I have. It tastes like slug bile."

"You don't drink. You're not a *connoisseur*." But he yawns and stretches. "That's why we make fine friends, though. You're the no-nonsense get-it-done bounty hunter, and I'm the soggy-but-lovable agent provocateur. They should do a HoloNet show about us now that the Empire's stranglehold over the media has all but fallen away."

"You're mad at me," she says.

"What? No," he lies.

"Was it Jom? Are you really mad about him?"

"Are *we* really doing this? Right now?" But he can see by the steel in her gaze that the Zabrak is quite serious, indeed. "Blech. *Fine*. No, it's not Jom. You do what you like when pantsless. It's . . ." He doesn't want to say it, so for a moment he just lets the words dissolve into a kind of throaty growl until he can finally articulate: "It's the plan. *Your* plan at Slussen Canker's fortress. You went ahead and played your little scheme and you told the boy but you didn't tell *me*."

"I should have. I concede."

"I don't like being in the dark. Not with you. It makes me *squirrelly*. And it's not just that. It's . . . I didn't *know*. I had no idea you were pulling a fast one on us all. That sort of thing, I can usually see it long before it drops out of hyperspace. But somehow you kept it from me. The boy did, too. I'm either losing my touch or—"

"Or you trust us."

"I do."

"That bothers you."

"It does." Now it's his turn to make a face. "Let me ask you something."

"Ask."

"Why do you do it?"

"Do what?"

"This. The team. The New Republic."

She cleans the tip of her blade with the pad of her thumb and shrugs. "I don't know. Credits. Debts."

"I don't quite believe you."

"So don't. Why do *you* do it?"

"I'm bored."

It's her turn to say it: "Now *I* don't quite believe *you.*"

"Maybe we both have debts that credits alone cannot pay."

She shrugs. "Maybe we do."

He sniffs and winces. This conversation has gotten far too serious, far too dour. "How'd you find me, anyway?"

"Conder told me."

"And how'd you find *him*? I didn't know you knew."

She smirks. "I know everything. I'm good at my job." She twirls her blade and shoves it back into the sheath at her side. "Which reminds me, we *have* a job. Norra called."

"I thought we had a few days of R and R."

"This is your idea of R and R?" she asks, gesturing toward the two figures at the other end of the bar. One of those figures is Browscar, who is belly-flopped across the bar top, flung there like a dead fish. Around his head are the broken remnants of a mug and the cooled puddle of liquid that was in it. The other is Scowlface, who lies supine in the sand, a bar towel held firm to her bloody nose. The woman moans.

"At least both of them are still breathing," Jas says.

"I'm not a murderer."

"What'd they do, anyway?"

He sighs. "They were rude."

"C'mon, Sin. Let's get to work."

CHAPTER EIGHT

Sloane comes up out of The Pit and steps outside, craning her neck and rolling her shoulders to get the tension out of them. How long was she in there, anyway? (The precise answer matters little, as the real answer is: *way too long.* So long that the lack of her presence on board the *Ravager* will be noticed by someone.) What strikes her immediately is:

It's dark.

That would be sensible on any other world, because it's late—or at the least, really, really early—but the thing about Coruscant is, it's a world that never sleeps. The power never goes out. The dark comes and the whole planet lights up. But here, in the Verity District, it's *dark*-dark.

It's also *quiet.*

The skin on her neck prickles. Something's wrong.

She has to move. But where? Her plan was to find herself one of the departing subgrav trains—the Black Line would take her right to the

Federal District, after all. But if there's no power up here, what about down there? And finding a taxi won't be an option . . .

Far down the block, three figures run between buildings. Ducking and darting until they're out of sight. They're not troopers—she doesn't hear the familiar clatter of their boots and armor.

We're under attack. The insurgents are here. Right now.

The only recourse is to get to her ship.

She hasn't been in action for what feels like too long—but the blade of her instinct hasn't gone dull. She feels suddenly hyperaware, and her mind goes through the cold, dispassionate calculations that are all too familiar: *Stay away from open streets, move between buildings, keep your head down, get your blaster out.* A grim realization crawls up inside her: This is what life on the throneworld is like now, isn't it?

Sloane moves fast. Across the street. Sliding through the alley between a commissary and BRAC (base realignment and closure) building. Ducking behind a compacting trash machine as she checks her blaster, then she's back up and moving. She winds around a med station, alongside a repair bay, under the black shadow of a communications array.

Whoom. Ahead, far ahead, the air lights up with a pulsing explosion—lightning crackles in its white-hot center, and then it's gone. Alarms sound in its wake. Down a nearby street, an ISB transport roars past, heading toward the source of the explosion. Sloane thinks: *I hope that wasn't my landing platform.* She takes a step forward, her eyes still adjusting to the white streaks pulsing across her vision. A sound behind her. She wheels—

Something clips her across the side of the head and she goes down. A boot presses on her hand and the chrome blaster slips from her grip. Another boot kicks her weapon away from her.

An absurd, defeatist part of her thinks: *This is fine.* The New Republic soldiers can take her in. Let it all be over. She will make a fine catch for some bush pilot or some hick commando—a guaranteed medal.

But a fire warms in her belly. Her heart goes supernova. *This is my*

Empire, she thinks. She won't leave it to these brutes. And she damn sure won't let someone like Rax crash everything she's worked for right into the heart of some star. No. Not tonight. Not if she can help it.

Sloane rolls toward her own pinned arm—causing no small pain— and reaches up with her free hand to grab at whoever is holding her there. Her fingers find the attacker's belt and she pulls hard, yanking him down to the ground. It's not even a New Republic soldier—she sees a dark dress and a blue-and-gold rag bundled around the arm. *Local resistance.*

The man, practically a boy, cries out for help. Other shapes move in toward her, but Sloane is up now in a crouch. Her body is coded with the memory of *how to fight.* Back in the Academy, she practiced and competed in NCB: Naval Corps Boxing. She was good. Never won the belt. But she always ranked.

And Sloane has kept up with it.

The first insurgent who comes at her does so with the inelegance of a drunken man groping for a kiss—she sidesteps him and jabs with a fist, catching him right in the eye. He flails and staggers backward as another one, this one in rough armor and a face-shield, steps in to fill the void. Sloane kicks out this one's leg, and her enemy drops, so she drops with her enemy, catching the person's arm as they fall. Sloane pivots herself into an armbar and yanks back on the insurgent's wrist hard enough that the arm dislocates with a grungy *crunch.* The terror- ist yells—and it's a woman's voice crying out in pain. Sloane kicks off the face-shield, then scoops it up and flings it at the next person com- ing in—

It catches the incoming terrorist in the face, and they spin and tum- ble. But Sloane is too slow and outnumbered. Someone tackles her from the side, and her shoulder crashes hard against the plastocrete. The breath blasts from her lungs as she scrambles against the ground.

Something presses hard against the side of her head.

A blaster.

"Don't move," comes a shaky, uncertain voice. That same voice calls out: "We got one. Imperial. Pilot by the look of her."

Sloane goes through a new set of calculations. She could fight back. But if they take her, will she play the role of Grand Admiral Rae Sloane, or will she instead aim to be Dasha Bowen, harmless pilot? The former has value, the latter almost none. What will serve her best?

Someone else moves in—a big man, half his face hidden behind a swaddling of blue-and-gold fabric. He reaches down with a wide paw and flips her so she's staring up. Sloane shows her hands. The woman with the blaster stands and stares, her face sooty, her eyes deeply set. "Get her up. We'll take her in. Garris will know what to do with her."

"We could just deal with her here," the big guy says. Others start to gather in behind them. Men, women, young and old. Half a dozen.

"Deal with her?"

"Yeah. *Deal* with her."

"That's not who we are."

"Maybe it's who we need to be."

Someone else from behind them, a gruff voice: "We're not soldiers. We're just taking back our home."

The blaster pointed at Sloane's nose wavers.

A new figure joins the group. Someone tall, thin. Arms extended out—a pair of batons held in hand. Hard to see anything but the cut of his silhouette. The batons twirl in his grip.

"What've we got here?" he asks.

"Caught us a fish," the big guy says.

But then someone asks: "Wait, who are—"

The new arrival moves like a cyclone. He ducks and spins, jabbing each baton into a different insurgent. The batons *bang* like slugthrowers going off, and it's a giveaway—those are concussive batons. And they are the signature weapon of someone Sloane has come to work with, recently:

The bounty hunter, Mercurial Swift.

The woman pulls her blaster out of Sloane's face to concentrate on the new attacker—and it's a mistake. Sloane gets up behind her and locks her arm tight around the woman's throat. Tighter, tighter, until the woman slides to the ground.

Swift, meanwhile, is up and down like a puppet on yanking strings, the batons jamming under chins and against ribs. Each time this happens, the baton cracks like localized thunder, and another enemy drops.

Until the only two left standing are Sloane and Swift.

"You," Sloane seethes. "You followed me."

"Do we have the time to discuss this right now?" The bounty hunter twirls his batons and clips them back on his utility belt. "I don't think we do. We need to go, Admiral. Unless you want to run into more of your friends?"

She does not. "You can get me out of here?" she asks.

Swift grins and licks his teeth. "It would be my pleasure."

The speeder skims the tops of the buildings along the Verity District, hugging it so close, Sloane is afraid Mercurial is going to scrape bottom and scrap the craft in a plume of fire. But he assures her—this makes them hard to see and, more important, hard to *hit*.

She smells burning ozone. And smoke. And hears blasterfire from somewhere behind them. Coruscant is a war zone. Has the Verity District fallen to the local resistance? Or is this just another random act of violence?

In the distance, the Imperial Palace. A massive, jagged thing. Like a mountain swallowed up by bruise-colored light. Spotlight spires shining up into the sky, painting the bands of dark clouds hanging far overhead with swatches of white. Suddenly two TIE fighters scream above them.

"You can tell your people that the resistance fighters are using the old cargo tunnels, the ones that run parallel to the subgrav tunnels." He glances at her, waiting for her reply.

What, though, could her reply be? The most pointed one, the one that sticks in her mind like a nail, is that these are not her "people." That is a thought that thickens and chills her blood, because what it means is that there does not exist one Empire anymore. There are several—fragments of the mirror broken. All reflecting something similar, but broken apart . . .

And, she worries, impossible to repair.

All Sloane can say in reply is, "Thank you." Two words that sound hollow. The bounty hunter must detect how little she means it.

"You seem not to care very much that I just saved your hide."

"I care. I also care that you have been following me."

"You summoned me, didn't you?" He flashes his white-toothed smile.

She turns and with a sudden surge of rage says: "When I summon you, I expect you to come as your name suggests: *swiftly*. Not skulk after me like a tooka waiting for a taste of milk."

They pass over the end of the Verity District and into the Federal— where the lights are still on. None will dare to breach this region, she suspects, lest they meet the full force of the Imperial Security Bureau. But then again: At the end of time, all mountains crumble and fall. They become hills and then dust and then the winds of change take them away. Most mountains erode slowly, but sometimes a tectonic shift can speed up its inevitable destruction. The galaxy is undergoing just such a shift.

"You have a job for me?" he asks. "Last one went fine. Our friend, the vice admiral, found that his addiction was *just* too much to bear. Nasty habit, that spice."

"I need you to find someone."

"I assumed that." He looks like he's about to say more—some snide or narcissistic remark. Even he is smart enough to know not to push the perceived head of the Empire too far. He clears his throat. "Who and where?"

"Brendol Hux. He's on Arkanis, at the Academy."

"Arkanis. Didn't the New Republic take that?"

"Not yet, but soon. It's under siege."

"You need him done in before then. Understood."

"No, not understood. I don't need him 'done in.' This one, I need brought back alive. And with good care."

He barks a laugh. "You want me to guarantee safe passage to some-one on a war-torn planet? I'm a bounty hunter, not a nanny."

"Then you'll be disappointed to learn that he has a son, and you are to retrieve the child as well." *The Empire needs children . . .* and with that, her mind flashes to the image seen back in the archives: a young boy on the cusp of manhood, standing there in an ill-fitting suit next to Palpatine himself.

"I'll need more credits."

"I can double the usual fee," Sloane says.

"Triple it."

"Or I could turn all the resources of the Empire against you. You would run and we could chase you. You would find no safe haven, and none would dare hire you for fear that the black miasma around you would capture and choke them, too."

"Bit of an empty threat, isn't it?"

"Is it? Do you not fear a resurgent Empire with me at its head?"

Moments pass.

"Double it is, then," he says.

"Good. Get me to the Imperial Palace. Then contact me when the job is done, and payment will be arranged."

INTERLUDE

THE ANNIHILATOR

Eleodie stands on the bridge, regarding their target.

It must be quite a surprise, zhe thinks, watching the Corellian CR90 ahead of them buck and shudder as the tractor beam lashes it. *Poor fools don't know what's coming.* They think it's the Empire. And why wouldn't they? A Super Star Destroyer cuts through space like a sword tip, its shadow falling over your ship—well, traditionally, that meant one thing. You were getting boarded. You were now guests of the Empire. You are no longer free people. Zhe knows that sensation. Eleodie belonged to the Empire once. In a way.

But those days are gone.

And we are not the Empire. Forming *an* empire is quite different from *the* Empire, after all.

Eleodie looks over at her second: an Omwati, Shi Shu, his splindly fingers running through the crown of feathers atop his head. Zhe asks him, "Remind me again what we're looking at, hmm?"

"The *Starfall*," he says. "Senatorial ambassador onboard—Tia'dor Emshwa."

Eleodie hums. "And also remind me why we are picking a fight with the New Republic so soon." The pirate's head is full of details and data, rife with debts and assets, thick with the names of those who betrayed zher. Eleodie is trying to seize an opportunity here—the slow death of the Empire and the rise of the revivified Republic leaves pirates and criminals such as zherself scrambling for a foothold. But Eleodie doesn't just want a foothold. Zhe wants the whole mountain. "This seems . . . unwise, and one hopes that here the juice is worth the squeeze?"

"It is," Shi Shu says, nodding. "They are on a mission to Ithor, hoping to, ahh, *seduce* them into joining the New Republic. As part of the seduction, they bring with them a ship full of wonders: reclaimed Ithorian artifacts, but also food, meds, and a bounty of tech. It would give our flotilla quite the edge. Even here, we stole this ship, but we still need to keep it stocked . . ."

"Good, good. And the ship is properly subdued?"

"It is."

"Comm array?"

"Fried like *ksharra* bread."

"No mistakes. Not like last time. The Rangs almost had us because *someone* forgot to seal the breaching airlock—"

"It is all handled."

"Then *let us plunder*."

The destroyer draws the corvette into its belly. Eleodie moves into place along with the others—they move to breach, and zhe stands just behind a pair of Weequay pirates with arc-lancers. As they burn a searing line around the edges of the door, Eleodie does a few vocal exercises and practices the speech in zher head. Zhe pops her knuckles and rolls zher neck.

And then, it is done. The door is opened. The way is clear.

Eleodie gives the nod.

The two pirates storm in, flinging flash grenades. They go off, filling the channel ahead with pulsing white light. Zhe stands aside as more of zher crew rushes in. From the entranceway come the sounds of yelling, crying, another flash detonator going off. Eleodie hums a song in tune with the universe, hands behind zher back, eyes shut tight. Waiting. Meditating.

The pirate ruler does not know how long this lasts.

Eventually, though, Vinthar gently pats zher arm. "It is time," the reptilian says. "The captives are secure. The ship is at peace. Your presence is required." He hands Eleodie a long, baroque staff. Zhe also takes from him a vocoder, which zhe secures around her throat like a choker necklace.

It is time, indeed, zhe thinks.

Vinthar steps onto the ship.

From back here, Eleodie hears his speech, a speech zhe wrote:

"Greetings!" he says, his voice deep and resonant—as if the reptilian creature is stepping out onto a stage to address an eager audience. The lizard announces: "I am Vinthar the Sarkan of Egg-Brood Xazin'-nizar, and I welcome you to this unscheduled boarding, friends of the spaceship designated: *Starfall.* I envy you today for the blessing you are about to receive as you are poised ineluctably to meet his highness, her glory, his wonder, her *luminous magnificence*—the picaroon! The plunderer! The pirate ruler of Wild Space! The glorious knave, Eleodie Maracavanya!"

Showtime.

As Vinthar presses himself against the hallway wall with a deferential swoop, Eleodie strolls onto the ship with a long-legged stride. Chin up. Eyes down. *Project confidence. You will one day rule this galaxy.*

Zhe eases zher shoulder forward and a cape of chromatic scales falls over half zher front—shimmering as a wave of colors sweep across it like a turning tide. Eleodie takes the staff zhe's holding and taps it twice against the ground, *thump thump*—

A swooping scythe blade snaps open. The blade thrums and crackles with threads of blue energy. An electro-scythe.

Zhe regards those bound before zher with golden eyes. These people are frightened of what is happening. Good. They should be.

Now it is time to soothe their fear. A balm to salve the sting.

The vocoder mutates zher voice as zhe speaks: Zher words are loud and alive, vibrating with a deep intensity. The voice that emerges is velvety and rich, and Eleodie can feel it all the way down at the ends of zher fingertips. Zhe hopes they can, too.

"I am Eleodie Maracavanya, child of Nar Shaddaa and captain of the Super Star Destroyer *Annihilator.*" Though here, zhe pauses and looks up to the ceiling, as if reconsidering. "I don't anticipate keeping that name. *The Annihilator.* Too final. Too murdery. Not really my *flavor.*" The pirate's hand fritters in the air like a fluttering moth. "As such, you may relax: If none of you try to kill me today, I will kill none of you. Such is our bargain. I will be taking your ship to join my fleet—our sovereignty requires vessels like this *and* the cargo it carries. But I am no murderer, and certainly no slaver, and so you are free to step to the nearest escape pod and be gone."

Vinthar steps in front and thrusts a claw-tipped finger in the air. "But!" he announces.

"*But,*" Eleodie continues, "while I will not press any of you into service, I will make the offer: join me. Come aboard our stolen destroyer. Live the life of a pirate. Enjoy a life of spoils and riches. *Be greedy.* Be self-interested. Life is far too short for all this . . ." Zhe makes a sour face. "*New Republic* nonsense. Do you really believe your precious foundling government will save the galaxy? Please. I think not. I am a precious realist, and what you get in this lifetime is purely the result of *what you take.* Come with me. Come to my nation. Become part of my fleet. Join my sovereign space. Enjoy the freedom that comes with taking whatever you want, whatever you can get, whenever the chance. Anyone? Anyone at all?"

Someone will take the offer.

Someone *always* takes the offer.

This time, the taker surprises Eleodie.

There, against the wall, is a young woman. A girl, really. Plain as dirt, plain as space, nothing exceptional but for the fire in her eyes. She stands up, pulling away from a woman who Eleodie suspects is the girl's mother, or at least her guardian—

The woman cries out: "Kartessa! Sit down—"

"I hate Chandrila," the girl snaps. Her voice shakes, but there's metal in there. It warms Eleodie. The confidence. The selfishness. Good. "It's dull. I want adventure. I want a *life*. I don't want to be cloistered anymore."

Yes, girl. That's it. Be who you want to be. Eleodie's growing pirate kingdom out there in Wild Space is all about the sovereignty of the self.

The woman pleads, of course: "No, Kartessa—"

But Eleodie shushes the woman. "Shhh. Let her be, woman. Are you her mother?"

Reluctantly, with spite shining in her eyes, the woman nods. "Yes."

"The girl has made her decision. Respect it."

The woman swallows. "Then . . . I will come, too."

"Mom!" Kartessa says. Eleodie pulls the girl close.

"Let her come. But she will govern you no more, Kartessa. The mother will find her way, and the daughter will find hers. Anyone else?"

No takers.

"Anyone at all?"

Fine.

Eleodie grins and says: "Then enjoy your intrepid escape-pod journey one and all. Thank you for the ship and your supplies. I have been Eleodie Maracavanya. It has been *your* pleasure." With a flourish of the cape, zhe turns and heads back through the airlock.

The girl, Kartessa, follows close behind. A small smile tugs at her cheeks even as her mother weeps.

Eleodie's own empire grows once more.

CHAPTER NINE

As the sunrise burns the edge of the Silver Sea, the team shuffles one by one into the belly of the *Halo,* gathering in the main hold. Jas comes up last. Everyone is talking—Temmin mumbling about how he doesn't want to miss X-wing practice, Jom chastising the boy because it's called training and not practice, Sinjir saying something about how he forgot to grab that bottle of tsiraki and hey does anyone have an extra bottle of tsiraki because tsiraki, that's why.

It's all background noise to the bounty hunter.

The noise in the foreground is the static of her own thoughts, crackling and snapping right at the front of her mind. Her skin tingles with an unusual kind of anxiety, one she's not used to, one that is born of a division inside her—a fissure she cannot seem to close, an injury that won't heal. At her core, Jas feels like two different people.

She has always told herself that everything she does is for her own-self. *I am not here to make friends* being an oft-repeated phrase—anytime some weapons trader or bartender or client wants to do more than talk about the business at hand, that's the line she drops in their laps. Not friends. Don't need them. Sorry, thank you, goodbye.

And she's never had much of a cause to carry, either—the only purpose she possesses is to pay her debts. Debts that actually aren't really her own at all, are they? They're her aunt's. Sugi's.

Damn you, Sugi.

Jas loved her aunt. Loved her more than words can say. And all the while she watched the woman fritter away her contracts. She'd bail on jobs if they violated her "honor." Or she'd do them her own way and burn the client in the process. Or she'd side with her team, or she'd take on rinky-dink low-pay (or no-pay) work to protect some new group of underdogs or slaves or pathetic deviants, or, or, or.

In the end, it all added up to one thing:

Sugi owed more than she took in.

Those debts mounted.

And now those debts belong to Jas.

She always told herself: *I'll never be like Aunt Sugi.* This job is a merciless one, and it requires rather extreme moral calisthenics. You go where the credits flow. You take the target out however you have to. She doesn't have to be friendly, but she damn sure has to be *fast,* and she has to be *good.* That's how you earn a name. That's how you get the next job.

Even still, she tells herself that she's here because right now, the New Republic is the winning side. They don't have the whole galaxy pinned down and buttoned up all nice and neat yet, no, but the stars are drifting in that direction. One by one, systems shake free the yoke of the Empire's oppression and move to independence—and the chaos of that independence drives them inevitably to the New Republic. A single banner. One government. A new galactic order.

Whatever.

And if that breaks apart and falls away, as it could? Then Jas tells herself: *I'll flip.* She can swing like a monkey-lizard from a broken branch to a safe one. From the Republic back to the Empire—or to a Separatist system, instead. Could be she'll tuck herself into the pocket of some credit-flush crime lord (long as it's not the Hutts, as Sugi never had luck with those treacherous piles of humid guano). Certainly there will be a number of ex-Imperial bankers striking out on their own. They'll need enforcers. They'll need someone to go secure their loans—break some legs, twist some tentacles, blacken an eye or another sensory organ.

She has always told herself: pragmatism above ideals. Self above others. The mind over the heart.

The job above all else.

This is that, right?

And yet . . . *and yet.*

Here she is. With a *team*, ugh. Sinjir looks over, gives her a wink even as she tries to remind herself *You're not here to make friends.* And across the table is Jom, who has this look in his eye, this hungry look like he wants to reach across the table and gobble her right up and may the stars help her she feels a rising heat and by all the gods of the great beyond, what happened to her?

Is this who she really is? Soft like Sugi? Maybe her aunt hides within her like a ghost, summoned to the flesh when she got soft. Or maybe Sugi knew something special all along. Something Jas is only just learning.

She doesn't like it. *Burn it out with fire,* she thinks.

Norra stands there—Norra! Whom Jas feels *warmly* toward, which makes her wonder suddenly if her brain has been taken by some kind of parasite, like that Neimoidian tick larva that makes you crave blood?—and spreads out a special deck of pazaak cards.

(Jas is thankful for the sudden distraction.)

These are not your standard cards. These are the New Republic's MOST WANTED. On each, a face and a name, listing the Imperials the New Republic wants captured. Some of them are big players presently operating within the known Empire. Others have gone AWOL, like Gedde.

Speaking of Gedde, Norra grabs that card and hands it to her son. "Tem, if you would?"

He nods and takes it over to a board hanging from the wall, next to the oxygen recycler. Temmin takes a little blob of tacky goo from a can, dabs it to the back of the card, and sticks it up there alongside nearly a dozen others. Among them: the targets from Akiva (Pandion, Tashu, Shale, Crassus), and those they've taken since (Commandant Stradd, Prefect Kosh, Moffs Keong and Nyall, Vice General Adambo, and ex-ISB minister Venn Eowelt).

Norra says what Jas already knows: "Gedde was poisoned. Likely the poison hidden in his spice." Jas asks if it was the fungus, and Norra confirms. *As if there were any doubt,* Jas thinks.

"I know who did it," Jas says.

Eyes turn toward her, expectantly.

"A bounty hunter, like me. Mercurial Swift. He loves poisons. And that mycotoxin is one of his signature favorites."

Jom grunts. Though he saves half a moment to pin his gaze on her. He smiles. She tries not to smile back, and fails. *Damnit.* "That means, what?" he asks. "The Empire is sending killers after their own?"

"We don't know the Empire engineered the killing," Norra says.

"But it makes sense, right?" Temmin asks. "I mean, c'mon. Gedde left the Empire and if we picked him up, maybe he'd flip on others."

"Good," Jom says. "That's easy, then. We suss out which ones are AWOL, and we concentrate on the others instead. Let the Empire eject its own garbage. Saves us the effort."

"Robs us of the credits, too," Jas says, her brow knitted.

"We're not doing this for the credits."

"*You're* not doing this for the credits. Me? It's the only reason."

"You don't care about the galaxy at all? Don't care about doing justice for the people and kicking the Empire out the air lock?"

She shrugs, even though inside that war between her two halves goes from a cold war to a very hot one. "No. I don't care. I care about the Me who is on this adventure. And besides, if all of you cared so much about the people of the galaxy, why did our last job concentrate on taking out Gedde instead of Canker? Gedde was just *sitting* there. High on spice, hurting mostly nobody. But Canker runs a slave network. We didn't take him out. We didn't free any slaves. What good did we do?"

"We had orders!" Barell protests.

"Spoken like a true Imperial," Jas snaps back. She's revving his engine, now, she knows that. But past the sharp teeth of her sarcasm lies a real question: What good are they doing?

The better question being: Why does she care?

Jom stands, his nostrils flaring. She's happy to have made him mad. It thrills her, inexplicably. She's tempted to drag him into the bunkroom for another, ahem, sparring match, but Norra suddenly raises her voice to say:

"None of this is relevant right now. We can talk about the *hows* and *whys* of what we do later. Right now, we've been asked—quietly, very quietly—to look into someone who has gone missing."

"Who is it?" Jas asks.

Temmin whistles. "I bet it's either Skywalker or Solo."

That earns him some looks—including a jaw-dropper from Norra—but Jas can buy it. She says, "That tracks. Two heroes of the Battle of Endor, and I haven't seen Solo around here in months. Skywalker for even longer."

The look on Norra's face tells the tale true—it's one of those two. She pinches the bridge of her nose and nods. "Yes. Han Solo is missing."

"General Solo," Barell corrects.

And Norra corrects him in turn. "He resigned his commission."

"Then he's just a smuggler and not our concern."

"I say he's our concern," Norra says. "Besides, this comes from on high, from a source very high up in the New Republic—"

"Leia," Jas says.

"That's *Princess* Leia to you," Norra says. "And how did you know that? Did you bug my chambers?"

"No. I know because I'm a professional. And because scuttlebutt says the two of them have been a thing since Endor or before. Makes sense that he goes missing and she's the one who wants him found.

Understandable she'd come to us. Smart credits say she's using Wedge as an intermediary."

"I heard they got married," Temmin says.

"Wedge and Princess Leia?" Jom asks, incredulous.

"*Solo* and Princess Leia."

"Oh."

Sinjir claps his hands. "Bonus trivia: She's pregnant."

A chorus of retorts and refutations rise in response. But Sinjir crosses his arms and jeers at them. "What? Don't look at me like I'm some malfunctioning protocol droid spitting babble. Whatever *your* jobs are, mine is to read people like they're a menu at the local automat. The way she dresses? The way she carries herself? The rosy flush to her cheeks? Her hands drifting unconsciously to her stomach? *Preg-nant*." That last word he says in a sing-songy way.

"PREEEEG-NAAAANT," Mister Bones echoes, also singing— except his song is a disharmonic glitch ballad. Everyone winces.

"Stop," Sinjir tells the droid.

"ROGER-ROGER."

All of this is melodramatic and insignificant, Jas thinks. "Do we have anything on Solo? Any leads at all?"

"We have one," Norra answers. "Leia sent over the *Falcon*'s movements. Solo was trying to single-handedly liberate Kashyyyk, but something went wrong and his copilot, Chewbacca the Wookiee, went missing. We have a pattern representing his search." Norra pulls up a holomap. It fills the air around them with orbs representing glittering systems, each linked by a shining, shimmering hyperspace route. Norra focuses in on a region near Wild Space. "He could be in one of a dozen systems."

"It's a start," Jom says.

Sinjir thrusts a long, pointy finger down on the table. He hops it from card to card. "Maybe some of our erstwhile Imperial guests have some information. I'll canvass our captives."

"I can check with some of my contacts in the underworld," Jas says.

"If Solo's truly desperate, he may have been clumsy enough to have drawn attention to himself."

"Good," Norra says. "I'll dust off the *Moth* and fly it out to where Chewbacca was taken by the Empire. Maybe if we can find a clue there as to where Solo's copilot ended up, it'll help us narrow down our options."

Jom nods. "Let's get to work, then."

They each know their job. Jas heads out—willfully getting ahead of Jom to make sure that he and the rest of the crew know she's no heart-swollen star-calf, no moon-eyed waif, no lust-struck fool. But again, that war of thoughts within her: *Why do you care what they think? Aren't you protesting overmuch? Admit it, right now you'd climb him like a ladder.*

It makes her grouchy.

Outside, Sinjir awaits to make her even grouchier.

He's grinning big and broad with the puckishness of a boy who hid his mother's creditspurse.

"What?" she asks, defensive.

"You," he says.

"Me what?"

"You never once asked."

"Never once asked what? Speak plainly, Sin, or I'll boot you off this platform. I'm in no mood for your brand of devilry."

"What it paid."

"I said, *speak plainly*—"

He rolls his eyes, obviously impatient with her lack of *getting-it*. "You never asked what it would pay to go find the missing Solo, Jas. You didn't ask about a bounty. Or a reward. Not any of it."

"I . . ." Her breath catches in her chest. A very real and very cold panic rises inside her like a cyclone of sleet. He's right. She didn't. Worse, she didn't even give a *thought* to it. "I knew there'd be a reward," she lies to him (and really, to herself, as well). "Leia's accounts run deep. Of course rescuing Solo would be a particularly big payout. And! *And* even if not, having an Alderaanian princess owe you a favor is not insignificant." She tells herself that all these things are so true that she must've just taken them on as assumed—*of course* it would be worth her while.

"Look at you. Such precious backpedaling."

"Eat *sleem,* Rath Velus."

He chortles and winks. She stomps off.

I'm not here to make friends. She repeats this in her head again and again, over and over, until it's all just gabbling noise.

CHAPTER TEN

Mas Amedda is troubled. He has not slept in days. He has hardly eaten. He is a creature who is trapped by the architecture of a government he helped create, a government that no longer wants him or needs him. For a time, Amedda hoped he had it figured out—he would give himself up. He would hand himself over to the New Republic and they could do with him as they chose. It was, he believed, a foolproof plan. And it was a plan that left him eerily comforted—at least it *felt* like he had agency. At least it felt like the choice to give up was *his*. Because everything else is out of his hands. Everything but minor administrative details.

It is lonely being the head of a dying Empire.

He is a figurehead. Or worse than one. They don't even trot him out for appearances. His office and his chambers make up his prison. It's here he mostly stays. Taking in his meals. Watching the HoloNet. Thinking about his future, or rather, the lack of his future.

It wasn't supposed to be like this.

Palpatine was supposed to remain. The Emperor was as certain a fixture in the galaxy as the Core itself. As fundamental as the Imperial Palace. Timeless and immortal.

But he wasn't.

He is dead. And Mas Amedda is alive.

Mas wishes he was dead, too.

And that is his plan when he returns to his office in the tallest spire of the palace. The office has a balcony over which one can regard the width and breadth of the Empire's throne room. It has a deflector shield, of course; the whole palace does. But that shield only stops energy blasts—it won't stop a physical being such as himself from passing through it.

He will go to his office. He will step out onto the balcony.

And he will jump.

None will care. Why would they? The illusion of a united, cohesive Galactic Empire won't last much longer. Already the schisms have begun. It's breaking apart like a delicate pastry in his fingers.

You're an administrator, Mon Mothma said. *So administrate.*

The only thing he intends to administer tonight is his own demise.

He steps into his office, distracted. It takes him a moment to notice the blue glow coming from the far side of the room, flickering before the massive bulging window that overlooks the Federal District like a great eye. It's a holographic image. An unmoving one: a static image captured. Amedda approaches the desk cautiously.

There, in its center, an image reader. On it, a crystal.

Amedda stares at himself. Because there he is, in that image. Like a ghost of himself standing there, with Palpatine and four others. Screed and Rancit, he recognizes, and Yularen, too.

The final, though—just a boy. It takes him a moment to recognize . . .

"Do you remember it?" comes a voice from the far corner of the room. He startles, though he tries not to show it. Amedda turns, attempting to demonstrate his implacable demeanor. As his eyes adjust, he sees someone sitting there in the far lounger, leaning forward. Hands clasped over his—

No, *her* knees.

"Grand Admiral Sloane," he says.

She stands up.

Here, before him, is the leader of one of those Imperial fragments— a rather considerable one. Perhaps *the* fragment of note. She controls what remains of the Imperial Navy, and their navy is dominant, so it is clear that whoever controls the navy controls the Empire. More or less. Still, it leaves her without the bulk of the ground forces, but rumor already has it that she's begun to bridge that gap and complete the deficit in her military presence.

Another rumor is that she has been cleaning house. Those who are not faithful to the navy find themselves at the wrong end of a blaster.

That's what this is, he realizes.

She's come to kill him.

And here, an ironic twist, because now Amedda is thinking: *I could kill her first.* He has a blaster holstered under the desk. If he could just skirt around, he could get it. He could defeat her before she defeats him. What a coup that would be—rather than the coup she intends it to be.

He begins to back toward his desk even as she advances.

"That image," she says. "That is you in it."

"Obviously." He's at the edge of his desk, now. His nails *tick* and *tack* against its hard metal surface even as he slides around the edge. Now the holographic image separates him from her—her image is warped by the hologram. Stretched and mutilated, at least until he eases around to his chair and begins to sit. "Let me take a seat and we can talk."

"Yes. Let's talk."

His hand eases to his knee, then in toward the blaster—

"Why do you bring me this image?" he asks.

"I want to know about it."

"I can't imagine why it interests you. It's archival. Meaningless."

His finger teases along the edge of the holster and he realizes—he's leaning into it too far. His movement is surely telegraphed. She's no fool. She'll see what he's doing. *You have to move fast.* And he does.

He reaches in—

And finds no blaster.

"I have your weapon," she says. She pulls it from behind her, letting it dangle like a tantalizing piece of fruit hanging from a branch too high to reach. "I'm not here to have a conversation with blasters. I'm here to have a conversation between two equals."

That last bit she says like she doesn't believe it, though Amedda supposes he appreciates the thought just the same.

Resigned, he sighs and eases back into his chair. He slouches. "Fine. I don't know what help I could possibly give you."

"It's the boy in that picture. Who is he?"

"I don't know." She can tell he's lying, can't she?

"You know something."

"Haven't you heard? I know *nothing.*"

She leans in, hands planted on the desk. "I have had a hard night, so spare me your appetite for self-pity." He notes, suddenly, that she *does* look rough. She's not even wearing her uniform. Sloane appears in the guise of a common pilot. What fresh mystery is this? "Tell me something."

Amedda chews on it. Why help her? She holds his fate in her hands. Mon Mothma's words revisit him: *so administrate.* If he wants to bring the Empire back into his grip, then maybe this is the way. An alliance with her. Or at least a favor done, which means a favor owed.

He hems and haws as he thinks. "I remember something. He would send his ship out. Always with proxies. Droids or advisers or, once upon a time, his Inquisitors. One time the ship returned with a stowaway. It was that boy, I believe. The one in the picture."

"And who is that boy?"

"You already know who."

"Gallius Rax."

A strange tremble presents itself in his many stomachs. An acid tingle, eager and excited despite the insanity of it. Since the destruction of the second Death Star, rumor has dogged every step of the Empire and come at him from every angle. Nearly all of these rumors could be discarded—Vader was surely not alive, despite what some insisted. Nor could Palpatine be giving commands after his death through coded droid messengers—how absurd a story was that! But one of them was that Rax had survived and was manning the *Ravager*, the Empire's last Super Star Destroyer. Then the truth came out that he was dead and Sloane had control.

"He's not dead," Amedda whispers.

Sloane says nothing. "Where did Rax come from?"

But he doesn't answer that. Instead he says, "If he's not dead, are you really in control, Admiral Sloane?"

She points his own blaster toward him. "I'm in control of this conversation. Of that you must be assured."

"Yes. Yes. Of course." He swallows hard. This is an opportunity. For a long time he felt himself sliding down the side of a mountain—a slow and unending slip down the scree. But here is a handhold. He doesn't understand it. He cannot say where it will take him should he avail himself of it. This isn't hope, not yet, but it's close. "I don't know where Rax came from. But I know how you could find out."

"Tell me."

"Those droids I spoke of. They might know the boy that Rax once was. Their memory banks might have data. If not the droids, then the databanks of the ship itself: the *Imperialis*."

"A slicer could access the data in those droids," she says. "If I knew where they were."

"I know where they are."

A cold silence stretches out between them. Finally she says, "Tell me where."

"And what will I get?"

"You will get *not shot*."

"Hardly good enough," he says. "My lust for life is a dead and withered thing, Admiral Sloane. I am a broken fixture on the wall of an empty palace. If you want my help, I want a place in your Empire. If it *is* your Empire. Well? Is it?"

She narrows her eyes, suspicious of him. As she should be. "It is. Or will be. I can give you a place. You know how to run an Empire, after all."

Yes, he thinks. *I know how to run one. Even if I don't know how to lead one.* "Rax is still alive, isn't he? You don't have to answer. I see the fear in your eyes. You're a prisoner of your own command, just like me. Perhaps we can plot our escape together. Perhaps we can take over the prison." He idly drags a nail against his teeth—*click, click, click.* "The droids are in storage. Along with the wreckage of the *Imperialis* itself."

"Where?"

"Where else? Quantxi, the Junk Moon of Ord Mantell."

PART TWO

INTERLUDE

THE ALDERAAN FLOTILLA

Asteroids tumble through space. They drift and spiral, and when one hits the perimeter shield, it breaks. Bits drift, pulverized, as the rest of the rock pirouettes away to join the rest of its crumbling brethren.

Every time it happens, it hurts Teven Gale's heart. Because that asteroid is a piece of his world. *Was* a piece of his world, anyway. Out there waits an infinite black space horizon of Alderaan, now reduced to rock.

The flotilla is safe, at least. Seven ships belong to the flotilla, now, including the Alderaanian frigate *Sunspire*. Another gift from the nascent Republic. Or, rather, another gift from their princess.

The ships float near to one another, gathering in a circle and protected by the deflector shield to keep out both the asteroids and, hopefully, marauders. *The galaxy is drifting toward lawlessness,* he thinks. Better that, though, than choked in the black steel gauntlet of Darth Vader.

Out in the black, demo-droids drill and dig into the asteroids, one by one—they look like fireflies out there with their bright-orange light flickering from their cutting lasers. Those droids look for anything of note from the world the Alderaanians lost: artifacts, remains, fragments of precious stones or minerals or metals. Even a single brick would be a find. Accessing any of this wasn't even an option under Imperial rule; the Empire blockaded all access to the Alderaanian graveyard.

Behind him, the argument—the one he tries to tune out—continues.

Eglyn Valmor is up and pacing, as is her wont. "This is our home. *This* patch of sky is ours. Our world was here. And the diaspora has returned us to this place. We are home and I will not leave it." She tugs on the loose braid from her ice-blond hair. *She's young,* Gale thinks, unlike himself. *But she's got a vital heart.* He likes her. She and the others are not royals—there exists only one of those, now—but they are what the world has left. Alderaan has to be ruled by someone, and the commoners are what remains. Valmor is not queen, but rather, regent administrator.

"Bah," says Icar Orliss—once a teacher at a university. The man sits back in his chair, idly scratching at the peaky beard rising up off his jowls like mountains of chef's meringue. "This is no world, Regent Administrator, forgive me for saying. It's just rock. Blasted, wretched rock. The Empire turned our world into salt and dust and though I'm old, I for one don't want to be like some geriatric clutching to his chest the remnants of *what once was.* It's time to demand resettlement. I've prepared a list of worlds we could colonize—"

"That's not how it works," chimes in Argus Tanzer. Argus is a young bureaucrat, possessing a handsomeness that looks less cultivated and more like someone simply carved him out of quartzine. Argus thrusts up a finger, gesturing with it as he speaks. "The New Republic won't be keen on us just picking some planet and resettling there. There's a process." He lowers his voice when he adds: "Not that anyone quite knows what the process *is.*"

Orliss barks: "All the more reason to seize the chance *now*. We can claim that the Republic simply did not have their bows tied and their knots cinched—we seize upon their ignorance."

"Besides," adds Janis Pol, an elder diplomat. A small woman, as sharp and as pale as a broken tooth, she steeples her fingers and stares over them. "We are not yet members of the Republic."

"We *are*," says Riyana Torr. She's young. *Too* young to be here, Gale thinks. But when the Empire destroyed their world, what was left but those who were living offworld? Riyana was with her missionary parents, part of a roving school dedicated to helping those in the galaxy who could not so easily help themselves. Now she's back and fulfilling a similar mission, isn't she? *We can't help ourselves,* Teven thinks. He reminds himself: *We are all just asteroids, tumbling into one another.* Riyana continues, visibly nervous as she says, "We are a member of the New Republic! Leia is one of their most vital members."

"And yet, we have no senator," Orliss says. "We've no representation. We've no *vote*. What has Leia given us? Is she even truly our princess? None of us are royals. Why do we think she would listen to us?"

It's time to speak up. Gale turns and offers words in a stern tone when he says, "Leia has already listened to us! She's given us this flotilla. Four of these ships are from her. The supplies we use to survive are from *her*. We exist, gathered together because of the efforts of her and Evaan Verlaine and the other Alderaanians working on Chandrila. I'll not have her name sullied in this room."

That earns murmurs and mumbles of both agreement and dissent.

He hopes the dissenters will change their tune soon enough.

As if on cue, the center of the korabite table—a table carved from one of the asteroids and formed of Alderaanian bedrock and schist—lights up with an incoming message. Above the table floats Rickert Beagle, one of the comm officers on the *Sunspire*.

"We have incoming ships," he says, visibly worried.

"Who is it?" the regent administrator asks, leaning in.

"I . . . we don't know. But the ships are *big*."

They damn well should *be,* Teven thinks. Hauling cargo that big, well, you can't just pull it along with a couple of tug-tugs.

The worry rises in the room. Whispers of pirates or bandits. Fear of a resurgent Empire—or, perhaps worse, some brutal fragment of what remains of the Empire. Certainly rumors have persisted of various worrisome remnants of the Imperial forces that have gone mad out there in space.

Rickert suddenly says: "Wait. We have a signature—code clearance says it's New Republic."

Beyond the asteroid field, ships begin to pop out of hyperspace. *Big* ships—cargo freighters whose cargo will not fit within those ships' bellies. Cargo so big it must in fact be contained in its own shield, lashed to the ships with magna-beams. The scrap they haul is epic in size: huge curved slices like the rind of some fruit designed only for the massive hand of an old god. Those with Teven gather at the glass, staring out.

"What . . . what am I looking at?" Valmor asks.

"It's a gift from our princess. I had to pull quite a few strings just to get this on the table, but as it turns out, nobody was really *doing* anything with it—it was just going to end up as scrap elsewhere. I started the ball rolling, but it was Leia who really made it happen. Her and Evaan."

Orliss growls, "I still don't know what that *is* or why we'd want it."

But Tanzer sees it. He smirks. "It's pieces of that damnable Death Star. Isn't it?"

"It is, it is." Teven laughs and nods. "They reduced us to scrap. Now we get *their* scrap as reparations for war. This is just the first lot of it, too. Quite a bit more coming if we say the word."

"We could build a whole space station of our own," the regent administrator says, beaming. She presses her hands against the glass, and therein lies the wonderment of a child, even though she is one no longer.

"That's my hope," Teven says. "What say the rest of you?"

Orliss grumbles some kind of reluctant acquiescence, then stomps off. Pol, another dissenter, shrugs. "We can try this. But resettlement will still be on the table. And we *must* be afforded a voice in the Senate if we are to aid the New Republic in any of its efforts to secure the galaxy."

Their conversation fades as Teven looks at the regent administrator—an untested, untrained, politically naïve young woman whose eyes are as big as moons and whose heart is as bright as ten suns. The awe in her eyes is so tangible, Teven thinks he could bask in it. Drink it up, even.

"This is our future," she says not to him, not to any of them, but to the glass and to the space beyond.

Yes, he thinks. *I hope it is.*

CHAPTER ELEVEN

The *Moth* drops out of hyperspace into the open black of nowhere—for a moment, Norra finds the open emptiness overwhelming. As if it's going to swallow her whole. Once upon a time, she found the expanse of space comforting: so much potential, so much freedom. These days, it only offers her terror, from which she must wrest her own respite.

She tries Leia's trick: closing her eyes, drawing a deep breath, exhaling slowly. Norra tries to reclaim that feeling of freedom, and, finding even *that* difficult, she just lets herself sit there.

In, out. Clear the mind. Become one with the stars.

And then—

It helps. She feels less . . . lost. Less overwhelmed.

More centered.

Thanks, Leia.

She cuts the engines and the ship floats there.

The *Moth* once belonged to the smuggler Owerto Naiucho, but he lost his life during the rebellion on Akiva after helping Norra get plan-etside. That left the MK-4 freighter up for grabs. Norra considered selling it . . .

But, truth is, how long can she live this life? She was a pilot for the Rebel Alliance and now leads a team of Imperial hunters for the New Republic. This work has to have an expiration date, she tells herself. (And yet she keeps coming back for job after job . . .)

Either way, it seemed like a good idea to have a ship of her own for once. Something that belonged to the Wexley name. If she dies—or *when,* since immortality is not likely—then Temmin will have some-thing to call his own. He is becoming a good pilot. He deserves it. Especially since his father is gone. He should have something of his *own.*

Right now, though, Temmin isn't here.

Though she's not alone, either.

"See anything?" Wedge asks, hobbling into the cockpit.

Norra points at the viewscreen. Out there, in the foreground of the glittering stars, float bits of gleaming metal. Wreckage.

"Giving her a little thrust," Norra says, and she does. The *Moth* eases forward. Wedge leans over her, accidentally bumping into her—they share an awkward laugh as he clears his throat and sets up the scanner.

After a few key-taps, a green beam—glittering like precious stones flung onto a cloth of black velvet—sweeps the void in front of them. First a vertical scan, then horizontal. Pulsing as it searches and cata-logs.

This space represents the coordinates of the *Millennium Falcon* when Solo and Chewie were trapped by the Empire. "The *Falcon* wasn't destroyed here, was it? There's a lot of debris," Norra asks.

"I doubt it," Wedge says. "Leia didn't say as much. Besides, the *Fal-con* has gotten out of more scrapes than the galaxy has stars, I think."

Norra can personally attest to that—she remembers watching the blue burn of the freighter's engines as it whipped through the narrow channels and conduits inside the belly of the second Death Star. The ship clipped a pipe and lost its rectenna array, the dish spinning off as Norra's Y-wing went past. Wedge goes on to say: "Something sure happened out here. Look at this." Data scrolls on the nav screens. "Wreckage from at least . . . four different ships. None of them the *Falcon*. Let's see what we have . . . three freighters, one fighter. Wait. Imperial wreckage, too. Scrap from a TIE's wing panel. What a mess. I don't know that we're going to find any clues to Chewie's whereabouts out here, Norra."

"Let's pull in the scrap, see if we can't eyeball something."

"I'll get the tractor beam cooking," he says. Wedge eases into the copilot's chair. As he spins up the beam controls, he looks over at Norra. "Thanks for having me along. It's nice being out in the black again. Planetside's all right, but out here? This is home."

"It won't be long before you're back in action."

"I hope so." He hesitates. He looks like he wants to say something. "What is it?"

"After this, after . . . we find Han, because I know we will, do you want to . . ." He coughs into his hand and wets his lips. "You wanna go out and get a drink sometime? I know this little cliffside cantina—"

Movement on the viewscreen. They both see it.

Norra says, "Did you see that?"

Something darts from one piece of scrap to another. It moves like a squid through water: tentacles pushing off, legs like a blooming flower whose petals are closing. There's a red glow before the shadowy shape is again behind another piece of scrap. Hiding there. Where the sensor beam wouldn't have found it. Wedge says, "Let's see what we've got."

The tractor beam hums as it fires up.

"I'm not your babysitter," Sinjir says.

"Good, because I'm not a baby."

Temmin and Sinjir head down the hall toward a door guarded by two New Republic soldiers with vibro-staves crossing the door.

"I never said you were a baby."

"Good, because I'm not."

Before they get to the door, Sinjir stops and plants a hand on Temmin's chest. "Listen. The pouty, angry teenage thing? It's tiring."

"I know. Does that mean you're going to stop doing it?" Temmin asks, crossing his arms and cocking his eyebrows.

The smirk that crosses Sinjir's face will not be denied. "Oh, ho, ho. You think you're clever, do you?" He sighs. *At least the boy told that mad droid of his to stay home when asked.* "Believe me. I speak from experience when I say that cleverness will earn you as many enemies as it does friends."

"So?"

"So, take it down a notch. We've got work to do."

"It's just—" But then the boy shuts up.

Sinjir knows he's going to regret this in much the same way one might regret sticking a hand into a hive of redjacket wasps in the hope that they make honey (hint: They don't), but he asks anyway: "Oh, fine, what is it?"

"I don't know what I'm doing here."

"We're here to visit one of our estimable prisoners."

"No, I mean like, *here*-here. Like, nnngyah." The boy makes a wild, frenetic gesticulation. That sound, that movement, perfectly articulates a specific feeling. That's when Sinjir understands the problem.

"Ah. The *existential* 'here.'"

"I don't know what that means."

"It means you're having a crisis of identity."

Temmin fidgets. "Yeah, I guess."

"Congrats, my boy. It means you've become a proper adult."

"So you don't have it figured out?"

"Hardly. I'm utterly bewildered nine times out of ten. I just happen to make it look good. I don't know what I'm doing here, either. I suspect that the moment I have it figured out, I'll probably die half a second later. Because if there's one mystical energy that powers the galaxy, it's not the Force. It's pure, unadulterated *irony*. Now let's go

talk to General Shale. See if she can't help us in our foolhardy quest to
locate the errant smuggler."

"I hate this place," Jom says, following Jas through a narrow, crooked
alley on Nar Shaddaa. Behind them is the mouth of one of the moon's
countless black markets. This one is lorded over by the maven, Nyarla
the Hutt—a slime-dripping slug-woman whose red tongue slathered
the nozzle of a bubbling spice-drip while she told them she didn't
know a damn thing about Solo, his Wookiee, or Imperial prisons out
in Wild Space.

"You want to hang with me," Jas says, "you should get used to places
like this, Barell."

At that, Jom feels mighty conflicted. He *does* want to hang with Jas.
His attraction to her is something on a whole other level. It's practically *feral*. His greatest desire right now is to grab her and pull her into
some dark alcove and have another go. And yet, why? She's nothing
like him. He's a man of order and principle. She's a fragging *bounty
hunter* of all things. A criminal haven like this is second nature to her.
Meanwhile he feels like a Mon Cala out of water—like he's drowning
in open air, totally exposed.

"This is a strange place for a date," he says.

"You're funny. It's not a date. Don't think that what we had will
happen again. It was just a bit of fun, is all."

They pass a stall full of wide-mouthed toothy aliens barking about
a table full of strange oils and unguents. He slaps their hands away as
they reach for him and he calls after Jas: "No reason the fun has to
end."

"Fun always has an end, Barell."

They push on toward the spaceport—really it's just a ship recepta-
cle carved out of the urban sprawl. Jas paid some crumple-headed
Weequay too many credits to keep their ship hidden and off syndicate
registers. She told Jom that Black Sun operates out here and the last
thing she wants is to be on their screens. Them *or* the Crymorah. *I*

have debts, she told him. He asked her what kind, but she didn't eluci-date.

As they duck under a ratty tapestry hanging from a fraying rope and enter the spaceport, Jom says, "This is the third time we've come up empty, Emari. Maybe it's time to realize that your underworld con-nections here are drying up. Time to go back to Chandrila and—"

The air warbles and something hits Jom in the back, knocking the air out of him. He pitches forward, chin hitting the ground and teeth biting into his tongue. Blood fills his mouth as he tries to summon his limbs to move, but they don't respond to his commands. *I've been stunned.* He barely manages the will to lift his chin off the dirty ground—

And he sees Jas pinned down by a series of red lights—beam-sights, he realizes. Dozens of them. All from weapons threatening to fire. Her hands are up in surrender as enemies close in from the shadows.

Frag.

The air lock shudders as the *Moth*'s oxygen cyclers pump air into it. Wedge steps forward, leaning hard on his cane. He and Norra share a look, then she jams the big red button with the heel of her hand. The door slides open with a rattle-bang.

There, inside, sit heaps of scrap drawn into the ship with the tractor beam. Already she sees plasma scoring and char marks.

What she doesn't see is anything moving.

"I know I saw something out there," she says.

Wedge nods. "We both saw it."

Just then—a piece of hull scrap shifts, groaning against the floor. Then all is silent once more. The two of them draw their blasters—

A faint scuttling and scraping.

And again, nothing.

Moments pass. Wedge starts to say, "Maybe together we could lift—"

The scrap piece flips up suddenly, slamming against the wall with a deafening bang. A dark shape, big as an astromech, takes flight, slamming into Wedge. He screams as he falls.

"The tea here, right?" Sinjir says, holding up his steaming cup as if to demonstrate. He takes a noisy sip while Temmin stares disappointedly down at his own cup. "It's a far sight better than what we got at the Imperial commissary, that's for certain."

Jylia Shale was once a general in the Empire's army—and legendarily one hell of a strategist. Sadly, her legend was habitually ignored by those above her. She sits with both of her small hands around a cup of her own. "It is something. But I had my own supply during the Empire days."

The apartment is spare, but functional. It's more than she'd get in a prison cell—she has a food prep station instead of a protein recycler, a proper bathroom instead of a vacu-suck porthole, and no interrogator droids hovering about. All because she has played along and given the New Republic true answers to the questions it has posed.

House arrest is quite nice, Sinjir thinks. *I should've gotten arrested.* He could live a comfortable life in one of these boxes. As long as they delivered liquor. Did they? He makes a mental note to ask.

Then he sets the tea down because tea is disgusting.

"So, nothing?" he asks, rapping his knuckles gently on the low table between them. He gestures toward the star map hovering there holographically. "You don't know anything about this space? We're looking for Imperials—any at all—you think might be in that area."

If no answers present themselves, that means Solo is—what? Investigating that region for his own daft giggles? Perhaps he's truly gone back to the smuggler life. Succumbed to the pressure of adult life and bailed on the wife and the coming child. Perhaps Solo kissed the straight and narrow goodbye and he's gone off to have his own illicit adventures.

It's what Sinjir would do.

It's what Sinjir *did*, at least.

Hm.

Still, Shale is lying. He can tell she's withholding.

It's strange sitting here, interrogating someone of Shale's stature. Though he supposes her stature has fallen considerably. Not in his mind, though. Interrogating her—and that's what this is, just a more polite version of it—makes him feel rather uncomfortable.

He tries not to show it, though.

"Do you miss it?" Shale suddenly asks.

"What's that?"

"The warm embrace of the Empire?"

"Ah, an embrace as warm as a hug from a slab corpse." He taps his thumbnail against the side of the teacup. *Tink, tink, tink.* "No. I don't miss it. I don't miss who I was or what I did in its service. I miss who I was once before the Empire turned me into *me*. Not that I much remember that version of myself, but I'm quite confident he existed. He may have even been nice."

"I don't miss it, either. What we did formed a scar across this galaxy, and I'm not sure it will ever truly fade." She sighs. "You should go and ask Tashu. I don't know anything, but he and his other sycophant advisers seemed awfully enamored of that region. Good luck finding whatever it is you seek, Loyalty Officer Rath Velus."

And with that, they are dismissed.

Wedge squirms and kicks under the clicking limbs of an Imperial probe droid—not a viper, but one of the smaller Prowler models. The droid's flat, disk-shaped body suddenly glows red around the margins and emits a high-pitched trill. Norra recoils from the sound, her ears ringing—it's a noise so terrible it feels like it's trying to bore into her skull.

All she can do is steady her hand, take aim, and—

Her blaster shot slams the probe droid back, sending its top popping off. Its spider legs, free from the body, come away in Wedge's hands and he flings them to the ground before kicking them away with his one good leg.

His hair is a mess. His cheek is bleeding. Norra rushes over, grabs a kerchief from her pocket, and dabs at it. "Hold still," she tells him. Thankfully, it's not serious—just a scrape from one of the thing's limbs.

The droid sits in the corner, sparking and smoking. The red light shines bright one last time then goes dark. At least the sound is gone. What was that sound? Self-defense mechanism?

The two of them are left sitting and staring at it.

"Why is there a probe droid out here?" he asks, panting.

She helps him stand. "Searching the wreckage like we were?"

"Could be. But why remain out here? That's a Prowler probe. They don't travel long distances. They're local."

"They forgot it," she posits. "It's easy enough to leave behind. Especially if things got violent."

"That doesn't sound like the Empire."

"Maybe not the old one. But in its current state? They're different now. Less efficient." Her brow wrinkles. "Hey, those probes don't travel far, but how's their transmission range? Could it have been . . . ?"

Wedge grabs his cane and uses it to move toward the droid. With the toe of his boot he lifts it. Sure enough, on the underside is a modular comm array: a little transceiver dish that would've been hidden by its limbs.

That dish is blinking green.

"It's still transmitting," Norra says.

"What could they possibly be—"

From the cockpit, a proximity alarm. Its presence could mean only one thing: incoming ships. Norra rushes out of the hold and into the cockpit, spinning the chair and plonking herself down just in time to see a Star Destroyer cut through space like a spear-tip.

Drool drips from Jom's chin as he grunts, pushing himself up on shaky arms. He falls back down, pain radiating through his old shoulder injury. With one hand he fumbles gamely for the blaster rifle hanging on his back—but the toe of a boot pries his hand away and gently steps on it.

It's Jas's boot. Her hands are still up. She looks down at him and shakes her head, clucking her tongue. "Now now. Stay still."

"Jas . . ." he moans.

"Shh."

And with that, they are surrounded.

Ridge-browed Niktos emerge, hand-cannons held aloft, beam-sights all targeting Jas. Their nose-slits flare, as if sniffing for her scent. Blunt-toothed mouths gnash and clamp open air.

They ease apart as a new player enters the scene:

A woman, by the look of her, face hidden behind a rust-pocked metal mask. The mask is curved, and the top of the metal is curled into the facsimile of curved horns. A pair of trillium lenses whirr and buzz as they focus in on Jas. The woman tilts her head and says: "Hello, Emari."

"Underboss Rynscar," Jas says. "Been a while."

"That's because you've been avoiding me. Playing Suzee Goodgirl with the New Republic, I hear."

"Job's a job. And last I checked, I need credits."

The masked woman stiffens. "You do. To pay me. You have debts."

"My *aunt* had debts."

"And now they're yours!" Rynscar barks, suddenly furious. "But since you don't seem to be able to pay, I have little choice here but to bring your head back to Boss Gyuti. Black Sun demands money or blood, bounty hunter. Will it be blood? There is a bounty on your head."

Jom thinks: *I won't let this happen.* He again starts to lift himself up—but Jas slams her foot down on his back. She hisses at him: "Stop. They'll kill you and kill me and then what? *I'll handle it.*" Then, to Rynscar: "Who sold me out? It was the Hutt, wasn't it?"

"The Hutts are in disarray. Nyarla has come back to Black Sun."

"I will pay you what I owe."

"We've all heard that one before."

"I'll make you a deal."

Rynscar sniffs behind the mask. The Niktos gathered all share looks and laugh. "What deal could you make me?"

"I'll pay you twice what I owe. And failing that, I'll turn myself in. And the group I work with."

She'd really betray us? He again starts to get up, protesting—

And she grinds her heel against the back of his neck.

"Interesting," Rynscar hisses. Her head tilts at a curious angle. "And all I have to do is let you scamper away, out of my grip?"

"Actually," Jas says, offering a nervous laugh, "there's one more thing. I need information."

"Don't we all." The underboss hesitates. "What is it?"

"I need to locate someone. The smuggler, Han Solo."

Imperial adviser Yupe Tashu was, is, and forever will be a wild-eyed religious zealot. His capture on Akiva did little to dampen his fervor, and in fact seems to have allowed it to further infect his mind.

That presents Sinjir with two problems.

First, Tashu's devotion to the Empire—or, more particularly, to Palpatine himself—is so intense it utterly overwhelms his fragile sense of self-interest.

Second, he's as mad as a spark-drunk mynock.

It's very hard to interrogate one who suffers from one of these problems, much less both of them. The deranged only offer cryptic or nonsense answers, while the self-sacrificial will gladly immolate themselves in the service of keeping their trap shut.

Sinjir hasn't gotten anywhere with Tashu since they brought him in. And by the look of his cell, things have only gotten worse.

The man stands there behind the buzzing laser shield. He paces the cage like a pilgrim who has lost his way, wandering the world with a vague sense of purpose and faith but no actual destination. The walls have been marked up in his food waste. Strange symbols and maps and other indecipherable gibberish are drawn there. Temmin stares. Sinjir sees that this is upsetting the boy.

That's interesting. Something about Tashu has gotten to him. It's cracked the boy's veneer of false confidence.

"I don't think I can do this," Temmin says.

"You don't have to," Sinjir says. "Run along."

"But—"

"Temmin. It's okay. Go."

The boy cannot seem to tear his gaze away, so Sinjir helps him by turning the boy in the other direction and urging him forth with a gentle push. It's enough. Temmin leaves.

The only other one that's left now is the guard: a Chandrilan man with a swoop of blond hair and a light scar along his chin.

"Is Tashu usually like this?" Sinjir asks.

The guard regards Sinjir with cold gray eyes, then reluctantly offers a curt nod. There's discomfort there, with the guard—and Sinjir's left to wonder why. Maybe the guard doesn't trust him.

That's fine. He shouldn't.

"Open the cage."

"I . . ."

"You have your orders, do you not?"

But still the guard hesitates.

And there, Sinjir realizes, is the glorious-yet-naïve failing of the New Republic. It isn't a fully fledged government. It isn't a proper military. In the Empire, you didn't turn down an order. You didn't hesitate. Hesitation meant reprimand. Failure meant Vader making three long strides into your office and pinching your windpipe shut with the power of his mind.

In the Empire, the chain of command was everything. Someone above you told you to drop your pants and spin around three times, you did it. You didn't ask questions. Here, though, individuality rules the roost. That was, at least on paper, a benefit, right? You get to think your own thoughts. Do your own good. If something doesn't sound right or smell right, you speak up.

But when that happens, order breaks down.

The saying might be *Too many admirals, not enough ensigns,* but here that's not precisely true, because in the New Republic there aren't enough admirals, either. And given that Mon Mothma has already begun trying to figure out how to demilitarize the galaxy . . .

How long before it falls apart? Before it spins off its axis and bounces away? It wouldn't take much. The Empire couldn't even keep it together and in that gap, the disease known as the Rebel Alliance formed—a disease that is presently killing its host. How long before the New Republic suffers the same gap? How long before the Empire returns the attack with its own infection?

The Empire pushed too hard.

But maybe the New Republic isn't pushing hard enough.

Ugh, he needs a drink.

Sinjir lends a Jom Barell growl to his voice and says: "You open that cage, guardsman, or I open your head."

"Fine," the guard says, staring balefully. He opens the cell.

"Thank you," Sinjir says, then steps inside. He tells the guard to turn the shield back on, which the man does, if reluctantly. Gently, Sinjir folds his hands behind his back. Best to give the veneer of authority here. Stand like an officer and maybe, just maybe, Tashu will fall into an old pattern—he'll conjure the sense memory of what it was to serve in Palpatine's Empire and he'll nod and smile, bow and scrape, and give answers to the questions that Sinjir will ask. "Hello, Adviser Tashu."

"I remember you."

"Yes. I imagine you do. Now, I'd like to ask you a little something about Imperial prisons."

"I know nothing of those."

"We shall see, Adviser." And so Sinjir weighs in—trying to pluck at the man's strings, hoping dearly to get him to confide (one ex-Imperial to another) just where the Empire might've taken a theoretically high-value target like Chewbacca, or if there's something, *anything* out there Solo might be looking for. And all the while, the man in front of him continues to break down mentally—until he's crumpled into himself, the barest human shape gutted of its stuffing. His shoulders rock as he laughs quietly to himself before that laughter dissolves into weeping. His hands pluck at each other. They pick at the nails until they've gone bloody.

Sinjir just stands idly by, watching.

He didn't have to do *any* of this. He didn't lay one finger on the man's messy, sweat-slick head. Tashu wound himself up to a complete and total freak-fit, babbling about how he keeps trying to "open himself" up to something, because we're all "bound in its web," but he cannot "hear its voice," cannot "feel its tremors." And how all he can do now is trust in his gut and trust in the "instructions" he was given.

And that's it, Sinjir thinks. The game is over. He won't get anything of value from this gabbling freak.

Sinjir's communicator pings.

"Pardon me," he says to Tashu, then steps out of the cell. The guard with the shock of blond hair watches as Sinjir talks into the comlink. It's Jas on the other side.

"I have information," she says.

"Good, because I'm not getting anything from this human methane fire. I would get better results if I asked a rain puddle."

"What I have isn't complete. Ask Tashu about *Irudiru.*"

"Is that some kind of delicacy?"

"It's a system near Wild Space."

"Irudiru, you say. All right."

Back in he goes, then.

The weapons at the fore of a Star Destroyer are many—the main battery alone presents a host of turbolasers that could tear an entire space station to ribbons. But therein lies the value of being in a smaller ship: Just as it's hard to swat a fly, it's hard for a Star Destroyer to eliminate a single small craft.

Provided, of course, that the littler ship acts like a fly. Sitting still—or even just retreating in a straight line—won't cut it.

Norra puts a hard spin on the *Moth,* corkscrewing it through open space even as the massive capital ship wastes no time unloading a fusillade of weapons fire at them. The dark vacuum of space lights up with ship-killing spears of laserfire tearing past them. Wedge braces himself against the dash as he straps in and operates the weapons system.

Time for a little *roll-off-the-top.* It's a maneuver she learned early in her days doing combat cargo runs for the Alliance, though some of the pilots call it an Eimalgan Turn, after the one who reportedly originated it: Cargin Eimalgan, one of the earliest Alliance aces. A hero. Now dead, like so many of them.

Norra accelerates forward, then pulls up hard. The *Moth* lifts through the open black, lasers chasing the space where the ship was only half a moment before. She brings the ship from level to a half loop, then a hard roll and turn so that the craft is now going the other direction entirely.

Which is to say, it's heading straight for the Star Destroyer. It's like facing down a monstrous beast poised to swallow you—and choosing to run *toward* its open maw rather than *away* from it.

"This is crazy," Wedge says with a smile of admiration.

"Let's hope it's the best kind of crazy," she says before giving the ship maximum thrust—

Just as the Star Destroyer ejects a swarm of TIE fighters into space.

Back on the *Halo,* Jom shakes his head, struggling to claw free from the mud that remains after being stunned by those thugs. Through blurry vision he sees Jas finish up her communication with Sinjir. Then she turns toward him.

She's clearly worked up. Her blood must be running hot.

Her hands flex in and out of fists. He can't tell if she's angry, excited, or both. "You sold us all out back there," he growls.

"Relax, Barell. I'm not giving up the team. I just needed to buy us more time."

"Buy *yourself* more time, you mean."

But she doesn't respond to that. Instead she says, "You think what she gave us is right? Will that lead us to Solo?"

"Slag if I know. Point is, I don't know if I can trust—"

She slams into him, knocking him back. He's about to protest when she mashes her lips into his. Her tongue snakes into his mouth.

"Hey," he snarls. "What is this?"

"No reason the fun has to end just yet," she says. *Sound logic,* he thinks, just before she renews her assault on his face.

Sinjir merely has to say the name:

"Irudiru."

With that one word uttered, Tashu freezes. He stops weeping and laughing. He stops biting at his fingertips. "Irudiru," he repeats.

"You know it?"

"I do."

"Is there a prison on Irudiru?"

"No."

"What is there, then?"

"Not a prison," Tashu says. "But a prison-*maker.*"

The TIEs form a screaming swarm behind them, spitting lasers. The *Moth* jolts and bumps as the aft of the ship is struck and stung. Wedge starts to spin up the nav computer, plotting a course through hyperspace even as Norra dives closer to the Star Destroyer—meaning any shots the TIEs take at her pepper the surface of their own capital ship. She banks hard past a turret, escaping its twin fire, then whips the ship back around, ensuring that the turret will be too slow to track her.

"Almost there," Wedge says.

"Gotta go faster," she says through clenched teeth, and nearly bottoms the freighter out against the surface of the Destroyer.

"There. Just get us clear."

To starboard, the massive towers and shield generators of the Star Destroyer loom over them like jagged cliffs. Dead ahead sits the end of the colossal ship: the bank of its engines. Norra intends to get clear of the Destroyer, then bank hard to get out of any wake from its engines, then . . .

All clear!

"Punch it," she says.

Wham. The ship rocks hard, its back end lifting high and sending them into a tumble before she realigns the stabilizers and gets them upright again.

"The hyperdrive," Wedge says. "It's out. Direct hit. We're toast, Norra."

"I've been toast before. So have you." She pulls up hard, moving back into another roll-off-the-top maneuver—they won't expect her to do it so soon, though that element of surprise will wear off fast. "And yet here we are." She flings the *Moth* back through the cloud of TIE fighters, moving the freighter as erratically as she can manage—the gamble works, and two of the TIEs try to predict and evade the *Moth*'s movement, smacking into each other, leaving behind a blossom of blue flame consumed by the void.

Wedge knows the score. He's been in fighters before, and he knows how to get out of the way of a big ship like this. They move fast but they turn slow. As the *Moth*'s weapons systems autotrack the TIEs, getting them off their tail, he narrates the plan: "All right. We need to go vertical. Perpendicular. You follow?"

"I follow." The underbelly of the Destroyer—that's where they go. She can slide the ship down over the edge, tucking it under, then launching it straight down through space. The TIEs will still be on them like a bad smell, but it'll give them a chance to get clear of the Destroyer—

More alarms.

Something else is coming out of hyperspace.

Reinforcements.

Two blips coming in, growing bigger—

A pair of *enormous* ships, no, no, no—

The reinforcements drop out of lightspeed.

Wedge whoops with sudden relief. Because the two ships aren't Imperial ships—they're *New Republic* ships. One of them is an Alderaanian escort frigate, the *Sunspire*. And the other is one of the brand-new battleships: a Nadiri Mark One Starhawk, one of a few capital ships constructed at the Nadiri Dockyards deep inside the Bormea sector. This ship, and all the ships there, are built from the disassembled Imperial craft the New Republic has taken since Endor. The literal spoils of war. Weapons turned by a savior's hand, pointed back at their masters.

This Starhawk, Norra recognizes as the *Concord*—which now operates under the command of newly minted Commodore Kyrsta Agate, who once commanded the frigate right next to it.

The front of the Starhawk is like an ax blade cutting its way through space. It is a foreboding ship, but regal, too, in its own way.

Sure enough, who comes crackling across the comm but Agate herself: "Hailing New Republic craft *Moth*. This is Commodore Agate. Time to come on board—we've got this."

With that, the *Concord* unleashes its fire.

CHAPTER TWELVE

Days have passed since her dalliance on Coruscant, and Grand Admiral Rae Sloane feels stuck in a waiting pattern. The pressures of leading an Empire have given her no time to take a side-trip to Quantxi, and she sees no way clear of the mire. Her last trip did not go unnoticed. She was able to deflect questions and criticism easily—after all, she is the operating military leader of the Galactic Empire, and many fear the power she wields.

The men at this dinner table, however, do not seem to fear her at all.

And that upsets her greatly, because they *should*.

This, then, is Admiral Rax's vaunted Shadow Council. She sits at the narrow head of one side, and the opposing head of the table offers only an empty chair where Rax has promised to sit (though he has yet to make a proper appearance). The others dine, all of them watching one another, uncertain as to what this even is. They are suspicious of one another. They are dubious of the situation. Surely each of them fears, quite fairly, that at any point the ground beneath their chairs will suddenly open up and they will be evacuated into open space, or dropped down into the crushing walls of a garbage compactor, or devoured by some slavering creature.

Problem is, none of them think *she's* the one to fear. They hardly give her a look. The empty chair at the other end of the table? Oh, they can't stop staring at that, can they? *Idiots.*

The Shadow Council, as arranged around the table, consists of five Imperials (including herself):

Next to her sits Brendol Hux, once-commandant of the Arkanis Academy. Mercurial Swift did his job and rescued the man (and she makes a mental note to get the bounty hunter paid for that work). Hux is a big, blustering, ego-fed pig. Gone a bit to pasture, that one: His gut strains at his buttons, his neck is fat, and his firm jaw has gone soft with an unshorn patchwork of facial hair. He looks haggard, lost, angry. Occasionally he seems to remember that this is a dinner, then dives down into his meal with sudden gusto, shoveling food into his mouth once more.

To his right sits Grand Moff Randd, special governor of the Exterior—a far-flung slice of the Outer Rim, and the only true Outer Rim sector remaining under Imperial control. His distance from the action explains his survival. The war burned bright across the galaxy, claiming the lives of many of the Empire's most elite members. Randd was not one of those members. He, like many, was at the edges.

And those at the edges were, and are, survivors. Sloane counts herself among those survivors—she had been pushed so far from center that her marginalization likely saved her.

Randd has the rigidity and the pointedness of a needle. He moves nothing but his eyes. His hands lie flat against the table, and he has not eaten a single bite. Prudent, that. Perhaps he thinks it's poisoned. Or maybe his nerves are just so jangled he cannot contemplate the idea of food.

Across the table: General Hodnar Borrum, though nobody calls him that. His nickname is "the Old Man," because of how long he's served the Empire—Hod Borrum actually served the original Repub-lic under Chancellor Palpatine. It was he who reportedly led the charge against the last stand of the Jedi at the close of the Clone Wars, personally marshaling clone troopers against the mountain fortress of—what was it? Her history training is suddenly failing her. Madar? Morad? It matters not.

Point is, he's a veteran in the truest sense, and she among others always wondered why Kenner Loring was made grand general instead of Hod Borrum. Some said he was too old, others said he was too practical. And he was known for making a show of how little regard he gave "the Force," which likely enraged Vader. Borrum *is* old, and his cheeks are marked with deep lines, craggy craters, and dark liver spots. But his eyes are still flinty—they are not clouded over with the fog of age. Those are a young man's eyes. A predator's stare looks back.

Last up is her favorite: Ferric Obdur. Imperial propagandist ex-traordinaire. He's the only one who looks happy to be here.

Nobody is talking.

She decides that has to change.

Sloane says to Hux: "I'm glad we got you off Arkanis."

"Yes." He pauses, looking down at the hunk of steaming meat at the end of his fork. He sets it down with a clatter as if suddenly not hun-gry. "I suppose I am, too."

"You suppose?"

"The Academy was my life's work. I was good at it. The best of the Empire came out of Arkanis. The *very best.* And now what?"

"Now we pick ourselves up," Randd says. "We fight back."

Ferric Obdur gestures with his own cutlery as if to make a point. Around a mouthful of food he says, "We show the rest of the galaxy how it's done and why we are needed." With the serrated knife in hand, he points it at Sloane. "Admiral, you have a good story about that. You should all listen, because when Sloane was a girl—well, go on, Admiral, you tell it."

Her face burns with the sudden attention of the whole table. The propagandist is both correct and obviously playing an angle here,

though she's not sure what it is. Either way, she does have a story—
a bad childhood on a lawless world, and the Empire swooping in to
bring order to chaos. She's about to speak and tell that tale when Hux
interrupts:

"These are dark days. Dark days for all of us."

Sloane bristles at being interrupted. Hux undercuts her because he
thinks she's not important. It is vital she make a show of counter-
manding that—honestly, her greatest desire right now is to slam her
fork through the back of his hand and chastise him for the intrusion.
But that would defy Rax, and she's aware suddenly of the keen and
delicate balance of power.

Instead, she does her own brand of undercutting.

"Brendol," she says. "I understand you have a son. Not of your
wife—an illegitimate child? Will *he* be the best the Empire has to
offer?" That is a stab from a double-sided dagger: first the fact that he
has an illegitimate son, and second the inference that no matter how
good the cadets at his academy became, they still weren't enough to
save the Empire from its fate.

His eyes pinch and blink as if he were just slapped. "I . . . Armitage
is a weak-willed boy. Thin as a slip of paper and just as useless. But I'll
teach him. You'll . . . you'll see. He has potential."

Around the table, the others chuckle.

A small victory, she thinks. But precious just the same.

General Borrum dabs at his mouth with a napkin. "From a military
perspective, we do have an interesting inversion here, don't we? We
went from being the prominent power in the galaxy to being second—
a far second, if the numbers hold. It happened fast, too, proving that the
war machine breaks down with too many hits. But I find that many in
the Empire still see us as the first and only law in the galaxy, when I
wonder if it would be far better to face reality. We have lost that edge."

"I agree," Sloane says. "It's high time we regard our place in the
galaxy with a full awareness unclouded by prejudice. And then it's
time to act accordingly—we are the underdogs fighting to save the
galaxy."

"Yes!" Obdur says, clapping his hands. "That's exactly it, isn't it? *We* are the rebellion. We're the resistance!" He laughs somewhat madly. "Think of it this way. Truth is given to us in two stages. All of this, *everything* anyone ever does, is only as true as the stories we tell about it. The narrative is the thing. We have to control the narrative. We can be the ones to swoop in and save troubled worlds dwelling in the shadow of the New Republic's ignorance. *We* put out the message. *We* control it politically. And *then* we enforce the narrative militarily, not the reverse. Too often we lead with aggression and then try to tell the story afterward—I say *no,* I say we get our story straight and then use what's left of our war machine to hammer that story into the hearts and minds of the galaxy and its people."

"And what story will that be?" Grand Moff Randd asks, his tone crisp, clipped, and sharply uncertain. "What is our . . . narrative?"

That showman's smile from Obdur when he explains: "It is exactly as Sloane said: We are the underdogs. Everyone loves an underdog. So we lean into that, not away from it. We play the wounded animal. The loyal hound who has been kicked out by a brutal, unjust, and altogether unready father."

From the back of the room comes a gentle applause—a sound that grows more insistent as it gets closer. And from the dark outside the dining table comes the fleet admiral himself, Gallius Rax.

It surprises her not at all that this is when he chooses to emerge. It's the most dramatic moment, isn't it? There sits Ferric, giving his speech about narrative and story, and oh how closely it mirrors Rax's feelings about artifice and the ephemeral, uncertain nature of truth.

"*This,*" Rax begins, "is precisely why I have selected you all. Such good ideas. Such impeccable wisdom. The truth of the matter is, we have lost this war. The Empire as we knew it is gone. Already we were letting it slip when the Rebel Alliance grew in unseen spaces like a cancer." Discomfort manifests around the table as those seated shift in their chairs. "For us, this represents an opportunity to reshape ourselves. That is why I have gathered you all here, a veritable brain trust of the first and most vital among us. It is on us to retake and control the narrative." In his hand he gestures with what looks to be a small controller. "What will our story be? What—or *who*—is the Empire?"

Hux leans in, desperation glinting in his eyes. "And how exactly do we retake our story? Propaganda is all well and good but we still need resources! It's not the *narrative* we're losing. It's people. And ships. And—" Here he looks to General Borrum. "And vehicles on the ground."

A slow, chilling smile settles across Rax's face.

Then he hits a button.

From a centerpiece in the table—hidden from view—a holo-lens projects images all around them. Above them, behind them, everywhere. What it shows is galactic space: stars and systems, clouds and hyperspace routes. It is not one map, but several slices of the overall galaxy.

"It is time," Rax says, "to expose my ruse."

He hits a button again. The air shifts and shimmers, and now they're looking at thick, interstellar clouds: nebulae. Like the one they're hiding in right now, the Vulpinus. Sloane knows her galactic map well; as a naval officer, it would do her little good to be ignorant of the stars. She spies five known nebulae: the red clouds of the Almagest, the bruise-dark striations of the Recluse's Nebula, the sapphire orb of the Queluhan, the spiraling Ro-Loo Triangle, and the bleak columnar plumes of the Inamorata.

What ruse will he expose? The truth of it reaches her even before he speaks: Just as they are hiding in one nebula, so, too, are other fleets.

They are not alone out here. They are *not* the last fleet.

Rax confirms exactly that: "Portions of our naval fleet have been hidden since not long after the destruction of our glorious battle station over the Endor moon. These fleets are not as large as the one we currently control here in the Vulpinus. Yet they are substantive just the same: hundreds of Star Destroyers, thousands of smaller craft."

Sloane is left reeling. She feels gutted—like a dolo-fish, its belly slit so that its steaming innards can lie on the dock while it gasps in the open air. Even now her lips work soundlessly in the same way. She tries to find words. Tries to find something. She *should* be happy, shouldn't she? That the Empire's demise is not so plainly written? But all she feels is disappointment. And anger. A red, rising anger.

She's about to erupt—

And then Rax says: "Admiral Sloane and I felt it was necessary to maintain this ruse. We simply did not know who to trust."

A second blow. He included her in the conspiracy—a conspiracy she literally *just* learned about alongside the rest of the Shadow Council. They're staring at her. Betrayal in their eyes. But something else, too.

Admiration.

That sickens her the most. They admire the plan *he* created, and she has been given undue credit for it. Why? Why did he do that to her?

All she can do is grit her teeth and nod. Exposing him now would seem untoward. Worse, it would show him for being someone gracious enough to give credit to an inferior and reveal her as unappreciative of a bone thrown in her direction. *But I want more than just a bone,* she thinks. *I want the whole damn animal.* That is the only way the Empire will be kept safe and strong: its leash held firmly in her grip.

Now is not that time.

Instead, she sucks it up and leans into it. She says, summoning a swell of false confidence:

"With Palpatine's demise, it was clear that some factions within the Empire would attempt to wrest control. Pandion was an excellent example of this—a greedy man using the chaos to extend his reach. Further, we had no way of knowing who would attempt to save their own skins by running to the New Republic. We had to be sure that we revealed this to those vital few we could trust. That's all of you."

Now admiration shines at her from a different set of eyes—from Gallius Rax himself. The corner of his lip is twisted up in a mischievous hook as he regards her. *He is pleased with me,* she thinks.

It warms her and chills her at the same time. *The fox is pleased with the hen.* Is she falling for his strange way? Does she admire him, now?

She might. Even as she hates him, she admires him, too.

"We need more than fleets," Borrum says. "We need boots on the ground and the armor to go with them."

"Good news, then," Rax answers. "The factories of Kuat have been bombed into submission, and the shipyards of Xa Fel, Anadeen, and Turco Prime are all either contested or already lost. But the Outer Rim will be our savior—and it will be the strangling cord we tie around the neck of the New Republic. We already have three worlds under our sway there: Zhadalene, Korrus, and Belladoon. The Empire has long—to its detriment—relied on third-party corporations to produce the pieces of our war machine, but that is no longer the case. Production is entirely Imperial. And on these worlds we have already begun to produce our weapons: all-terrain walkers, new TIE starfighters, E-11 rifles, and the other necessities of war."

Hux sits stunned. "We still need personnel. We need new academies—"

"In due time," Rax says, sharply.

Sloane is so busy watching the reactions of the men at the table to this news, spying the competing emotions of relief and fear and rage on these men's faces, that she fails to notice someone else come into the room. Someone who steps up behind her and places a gentle hand on her shoulder.

She startles as Adea whispers: "Admiral, we have a situation."

A hot flash of anger rises in her, and for a moment she's about to chastise the poor girl in front of everyone. But that won't do. It isn't earned. Sloane is on edge, and if Adea says that a situation demands her attention, then she must trust it to be true.

It takes every ounce of willpower to get up from that table—excluding herself from the meeting, even for one second, will make her feel robbed of information. And in this Empire, information is power.

CHAPTER THIRTEEN

Out there, the Star Destroyer is in the slow-motion midst of its destruction. The elimination of a capital ship like that is rarely fast—it's bled like a great beast, like a purrgil punctured over and over by hooklashes before it can be brought up on deck. Missile streaks and laser-fire crisscross the endless dark, and slowly but surely the Destroyer is ripped asunder as the vacuum of space sucks great gulps of fire from fissures in its hull. And then like that—

It's over. Through the dark cascades a great pulsing flash from engines gone supernova. It burns its image into Norra's retinas, and now when she blinks she sees the skeletal frame of that ship just before it's gone.

All that's left out there now is debris. And though she cannot see them from here, bodies.

"At the Empire's peak, a Star Destroyer played host to around forty thousand crew," Commodore Agate says, walking up behind Norra. "Our best guess was that the ship out there, the *Scythe*, had far fewer than that on board—closer to fifteen thousand. That's still a great many lives lost."

Agate is tall, rail-thin, with broad shoulders and long legs. Her chin is held high. Her hair is short—a dark curl around each ear is as ostentatious as it gets. The commodore keeps her hands held behind her back—Norra knows the woman has a reputation for her trembling hands. Once it earned her dismissiveness and doubt, but that has changed. Kyrsta Agate has proven her place time and time again. Many admire her earnestness.

Though now, Norra wonders what the woman is getting at.

"I don't understand," Norra says. "We did this. This is war."

"That's exactly right. *This* is war. It's easy to get caught up in the swell of it. The medals, the parades, the garlands of lorachid petals on the victors' brows. But it's important to remember that war is mostly this: destruction and death. We are killers."

Norra fails to suppress a tremor of her own. "I . . . are you saying we're in the wrong? With all due respect, Commodore Agate, I can't believe that."

Agate turns. Her smile is sad. "No. We are doing just work. Those on board the *Scythe* knew who they were and why they were there. And they were not ignorant of the cost of war. I just want my people not to be ignorant of it, either."

"You want us to regret what we've done?"

To her surprise, Agate nods. "I do. A little. We should. I don't want unrepentant killers, Lieutenant Wexley. I want soldiers who hate what they had to do and fear having to ever do it again."

"And if that means we lose the war?"

"Then we lose the war by keeping ourselves."

That hits her like a fist. She feels staggered by it—dizzy, almost.

"Thanks," Norra says. Though the way she says that word, Norra frames it almost as much a question as a statement of gratitude.

Agate nods. "I spoke to Captain Antilles. He told me why you were out here." Norra wonders idly if he told a lie, given that their purview to track the missing Han Solo was not exactly official. But when she hears the tale told true, she knows Wedge may not be capable of such an easy lie: "Han Solo is missing?"

"He is. And there may be Imperial entanglements."

"Let's hope you find him."

"Let's hope they continue to let us find him. He resigned his military commission."

Agate sighs. "That may complicate things."

"I'm betting on it."

In front of the *Moth* on one of the decks of the *Concord,* Wedge meets Norra once more. He's nervous. He looks around at the bright, clean curves of the *Starhawk*'s interior. "One helluva ship, huh?"

She agrees, and she tells him so. It's different to be in a ship that feels so *new.* It almost feels fake, somehow, or like she doesn't belong. Even something as simple as a docking bay—above, the ceiling is sculpted in white scalloped edges, and all is lit with a warm glow rather than harsh lighting. The floors are lit, too, from underneath.

"Listen," he says, leaning forward on his cane. "I told Agate."

He doesn't have to say about what. "I know. She knows we're looking for Solo. It's fine."

"Ackbar's going to want to have a conversation."

"I accept that."

"You should be steamed."

"I'm not. Really."

"I just figured if anyone was going to betray Leia, I'd rather it be me and not you. Though that means I had to betray you, somewhat . . ."

"Wedge, it's okay."

"Promise?"

"I swear by all the stars in all the skies."

He raises an eyebrow. "About that drink—"

Norra kisses him. She does it before she even realizes she's doing it. Her eyes close. She draws a sharp intake of breath through her nose as they hold the kiss. Her heart feels heavy in her chest as for just a fleeting moment, she thinks of her husband, Brentin . . .

When she finally pulls away, it feels like forever has eclipsed them, that so much time has passed that the war may be over and all that has come before can be willfully forgotten. An illusion, she knows.

But a comforting one.

She smiles.

He smiles, too.

"About that drink," she says, aiming to put some Sinjir swagger in her voice. "I'm sure they have a bar somewhere on this ship. I say we find it."

CHAPTER FOURTEEN

For the first twelve years of Gallius Rax's life, music was a thing that simply did not exist. Yes, the music of his surroundings played: wind whistling through the stone spires, the jostling of rust-bone chimes made by the anchorites, the melodic hum of a speeder cutting a swath across the hissing sand. But real music, *true* music orchestrated willfully by the hands and the breath and the sheer bloody desire of *sentient beings* . . .

That was unknown to him.

The first piece he ever heard as a boy plays in his chambers now: *The Cantata of Cora Vessora,* an Old Republic opera of a dark witch on an unnamed world who refused to become Jedi—but neither would she join the Sith. It is a tale of birth, death, and all the glories found between those poles: love, passion, war, and above all else revenge. Revenge against the Sith who took her loved ones. Revenge against the Jedi for standing idly by and refusing to protect her because she would not join their ranks. Revenge against the galaxy for being as imperfect and impure as she had feared.

The tale itself was something he didn't learn until much later. The story mattered, of course. But as a child taking his first flight off a grim, dust-choked planet that he thought (or feared) was the center of the galaxy, it was the sound of the music that haunted him. Now as much as then.

The light pluck of the moda khur's strings.

The crash-and-clamor of the denda drum's glass breaking and re-making and breaking over and over again.

The vibration formed of the choral ululations from the unglanded tucari singers—a vibration that can be felt as an intense buzzing in one's temples and jaw, a vibration that can make one feel almost *drunk* on it.

He lets it wash over him, standing in the center of it. Almost as if the music can pick him up and lift him higher.

Rax is aware of someone in the room with him. Likely, it's Sloane. Here to ask him about the destruction of the *Scythe*. She won't accuse him of anything; Sloane is too smart for that. Though he fears that day is coming.

He will not have the *Cantata* interrupted, though, not for her. Not for anyone. So he stands, swaying gently, and he holds up an insistent finger demanding patience above all else.

It plays out into silence, and only then does he turn.

It is not Sloane standing there. Rather, it is her aide, Adea Rite.

"Miss Rite," he says. "I am surprised to see you here and not her."

"She chose not to come."

He lifts his brows. "She discovered the destruction of the *Scythe*." Adea confirms with a nod. "And she learned that I sent out a trans-mission."

"Both transmissions."

It is a shame that Admiral Sloane has not come to talk this through with him. He understands why, of course. She feels lied to because she has absolutely been lied to. And that deception will not end anytime soon. It cannot end because she cannot know everything. Not yet.

If only she would *trust* him. An ironic statement, he knows, given that all she has on him are mounting reasons *not* to trust him. But leaders are like this, sometimes. You must place trust in them even when you are uncertain that they are making the right choice.

No. Not trust.

Faith.

"Rae Sloane will come around," Rax says, suddenly confident. He reaches out and takes both of Adea's hands. Her eyes shine with veneration. Though in there he sees something else: a conflict. Adea respects and admires Sloane, too. This is hard for her. Good. It should be. "We do what we must. The sacrifice of the *Scythe* was a necessary one. Besides, Commander Valent was conspiring with Loring—we cannot stand any more needless fractures in this, and he was too stubborn to be brought into the fold. Not to mention incompetent."

"Can I share this information with Admiral Sloane?"

He pulls her closer, gently easing her so that her chin is on his chest. "Yes. You may. But not yet."

"I . . . should be getting back."

He can feel her heart beating against his own. Faster, now. A rabbit's pace. Rax gently places a finger under her chin and lifts it toward him.

"Will you stay the night again?" he asks.

"I . . ."

"You must. I insist."

He eases forward to meet her. He presses his lips against hers. Cold against warm. The kiss of fire against a shard of ice.

The *Scythe* is destroyed. Commander Valent and all those on board are dead. And it's her fault. Or, it was made to *seem* like her fault.

There, on her comm, a message sent to the *Scythe* from *her* station and with *her* clearance codes—text only, no visuals, no audio. That message asked the *Scythe* to respond to an alarm signal sent from a Prowler probe droid.

Then someone went ahead and blocked all incoming messages from the *Scythe,* so that distress signals from the Destroyer failed to arrive.

And finally, the last piece of a troubling puzzle—yet another missive sent out through heavily encrypted channels, onward to the New Republic.

That's him. That's her so-called adviser—Fleet Admiral Rax. He's been stringing along the New Republic as a character he called the Operator now for the better part of three months—but it seems he's more interested in maneuvering the Empire into cannibalizing itself, giving the fledgling Republic a much-needed edge. He's *handing them the weapons* and then shoving Imperials into firing range. Before, she could maybe excuse it—certainly remnants of the Empire truly *were* out for themselves. May the stars help them all if someone like Pandion were to capture the Imperial throne.

But this? The *Scythe*? That was an *execution.* Because surely it was the fleet admiral who summoned the New Republic ships under the guise of the Operator. Him tugging their leash and giving those scum the scent of another good Imperial target. Thousands of soldiers are now dead because of it.

And why? For what purpose? Shaking, Sloane paces her office, trying to figure out exactly that. Valent. He was loyal, was he not? Maybe that's an overestimation. She sits down at her holoscreen and pulls up all the information she has on the *Scythe* and Commander Valent. Everything seems standard—but there. Wait. Valent didn't go to the naval academy first, did he? He went to the officers' school on Uyter . . .

. . . along with Grand General Loring.

So that's it. Another rivalry extinguished. One more potential dissenter whose throat is metaphorically slit. Instead of trying to bridge the divide and lead from the center, Rax is happy to drift to the edges—and those who don't follow him will be shot like dogs.

Sloane cries out in rage and sweeps everything off her desk. A tumbler of water spills and rolls away. She is left seething, her chest rising and falling as she envisions marching into Rax's chambers and putting two blaster shots through his forehead. All for what he's done.

This is not my Empire, she thinks.

But how to reclaim it? Exposing Rax is an option, but the consequences of that may not play out in her favor. First, she'll have to openly admit that she does not control this Empire. Second, he's a war hero, and no matter who you are, as an Imperial, those medals *matter*. Third, the response might be an overwhelming shrug. So what, they may say, that he's a manipulator? Palpatine was, too. In its earliest days, the nascent Empire grew strong precisely because he let the Republic and the Jedi destroy each other—and then he simply seized the preexisting war machine for himself, uniting the fissures in the galaxy under the Imperial banner. They might have faith in Gallius Rax's choices, however grim, however strange. Exposing him exposes her, too. Worse, it potentially pushes the Empire into its own internal civil war.

It's time to stop dithering. It's time to head to Quantxi and find the wreckage of the *Imperialis*. If droids remain, even in scrap, maybe she can find something, *anything*, that can shed light on who Rax is or what his true intentions may be.

With that, Sloane launches up out of her chair, renewed with vigorous purpose. She strides to the door, opens it with a hiss—

There stands Ferric Obdur. He gives an obsequious smile. "We have another meeting regarding information dissemination. And we should prepare a statement regarding the loss of Arkanis. Oh, and it's vital we establish some *vague* sense of the future of the Empire—we can discuss the new breeding initiatives, for instance, and . . ."

As he goes on and on, she nods gamely. All the while, Sloane feels like her boots are stuck in a mire, and the mud keeps pulling her down, down, down, until her mouth is full of it and her lungs are full, too, and all she can do is drown in the muck as the Empire she loves slips away.

INTERLUDE

TAKODANA

There's only one rule in Maz Kanata's castle.

(Well, okay, there are dozens, even hundreds of rules. *If you get up on stage, you have to perform; don't drink what's in the brown jug; don't go downstairs; if your animal drops a pile anywhere, you're out; all deals need the approval of Maz before they're done, and if you try to go around her back she'll take what's yours and what's his and sell all of it to the highest bidder; and for the love of all that is holy don't mention Maz's eyes unless you want to get into a* very *long conversation.*)

But there's only one spoken rule—written, too, in a hundred languages (many of them long-forgotten) on the wall beyond the bar: ALL ARE WELCOME. (NO FIGHTING.)

That rule is simple on the surface, but not easy in the execution, because Maz Kanata's castle has been a meeting place since time immemorial—a nexus point drawing together countless lines of allegiance and opposition, a place not only where friend and foe can meet, but where complex conflicts are worn down flat so that all may sit, have a drink and a meal, listen to a song, and broker whatever deals their hearts or politics require. That's why the flags outside her castle represent hundreds of cities and civilizations and guilds from before forever. The galaxy is not now, nor has it ever been, two polar forces battling for supremacy. It has been *thousands* of forces: a tug-of-war not with a single rope but a spider's web of influence, dominance, and desire. Clans and cults, tribes and families, governments and anti-governments. Queens, satraps, warlords! Diplomats, buccaneers, droids! Slicers, spicers, ramblers, and gamblers! To repeat: ALL ARE WELCOME. (NO FIGHTING.)

You fight? You're done.

How *done* you are is a permutation left to Kanata herself. Maybe that means you're out on your can. Maybe it means you end up locked away for however long she chooses. Maybe, just maybe, if she *really* doesn't like you, it means she takes you up on one of her many ships— the *Tua-Lu*, aka the *Stranger's Fortune*—and forces you to walk the air lock and meet the stars.

Sitting at the bar presently is an Imperial officer in the ISB. At least, he *thinks* he's still with the ISB. Truthfully, Agent Romwell Krass doesn't even know if the ISB is functioning fully anymore. He had been stationed on the Hyborean Moon at a black-site prison. His family lived there on that moon: his wife Yileen, his son Qarwell, his father Romwell Senior. His friends in the bureau lived there, too—Krass worked very hard behind the scenes to ensure the transfer of those he came up with in the Empire, because the Hyborean Moon was a cushy, easy job. The prison was locked up tight. The work was clean and simple. You got housing by the shore of one of the hot spring lakes. And at the end of it all, a commendation awaited for work performed, for loyalty sustained, for virtue upheld.

And then the rebels came. He won't deign to call them the Republic new or old—they are anarchist scum undeserving of the dignity. They came in out of hyperspace with a small fleet of ships, and before anyone knew what was happening, hell rained on them from above.

They fired on the remaining structures.

They fired on the *houses.*

Spears of scourging light rent Romwell's home from the surface. His family was inside when it happened. They are dead now and he is alive because as rebel scum flooded the prison, he fled to the nearest ship and escaped to hyperspace before they could disable the craft.

That was a month ago. He contacted Coruscant—the bureau there was under siege, and he told them he would show up, provide backup. But he didn't. Instead he just wandered. Floating for a while. Weeping over the pictures of his family. Screaming in rage at those who had done this. Even now, his eyes grow wet at the thought of it. It's like something wants to crawl up out of him: a screaming monster with breath of fire.

He washed up here two days ago. He wanted information on whoever did this. Who gave the order to wipe out his home? The Republic prides themselves on being noble—their snotty noses thick with the mucus of righteousness. And yet, how do they justify what they did?

Why did they kill his family?

His son, Qarwell, was only five. He liked to draw in moon-dust. He had an MSE mouse droid unit as a pet. The boy was sweet and fun and he had a big vocabulary and an even bigger heart. He would one day have made a most excellent Imperial Security Bureau officer. Better than Romwell. Better even than the boy's own grandfather.

Now that boy is gone.

And it is the rebels' fault.

Wonder of wonders, right here, right now, Romwell sees such a rebel.

There, on the far side of the bar, closer to the stage, sits his enemy. The rebel is a lean fellow with a pretty-boy jaw and a swoop of dark hair. On his pilot jacket's sleeve is the emblem of the so-called New Republic. He's there with a woman. Their heads nod to the music—some mad-sounding song from Minlan Weil and the Tam-honil Three.

Romwell can read the sign not far away. All are welcome, no fighting, blah blah blah. He knows it. He *comprehends* it.

But . . . he's been drinking.

And that rebel is a pilot. The Hyborean Moon fell to the rebels. Pilots made that happen. Even now he remembers the trio of Y-wings roaring above his head, dropping their payload. He bets *this man* flies a Y-wing.

Krass decides rather immediately—

That rebel scum was one of them. One of his family's *killers*. Anarchist! Murderer! He's sure of it. He has no *reason* to be sure of it, but the more he drinks, the deeper his certainty.

There comes a moment when the band stops playing and there's a pause between sets, and once more the sound of the crowded castle fills his ears, and it's enough to get him to stand. He pays up, slapping a handful of Imperial credits flat on the bar top. Then Romwell pushes his way past a trio of screeching Chadra-Fan throwing dice in a gambler's trap. He bumps a table of Bravaisian guilders licking palmfuls of glittering gems—they squawk at him as he passes. Not that he cares. Passing by a sad-faced Skrilling sleeping next to a round jug of bubbling wine—Romwell hooks a finger around the jug handle and lifts it. It's full. It's heavy. It's perfect.

The woman sees him first. Romwell's still in his officer's black—he hasn't changed out of it in a long time. Her eyes go wide and she grabs the pilot's elbow, and just as the rebel thug turns, Romwell says, his voice oozily slurring from all the drink—

"You killed my family."

Then he clocks the rebel across the head.

Or, rather, he tries to. The jug is heavy and the rebel traitor isn't drunk, so the pilot moves fast enough to take the hit on the shoulder. He still goes down, though, and Romwell barks a muddy laugh.

What surprises him is when the woman stands up and throws a hard straight punch to his chops. His nose pops like an overripe fruit and he cries out, staggering backward. "That's not how a lady is supposed to act," he says, but between the inebriation and the blood running down his face it comes out, *Thasshh nah how a dady is thupoothed to ack—*

Someone grabs his ankle. The rebel! His enemy pulls hard. The whole world goes tipsy-tumble as he falls, crashing hard against a chair. By now patrons of the castle stand, watching: freaks in masks, disgusting aliens, sneer-lipped mercenaries. Criminals, the lot of them! He's about to yell at them all to stop their damn staring when the rebel rolls on top of him and starts dropping fists into his gut.

"You blasted Imperial pig!" the rebel yells, raining punches.

Romwell spits his own blood into the rebel's face, then shoves hard with both hands—the pilot crashes backward into a table. Glasses roll and shatter. And then everyone around starts gasping and moving aside.

It takes Romwell long, *too* long, to figure out why.

Above him stands a droid. Strangest damn protocol droid he's ever seen—an exoskeleton like burnished bronzium, and peaky spikes coming off the robot's legs, arms, and skull.

It chatters at him in some machine language, then repeats in Basic with a mechanized female voice:

"You have violated the Castle's law. The Castle is all. Castigation is now imminent."

"And I'd violate it again, you damn, dirty—"

The droid points her hands at him, the fingers splayed out. The tips of those fingers suddenly fire at him like little rockets, each sticking in the fabric of his shirt—he spies five thin golden filaments now connecting his chest with her hands via those fingertips.

The droid's hands glow. Electricity courses along the filaments. Everything lights up like a supernova.

And then it goes dark like the deepest night.

Next thing he knows, he's gasping awake on a filthy cot matted with stinking straw. The chains holding the cot to the brick rattle as he rolls off. His head feels like a kicked pumpkin. He vomits onto his own hands.

The floor is damp and cold. There—*a door*. Old wood, held fast with hinges of ancient iron. At the top of the door is a small window, and Romwell crawls to the door and pulls himself up to that opening (all the while his brain feels like it's trying to ram its way out of his forehead). He pushes his face against the smaller bars in the window.

"Help," he says. Louder, again: "Help!"

"We're done for," says the rebel—who stares out a similar window behind a similar door across the hall. Water drips from the vaulted ceiling above. "Face it, pig, we messed up. Now we have to pay for it."

"You don't know what you're talking about," Romwell says, then feels his gorge rising anew. He chokes it back and burps into his hand.

"I know there's one law and we broke it. Why'd you come at me like that? I didn't kill your family."

Romwell thinks: *Did I say he did?* Maybe he did. "Fine, not you specifically, but your *people*, they killed my family. My *boy*."

The rebel frowns and looks down at fingers gripping the bars. "If that happened, then I'm sorry it happened. But war isn't exactly a game of precision, much as we hope it would be."

"Whatever helps you sleep at night, scum."

"Hey, we didn't blow up a whole planet. That was you."

"I didn't authorize that!"

"And I didn't kill your family."

"But your belief in this nonsense 'Republic' contributed to—"

From farther down the hall, a sharp voice commands: "Silence!" It's a woman's voice. Sounds old. Footsteps pad on the stone toward them.

The wizened woman, Maz Kanata, reveals herself. She's withered and shriveled like a fruit left too long on the vine. Her hands are behind her back and she looks to both the rebel and the Imperial with puckered eyes pressed behind round, moon-sized lenses.

"Hm," she says.

"Listen, Miss Kanata," the pilot says. "Missus Kanata? Whatever, we're really sorry for what we did—if that brute didn't think to attack me—"

Romwell interrupts: "Brute? *Brute?* You and your rebels are the brutes. Indiscriminately bombing—"

Another shush from Maz Kanata.

It echoes like a serpent's chastisement, and Romwell is surprised at how effective it is at clamping both their mouths shut.

Maz goes over and grabs a two-step stool from against the wall, then drags it to the door in front of Romwell's cell. She clears her throat as she steps up onto it. With the boost, she can stare in through the portal.

"Let me see you," she says, adjusting one of the lenses around her eyes. "Come on, come, come. Closer, now."

What is this mad old pirate going on about? He keeps his head back and she clucks her tongue. "You either come closer or I'll send Emmie down here again to give you a proper shocking. Mm?"

Grousing, Romwell does as she commands. He leans in.

Her little raisin eyes pinch to slits and she wets her lips with a dark-purple tongue. "I see pain in your eyes. Loss. Regret. You have caused pain, too. You have given loss." She puckers her thin lips. "The scales are balanced, it seems. As for your people . . ."

"What do you mean, the scales? What about my people?"

"The Empire is dead," she declares. "You may think it has life and everyone else may think it is dying but I say that it is dead. But just as a carcass gives way to new life—flies and fungus and whatnot—so, too, will the corpses of the Empire birth new creatures. For now, though, it is dead." Her hand rattles the lock by the door and then frees it. She steps off the stool and then lets the door drift open. "You are free to go. Do not come back here. And I advise you not to share your pain with the rest of the galaxy. Find peace for yourself or no good will come to you."

Romwell doesn't know what to say. Should he thank her? Condemn her? Better still to say nothing at all? Instead he flits his eyes toward the rebel. It's as if she's reading his mind.

"Do not worry about him. I'll let him go, too, but only after I see your ship in the sky above my castle."

Romwell nods. And Romwell leaves.

Later, when he's gone *and* when the rebel pilot has gone, too, she stands alone on one of her parapets overlooking the waters of Nymeve Lake. She feels pushed and pulled from all sides, and so she goes with it, letting her body sway. ME-8D9 comes up alongside.

She asks the old droid—a droid who has been at this castle longer than Maz herself has been, a droid who has seen so much of this galaxy that to plumb the depths of her databank would be an effort of futility and madness—if Minlan Weil and his band have their beds for the night, and the droid replies that they do.

"Peace has returned to the Castle," 8D9 says.

"Good, good, good. Still. Peace has not returned to my heart. Something is off balance. Some stirring in the Force has made the water turbid. Hard to see. But I think it best we be prepared."

"Please define the next course of action."

"Get the *Stranger's Fortune* ready for flight. I want to have a look around the galaxy. See just what I can see."

"Acceptable."

The droid does not belong to her. ME-8D9 does not belong to anybody—the droid is her own master. As it should be. Maz listens to her go, then closes her eyes and tries to feel the tremors in the galaxy—the weave and weft of a changing Force.

CHAPTER FIFTEEN

One by one the team members arrive in the Skygarden above the Polis District of Hanna City—it's where the citizens often gather to openly debate politics, which is apparently a favored activity here on Chandrila. To Norra's mind, it just sounds wearisome. She'd far prefer going home and fixing a meal, or being out *doing* something. Anything other than discussing politics. Yes, she recognizes that such a discussion has value, participating in democracy and all that. Just the same, she'd rather be a hundred parsecs from it.

Thankfully, today, no such debate is present. The Skygarden has been sealed and they are, for the moment, alone with one another.

"Something's going on," Jas says, leaning up against a planter. Her arms are crossed and she's chewing a pizo stick—a dried, cured branch from the slickbark tree. Chandrilans chew it and suck the juices to stay awake. Pilots in particular love them when they can get them. "It's a little too strange that all this stuff is happening. Two heroes of the Rebellion go missing. Then the probe droid signaling a Star Destroyer? And with Tashu somehow wound up in all this? I don't trust any of it."

Sinjir drapes himself backward across a bench. He spins the cap off a tarnished mercurium flask and nips at it, smacking his lips. "Tashu's a bird trapped in a turbolift. Barking, flogging mad, that one. Still. He gave up the answer to my question without a second's thought. He *wanted* me to know. Which makes me think Not-Actually-A-General Solo is in a deep dive."

Norra nods. "Either he's in trouble, or *we* are."

She expects her son to come back with some whipcrack sentiment— he's good at those when all the chits are on the table. But instead he sits off to the side, staring at nothing. Distracted. Sullen. Norra thinks: *I'd better get ahead of that when we're done here.* And then she wonders: *Should I tell him about Wedge? What will he think?*

Panic assails her.

Meanwhile, Jom paces, craning his head and stretching. "Those bounty hunters did a right nasty number on me." His joints pop and crackle as he moves them about. He grunts and shrugs. "Maybe it's high time we realize that Solo is not our mission. We've got real targets to look after. Need I remind the lot of you that we had Admiral Rae Sloane in our sights back on Akiva—and as it turns out, she's basically the military head of the Empire these days. Let Solo be Solo. I want another shot at Sloane."

Behind them all, Mister Bones chases after a butterfly. He catches it gingerly in the cup of his clawed hands. Then he tears its wings off.

Norra refocuses and jumps in, saying: "I'll remind you that if it weren't for Leia and Solo, that shield generator would've stayed up and the Death Star would remain." Her insides twist at the thought of how that would've played out. They were already outnumbered and outgunned before the beam from the battle station lit up the black and destroyed both the *Liberty* and the Mon Calamari cruiser *Nautilian*. It takes everything she has to hold it together, and she can't stop injecting a little venom into her voice when she says: "We wouldn't be standing here if it weren't for him, so a little loyalty wouldn't go amiss, Barell—"

Nearby, there's a soft chime as the turbolift platform at the center of the park begins to rise, bringing with it a small group.

Ackbar leads, striding in his way—his head pointed forward as if drawn forth by the gravity of sheer purpose. Leia walks with him, speaking animatedly, worriedly. Wedge trails alongside Commodore Agate.

Wedge. He lifts his gaze and meets Norra's. And for just a moment, all her anxieties and all her worries fall away like a heavy rucksack allowed to slip from her weary shoulder.

That ends with the brusque sound of Ackbar clearing his throat. His lips press together and he seems poised to speak.

Sinjir whistles low and slow. Norra leans forward and kicks his shin. The ex-Imperial grouses and sits up, wiping a line of liquor from his lip. Deep in his cups, he noisily whispers to the others: "We are about to be reprimanded by the academy commandant, children. Shhhh."

"This is not a reprimand," Ackbar says gruffly.

"You were operating under my request," Leia says. And then adds with a crisp shot of bitterness: "I'm the one who received the reprimand."

"Sir," Norra says, "with all due respect—"

But the Mon Calamari does that thing he does where he shuts you up with a look. His bold, golden eyes fix on her. "Han Solo, as I understand it, has resigned his military commission. And even if he had not, we cannot pivot the entire New Republic to search for one man willfully gone off the reservation. We are already overextended. Our reclamation of systems is slow, our grip tenuous. Your team, Lieutenant Wexley, is designed to serve a single purpose, and finding a smuggler—however goodhearted and helpful he is—is not that purpose. Your search for Solo ends now. You will return to pursuing Imperial war criminals posthaste."

"No."

That single word comes out of nowhere. Norra wonders who even spoke it aloud, until she realizes . . .

It was her own voice.

Ackbar seems taken aback. His nostrils flare as he scowls.

She says it again, wishing desperately she could catch the words before they leave her mouth and shove them back down into her throat, but the effort is futile. "No. We won't. The New Republic owes Leia and Solo a great debt. He's missing and I think he's in danger. The Empire doesn't want us to find him, and that's all the more reason we should be looking. So, with all due respect, we will continue our search for Solo."

Oh, no. What am I doing? Shut up, Norra. Shut! Up!

Her fears are reflected back in Wedge's eyes, now as big as moons. He shakes his head at her, trying to tell her to stop.

"Are you disobeying an order?" Ackbar asks.

No, she thinks. *I would never. I'm a pilot. I'm a soldier. I—*

I'm a rebel.

Oh.

"Yes," she says, the word erupting out of her. "I am disobeying your order. I resign my military commission. This is the right thing to do and I aim to do it, no matter who stands in my way. I'll find Solo myself."

Sinjir sits forward, grinning like a maniac. "Well, this just stopped being tedious." Jas, too, looks on with a smirk twisting the ends of her mouth (though Norra doesn't know if that smirk signifies approval or amusement or something else entirely).

Jom on the other hand looks like he just ate a piece of rotten meat.

And Temmin? He's already at her side. "I'm in, too, Mom."

Leia steps forward. She clasps Norra's hands in her own. "Lieutenant Wexley—"

"Norra."

"Norra, please, reconsider. Don't do this to yourself. Not for me."

"Why not? You'd do it for me. For all of us. That person, the princess and general in all the holovids? That's not some creation. It's not propaganda. It's you. You gave up so much for us. You lost your world. At least let me get your husband back." Norra leans forward and in a much lower voice says: "And a child needs its parents. I know that now."

Leia appears speechless. All she can do is acquiesce with a small nod.

"That's done, then," Norra says as her heart churns excited—and panicked—blood through her veins. She feels woozy, like she's on the edge of something. But it feels good. It feels *right*. "Private citizen Norra Wexley. I suspect this meeting no longer involves me. If you'll excuse me, Admiral, I have matters I must attend to."

The matters Norra must attend to include, in order:

a) Trying very hard not to vomit.

b) Trying doubly hard not to pass out.

c) Feeling both lost and free at the same time, which is probably why she feels like vomiting and passing out.

She stands at the far side of the Skygarden, away from the others, just out of sight. She can't go, not yet. Her legs are too wobbly. And she's not really even sure where she's going.

That's the thing. For so many years now, she's been on rails. Fixed to a track not of her own making. She almost jumped that track on Akiva, but it wasn't long before duty called and once again she was swept up in someone else's cause. Admittedly, it felt comfortable. It felt *easy*.

Following orders is simple.

But the galaxy isn't simple, is it? The Empire is about following orders, but the Rebel Alliance was about changing all that—tossing it on its head and flipping up an obscene gesture before walking out of the room. The Empire didn't care about individuals. It cared only about itself. Still does. But Norra wants to care about people again. Not orders. Not governments. She adds a new "matter she must attend to" when she tries not to cry.

She fails. Norra sobs. Her shoulders hitch and what comes out of her is a desperate, animal sound. *Brentin*. Her husband. Temmin's father. Brentin is lost precisely because she got swept up in someone else's cause. And now her chances of getting him back are gone. Because she chose a path bigger and greater, even if it wasn't her own.

It was *his*. It was Brentin's cause. He was the rebel. She just wanted to be a mother to her son. The galaxy, she hoped then, would sort itself out.

She leans forward, wiping up tears with a drag of her forearm.

A hand falls upon her shoulder.

It's her son. She sweeps him up into a hug. He *oofs* a little and then goes with it, hugging her back. Approaching under a copse of flyleaf trees are both Sinjir and Jas, with Bones toodling behind.

Norra says to them: "Sorry to do that back there, I know I'm abandoning you and the team—"

"Shut up," Jas says, rolling her eyes. "We're in."

"What?"

"We're going to help you find Solo."

Sinjir snorts. "Little Miss Bounty Hunter here even negotiated a *truly* impressive fee for the job."

"Shut it, Rath Velus."

"Ten credits. *Ten*. We're all getting paid enough that we can probably split a steaming kofta-bun or all buy four bottles of jogan juice. Small bottles. We'll be richer than in our wildest dreams. Provided that our wildest dreams have us living in total destitution. You've gone soft, Emari."

"Like the lady said, we have debts. I pay mine."

"And Jom?" Norra asks.

Jas scowls. "No. The coward is sticking with them. Antilles, too."

"That's fine. They have to follow their path. We have ours. So let's get to work." She draws a deep breath and wonders exactly what they're getting themselves into. "Han Solo is apparently not going to find himself."

PART THREE

CHAPTER SIXTEEN

The veldt stretches out before them.

The *ki-a-ki* bushes tremble in the warm wind, dark thorny scrubs whose gentle tremors call to mind an animal trying very hard not to be seen. The thirstgrass conspires with the breeze: whispers and shushes and hissed hushes. Red, feathery clouds streak across the open sky, a sky the color of blush and bloom. A lone ship crosses it— some cargo ship, probably, one of the few travelers to this distant world of Irudiru.

Down there, among the grass and the scrub, sits a compound.

The compound has seven buildings. Each sits squat and rectangular, each made of blond brick and blood-red mortar, each with rail-top roofs and round porthole windows and water catchment tanks. One of the buildings is different, though: a manse larger and more ostentatious than the other, more austere buildings. The house is surrounded by a screened-in-porch, a xeriscape garden, and a series of shimmering and shifting holostatues. A droid with many extensor limbs flits about, tending to the garden and tuning up the statues.

Otherwise, the compound is silent and still.

And it has been for the better part of the last day.

This is the compound of Golas Aram.

What the crew knows about Aram is little, but perhaps enough: The big-headed Siniteen was once employed by the Galactic Empire as an architect. A *prison* architect, in fact. Aram designed some of the Empire's most notable prisons, including the Lemniscate beneath Coruscant, the floating asteroid prison of Orko 9, and the Goa Penal Colony. Aram's reported specialty was making prisons that were self-sustaining and inescapable. He considered it his "art."

Thing is, he didn't work only for the Empire. He operated freelance, too—helping design and build prisons for the Kanjiklub, for the Junihar Cartel, even for Splugorra the Hutt.

Aram is retired, supposedly.

Just the same, Aram is the only Imperial connection out here on Irudiru. He's the one good lead they have. But what happens when they go pulling on that thread? Will they find Han Solo? Or will the whole thing fall apart? Could they be putting Solo in danger?

The narrative they can put together for Solo is shaky, at best. The *Millennium Falcon* got into a scrap not far from Warrin Station. Han had transmitted after that—but whatever he was investigating sure stirred up trouble. Given the presence of that Prowler droid, plus the information from Black Sun and the sheer manic glee of Tashu regarding Irudiru, there's cause to worry. So if Han was here investigating Aram, then what? After that, the narrative frays. Why look into Aram at all? Did Aram catch Solo sniffing around? Is Solo in prison—or is he looking for someone in prison?

Either way, it's what they have, so here they are.

From their hiding spot atop a gentle hilltop plateau, Norra leans forward, parting the sharp-bladed thirstgrass like a curtain and peering out through a pair of macrobinoculars. Using the dial on the side, she scans through the heat signatures then clicks over to electric and electronic indicators. The binocs highlight a series of danger spots all around the compound; they glow red in the viewscreen. "I see them," she tells Jas—Jas, who lies unseen in the tall grass even though she's only a few meters away.

The binocs highlight that the compound is ringed by an invisible perimeter fence: a barrier of ghosted lasers, impossible to see but sure to cut you apart if you marched through them. The ground leading up to the compound, both in and out of the fence, is littered with land mines. Then, located throughout the compound are turret-droids. Each hides in plain sight near vaporators, looking like part of the mechanism. Stealthy buggers, those.

Through the grass, Jas says, "The place is loaded for war. Aram's protecting himself. I get that he's paranoid, given the changes cascading through the galaxy, but this is a whole other level. He's afraid. And he hasn't come out in days." From behind them, Norra hears Temmin working on something—a *tink tink tink* followed by a buzzing twist from a microspanner. What is he doing back there? Norra's about to ask, when—

The grass swishes and shakes as Sinjir crawls up on his belly. "Ow!" he says, flexing his hand and popping the knuckle of his thumb in his mouth. "This grass is slicing me to bits."

"It drinks your blood," Jas says, easing closer. "Thirstgrass sustains itself on the creatures who walk through it. Little sips from little cuts."

He frowns. "Lovely. I'm here for my hourly update. And my hourly update is: I am bored. Bored out of my skull."

"That's always your hourly update," Norra says.

"Because it's true every hour."

"It's my update, too," Temmin says, crawling up next to them. "Seriously, this is awful. I want to burn all this grass. And the thorny bushes. And the flies." As if to demonstrate, he swats at the back of his hand. "See? Ugh. I should've stayed on Chandrila."

"Can't we just go back to Kai Pompos?" Sinjir asks. "We'd make it by nightfall. There's a little drinkery around the back of the town. They have a still where they ferment this root, this korva root. So we go back, we tip back a few under the Irudiru moons, we reformulate our strategy—"

"This is a fact-finding mission," Norra says, feeling like a mom commanding a child to stay put. "We stay here until all the facts are found."

"Facts are," Temmin says, "the guy isn't coming out. He's dug in like a blood-bug." They'd heard rumors that Aram was a big-game hunter, and thought maybe that would afford them an opportunity to get close to him. But so far, no go. Nor has he gone out for supplies. Or even a breath of fresh air. They've seen neither hide nor hair of the man. Just droids. "Here's what we do. We take Mister Bones—" Bones sits crumpled up behind them, his skeletal body folded tightly with his head bowed and his arms enclosing his knees. "And we let Bones march down there, find the guy, drag him up here onto the plateau, and we question him. Simple."

"As simple as chasing birds with a hammer," Sinjir mutters.

"Everyone hush," Jas says. "Temmin, did you build my thing or not?"

"Yeah, yeah." He fishes around in his pocket and holds up a pair of devices in the palm of his hand. One looks like a round from a slugthrower, but it's been modified—the shell casing crimps around a circuit bulb, and the tip of that bulb has four little prongs. Like insect mandibles. The second device is round, no bigger than a button, with a little zigzag antenna sticking out.

"It's a bug," Temmin says, sounding impressed with himself.

"This planet has enough bugs without us adding more to it," Sinjir grouses. "And before anyone corrects me, yes, I know, it's a *listening* bug and not a *real* bug and—oh, never mind. Good job, Jas. Now what?"

"We can't get eyes on, so we need to get ears on. I load this into my rifle and fire it right at his manse. Then—" She grabs the second device. "This jury-rigged earpiece with which to listen in."

"Clever," Sinjir says. "Still not sure what *I'm* doing here."

Jas hands him the earpiece. "*You're* going to do the listening."

"Joy." He makes a face as he takes it and screws it into his ear.

The bounty hunter unslings the slugthrower from her back. Norra again grabs the binocs and focuses them at the compound.

A herd of animals have come up alongside the invisible perimeter—long-limbed, long-necked leathery things, these beasts. They number in the dozens. Some stop to nip at the tufts of *ki-a-ki* bushes, while the others bat at one another with bony protuberances atop their narrow snouts. Norra is pretty sure they're morak. Big things, but herbivores. Though she'd hate to get stomped under those long legs—legs that end in claw-tipped feet.

Jas pulls the slugthrower close and uses her thumb to pop open a bipod at the end of the barrel, giving it stability. She tugs the scope tight against her eye. Norra watches her through the grass—the way Jas draws a breath deep, then slowly exhales it until no breath remains and she is still . . .

It's surprisingly close to what Luke taught Leia, isn't it?

Shut out the world. Be mindful, but empty.

Like a cup to be filled up.

(Of course, Jas does this in order to kill people more efficiently.)

The bounty hunter's finger coils around the trigger.

But then—

The morak all look up at the same time. A gesture of alarm.

Norra reaches out and touches Jas's shoulder. "Wait."

"What is it?" Jas asks.

"Something's up."

Sinjir plucks the earpiece out of his ear, scowling at it. "This thing is fritzing out. It's making this . . . high-pitched whine. Wretched sound."

Down below, the morak begin to move. All of them at once, a herd movement. They go from walking to galloping, their long bony legs launching them forward with a swiftness that surprises Norra.

The animals are headed toward the hill where the crew is waiting.

Closer, closer.

The ground begins to vibrate beneath them.

It's too steep, surely. They can't—

The animals reach the bottom of the hill and begin to scramble up the side of it. Their clawed feet make great haste, and now Norra knows what those claws are for. Dust spirals behind them.

They're coming right for us.

"We have to move," Norra cries. *"Move!"*

She and the others spring up out of hiding and turn tail, bolting through the grass. The morak crest the hill, bleating and blowing mucus from their snouts. The ground rumbles as the herd stampedes.

The grass slices at Norra's arms, but she can't waste time caring. Everyone moves fast—everyone except Bones, who sits somewhere under cover, and is hopefully resilient enough to suffer the knocks and blows of the morak. She's not even sure where they should go. Run straight? Turn to the side? The morak are coming right up behind them—

One lopes past Norra in a lumbering gallop, swiping at her with its long neck—the thing is twice her height and she just barely darts out of its way even as others come up behind her. Ahead, though she can't see it, the far side of the hill awaits. What then? Run down it, trying not to fall? Duck and pray the charging morak go over the edge?

The bounty hunter runs next to her, and when one morak comes behind her, Jas jabs at it with the barrel of her slugthrower—and the beast roves drunkenly toward Norra. It clips her and she staggers—

Her legs go out from under her—

There's Temmin, grabbing her by the belt to keep her from falling. It's just enough to help her get her legs back under her. Norra is about to thank her son—

She doesn't get the chance.

A sound hits them, a sonic hum. Suddenly, the morak are squawking and turning sharply away, the herd splitting in twain as if by an invisible wedge. Norra thinks, *Thank the stars for whatever is doing that.*

But then something lands in the grass in front of them—the thing rolls a few times like a flung rock. It beeps three times in succession. Then:

An implosive sound—*foomp.* The air lights up around them, a hard pulse of bright light. It concusses the air, too, hitting her like a thunderclap. Norra is suddenly blind and deaf, her ears ringing, her vision washed away in a tide of searing white. She fumbles for the blaster at her side—she whips it out, and it's suddenly rocked out of her hand, clattering away.

A shape emerges in front of her as the white light begins to recede: a person-shape. Norra thinks: *Aram has us. We thought we were watching him, but he was watching us.*

She leans forward, starts to stand.

"Don't move," comes a voice. Quiet, but urgent.

Norra asks as her eyes adjust, "Who is that? Who's there?"

The figure steps forward. She spies two blasters held aloft, one in each hand, and one pointed right at her. "Name's Han Solo. Captain of the *Millennium Falcon.* Who the hell are *you*?"

CHAPTER SEVENTEEN

The little cantina here is less a bar and more a ragtag collection of debris and detritus. The crew sits under mesh netting in an alcove formed by old junk: the war-scorched foot of an AT-AT walker; a stack of tire treads looped end-over-end; crates whose lids are pulled back just enough to reveal the haunted dead eyes of forgotten, deactivated droids.

They sit and they watch the man known as Han Solo.

When they saw him on that plateau, he was barely recognizable. The scruffy beard made it hard enough, but then he was dressed in a set of ratty rags: rags, Jas realized later, that matched the color of the thirstgrass. Smart. His hair is longer, too. Shaggier. Unkempt.

Here, now, Jas recognizes in him that smuggler's lean—an easy swagger that the man doesn't have to try to manifest. It's just part of who he is. Part of that bona fide Han Solo *charm*. He's certainly handsome. A boyish rogue. Jas would, given half an invitation, mount him like a turret. Though here her mind wanders to Jom. *That coward,* she thinks. She tries to make her fury at the old commando burn hotter than it does. She fails, and misses Jom Barell regardless.

Solo sits back, arm over an empty chair. There's something else there, something beyond his swagger and his charm, and her shared looks with Sinjir tell her that he sees it, too: Solo is on edge. He's wary, but a smuggler is always wary. This is different.

Han Solo is *angry.*

And not just at them, she thinks.

The Bith bartender shuffles up, his one leg little more than a crudely fashioned metal prosthetic, and pops glasses in front of all of them. Korva. The stuff Sinjir was talking about. The smell coming off the glasses is enough to fry an astromech's circuits. The vapor blurs the air above the liquid. The Bith sets one down in front of Temmin, and Jas watches Norra rescue the glass before the boy can grab it. He pouts in response.

When the Bith is gone, Solo regards them.

"Who are you, and what do you want with Golas Aram?"

The crew shares uncomfortable looks.

It's Norra who speaks up: "We're not interested in Aram. We were looking for you."

It takes a moment for that to register on his face. He laughs, then, though no mirth dwells in the sound. "Well, congratulations, lady, you found me. You can collect your prize at the door." He clears his throat. "On your way *out,* if you get my meaning."

"*You* are our prize," Jas says.

His hand is no longer on top of the table.

She knows he's going for his blaster. The others don't get it. They don't understand that he'll clear them with his DL-44 before they even think to unsnap their own holsters. Probably a good idea to get ahead of that.

"We're *not* bounty hunters," Jas says, holding up both hands, palms out. A sign of acquiescence and surrender.

Sinjir wrinkles his brow. "Jas, you, ahhh. You *are* a bounty hunter."

"Shut up, Sinjir."

Han's gaze flits from each to each. "Who sent you?"

"You know who," Norra says.

There. That wariness, that anger, that edge: It softens and dulls, just for a moment. Like a mask sliding away, showing his true face. He says what he surely already knows: "Leia."

"Your last transmission ended abruptly. She thinks something happened to you."

"It did. I was on my way here and crossed paths with a slave-hauler run by the Dodath Raiders. Without Chewie in the copilot's seat I missed that they were coming up on me fast, and they fired on me and took out my comm array. Again."

"You could've found a way to contact her."

He hesitates.

Norra fills in the blank: "You didn't want her to come after you."

"Of course not. I got my things to take care of and she has her things and then, when all that shakes out, I'll go back."

"You have things to take care of back home, too." A moment passes between him and Norra with that exchange. She struck a nerve. Jas wonders if the woman is playing a dangerous game. Solo is angry, and anger is irrational. Here is a man backed into a corner. Pinned down by his debts.

Norra says: "We'll help you find your Wookiee."

"He's not *my* Wookiee. Nobody owns Chewbacca, you can be sure of that, sister." And once again, that war plays out across his face. A softness and a sadness give way to fresh anger. Han suddenly takes his glass and pitches it over the small wall of junk. Somewhere in the distance, a faint sound of glass breaking: *ksssh!* "I screwed up and now Chewie is gone."

His guard drops. He breaks down. Solo tells the story.

"A little something came across our dash. An opportunity. And no, before you go looking at me like that, not a *smuggler's* opportunity, but a real one. The kind that matters.

"Chewie and me, we've been kicking around now for a long time. He's my partner. He's not just some sidekick. He's not a *pet*. And he's damn sure not my slave. It's equal between us. We always split everything, you understand? We split our share of every job. We split our share of the injuries, too. And sometimes we take on . . . each other's burdens.

"He's a Wookiee, right? Kashyyyk, that's where he comes from, that's his home. But it's not his anymore. I've been there. I've seen what the Empire has done. They ripped down the trees. They put cuffs and collars on all the Wookiees. Some of them they cut open. Others they ship off to work the worst jobs the Empire has on offer. They took his home from him. I can't abide that. I don't have a home anymore besides the *Falcon*, but him? He does. And he deserves to go home. He has a family, too, you know.

"I saved him, at least that's what he says, the big fuzzy fool, but really, he saved me. I was on a bad path, and Chewie, he put me straight. Saved my shanks more than once, too. He said it was part of some *life debt*—he has a word for it, but if I try to say it in his tongue I'll probably strain something. Even if I can't say it, I know what it means. It means that he owes his life to me.

"But that's a hot cup of bantha spit, is what it is. He doesn't owe me. *I* owe *him*. I got a debt to Chewie to get him his home back. So when this chance came up, I leapt at it. The rebels, or the Republic, or whatever they want to call themselves? They didn't want any part of it. I made it clear, we need to make Kashyyyk a priority, but they waved me off. *Not strategically significant*, they said. *Not yet. Soon.* Blah blah. Bureaucracy and strategy and war planning? They made me a general but I didn't know a thing about any of that. I don't follow what's on some . . . *schematic*. I follow what's in here. In my gut. My gut always knows the way.

"Or so I thought. I leapt at the chance but didn't look first. Imra, the smuggler who *presented* this little gift-wrapped opportunity—turns out, she was on the wrong side of things. The Empire must've had something on her, and she set up this trap for me. Not just for me. For all of us. I called in favors, brought a bunch of smugglers to a space not far from Warrin Station, and worse, I called in a few other Wookiee refugees, too. Ones I knew would want to scrap with the Empire. Ones who would want to go home.

"We all got in one place—half a dozen ships of people willing to work for me, and okay, yeah, maybe I promised them a pardon even though I didn't know if I could make that magic happen. I mean, I'm no Jedi. I can't just wiggle my pinkie and make someone dance. But there we all were. I sent Chewie to board a gunship captained by this Wookiee pirate, Kirratha. Next thing I know, we're blown. Two Star Destroyers, plus a swarm of Imperial starfighters. They're all over us. Cutting us apart. They shot out Kirratha's engines, hobbling her on the spot—with Chewie still on board. Some ships they wiped off the map. Others they nabbed with tractor beam. And I . . .

"I beat stardust and got the hell out of there. I didn't know what else to do. I thought that my best bet of getting Chewie and the others back would be from inside the cockpit of the *Falcon* and not stuck in some cell on board a Star Destroyer. But now I know: I was a coward. I should've sucked it up, found a way out from on board. I didn't share the burden like I was supposed to. And now Chewie's out there shouldering it all on his own.

"Ever since, I've been tearing up the galaxy looking for him. Every two-bit Imperial officer I could find told me what I wanted to know or got his teeth knocked out of his head. Finally, I figured out where they took him.

"They took him back to Kashyyyk. They took him home."

His eyes shine. His lip purses and twitches even as he fidgets and scratches at his beard. It's then that Jas gets it.

Solo is angry.

But he's angry with *himself.*

"So why Golas Aram?" Norra asks. "Why are you out here?"

The smuggler hesitates. He's still not sure if he can trust them, maybe. Jas gets it. Trust is hard. It feels like falling.

Finally, Solo says, "Story goes, Chewie found himself on board a prison transport. A ship bound for a place called Ashmead's Lock: a prison on the far side of Kashyyyk. Don't know much about it except who built it."

"Golas Aram," Jas says.

"Right. I've been watching him. Then *you* bunch come along, damn near mucking everything up. If I hadn't summoned that herd of morak, you woulda fired that tracking bug on his house. But Golas? He's paranoid. *Real* paranoid. He does routine sweeps. He'd have found that bug before nightfall and sent out tracker droids to hunt you—and by proxy, *me*—down." He kicks his chair out and stands up, arms out. "So, you found me. Great. Now go away. Tell Leia . . . well, tell her what you want, but I can't have her thinking she needs to fix this. I can't have her in danger. Just tell her I'm okay and I'll be home soon."

"When?" Norra asks.

"Just tell her I'll be home *on time.*"

With that, Solo pushes past them and heads out of the junk alcove.

"Well!" Sinjir says. "That solves that. Time to celebrate." He blasts the glass of korva down his throat and has a small spasm as it hits him. He coughs so hard he has to wipe his watering eyes. "Oh, this stuff is uniformly terrible. It may—" He *urps.* "It may be poison."

The rest of them sit quietly, unsure what to do.

Norra says, finally: "I think we need to—"

From close by, the sudden sounds of a scuffle arise. The noise is short—a cry of alarm, a hard *thwack,* and a subsequent *thud.*

They rush out of the alcove. Just around the corner, near the korva still, lies a body. Han Solo's body.

Mister Bones stands astride the smuggler's supine form.

"I SUBDUED THE TARGET WITH VIOLENCE," the battle droid chirps, his words punctuated by bursts of sharp static. "MISSION AC-COMPLISHED. VICTORY FOR ALL."

CHAPTER EIGHTEEN

Leia hears voices through the door. She leans in and listens, and as she listens, she finds herself growing furious.

Ackbar: "Alliances across the galaxy are patchwork. Too many systems stand alone and are falling between the widening fissure between our power and the Empire's own influence. We are not growing swiftly enough to match their decline. We are not bridging that gap."

Mon Mothma: "This is why we must concentrate our efforts helping those worlds that offer a likelier chance of joining the New Republic in order to have a voice in the Senate."

One of Mon's advisers, Hostis Ij: "Our resource reserves are stretched thin, Chancellor! But there remains one simple way of obtaining new lines of food, fuel, and other vital supplies—"

Mon's other chief adviser, Auxi Kray Korbin: "Oh, please, let me guess: A stronger military? Tell us. How will a more robust military help?"

Hostis: "If we step up recruitment, we will have more soldiers to secure supply lines once possessed by the Empire—such resources are out there in the wind, and who knows who will possess them."

More bluster and clamor. It's time to step in.

Leia palms the door panel, and the door hisses open.

The metal shutters of the meeting room window are closed, though light from the bright Chandrilan day outside bleeds in at the edges like magma. All around them float various holoprojections: datagraphs, system maps, planet maps, schematics. It adds up to a galaxy in chaos. A galaxy whose allegiance is divided—not divided merely between the two warring sides of the New Republic and the Galactic Empire, but diced up finely into factions. Those factions will fight. They will fall to one another. They will form their own power structures. Warlords will lead them. As will despots, crime bosses, cult leaders. The galaxy will go from suffering the cruelty of the Empire's order to being thrown into the maelstrom of disorder and madness. It will be an ugly time, Leia knows, if the New Republic cannot see its way clear through this labyrinthine tangle. A *dark* time.

As she steps into the room, all eyes fall to her.

They are surprised. Surprised even though she has a chair of her own in this room, a chair that presently sits empty between Mon Mothma and Admiral Ackbar. The chair sits empty because no one told her of this meeting. She was kept away on purpose.

"Leia," Mon Mothma says, standing up. "Welcome. Sit."

"I'll stand." She hears the frostiness in her own voice. Leia thinks to control it, then decides against it. *Let them be frozen out the way they are trying to freeze me out.* "Having a meeting?"

"Please understand," Mon says. "You're going through a hard time. With your husband gone, and that unfortunate situation with that crew—"

"Yes. How unfortunate."

"I . . . you are of course welcome to sit, join us, offer your thoughts."

"I told her," Ackbar says, his voice a gruff gurgle.

Mon nods. "Of course. It was my mistake, Leia, for not inviting you. I simply thought you had a great deal on your mind already."

"Leia is more than just the face of our efforts across the galaxy," the admiral says, giving a little nod as if to agree with himself. "She is also a precious resource unto herself. Smart and savvy and a needed voice."

Ackbar, Leia realizes, is a good friend.

Mon is, too. She has to remind herself of that.

But Mon is a realist. Sometimes, that seems cold. And Leia is an idealist—her passions can run hot. They will remain friends through this, but that doesn't mean Leia can't—and shouldn't—push back.

This is a delicate time for the New Republic. When Palpatine founded the Empire, he did so like a parasite: a creature growing inside the body of a stronger host until it could burst free from the skin and take control. The Empire emerged from this brutal chrysalis fully formed—and all it had to do was claim the resources that the winnowing Republic already possessed. Ships, weapons, soldiers, supplies. The New Republic has no such advantage. It must claw and scrape for every ship, every weapon, every scrap of food, and every willing soldier.

Mon wants this transition to be as peaceable as possible. That is, of course, a noble goal. And in late nights the chancellor confided in Leia that she is wisely struck by the fear of what happened the first time the parasite of Palpatine squirmed under the skin. How easy it was for him to prey on the anxieties of the galaxy. How simple it was for him to turn system against system by stoking the fires of xenophobia, anger, selfishness. (And here Luke's voice echoes in her mind: *The ways and tools of the dark side, Leia.*) How do you form an Empire? By stealing a Republic. And how do you steal a Republic? By convincing its people that they cannot govern themselves—that freedom is their enemy and that fear is their ally.

Palpatine was an able puppetmaster. He gave himself the power. He pulled on all the strings. And the galaxy danced to his whims.

Mon, thankfully, wants no such power.

And so she's already begun ceding it. As chancellor she's put up votes that have begun the path of demilitarization. That presents a sign of moral strength, but also sends up a signal of defensive vulnerability. (That means getting her to approve new military contracts—like the creation of the Starhawks—is like pulling the teeth from the mouth of an ornery tauntaun.) As to defeating the scattered remains of the Empire, Mon seems of a mind to let that infection burn itself out. Strike when necessary, and otherwise sit back and let the antibodies of a free galaxy do the work.

That, Leia believes, misunderstands the infection. It won't take much for the disease to again take hold. And sometimes, diseases *evolve.*

Worse, what does it say to those systems that need the New Republic right now? The Empire still enslaves whole worlds.

Like Kashyyyk, she thinks.

Kashyyyk: one planet where the New Republic is content to let the Empire burn itself out. That comes with an undercurrent of grim, overly pragmatic reality: The Wookiees are not a meaningful resource to the New Republic. Not militarily, not governmentally. Kashyyyk has resources, but none so dramatic that the New Republic is willing to sacrifice ships (and besides, the Empire has plundered most of those resources already).

But sacrifice is everything, isn't it?

It means the willingness to leap into the void to save those who need saving. To save your *friends.*

"We argue," Leia says suddenly, "about whether it is the time to build up the military or to dampen its effect. And all the while we forget that we have the privilege of arguing from comfortable chairs many parsecs away. We argue about what's prudent or what's practical while people suffer. Do you know what people want to see from the New Republic? Do you, truly?"

Mon cedes the floor. "Please."

"They want us to be heroes."

A moment passes where everyone chuckles uncomfortably. At least until they realize she's quite serious.

Mon says: "I know. You're not wrong. And you are a hero, and you helped us all be the heroes needed to get to this point. But such passion and idealism have to be tempered by reality. This is a government. It has a lot of moving pieces."

Leia stiffens. "And that is where we'll fail. This isn't a machine, Chancellor. When did we start to see this as a government and not a collection of people helping people? We've started seeing . . . territories and battle logistics and *votes*. We've stopped seeing hearts and minds and *faces*. The more we do that, the more we lose. Of ourselves. Of the galaxy."

"Running a galactic government is complex."

"Then I don't want to run a *galactic* government!" Her words come out louder than she means them to. All in the room seem startled by their intensity. *Empty yourself. Center yourself.* She must. But she can't.

Mon says softly, "This is about Kashyyyk. About Han."

"We should have helped the Wookiees." Her voice trembles with rage and sorrow.

"I understand." Mon speaks like a mother to a tantruming child: slow, steady, and with a condescending tone. *She's talking down to me. My own friend is talking to me like I'm a youngling.* "But as we discussed, we ran the numbers, we performed the simulations, and now is not the sensible time—"

"Sensible!" Leia barks. "We've lost all sense, I fear. You're right. I shouldn't have come to this meeting."

Ackbar calls after her, but she doesn't stop. Leia turns heel and marches back out of the meeting room.

If only she could slam the door, but it whishes gently shut behind her.

A transmission shimmers into being. There, projected above Rax's desk, is the visage of a Bith. A drink-slinger from the distant planet of Irudiru. His appearance can only mean good news.

The Bith's massive cranium turns left and right as if to make sure he's alone. Satisfied, the bartender says: "They're here. And they're together."

A smile spreads across Rax's face like a consuming fire. It warms him, this news. It's taken too long to get here. So many puzzle pieces to nudge into place. And my, how those pieces were *stubborn*. Setting up a convincing mystery and threat is delicate work. One must commit to the theatrics but never overdo them; if any detected his shadowy hands above all of it, directing the stage, they would buck like an ill-saddled beast.

The Contingency continues, he thinks.

"Good," Gallius Rax says. "Continue monitoring. Credits will be forthcoming." Then he ends the transmission.

He wonders if Golas Aram is a piece deserving of a nudge or two. *Patience,* he chides himself. Let the mechanism work.

Part of that mechanism is Sloane.

She is one who has detected his shadow behind it all. That is a problem. Maybe one he can use to his advantage yet.

It is time to call her in.

Time, too, for one last test.

The room is white and mostly empty. The walls are padded. The windows are many, and the sunlight streaming in is bold and bright.

The only things in this room are Leia and a potted plant.

The plant is a sapling of the sanctuary trees of Endor, though some call it a serpent's puzzle, named so after the way the dark branches weave together in a kind of organic knotwork.

She grew it from a seed—a small knobby acorn given to her by the little Ewok known as Wicket. She grew the plant in a pot of Chandrilan soil, and to her shock and delight, it took.

It has become a focus of her meditations, as suggested by Luke. She decided, after storming out of the meeting room, that it was best to come here. Best for her to focus on something that wasn't the state of the galaxy, or the nascent New Republic, or that nagging feeling in the deep of her middle that Mon has betrayed her in some small but significant way.

She sits with it in the middle of the room.

She clears her mind.

And then she tries to *feel* the tree.

She does this at least once a day.

Leia has never felt the tree.

Not for lack of trying! She sits here. She empties herself of breath, and then she tries to free herself of thought. Just like Luke taught her to. That part works fine most of the time. But he said it was possible to feel the lifeforce of things with the Force.

She swore to him that she just doesn't have it. *It* being that mystical, intangible power that her brother possesses and (this thought comes with a set of chills grappling up her spine) that her father—her *birth* father—possessed, too.

Luke continues to swear that, with time, she will come to feel the Force just as he does. He explained that it was how she felt his pain back during Cloud City—him hanging there, wearied and beaten and about to fall into the roiling clouds below. He said he'd teach her.

And he did teach her. Some things, at least.

Then? He left.

Just like Han left.

Luke . . .

She finds her mind wandering to him now. Her thoughts reach for her wayward brother like a living thing, like branches seeking the sun. *I need you here. I need your help.* Luke sometimes had a farm boy's naïveté, yes, but right now she feels she could use a little of that.

Her mind is a tangle of thoughts. The complexities of politics, the love of (and anger over) Han, the loss of Luke, and above all else the ever-persistent worry about the life she carries—

Her skin tingles. Her mind feels suddenly unmoored from the rest of her. Leia feels dizzy enough to fall over.

Oh.

Oh, my!

There! There it is. Washing over her and through her—an awareness unlike any she's ever felt before. A pulsing glow, flickering and strong.

It's not the plant. It's not Luke. It's not even Han.

It's her child.

This isn't just a mother's recognition of the life inside—that, she already knows. She's already well aware of the bump and tumble of that little person she carries. (And she already knows about the heartburn, and the pre-breakfast nausea, and the post-breakfast nausea, and the post-post-breakfast hunger . . .)

This goes beyond all that. This is something separate from her. It isn't a physical feeling. It is all around her. It suffuses her like the perfume from a jungle of flowers. As such, she is suddenly aware of her child's mind and spirit: She senses pluck and wit and steel blood and a keen mind and by the blood of Alderaan is this one going to be a fighter!

Wait.

He?

It's a boy.

It's a boy.

Her hands fly in front of her mouth as she both laughs and cries at the same time. This, she thinks, is the light side that Luke always goes on about—the promise of light, the promise of a new life . . .

And then, the black edging of the dark side encircles her bliss like a noose. Because what rides swift on the heels of hope but fear—a fear that stretches out far and wide like a growing shadow. Fear of having a child in an unstable galaxy. Fear of whether or not Han is alive—or Luke, too. Will the child grow up with a father? An uncle? A mentor? What is her legacy and what will her boy's legacy be?

Her breath catches in her chest. She has to force herself to breathe.

Clear your mind. Clear it all. Focus, Leia. Focus.

Are those her thoughts?

Or are they Luke's?

The Empire cares little for the fripperies of life, preferring instead to put a cold gray veneer on just about everything, but Gallius Rax grew up in a dead place, and so putting in this garden here on the upper echelons of the *Ravager* gives him a source of solace.

From behind him, Rae Sloane clears her throat.

He does not turn. He suspects she has brought a blaster. Sloane does not trust him, but he suspects she feels trapped by her options. The one option that makes the most sense—the one that would demonstrate strength that few others would deny—would be to burn a hole in his back.

Fleet Admiral Rax hopes now to change that.

"You despise me," he says, staring at the stalk of a red-tongued kubari flower—its petals have many layers, each folded against the next. The prettiest, most crimson petals in fact remain hidden from view.

"No," she says. A lie, certainly. "Of course not. I respect you."

"You can respect me and despise me at the same time. I felt much the same way about our former Emperor. He was mighty and deserving of praise. He was also a monster, and one who made mistakes."

That would've been heresy if Palpatine were still alive.

Still might be, if those words were uttered to the wrong person.

"Be that as it may," she says, suddenly uncomfortable, "if you worry about me, please. Don't."

"And yet I do. I know you've been to see Mas Amedda. I know you've been investigating me in a way that goes well beyond cursory checkups. And I would guess that right now, feeling cornered, you are reaching for that elegant chrome blaster you keep at your hip. But I ask you to wait."

In the reflection of the blast-glass enclosure, he sees her hand hovering near the weapon. So close.

To her credit, she denies nothing. Good. He likes her. He would hate to have that feeling diminished by something so weak as a common lie. Lies must be big, grand, *full of purpose.*

"Go on," she says.

Now, *now* he turns. His arms spread wide and welcoming. His mouth pulled tight in a cold rictus grin. "I want to tell you my plan."

Confusion flickers on her face like a short-circuiting holovid. "Why? Why now? You've kept me at arm's length."

"Yes. Because I am distrustful by nature. And because the future of this Empire traipses delicately upon a wire. The chasm beneath it is deep and I don't wish to shoulder it into the abyss by trusting the wrong people."

Sloane narrows her eyes. "You're pulling strings, Admiral. I don't know what they're connected to or why you're pulling them. I don't even know who you are or where you come from. You are little more than a shadow—and yet you lead the Empire."

"Secretly. *You're* the grand admiral here, I'll remind you."

"In title, yes. And your leadership is not *that* secret. You're out in the open more than you think. Word will get out."

"And when it does, I will confirm that I remain your most trusted adviser—a war hero who supports your own candidacy for Emperor."

"Who are you, Admiral?"

Rax rolls his eyes. Such a brutal, worthless question. He doesn't care to waste time on it. As if the identity of one man is really all that special? The beauty is in the total mechanism, not the parts pulled out of it.

Instead, he cuts to the quick.

"I plan on attacking Chandrila," he says.

The shock on her face—he won't lie and say it doesn't please him. It means she didn't see that coming. If she didn't, nobody will.

"For so long we've remained still, patient, waiting . . ." she says.

"And now it's time to return to the galaxy and strike at the heart of the New Republic. Our attack will stagger them."

"The fleets hiding in the nebulae? Will you utilize them?"

He offers another vicious smile, and she mistakes it as confirmation.

"When?" she asks.

"Soon. All the pieces are almost in place."

"What pieces?"

"In time, you'll see."

Sloane bristles at that. "I need to know—"

"And *I* need you to trust. All will become clear in time. I want you with me through all of it, Grand Admiral Sloane. You are a vital re-source." He says that last sentence as something he hopes is true. He will have to test her this one last time. Just as he was tested many times. "Do you trust me?"

She hesitates. "I don't know."

"An honest answer. Good. Tell no one of this little talk. I'll let you know when it's time. Be ready."

And with that, he walks past her, because the conversation is over.

INTERLUDE

TATOOINE

It is a difficult thing being a creature without purpose.

The purpose of the man, Malakili, was once to *give* purpose to such creatures. He was always good with beasts. As a child in a Nar Shaddaa slum, he taught vicious gugverms to stop stealing from the food stores—and over time they became his pets, his friends, his protectors. Later, he would help tame and prepare a variety of beasts for the Hutt circuses: sand dragons and kill-wings and little womp rats in their little outfits. And then later, his precious joy, the rancors. Those, the monsters none could tame but he.

And now his last rancor, Pateesa, is dead.

Crushed by a lucky fool in black.

Worse, his employer is also gone—eradicated by that same lucky fool and his cruel friends. Malakili and the others were left in the palace after Jabba's sail barge erupted in belching fire, all of them unsure as to what exactly to do now. A new Hutt would come to occupy the dais, they said. And so many stayed as the food dwindled and the water ran out. Soon those left began drifting away, too, off into the sands and away across the dunes. No Hutt was coming. The galaxy was changing. Could it be that the Hutts were fighting? Some underworld war pitting slug against slug?

Malakili was one of the last in the palace.

And then one day, he left, too.

He thought maybe to tame the glorious monstrosity at the bottom of the Great Pit of Carkoon (and, failing that, to throw himself into its maw), but the mighty Sarlacc was injured. Burning wreckage from the sail barge had rained upon it. Already its body—considerably more massive than the mouth exposed from the sliding sands—had been partially unburied, its stoma-tubes slit open, its digesting innards pillaged by industrious Jawas. They pulled out weapons and armor, droids and tools. And skeletons, of course.

The creature of Carkoon had a pure purpose, to wait and to eat, and now it was left to thrash and wail in the grip of pillagers. Malakili wept at another life without purpose.

He wandered, as many do. He felt like a scrap of cloth or a wad of trash blown across the desert, pushed this way and pulled that way. Rolling without destination. Without meaning.

And now, he thinks, *I am going to die.*

The Red Key thugs found him wandering toward Mos Pelgo. They gave chase, but he is older and slower than he used to be. One hit him from behind and now?

Now his face is pressed into the hot sand. A boot pushes on his neck, and the bones in his back grind. One of the Red Key Raiders— men who claim to work for the new mining conglomerate, a conglomerate even naïve Malakili knows to be just a front for a criminal syndicate—rips off his leather hood and presses a blaster into the back of his skull. They rip his satchel from his shoulder and empty it onto the sand. His waterskin finds its way into one of the thug's hands, who parts the leather from in front of his face and drinks what little is left. The rest of Malakili's belongings decorate the dirt: a lucky braid of bantha fur and teeth; a small water shiv made of dewback bone; a few droid gears and shiny chits to give to the Jawas or to pay off the grunting Tuskens.

A man who introduces himself as Bivvam Gorge rasps in Malakili's ear: "What else you got, wanderer? These sands are Red Key sands and Lorgan Movellan is taking his cut. Wouldn't want his cut to be your ears, or your tongue, would you?" The second thug chuckles through a respirator.

As if to demonstrate, the first thug stabs a gleaming hunting knife down into the ground. It hits the sand with a hiss.

Above them, the shriek of a blaster bolt—

And then, the thug hits the sand, too. He topples like a vaporator knocked flat by a stomping bantha. His head turns toward Malakili as smoke rises from a patch of burned hair and skin on the far side of his skull. The thug's mouth works soundlessly. Then his eyes go dim.

Suddenly, the air erupts with blaster fire. The second thug gargles rage through his respirator, but even this is short lived. He staggers backward, arms flailing, the rifle dropping out of his hand.

That thug joins his friend. The suns will claim him.

Malakili does not move.

Whoever is coming is worse than these two, and so it seems better to play dead. That, a trick he learned from many of the beasts he trained. Prey knows that the best costume from a predator is the *already-dead*.

Please let me be, please let me be, please . . .

But why? To what purpose? To be saved—to be spared—is a privilege that should belong to one with purpose.

Footsteps approach. Boots thumping on the sand.

"You can get up." A voice. Male. Gruff, plain, clear.

Another voice: a woman's voice, "Relax. We're not raiders."

"We're law."

Law? On Tatooine? No such thing. The Hutts *were* the law. *Jabba* was law. But now, with Jabba dead . . .

Malakili rolls over and sits up.

There, a man in Mandalorian armor, the suit of it pocked and pitted and streaked with scars. Armor that looks eerily familiar, and Malakili's innards clench at the sight of it. A carbine hangs at the man's side.

Next to him stands a tall woman. Head-tails which means she's Twi'lek—though one of those head-tails is mangled, its end puckered with scar tissue. At her hips hang twin pistols.

"I'm Issa-Or," she says, a sneer to her lips.

The man removes his helmet. His cheeks are lined with salt-and-pepper stubble. He winces against the double suns. "I'm Cobb Vanth. Lawman and de facto mayor of what used to be Mos Pelgo."

"Freetown, now," the Twi'lek says. "A place where good people can come if they're willing to work. If they're willing to stand tall against the syndicates. Against folks like Lorgan and Red Key."

Malakili nods as if he understands. But he doesn't. Not yet.

Cobb kneels down. "You look familiar to me."

"I am no one."

"Everybody's someone, my friend. Thing about Freetown is, to live inside our walls means to be useful. Are you useful?"

And here, Malakili's spirits sink. He is not useful to anyone. He admits as much, his dry eyes going suddenly wet with tears. "I have no value to you. Kill me. My creature, Pateesa, is dead. All my beasts are gone—"

The Twi'lek says, "You a beastmaster?"

Master. If only he deserved such a word. But he gives an uncertain nod. "I train beasts. Yes."

The two share a look. Vanth chuckles: a dry sound like rocks rolling together down the side of a cliff. "We got a couple unruly rontos that could use a steady hand. Can you handle that? There'd be payment. And a homestead for you if you care to claim it."

His sinking spirits are suddenly buoyant. Purpose dawns inside his heart bringing light to darkness once more. "I . . . can."

"There's something else," Issa-Or says.

"Should we tell him?"

"Why not? If anybody can help . . ."

Cobb leans in close and as he helps Malakili up, the man says in a low voice as if the sand might be listening: "You know much about Hutts?"

"I know quite a bit."

"You think you could train one?"

"I . . . they are sentient beings, not pets."

"Fine. *Teach* one, then."

"I could. I believe. But why?"

Issa-Or grins. "Because we have one at Freetown."

"A *baby*," Cobb says, scratching his jaw. "Seems that Red Key was trying to sneak one in, install it onto the palace dais. We interrupted that little plan, and now we got this . . . slug, and not sure what to do with it. If you can help us with the rontos, maybe the Hutt, you've got a place at Freetown. How's that sound, friend?"

"It sounds . . ." *Like purpose.* "Most excellent. Thank you."

"You can thank me by doing your job."

"Let's go," Issa-Or says. "Leave the corpses for the others to find. Let them see that law, *true* law, is spreading across the land."

CHAPTER NINETEEN

Sinjir assured Norra that a glass of the korva would do it, and he was right. As soon as she eases the glass under Solo's nose, the vapor hits him. The smuggler's eyes bolt open and he stares back with a turbolaser intensity.

"Wuzza what the," he says, suddenly scrambling to stand. "Leia?"

"No," Norra says. She's alone with him in the main hold of the *Halo*. "It's Lieu . . . it's Norra Wexley. We're on Irudiru. Remember?"

He winces. His hand moves to rub the lump forming under his hairline. "Attacked by a droid. A . . ." He scrunches up his face in disbelief. "An old Clone Wars battle droid of all things. I must be hallucin . . ."

Movement from behind her. Mister Bones leans around the corner, poking his vulture's-skull droid head out. Han paws at his side for one of his blasters, but Norra holds his wrist and moves to block the view of the droid.

"Go away," she spits at Bones. "Go! Shoo, you bag of bones."

"ROGER-ROGER, TEMMIN'S MOM."

The droid recedes.

Han growls: "That droid is *yours*?"

"My son's."

"Damn thing knocked me out cold! You bring that rickety clanker back here. I want to shoot its arms off. Then I want to beat it with its own arms. Then I want to take its head—"

Norra eases him back into the chair. "I apologize for the droid. We looked at your head—the injury is superficial."

"Great. Thanks, *Doc*. Now do as I said: Get out of here and let me get back to work. You're slowing me down."

"We want to help."

"I don't need your help, lady."

"You're alone out here. I think you do."

He scowls at her and sits forward. "Why? Why help me? I don't know you. I didn't do anything for you. And I'm tired of owing people."

"We owe you."

"Not according to my tally," he says, tapping his temple. "I keep the ledgers up here and your name's not in it, honey."

"We could've just shipped you back to Chandrila, you know. Tied you to a chair. But you're a hero of the galaxy. You and your friends. You saved us all. This is how we pay you back." She stiffens. "Also, please don't call me honey."

He stands up.

"I can do this by myself."

No, you can't. But she placates him anyway. "I'm sure you could."

"I work alone."

"Obviously."

His eyes pinch and his hand idly scratches at the beard growth along his jaw. "But I do need Chewie back."

Norra understands—he's trying to ask for help, but he's too callused, too gruff-and-tumble to really *ask*. She offers it again: "So, let us help. We can offer extra hands, extra guns. We'll follow your lead."

"That might make it easier." He sizes her up with his eyes. "*Might.* But like you said: You need to follow my lead."

"Done."

"Fine. You can help me get Aram."

Norra stands up, too, offering her hand. "We'll help you get Chewie back, too."

"Well, then. In for a credit, in for a crate." He takes her hand. "Welcome to Team Solo. Hope you can keep up, Norra."

CHAPTER TWENTY

Everything's going according to plan.

That thrills Jas in no small way. The plan is everything. Designing one is like making a clock: all these little parts working together, turning, tugging, ticking. And at the end of the day, it either tells time or it doesn't.

And this plan, it's going along like clockwork.

She got to take out the pulse mines first—Jas took up the same place on the plateau overlooking Golas Aram's compound, and she used the scope on her slugthrower to identify the electronic signatures from each of the mines. Then it was the simple act of pointing the gun, emptying herself of breath, and pulling the trigger.

The first one did what it was supposed to do:

It went *bang*.

And that sound was a signal to get the rest of the plan going.

Kilometers away, Temmin and Bones got to work on cutting the conduit from the wind farm that Solo had identified. That knocked out the fence *and* the turrets. And it's allowed Sinjir to head down under the cover of night to Aram's compound. She spies his shadow darting through the fence now.

To keep him on his toes, Jas pops off more mines ahead of him—the pulse mines detonate with buzzing explosions, leaving behind small craters and a crackling haze of ozone smoke in their wake.

He's closing in on the compound—

Suddenly, from all around, shutters and doors open up. New shadows emerge, shapes that seem human but move with an inhuman stutter-step. *Droids,* she thinks, and that's confirmed the moment they ignite fire-red vibroblades from their hands. She sees a dozen of these droids. Maybe more.

Advancing on Sinjir's position.

And now, the clock is threatening to break.

Down there, outside the compound, the darkness is lit up by strange, glowing vibroblades. They draw glowing arcs through the air as they advance toward Sinjir—the ex-Imperial dashes behind an old motor-vator tiller, peeling off shots from his pistol. But it's not enough.

That is where Jas comes in. Her slugthrower kicks and barks as she takes out one droid after the next. Hard to see in the dark, but she does her best. The droids offer a satisfying rain of sparks every time she peels the skull off one with a hot tanium-jacketed projectile.

She thinks: *I got this.*

Confidence, or rather overconfidence, is a blinding force. And it doesn't help that she's got one open eye pressed against the ring of the rifle scope. Which means she hears what's coming one second too late.

Soon as the thirstgrass shakes and whispers, Jas quick rolls over onto her back and points her rifle up—but a thrumming vibroblade ignites in the darkness above her, whipping forward and slicing through the barrel of her slugthrower. It gets stuck there, buzzing and grinding, sparks flying, and the weight of the commando droid presses down against her.

She tries kicking the thing off her, but it's like trying to kick an astromech with its legs grav-bolted to the floor. As she struggles use-lessly, the droid's second vibroblade lights up and plunges toward her.

Jas jerks her head to the side just as the blade sticks into the hard-scrabble ground. Dust and debris sting her cheek.

The droid starts to spasm.

And glow.

Its mouthpiece offers a loud announcement:

"DESTRUCT SEQUENCE ENGAGED."

Oh, slag.

The commando droid shines like magma through a broken mantle of stone, and it's vibrating so hard now that Jas feels like she, too, will rattle to pieces. She struggles to shove the thing off before it detonates—surely taking her with it, leaving her little more than a red streak in a smoking crater. In the distance, she hears Sinjir yelling for her.

I have my own problems, she thinks.

If she can just pivot the gun . . .

The barrel is broken, the vibroblade still stuck in it—but firing a round out will still make a mess of the droid, maybe. But she needs to aim it toward the thing's head. Her muscles scream as she willfully turns the gun centimeter by miserable centimeter . . .

"DESTRUCTING IN THREE . . ."

She grits her teeth, turning the weapon—so close, *so close.*

". . . TWO . . ."

Her finger searches for the trigger.

". . . ONE . . ."

No. I'm too late—

A laser lances through the air, cutting clean through its steel neck. The droid's head tumbles off its shoulders. Searing metal bits seem to burn holes in the air as the mechanical skull rolls away into the grass.

The commando droid's body slumps to the side.

That wasn't the culmination of a self-destruct sequence.

Someone did that. Someone who steps up to Jas, standing over her and offering a hand. The rich baritone of Jom Barell's voice reaches her:

"You know, Emari, I leave you alone for a second and you go make sweet with a droid. You're lucky I'm the jealous type."

"Shut it, Barell. Fall in line—Sinjir needs our help." She pretends like it's nothing at all that he's come back—that he's chosen loyalty to their little team. She'll never tell him about the flutter in her chest at hearing his voice again. She'll hardly acknowledge it herself, even though it feels like she has a flock of birds trapped inside her rib cage.

Inside the house, now. Inside Aram's *compound.*

Outside in the dark lie the sparking bodies of Aram's droids, and the smoldering craters of where the mines were.

Inside, though, there's nothing.

Or, rather, no *one.*

"Blast it," Sinjir says, coming back through the house.

Jas warns him: "Be careful. We don't know that he didn't trap this place."

"Is he here or not?" Jom Barell asks.

To which Sinjir responds: "No, he's not here, and by the way, when the hell did you show up?"

Barell grunts and shrugs.

"He's gone," Sinjir says. "Half his computer systems are fried. His droid docks are empty—either we met the clanking monstrosities that were in there, or he's got a whole gaggle of them marching with him somewhere."

"Where'd he go?" Jom asks.

"I don't exactly know, do I? My job is to ask questions, and it's bloody hard asking questions of someone who *isn't here.*"

Jas says, "We know he has tunnels dug under this place." Han and Norra went down to intercept him in case he made it that far. She pulls up her comlink. "Solo?" Nothing but a crackle. "*Solo.* Report in."

"Nnnn," comes a voice.

Sounds like the smuggler. And he doesn't sound good.

"What happened?" she asks.

"That . . . big-headed freak surprised me. Was . . ." Over the comm come more groans, followed by a fit of coughing. "Was riding a hoverchair, and the damn thing shocked the hell out of me when I reached for him."

"What happened to Norra?"

"I don't know where she is. Before Aram came through she said she was going to check something out and then—then I got suckered."

She has to remind herself: Aram really isn't their mission. He's Solo's problem. And if Solo let him go, well, that's that. Jas will tell Temmin to have Mister Bones bag and tag the smuggler, they'll toss him in the back of the *Halo* and fly him back to Chandrila.

Just the same: Where is Norra?

As if on cue, another crackle as Norra's voice comes over the comm: "I got him."

"You got who? Aram?"

"I did."

"How?"

"I followed one of the subtunnels out. It ended up at a small solar shuttle prepped on a platform. The nav computer was already loaded with a destination: Seems Aram has family on Saleucami. I hid. Aram hopped in, tried to take off. I stunned him. He's heavy, though—I could use a fly-by. Bring the *Halo* in to pick up the prize?"

Jas grins ear-to-ear. "You got it, boss."

CHAPTER TWENTY-ONE

The prime operator within all Imperial ranks was the human being. "Aliens" were by and large unwelcome within its labyrinthine order because aliens were seen as different. They were serfs and slaves or, at best, obstacles. They needed to be tamed, removed, or ignored.

At least, so spoke the propaganda.

Sinjir felt the tug of that prejudice himself from time to time, for it was so programmed into them that even *near*-humans were to receive a measure of distrust. Palpatine and his propaganda machine worked to drive that nail of bigotry deeper by demonstrating how the old Jedi thugs and the scumfroth rebels consisted of many more *non*humans than humans. You could trust a human, the Empire said; aliens would always betray you.

Of course, over time Sinjir learned the foolishness of that, because as it turned out human beings were fairly horrible. Full of treachery! Just brimming with the stuff. He came to believe that the Empire's corruption was precisely because it was xenophobic. It afforded no one any other voice, and so man and machine ruled the Empire together while the rest of the galaxy—despite being predominantly nonhuman in origin—suffered, powerless while under the twisting heel of the Imperial boot.

Whatever the case, Sinjir's training as a loyalty officer gave him little opportunity to, ahem, *extract* information from nonhumans. He was acutely aware of the physiological pain points of the human animal.

Aliens, not so much.

And so when presented with a Siniteen, it took him some time.

The Siniteen frame is similar to that of most human beings, with the exception of the cranium. There, the alien's head is large. Twice that of the average person's skull, and, well, *squishy.* The human head is protected by that precious mantle of bone, but the Siniteen head seems like little more than a leather sack full of meat. The creature's brain is so immense that it literally *strains* against the inside of the wrinkling skin.

No way to know then if Golas Aram's attitude was typical of the species, but the Siniteen cared little for the sanctity of his body. Sinjir threatened to pull the alien apart like a warm sweet roll, but Aram was not forthcoming. The threat failed to land. Aram's legs were already ruined, and he traveled around on a hovering repulsor chair.

Sinjir decided to go back to his own instincts, then. This he learned from practice and not the *ISB Loyalty Manual,* but sometimes it was valuable just to let someone talk. And so he talked at some length with Aram. About the droids. His compound. His ship. The planet Irudiru. Anything and everything. Aram didn't want to talk and remained belligerent the whole way. He infused even the stiffest rebuke with alarming ego.

My droids are custom-built, hand-programmed in a way that no one else in the galaxy could duplicate.

My compound was designed to be impenetrable! You primates were beneficiaries of luck is all that it was.

Irudiru? Better here than anywhere else in the galaxy—seems every other system is choking on the fat and stupidity of a torpid, indolent population. Fools, fools, everywhere!

Golas Aram thought very little of the rest of the galaxy.

And quite a lot of himself. In particular, his intellect. He cared very little about his body, true. But he cared a great deal about his *mind*.

That, then, is the approach Sinjir takes. He tells Aram: "I wonder, Golas, what would happen if I took, say, a knife—or something long and sharp like this bit here?" He snatches a small antenna off the top of one of Temmin's crates of random parts here in the main hold of the *Halo*. He twirls it about, then *tap-tap-tap*s it against the Siniteen's head. "And I wonder, what if I pressed it through the folds? Or inserted it through one of your earholes? An urgent push and then a *pop* as it sticks into your brain."

He teases it around the Siniteen's earhole. Working it just inside.

"What? What are you doing? You ape. Stop it!"

Sinjir slides the antenna deeper. Pushing. Aram cries out.

"It would be a terrible thing. I'm just some clumsy, graceless primate, right? I would have no idea what I was even accomplishing. One *wonders* if it would have a deleterious effect on your own intelligence, hm? I might even suggest it could turn you as lack-witted as someone like me. All that genius stored up—if I popped that balloon, would it come leaking out?"

There. Fear in his eyes. Bright and alive like light reflecting off rippling water. Every person is a lock, and Sinjir is adept at finding the key—the one that undoes them, unbundles them, opens them up so that all within is fresh for the taking.

It is a moment that has in the past given him great joy.

Not this time.

Instead, he pushes out of the hold and steps out of the ship. To the others gathered in the morning light of Irudiru he says: "He's ready. Go ask him whatever." Then he staggers forward through the thirstgrass, failing to feel the pain of its blades.

The sun is over the horizon now. Gone are its gilded fingers splaying across the grass; it's just a throbbing white ball in the sky. Sinjir sits outside on a stack of boxes, staring off at nothing.

Someone blots out the sun. It's Solo.

"You did it," the smuggler says.

"Aram? I know."

"He gave us everything we needed." Solo has a ragged, feral grin. He's excited. Raring to go like a hound straining at its leash.

"Very glad to have been of service."

"You're Imperial."

"Ex."

"I don't like Imperials."

"Join the club. Even Imperials don't like Imperials."

"You did good. Get yourself cleaned up. Me and Norra are going to head into Kai Pompos, do a quick supply run. Then we're off to the races."

Sinjir offers a weak thumbs-up. *Yay.*

Solo is gone. Soon replaced by Jas as she comes off the ship, bantering with Jom Barell—oh, joy, *he's* back. The two of them came down off the plateau last night just as he was about to be overrun by a pack of commando droids. Ones apparently set to cook off like fireworks. Jas and Jom saved him. Sinjir supposes he should be grateful. And he is. Maybe.

Eventually, Jas gives him a wink. "You okay?" she asks.

"Golden," he responds, summoning a liar's smile.

Then she and Barell are gone. Off to do whatever it is they do. Probably thump like engine pistons.

"Hey, Sinjir," says Temmin, coming up from behind him.

"Hello, boy."

"You don't look so hot."

"That's rude."

"No, I mean—" Temmin laughs, nervously. "You seem like something's bothering you."

"Something's always bothering me. The sun. The air. Other people. Nosy younglings who pop by with rude questions."

"I don't know what crawled up *your* exhaust port and died, but fine, I'm outta here. See ya, Sinjir."

"Wait."

The boy pauses and looks back. "What?"

"Back on Chandrila. Looking in on Yupe Tashu. That bothered you."

"Yeah, sure."

"Why?"

"I dunno. Woulda bothered anybody."

"Mm-mm, I don't buy that answer. It hit you like a fast little meteorite fragment—*pop*, right between the eyes."

Temmin kicks a few stones, then says: "Okay. You tell me what's bothering you, I'll tell you what bothered me."

"A little tit for tat, hm? Fine. I don't want to be who I am anymore. I want to be someone different."

"You are. You're one of the good guys now."

"And, *as* one of those good guys, I just threatened another sentient being with the act of sticking an antenna through his ear and into his brain."

"So why'd you do it, then?"

Sinjir scowls like he's tasting something foul. "Because history demands distasteful things be done to preserve it. Because being good sometimes means still being bad. Because it's who I am and if I didn't do it, we'd probably still be sitting here scratching ourselves wondering whatever could we do? I am here for a reason. I am a tool that fulfills a very exclusive function. What good am I if I don't fill it?"

"You're good in a lot of ways."

"Such as?"

"Uhh."

"Right. Your turn."

"No, wait, I feel bad, you're really good at—"

"Too late. Buzzer is buzzing. Alarm is alarming. Your turn, I said. You. Me. Yupe Tashu. You were upset. Why?"

"Because."

"Because is not an answer. It's an empty word."

"Because of my father!"

Sinjir cocks an eyebrow. "What about him?"

"He's . . . maybe out there, too. In a cell just like that one. I think, who knows what happened to him? What happened to his mind? It made me worry that he might be broken, too. And if I ever find him, maybe he won't even recognize me. Maybe even if we find him, he'll still be lost. Y'know?"

"I do know. Quite profound, actually."

"It is?"

"For a nosy youngling."

"For the record, you're good at this kind of stuff. Talking to people."

"Oh, gross. I'd rather be good at *torturing* them."

"Jerk."

"Twit."

Temmin laughs. "Thanks, Sinjir. I feel better."

For a time, so does Sinjir. He'd never say as much out loud, of course. He tries to enjoy the respite from his own foul mood, because he wonders: What comes now?

PART FOUR

CHAPTER TWENTY-TWO

The *Falcon* slices through hyperspace.

"You look nervous," Han says to Norra, sitting in the copilot's chair—a chair that has a very deep seat and is lower to the floor than the other. A chair worn most often by a much bigger individual.

Like, say, a Wookiee.

"I'm not nervous," she says.

She's nervous.

It's hard not to be. She's admired this ship a great deal from afar—how could she not? This should be a clunky, junky freighter. But she's seen it move. The way it whips and dips through the chaos of battle is a thing to behold—performance like that steals your breath just watching it. She in her Y-wing followed the *Falcon*—then piloted by Calrissian and his Sullustan copilot—into the mazelike innards of the second Death Star. It was a thing to marvel. A sight she will never forget.

That's from the outside.

On the inside? She's surprised this thing holds together. It's got the structural integrity of a sack of spare parts. Nothing matches. Things dangle. Wires lie exposed. Panels don't match their moorings. The console doesn't even look original to the ship—it's like her son built it in his workshop back on Akiva. Bits sit welded to other bits or, worse, are stuck together with wound-up wads of bonding tape and shellacked over with shiny epoxy.

Norra is afraid this thing might break into pieces right here in the middle of rocketing through hyperspace.

Solo, for his part, seems like he's embraced the chaos of it. Sometimes an alarm goes off, or part of the dash goes dark—and then he pounds it with the side of his fist or jiggles the wires hanging underneath. Then it all comes back online. He smirks and winks.

Norra, in order to not talk about the orbital garbage fire in which they are currently traveling, says: "We sure Aram gave us good info?"

"We'll find out, won't we? If his codes don't check out, we're going to have to get out of there fast as a blaster." He closes his eyes and pinches the flesh at the center of his brow. "You know what? It'll work. It *has* to work." Because, she knows, this is their only shot.

Kashyyyk is a prison planet. A worldwide labor camp. The Empire, in its xenophobic monstrousness, saw fit to imprison and enslave the Wookiees there not because they offered a meaningful threat to the Emperor's ascendancy—but because they were different, and because their massive, robust physiology would allow them to work long and hard in extreme conditions. Probably took rather epic effort to work a Wookiee to death. Not that the Empire wouldn't try, she wagers.

At that, she fails to repress a shudder.

"It'll work," she says. *Because it has to work.*

Solo reaches above him, sets the stabilizers with a few flips of a few switches. "We're coming up on it. You ready for this?"

No. "Yes."

"Dropping out of lightspeed."

He gives a quick tap to the nav computer screen, then eases back on the throttle. The long light-lines go from streaks to stars.

And there, ahead, is their destination.

Kashyyyk. A green, verdant planet. She spies snowcapped mountains and snaking rivers leading to oceans of dark water. But above all else are the forests. Even from here, the forests pop. The clouds swirling above the atmosphere have to swirl *around* and *through* the trees.

But look closer, and you see devastation: Patches of forest gone dark and gray. Rivers stemmed to a trickle. Black dots across the seas: Imperial undersea mining platforms, she guesses. White clouds swirl into hurricanes of black smoke. If she can see the destruction from all the way out here, in space, how bad is it on the ground? What have they done to this world?

All around the planet hangs the Imperial blockade. Dozens of ships: a pair of Star Destroyers, a handful of battleships, plus shuttle traffic and patrols of TIE starfighters.

"We should've come in an Imperial ship," she says.

Behind them, a blip on the scanners. Another craft dropping out of hyperspace. Her heart tightens in her chest even though she knows that ship: It's the *Halo,* following behind. Jas is piloting it. The rest of the crew is with her, leaving Norra to accompany the smuggler.

"I said, it'll be fine," Solo says. "We didn't have time, anyway."

"Surely they know your ship."

"They do, but we got Aram's Imperial codes, remember? Besides, they think the *Falcon* is destroyed."

"How's that?"

"After I lost Chewie, I hired a slicer to hack the Empire's networks, see if I could find out anything. While in there, she did me a favor and 'updated' their records on me and the *Falcon.* I'm listed as dead, and this ship is listed as *having gone kaboom.*"

She hesitates. "And our gunship?"

"Like I said, your gunship is an SS-54. Fortunately for us, Imperial bureaucracy is an immovable object. Once upon a time, the Empire classified that ship as a 'light freighter.' Would take mountains of paperwork and official approvals to get it redesignated in their databases, so? They don't see a gunship. They see a freighter."

"That keeps our story, then."

"Sure does, lady. Sure does."

That story: They're bringing parts and a repair crew down to the surface of Kashyyyk to do repairs on the prison known as Ashmead's Lock at the behest of the prison's designer, Golas Aram. Simple. Clean.

As if on cue, the comm crackles:

"This is Star Destroyer *Dominion*. You are in illegal approach of Imperial territory G5-623. Identify yourselves and transmit clearance codes or you will be marked as a trespasser and in violation of Galactic Code."

Han clears his throat and gives a nervous smile to Norra—possibly meant to reassure her?—before speaking. "This is light freighter *Conveyance*, accompanied by light freighter, uhh, the *Swan*. Stand by for code transmission."

He gives the nod, and Norra uploads the codes.

Silence on the other end.

"They're not buying it," she says.

"They're buying it."

More silence.

"They're *not* buying it."

"They haven't charged up their weapons—"

A burst of static across the comm, then: "What is your purpose on the surface of Imperial territory G5-623, *Conveyance*?"

"We're, ahh, we were sent to do repairs on an old prison. We were sent by Golas Aram at the request of the Empire. We have technical parts and the crew to install them. Uh. Sir."

More silence. Norra hears only the blood rushing in her ears.

"Not today," returns the voice. "Turn your ships around and please exit Imperial space."

Han's brow furrows with frustration. He gets back on the comm: "I apologize, I don't understand, sir. The code clearance—"

"The planet is on lockdown, freighter *Conveyance*. No one in, no one out, by order of Emperor Palpatine himself."

Palpatine. Norra sits forward in her pilot's seat. Chills run roughshod over her skin, and she can't shake them off. Could he be alive? After all this?

Solo whispers to her: "He's dead. Relax." Then, back on the comm: "Sir, I apologize. I was to understand that the Emperor did not survive."

"Then you understand poorly. The Emperor is alive and well. Imperial territory G5-623 is under quarantine. I repeat: Turn around or we will be forced to open fire."

Panic traps both of them in its grip. Han and Norra look at each other. His eyes are wild. He's like a caged animal desperate to chew its way through the enclosure. He reaches for the weapons systems—

Norra catches his hand. "What are you doing?"

"What do you mean, what am I doing? We're gonna blast our way through this. You know. The *old-fashioned* way of doing things."

"They've got two Star Destroyers there."

"Oh, hey, thanks for that update. By the way, the *Falcon*'s punched its way through a lot worse. We'll make it to the surface."

"And what then?"

"Then we head to the coordinates Aram gave us."

"With half the Empire on our tails!"

"I don't mind those odds, sister!"

She grabs for the comm and speaks into it, desperate for a solution— except it's not the Imperials she hails. Instead, she routes her comm through to the *Halo*. Jas answers.

"Norra, I don't think they're interested."

"I know. Get Sinjir."

The shuffling of fabric, then Sinjir's voice crackles over the dash. "You called?"

"I need something. A code. Imperial. Emergency, um, high ranking, something, *anything*, that will get us planetside."

"Oh. Ahh. Damn, it's been a while—oh! Tell them it's a triple-9, 327. That's a classified work order code."

She flips the comm back.

"Star Destroyer *Dominion*," she says. "This is the *Conveyance*. I'm told to try one last time, sir—we are here at the demand of Grand Admiral Rae Sloane and Imperial Adviser Yupe Tashu." It's a wild shot in the dark—her plucking two names of powerful people, two of whom she has personally encountered, and hoping those names have enough power. "We are here to service Ashmead's Lock, a prison that contains high-value prisoners. Prisoners assigned to this prison by the Emperor himself. Sir. We have a work order. Triple-9, 327." She repeats it.

Even as she speaks the words, she knows how little a chance it gives them. So, what then? Blast their way through, apparently.

Which she is pretty sure will be a death sentence.

"Hold," comes the voice.

Han gives her a look. "They're not gonna buy it."

"I know."

"When they don't buy it, I'm gonna blast our way onto that planet."

"I know that, too."

"Better buckle up, then. It's about to get—"

Crackle. "*Conveyance*, this is *Dominion*. You are clear to land."

The breath that leaves Norra's chest leaves her shaking. "You were saying, Captain Solo? About to get what?"

"Don't get cocky, lady. Nobody likes a preening peacock. Let's get planetside before they change their mind."

The call comes across her holoscreen in the middle of a meeting with the Shadow Council—Brendol Hux is at one end of the table bellowing at Randd, the former red-cheeked and with a vein throbbing across his brow, the latter standing stiff as a flagpole and looking rather bored.

Sloane's device pings with the call from a Star Destroyer—

The *Dominion*, in the Kashyyyk system.

"If you'll excuse me," she says, and the men all stop and give her a quizzical, irritated look. Idiots. She steps out of the room and into one of the *Ravager*'s austere steel hallways.

She takes the call.

On her screen, Rear Admiral Urian Orlan appears. He's a plastic-cheeked, bird-nosed little man. She never much cared for him. He was a hesitant commander, one of the weakest she knew, and yet he accelerated past her in years previous—ironically given command of a Star Destroyer named *Dominion*. Orlan has dominion over very little except his hair, which is so perfectly placed against his brow she suspects it's fake.

"This is a courtesy call," he says.

"Not courteous enough to defer to my authority," she says. "Here, let me help you: *Greetings, Grand Admiral Sloane. It is my most distinct pleasure to be speaking to you today, sir.* Try that on for size, Urian."

He licks his lips and says: "Yes. Of course, Grand Admiral. It *is* a pleasure." The truth is, G5-623 is one of those Imperial territories that has not yet properly fallen in line with the rest. Like Anoat, they're still telling the myth that Palpatine is alive and well—that he's not merely some demonic ghost commanding an Empire from beyond the grave, but he escaped the exploding Death Star by improbable, even miraculous means. They remain fairly self-sufficient—so much so that this remnant has holed up there, protecting itself overmuch from outside influence.

"What is it, Urian?"

"I was wondering about the prison."

"What prison would that be?"

"Ashmead's Lock. Here on G5-623."

"I'm not familiar with it."

His nose twitches. "Are you quite sure?"

"Do you think me a fool or a liar?"

"I do not. Of course. It's just—we had two ships. We turned them away, but they insisted they had code clearance from, well, *you*."

"Describe these ships to me."

He does, sending rudimentary schematics to her screen.

Two light freighters—a YT-1300, and an SS-54. The latter is really a gunship misdiagnosed as a freighter. It's not for carrying parts.

She's dealt with two ships of those models before. It's an unusual combination—too unlikely to be a coincidence.

Could it be? The *Millennium Falcon and* the ship belonging to the bounty hunter—the *Halo,* is it? That's the same crew that slipped from her grip on Akiva. The same crew, in fact, that's been hunting down Imperials, often getting to them before she could. (At least Mercurial dispatched that last one right out from under them.) And the *Falcon* belongs to General Solo. Robbing the New Republic of someone like him isn't militarily significant, but the damage it would do to their morale . . . though, it could also provoke them into a fight for which they aren't yet ready.

Whatever the case, the incursion cannot stand.

"Sir?" Admiral Orlan asks.

"Send a team to investigate," she tells him. "Report back."

He hesitates. The chain of command is no longer what it used to be. Orlan is a man of different masters. Why even call her, then? Perhaps to stay just enough on her good side in case he's forced to make a choice.

"I'll have to check with Grand Moff Tolruck. If he approves—"

"Tell him he *will* approve or he will see a visit from me."

"Yes. Yes, sir. Of course, sir."

And then Admiral Urian Orlan is gone.

She turns around—

And finds she's not alone.

Admiral Rax stands there. Silent as a specter. His black-gloved hands are clasped in front of him.

"Everything all right?" he asks.

She might as well tell him. He probably already knows. So Sloane spills the story. His face registers no surprise.

"Call Orlan back," Rax says. "Tell him we *did* approve the repairs on the prison."

"But we did no such thing."

"No, but we're doing it now."

"The two ships? I believe they belong to known New Republic

malefactors—the crew of Imperial hunters seems to have joined ranks with one of the Rebellion's cultural heroes, General Solo. Taking them out—"

"... Is the wrong fight."

"How is that, exactly?"

He rests a gentle hand on her shoulder—though it feels to her like it weighs a thousand kilograms. A light touch that could crush her. Placating and condescending, to boot. "Admiral Sloane, we do not want to goad them into a fight right now. We are on the cusp of making our attack on Chandrila. We don't want to give them any sign that it's coming—no preemptive attacks. We must appear weak. They must be bloated with overconfidence."

"This is wrong."

"Trust me. I have it all in hand. Which reminds me, the instruments are nearly all lined up and the music has been written. It is time to perform the song. Chandrila must fall, but first, I need your help."

She hesitates. It feels like she's getting into bed with a viper. "How?"

"I have a task."

He tells her what it is.

And when he does, she cannot help feeling like she's being ushered toward another test—or worse, a trap.

"I'll do it," she says. "And I'll make sure Admiral Orlan knows that we did, in fact, approve of the work on G5-623."

"Good," he says, and reaches forward and kisses her brow. His lips are cold. Her whole body tenses up as he performs the gesture— a gesture made as if he is blessing her, somehow. She wants to vomit.

When he's gone, she does indeed call Orlan.

But then she makes another call, because *someone* is going to go to the Kashyyyk system on her behalf. She will not let this opportunity escape her—it is her life preserver, and she will hold on tight.

CHAPTER TWENTY-THREE

Jas has a bad feeling about this.

She eases the *Halo* along, following the path set by the *Falcon* just ahead. It's night, but even in the half dark, it's easy to see:

This planet is sick.

The trees here are some of the biggest she's ever seen. Bigger than some of the skytowers and complexes of Coruscant. But the trees are dead. Their massive trunks are splintering, and in those fissures shine the kaleidoscopic bioluminescence of spores and fungus, painting the trees in a diseased glow. The branches are skeletal things, reaching for the sky as if to drag the stars down to the ground and bury them in grave-dirt.

The *Falcon* winds through those dry, decrepit branches. The *Halo* follows close. It's Jom who says it:

"There's nothing here. Nothing and no one."

He's right. No other ships. No lights beneath the dead canopies. Just that swimmy, contaminated glow.

The others gather behind her in the cockpit. She grunts at them to back up and back off, but of course, nobody listens to her.

They're all too busy gaping.

Where are the Wookiees? The Imperials? Anything?

This is just one part of the planet, she knows—and Kashyyyk is a big planet. It has *cities*. This is as far flung from any of those cities as they'll get, according to her (admittedly outdated) maps, but just the same—

This is where they're supposed to be, and it is a lifeless place. What could the rest of the world look like?

"There," Temmin says, pointing over her shoulder. She swats his hand away but follows his finger regardless.

Jas can barely make it out, but way down on the surface she sees it: a faint shape of something big. A structure. *Ashmead's Lock*. It must be. The coordinates Aram gave them are right on, then.

Solo and Norra must see it, too, because the *Falcon* swoops low. Jas turns the gunship's engines vertical, bringing it in to hover.

As they descend, they move past crooked, busted platforms and rotten structures barely hanging on to the side of the trees. Jas flips on a narrow-band spotlight so they can see what they're looking at. Ahead is an old gun emplacement: a massive bolt-thrower hanging loose from its mooring, swinging gently from tangled vines. It's a Wookiee weapon. Like a bowcaster, but big enough to take down a craft or a small ship.

Then they pass another structure—not big enough to be a house. A guard station, maybe. It clings to the side of the tree, lashed there with fraying rope. A corpse hangs out of the doorway. A desiccated carcass, the hair on it gone dry as broom bristles. Mostly it's just a pelt stuck to bones. *A dead Wookiee,* she thinks. A gun still dangling from its shoulder strap.

The ground is a long way down. They see more dilapidated structures. More bodies. More rot and more ruin.

And then the ground eases up to meet them. The *Falcon* finds a proper landing platform—a concrete abutment jutting up out of a tangle of twisting thorn. Jas finds a clear spot of ground and settles the *Halo* into it. The engines burn and blast away some of that unruly underbrush.

Ahead, by a quarter kilometer, is the prison.

Or, rather, prison *ship*.

It looks like what Aram told them is true: Ashmead's Lock is not a prison he built. It's a prison ship from the Old Republic days. A ship run by some rogue empire—an enemy of the Republic, he said. The Predori, he called them. Whoever they were, they're gone now.

The ship once held captives of the Old Republic and sat in the center of some massive gravity well—how better to keep prisoners from escaping than by sticking them into a ship capable of resisting the crushing, implosive force of a gravitational hollow? Easy to get in. Impossible to escape. But one day, everything fell apart. Aram said that well must've fallen in onto itself, sending the ship plunging to the world below—

And it crashed into the surface of Kashyyyk, where it sat for hundreds, even thousands of years. The Wookiees believed it cursed: a place haunted by bad spirits. They made it forbidden to come here. They stood vigil in case anything ever came out of it.

And then, one day, the Empire came.

The Imperials found no such fear of the artifact, and were instead more than happy to refurbish the old ship into performing its task once more—and who better to turn it into a black-site prison than Golas Aram?

The prison ship sits in the distance illuminated with but a single light atop it: a shimmering blue crystal, bathing everything in an eerie radiance. It matches the creepy fungal glow from above, and serves well to further stir the septic feeling roiling around in Jas's stomach.

They all exit the *Halo*. Beneath them, the ground is hard and dry and cracked—the undergrowth is brittle, snapping like little bones as they walk.

They gather together behind the trunks of one of the gargantuan trees.

"This is it," Solo says.

"Doesn't look like anybody's home," Norra says. "You're sure Chewbacca is in this place?"

He scowls. "He has to be. All the records pointed me here."

"Can we all reach the uncomfortable agreement that this is very likely a trap?" Sinjir says. "I mean, the records 'pointed you' here—some old derelict ghost ship in an obliterated bit of forest—which says to me that we're about to stick our foot into an ill-concealed snare. Yes? Hello?"

"It's *not* a trap," Solo growls. "Can't be. Chewie's in there. I can *feel* it. The Empire doesn't have it together enough to put a . . . a trick together like that anymore. And if they wanted us dead or in shackles, they coulda done it before we ever got down here to the surface. We're doing this."

Jas hesitates. "I don't think we should."

"Then stay out here. I don't care. I'm going in."

With that, Solo steps out from behind the tree and begins his march toward the prison. He ducks his head low and darts forward, blaster in hand.

"Norra," Jas says. "Something's up, and he's blind to it."

"I know. But he needs our help." Norra sighs. "Tem, you and Bones stay out here—"

"Whoa, c'mon, we want in on the action."

"No, you don't. And the action might come up on our tails while we're in there, and if it does? You're our rear guard."

He rolls his eyes. *"Fine."*

"The rest of us? We're with Solo. But stay frosty. I don't know what we're expecting to find in here. Aram said the prison was automated—but that it had defense mechanisms. Thankfully, his codes are supposed to get us *past* those mechanisms. Cross your fingers, toes, and tentacles." Norra draws her own blaster. "We're going in."

It's Bones who opens the door. One of the talon-tipped claws on his hand flips back, and a datalink adapter emerges. He hums to himself as he jams it into the port—the interface mechanism spins right, then left, then buzzes all the way around as the modded B1 battle droid uploads the code.

It works. The door slides open.

Norra tells her son: "Stay here. Use the comlink if you need us."

Temmin wants to go. He's good at this sort of thing. Staying out here will be boring. (And, though he wouldn't admit it out loud, creepy.)

But he decides to play nice. He is learning to trust his mother.

He gives a reluctant nod, and then the rest of them go inside as he and Bones wait by the door.

The droid sways back and forth, rocking to some imperceptible tune. He clicks and clacks his talons against his skeletal legs, creating an erratic beat. Temmin shushes him. "We gotta be quiet, Bones."

"ROGER-ROGER, MASTER TEMMIN."

"Just . . . keep an eye out."

"OKIE-DOKIE."

"And be ready for anything."

"READY TO EVISCERATE ANYTHING."

"That's not exactly what I said." He shrugs. "But close enough."

Inside: darkness. Complete and total. Norra can't see Solo in front of her, can't see the others behind her. How could a prison like this sit here in the dark for so—

Click. Click. Click.

One by one, the lights come on, cascading down a long hall, fixture by fixture. The brightness washes everything out and Norra winces against it. As her eyes adjust, she can start to make out the layout of the ship. The hall ahead. Two sets of stairs going up on each side. Metal walkways above, each illuminated by lines of red light. Beyond that, above, are porthole windows glowing blue.

Everything is shiny and chrome. Walls like black mirrors.

Han blinks, then cocks an eyebrow. "All right. We're in." He keeps his voice low when he says, "We're going to split up. Me and the bounty hunter are going to stay on this floor. Norra, you take the Imperial and the new guy—"

"Hey," Jom protests. Jas snickers.

"—and head to the upper floors. We're looking for . . . I dunno what. The bridge. A control station. Above all else, we're looking for Chewie and the other prisoners the Empire took that day. Clear?"

"As a sunny day," Norra says.

"Let's do this." Han and Jas skulk off, sticking to the lower level. Norra has Sinjir and Jom form up behind her as they take to the second floor.

Norra keeps her blaster out—not pointed at anything, and her finger on the guard, not on the trigger. Wedge was fond of giving everyone lectures about *trigger discipline,* which means not putting your finger on that trigger until you're just ready to pull it.

Wedge.

She misses him.

She understands his choice not to come along. He's a pilot for the New Republic. He has his loyalties. And yet she's angry at him, too. Because he's a part of this. He should do like she did, and follow her heart—

Oh, that's just absurd, isn't it? She chastises herself for the thought. Follow her heart where? To a prison ship on a slave planet?

Maybe Wedge had the right idea after all.

The moment they reach the second floor is when the silence of the ship is suddenly broken.

A voice comes over the comm speakers, filling the whole ship with its booming presence, a voice that vacillates between male and female as it runs through a series of babbled languages. Norra recognizes some, like Ithorese, Gand, and Huttese, but not all. It races through them, almost as if calibrating itself—

Then it begins to speak in a language they all understand.

"Life-forms: eighty percent human, twenty percent Zabrak. Attuning language to Basic. Greetings, trespassers! This is Predori Prison Ship,

Ashmead's Lock. *I am the ship's IPU, or Intellectual Processing Unit, designation SOL-GDA: Synthesized Operating Layer, Grid-Based Drive Array. Welcome to my ship. Please speak the passcode aloud to continue."*

Sinjir almost laughs. "What did it say?"

"*'What did it say' is not an acceptable passcode. One out of three attempts used. Please speak the passcode aloud to continue."*

Norra sticks her finger up against her lips to shush Sinjir and Jom before they say anything else. Whatever this passcode is, Aram never gave it to them. That means he set them up. Because *of course* he did. Damnit! Why did the system trigger so late? Why not when they first stepped inside? A grim thought enters her mind: *All the better to trap us here.*

She starts to flag them to turn around and head back down the steps. Best to leave now and reformulate the plan.

But then the computer—now settling on a female voice—says:

"*'What the hell is this?' is not an acceptable passcode. Two out of three attempts used. Please speak the passcode aloud to continue."*

Who the? What the?

Solo.

Damnit! She mouths the word *move* three times over, and they start heading back down the steps—

A voice bellows from somewhere below. Solo again.

"Gimme the damn Wookiee, you crazy computer!"

And of course, SOL-GDA's response is:

"*'Give me the damn Wookiee, you crazy computer' is not an acceptable passcode. Three out of three attempts used. Passcode failed. System moving to lockdown. Please remain still for incorporation."*

Lockdown? Incorporation?

That doesn't sound good at all, does it? Norra waves her arms, urging the others forward—

The ship begins to rumble: a low, mechanized growl accompanied by a high-pitched whine that drills deep into her ear.

Above them and alongside them, the black mirrors begin to slide back with a whir. Out of each newly exposed chamber steps a pair of droids. Their faces are polished mirrors—not black like the walls but rather, a burnished gunmetal. The arms of the droids are configured like skeletal spines: countless joints allowing the hyperflexible limbs to drag behind them like tentacles. They lean forward with the predatory gait of a hungry beast, feet clicking as they begin to lope toward Norra and the others. Already she hears Solo's blaster and the bounty hunter's slugthrower—she fires her own. "Run!" she screams.

But down below, more droids are rushing up to meet them.

The way out is locked and blocked. So the bounty hunter and the smuggler go the only direction they can: They hard-charge it deeper into the bowels of the prison ship. Solo's just ahead, bolting forward, his blaster spitting lasers. Jas fires her slugthrower from the hip as she follows. Ahead, droids lurch and lunge, their whiplike arms lancing the air—

But they go down, one by one. Solo's lasers take their legs out from under them. Her slugs punch holes through those mirrored masks as they fall—droid heads whipping back and vomiting sparks, the machine-beings clattering hard against the floor and skidding.

One comes out of the wall at the smuggler—

The tip of its segmented arm glistens.

A needle, she thinks. It stabs toward Solo's neck.

No time to do anything else. She fires. The slug shears off the end of the attacker's limb, sending up a spray of hot metal chips. Solo cries out, clapping his free hand against his neck as he staggers against the wall.

"Keep moving," she hisses in his ear as she comes up behind him, shouldering him forward.

"You shot me!"

"I shot *near* you."

His hand comes away wet with red.

Ahead, more droids—he sneers and draws the second blaster at his hip and peppers the hallway ahead with searing light. Droids spin and spark.

They pass an adjoining passageway, and she catches his elbow with her hand. "There!" Down that way: an open space and what looks to be some kind of command center.

Han Solo fires off a few more shots and follows after her.

Jas hopes the others have found somewhere safe, too.

They're everywhere.

Norra's on the ground—her back against the metal, her blaster up and firing at a droid diving toward her. Her shot tears the thing's face-less mask off, exposing a sizzling circuit board. It collapses against her, limbs flailing uselessly against the metal—she rolls it off her and fires two more shots into its open skull. It stops moving.

Jom is just ahead, thrashing about as two of them crawl up on him, pinning him to the wall even as he bashes one in the skull with the butt of his rifle and kicks the other away. Two more swiftly replace those that fell—a segmented arm coils around his blaster and twists it from his grip.

He head-butts the thing in return.

It bloodies his nose. His skull cracks the thing's mask in two.

Norra stands steady and lines up a shot—

She hears the *click-clack* behind her just as something—a lashlike limb—curls around her neck and tightens. A sound comes out of her—*gkkk!*—and instantly her head starts to pulse and throb as the blood pools and her airway closes. Everything seems to go oozing and slow; Jom goes down as one of the droids sticks a needle in his neck; she can't even see Sinjir, but then when her head is wrenched back, she spies the ex-Imperial up, up, up above her as the droid crawls up the walls, carrying him with it toward an open portal glowing blue; then a needle sticks into her neck with a stabbing prick. She tries to cry out, but can't . . .

Her body goes weak. It's as if her limbs aren't even hers anymore—

like they're just sacks of meat stapled to her torso. She tries to do something, anything, but the blaster clacks against the ground and her vision starts to smear like grease on a window. She begins to fly, lifting up off the ground, and for a moment she feels giddy—*I'm escaping, I'm flying*—but that's not it at all. They're carrying her just like they did Sinjir.

Where are they taking me?

What are they going to do to me?

Help—

Someone—

Anyone—

She chokes.

And darkness sweeps the light aside.

Mister Bones sits cross-legged on the ground in front of the door. He has his vibroblade out, and it crackles and spits as he saws through a stick, one cut after the next, until he's got a little cairn of equally sized stick bits in front of him. *Bzzt. Bzzt. Bzzt.*

He sweeps the pile away, then grabs another stick to begin anew.

"What are you doing?" Temmin asks.

"CUTTING THINGS."

"Why?"

"I ENJOY IT."

He shrugs. "Fair enough." The droid is weird. He knows that. He programmed Bones to be functional, yes, but also . . . independent, in his own way. Problem is, Temmin isn't really sophisticated enough to know *exactly* what he did when creating his bodyguard's personality matrix.

So what he got was . . . *this.*

Whatever. That's not important now.

What matters is: "They haven't come out yet."

"THIS IS A TRUE STATEMENT, MASTER TEMMIN."

"They should've come out."

The droid suddenly stands. As if eager. "YES."

"Which means they might be in danger."

"I ENJOY DANGER, MASTER TEMMIN." The battle droid's vulture-like head tilts back and forth on its axis with little whirs and ticks. His jagged teeth gleam in the half-light. There's an eager tinge to the droid's discordant voice.

"If they're not coming out, we may have to go in."

"WILL THERE BE VIOLENCE?"

"If they're in danger."

Bones's fingers tickle the air. "THEN LET US HOPE THEY ARE IN DANGER SO THAT I MAY PERFORM EGREGIOUS VIOLENCE." One finger flips back and the datalink emerges, its fiber-optic tip glowing. "MAY I OPEN THE DOOR NOW?"

Temmin snaps his fingers, suddenly nervous. "Yeah, Bones. Open her up." *Please be okay, Mom.* Before, he was excited for the promise of action. Now, though, that rush of excitement has been replaced by a river of fear.

The door mechanism is cratered from one of Jas's slugs, and static arcs of electricity jump from it as it sizzles. She and Solo crouch down behind a bank of computers as the droids work to cut through the door.

The room they're in is hexagonal. It's out in the open—in a massive central area seen easily through the scalloped windows that surround them. The windows are thankfully impenetrable blast glass; the droids continue to hammer against them with their lashing arms, but so far they've only served to scratch the surface. The door, though? They'll come through that soon.

The computers aren't like anything Jas has ever seen: no keypad, just a smooth convex bubble sitting in front of a green holoscreen. When Solo's hands move across the bubble, the monitor flits from screen to screen. None of it in Basic. None of it making any sense to them.

"I . . . I don't know what I'm looking at," Solo says, exasperated. "I'm a smuggler, not a damn slicer. This is some kinda . . . machine language, maybe, or something old, real old." He roars in frustration—sounding not unlike his Wookiee copilot—and brings his fist down onto the control pad. "Blast it!"

His neck is still bleeding. But not gushing, though—so, thank the stars for small favors, right?

The door bangs as it rises up a few centimeters off the floor. Segmented droid arms slide in under the gap, whipping across the floor like agitated serpents before finally pausing to lift. The door groans and moves up a few centimeters more. Jas says: "They're coming in."

She leans around the side of the computer bank.

Bang. Bang.

Two shots in quick succession, and the arms break apart into metal vertebrae that spin and slide across the metal floor.

Through the window, she sees dozens of mirrored masks staring in at them, now—implacable and emotionless. Like drones. They've stopped bashing at the window. Now they're just waiting.

Above them comes the voice of SOL-GDA, the ship intelligence—

"*SOL-GDA welcomes you to lay down your weapons. You will be intercepted and held in stasis until your purpose here can be determined.*" It repeats that phrase in Zabraki: "*SOL-GDA thisska chu hai gannomari. Chu tai captak azza kan chutari geist fata-yith-ga.*"

"Computer!" Han barks. "You give me my friend, Chewbacca, or I'm gonna tear your IPU right out of its brain hole and throw it into an engine fire! You hear me!"

"*SOL-GDA possesses a wide variety of prisoners, all of them held in eternal stasis. They invite you to join them.*" This, too, she repeats in Zabraki.

Solo stands and fires his blaster at the computer. It peels back like a metal flower, and a small electrical fire burns.

"We could've used that," Jas says.

"Be my guest. I improved it."

The door lifts up another dozen centimeters. Mirrored faces now stare through that gap, gleaming. One struggles to get its head underneath the door. Jas bares her teeth and lines up another shot—

Suddenly the droid in her scopes hitches and shakes. Its mirrored mask vibrates and pops off as an ember-hot vibroblade bisects the machine's skull. Cinders rain before the droid goes dark.

Jas pulls back on the rifle.

Could it be?

Out there, through the window, the mirrored droids noticed the defeat of their fellow. But they're too slow.

A pair of glowing vibroblades spins through the air as Mister Bones dances through the droids, pirouetting—mirrored skulls popping free like a child flicking the heads off bugs.

"That who I think it is?" Solo asks.

"It is."

"That thing is terrifying."

"Just be glad it's on our side."

The mirrored droids mob Bones—their arms lashing at him. He ducks and leaps, slicing off segments of limb bit by bit with his blades.

"The door," Solo says. "Let's get it open while we have a chance."

She nods—

But the door is still opening of its own volition. It cranks up another few centimeters—which is enough for someone to slide through. She takes aim, but Solo palms the barrel of her rifle and pushes it to the ground.

"Whoa, hold up, Emari. Look."

It's Temmin. He smiles sheepishly, his hair stuck to his sweat-slick forehead. "Hey, guys. Need a hand?"

Impossible visions.

Norra drifts along, stitching in and out of consciousness, her breath coming in a keening wheeze. She feels loose, unmoored, utterly disconnected from the world. She floats through a dark room. She hears a song played on a valachord. Brentin is home. Lightning flashes at windows that weren't there moments before, and she sees the skull masks of stormtroopers staring in—Temmin is crying, Brentin is yelling, and the Imperials kick in the door and drag him away. Outside isn't outside. Outside is inside: the tangled conduits and piping of the Death Star battle station's interior. Power cablings spark and energy lines shine red and now she's in her Y-wing again, and she turns to peel away down a passage in order to lead the TIEs away from the *Falcon* but the flight stick is reversed and she pulls right but the fighter tugs left—her ship clips the *Falcon,* putting both of them into a spin. She sees the freighter slam into a massive concrete-and-steel post, dissolving into a ball of fire and debris.

Then her eyes are open—torn wide in a paroxysm of fear.

She's being carried. A mirrored mask regards her. She starts to struggle, but the segmented arms tighten around her in a vise grip.

Her head twists to look for something, anything that can help her. And she sees the circular windows peering into closed chambers. Pods sculpted into the walls. Hard to see from below—but these were the blue lights, the portholes seen. She sees faces pass her. A Rodian. A woman she doesn't recognize. Sinjir! Oh, gods, no, Sinjir—his eyes are shut, his mouth slack, a tube snaking toward and pushing up his nose—

Then something sticks into the side of her neck again.

A flush of fatigue washes through her, empties everything out.

They carry her toward an open chamber.

And she sees one more face as she passes—it's him. It's Brentin. Staring out from behind the window. His eyes are open. His mouth is working soundlessly in a scream. But she can hear his voice in her head: *Why didn't you ever come for me, Norra? You never looked. You never came. But now you're here to join me at last . . .*

Outside the windows of the control chamber, Bones is besieged. The droids are mobbing him, capturing his limbs before he can strike.

One of their arms whips around his neck, lifting the B1—Temmin watches as Bones wrenches upward, about to be torn off his spine.

But then Bones pulls his body up, kicking out with both legs—those wretched feet sinking claws into the masks of two drones. With a scissor motion, Bones smashes the droid heads together. The lash leaves his neck and Bones drops to the ground in a crouch—but quickly he's mobbed anew.

He doesn't have long.

Temmin has to move fast.

"Kid, I hope you got some kinda idea," Solo says. "Otherwise, you're trapped in the fishbowl with us."

"I . . . sure, yeah." He has *no* idea. They can see that. He didn't have time! Outside, Bones screams a mechanized sound—

One of his arms clatters against the window. Separated from his body.

Think, think, think!

He can't think. All he can do is panic. He can't do this. His droid is getting torn apart in front of his eyes. His mother isn't here. He's trapped in this . . . room and he doesn't have the power to change anything.

Wait.

The power.

Power.

That was the key to Aram's compound, wasn't it? Cutting the power. How is this place powered? Is it offsite? If it is—

"I say we shoot our way out," Jas says.

Solo nods. "I can get behind that."

"Wait!" Temmin says. "Hold on. Look-look-look." He points out the window, snapping his fingers—there, along the far side of this room, nestled in the wall joint and running up along the eaves is a thick bundle of cable. As it gets higher, those cables break from the bundle and spread out like the branches of a tree—leading to a series of pods lining the ceiling, pods that . . .

Oh, no. Those pods contain *people.* Faces stare back. Distant, but plain to see now that he's looking at them.

Those are the prisoners.

Jas says it before anybody else does: "They're powering the ship with the captives. They put them into stasis and they become . . . *generators.*"

"Human gonk droids," Solo says. "Disgusting."

And genius, Temmin thinks. "Which one of you is the better shot?"

Jas and Solo both raise their hands at the same time.

"Aygir-dyski," Jas curses with a sneer. "I am."

Han waves her off. "Keep dreaming, honey. I'm the crack shot around here. Hell, maybe *I* have the Force. I should have Luke check."

"Never mind," Temmin says. "Both of you, get out there and shoot that cable. *Now.*"

It's like sinking into dark water. Norra can't breathe. Panic chews through her like parasites. She feels herself settle into some kind of cradle. There's a tickling sensation up her jawline, up her cheek, toward her nose. In front of her comes the hiss of a door closing—

It's my tomb sealing up.

Thoughts chase one another in her mind like starving rats.

Temmin. Brentin. Leia and her child. Solo, Jas, everyone, anyone. I'm disappointing them.

She remembers a game as a child, a handheld game where you played these adventures and you got to choose where to go next— fight the monster or run from it, go through the swamp or run through the forest, choose a blaster or a sonic knife, be a pilot or a pirate . . . and now she realizes life is just like that. Just a series of choices. Sometimes you make the right ones and you get the good ending to the adventure. Other times you're eaten by a rancor in the dark.

She never did those games right.

Maybe she didn't do her life right, either.

Then, up through the darkness, a sound.

No. A *voice*.

The voice is distorted and mechanized—

She knows that voice. It belongs to a B1 battle droid.

Her *son's* creation—a cobbled-together robot monstrosity that will protect her child to the point of its total obliteration. Just as she would. Just as she must right now because—Temmin's here, isn't he?

She couldn't save Brentin. But she can save her son.

She fights her way through the dark water of her own drowning mind—Norra swims up through that septic layer of regret and fear, and she wills some part of her, *any part of her*, to wake up, to *move*. Her hand twitches and then the arm follows—before she even knows what she's doing, she's catching the door of her cradle just before it closes on her. She forces her eyes open, an act that is far more epic than it should be—but she manages it just the same. Her other hand flies to her face, where it grabs the tube snaking its way toward her nostril and yanks it away.

The ship's voice cuts through the air—

"*SOL-GDA has identified a perilous course of action and asks that you refrain from further violence against Ashmead's Lock. Please lie down on the ground now with your hands at your sides. Thank you for your understanding.*" Then she repeats it in a language Norra can't understand, nor does she care to try. All she can think about is finding the processor matrix of this IPU and emptying her blaster into it.

Norra struggles out of her chamber, pushing the door wider—

One of the mirrored droids appears. Its arm is tipped with another needle, and it plunges it toward her—

Norra skirts to the side, and the needle sticks into the cushion just behind her. Then she growls one word—"*No*"—and leaps.

She tackles the droid. Unprepared, it scrambles to stay clinging to the pod, but it's off balance—and its arms catch only open air as the two of them fall.

Norra winces, the air rushing up around her. She pivots so the droid is beneath her—and just in time, too, as it slams into the railing on one of the staircases. The droid's back snaps with the sound of a tree breaking in half, and next thing she knows, she and the shattered droid are tumbling down the steps, end-over-end-over-end until—

Wham. They hit the bottom floor. The air blasts out of her lungs, leaving her gulping for breath. The droid beneath her hitches and twitches, its head bent at a ninety-degree angle. Norra tries to stand—

Pain lances through her side and she collapses.

She lies there on her back, clutching her middle. The world blooms around her in light and dull sounds. She hears her son yelling—and then blasterfire and booming slugs tear apart the air over her. A droid descends upon her, its whipcord arms slashing at the air—and it's suddenly knocked aside by Bones. Bones, whose one arm is gone and whose leg is bent at a funny angle. Bones, whose own side is cratered in, dented like a kicked can. The B1 droid tries to say something but the sound only comes out as a garbled scream. Above them all, SOL-GDA narrates a constant warning for them to stop, lest they be destroyed.

Next comes a flare of light—and a crackle of little lightning filling the air above her. Norra rests her head, and once more, all goes dark. And yet—

She's awake.

She didn't go dark. The *ship* did—

The power has gone out.

Temmin grabs her hand. "I'm here, Mom. I'm here."

And with that, Ashmead's Lock goes dead and SOL-GDA goes silent.

INTERLUDE

THE CITY OF BINJAI-TIN, NAG UBDUR

The jagged campanile towers of the Ubdurian homes lie shattered. Bodies lie underneath, crushed, shot, lanced. Dozens of them. The stink in the air is strong. Rot-wings form blurry clouds above the corpses—the insects buzzing with endless hunger.

Tracene Kane pulls the white cloth over her mouth. Her nostrils are rimed with salt-dust; Commander Norwich said it would help prevent the smell from reaching her, and though it has diminished it considerably, still she smells the pickled, rotten stench of the dead.

She lifts a finger and waves Lug toward her. The Trandoshan stomps over. None of this seems to bother him. He's fond of telling her about life among his people: hunting and killing and reveling in death. He's not like that, not like the other reptilians, but it was still part of his childhood. "You want the shot set up, boss?"

"Right here," she says, holding the cloth over her face. "Get that collapsed wall in the frame." It has a dynamic shape—the tower broken, the wall shattered in just the right spot, and one body slumped over it.

Lug grunts a command to the cam droid—it's an upgraded model, ruggedized and battle-hardy. The little floating droid with one telescoping eye hums along, pulsing flashes as it takes a series of still shots to frame out the hologram. *Foomp, foomp, foomp.* It burbles and bleeps.

"I'll get Norwich," Lug says.

"No," Tracene says, shaking her head. "Go get someone . . . more common. We need to sell this to the common citizen, and that means putting the common citizen on cam. Get me a soldier, a private, a trencher." As the big reptilian grunts and starts to walk off, she catches him by the arm. "How's my hair?"

"I don't know. It's hairy?"

"I'm going for *battle-frizzled,* but still . . . well kept, you know? An order to the chaos. A well-designed non-design."

"Sure?"

She rolls her eyes. "Thanks, Lug."

"You got it, Trace." He winks one of his eyes—an unnerving gesture, as a nictitating membrane slides sideways over the eyeball. It's meant to be playful, but it only comes across as monstrous. He saunters off.

Things have changed for her in the last months. She's gone from the cushy platform of safe worlds and out into the galaxy—the war between the Republic and the Empire has gone hot. The New Republic keeps pushing the Empire back, and the Empire grows more and more desperate, like a cornered feral. Plus, the HoloNet's mandate has changed—with the Imperial controls on what can be broadcast broken, the network is free to show the *real* story, free to get into the middle of the fight and reveal the truth.

Tracene said she needed to be on the front lines.

So, by all the gods of all the stars, they put her on the front lines. Now it's her and Lug out here in the thicket of war.

Nag Ubdur in the Outer Rim—home to the native Ubdurians plus the transplanted Keldar and Artiodac refugees—has seen a brutal pushback by the Empire. That, most likely because the bedrock of Nag Ubdur is flecked with zersium, an ore essential to the making of durasteel. The Empire has strip-mined this world down to its nub, and still it keeps finding ore. As such, they're not keen to give it up—so they've bitten down hard and won't unclench.

Norwich said he suspects that the forces here aren't really under anyone's command beyond what exists in the Ubdur system: meaning, they're cut off from the Empire proper. Making this yet another rogue Imperial remnant hunkering down, taking control, and either waiting for backup or carving out their own mad little fiefdoms.

As such, the Imperials here have grown more and more brazen—driven, it seems, by desperation and fear. The massacre here in Binjai-Tin is just one such example. They came in, swept through like unholy fire, killing everything in their path. That is unlike the Empire. The Empire has always been known to keep its populace in check—punish 10 percent to keep the 90 in line. This is not that. This is a whole other level: murderous and foul.

Right now, she knows that only ten klicks away, over the tussock and past the sedge, the Imperials have dug in. They've excavated trenches. They've got walkers, TIEs, a new garrison. A fight is coming. Maybe not today. Maybe not tomorrow. But soon. And Tracene will be along for the ride. Her and Lug, filming it all so the galaxy can see the valiant Republic against the venomous Empire.

Speaking of her Trandoshan cam operator, Lug returns, hauling a New Republic soldier by the arm. It's some young, wide-eyed Kupohan—his face pelt hangs bound up in a series of braids, helmet askew and pushing forward his eyestalks. He looks lost. Shell-shocked, even.

"What's your name?" she asks. He blinks at the camera, then at Lug, then at her. The Kupohan has the look of a lost child. She pats his arm. "It's okay. We're not on cam yet. Can you tell me your name?"

He says, "Rorith Khadur. Private in the NR." His voice is a tremulous growl. He's not comfortable. But he'll have to do—the rest of the soldiers are counting the dead, setting up triage, building a camp. More women and men of the Republic keep trickling in, and will over the next several hours, given the long line of them outside the city's shield-gate.

Without warning, she holds up three fingers, then counts down— Lug raps a knuckle against the cam droid, and its eye-lens goes from red to green. "And we're on," she says.

The soldier looks flummoxed, but then he nods.

"Tell me about yesterday, Private Khadur," she says.

"Yesterday." He blinks. "Right. We encountered Imperial forces on the Govneh Ridge—it's a, like a plate shift where the ground bulges, and these tall crystals grow alongside it, and the Imperials were . . . they were waiting for us. They came out of nowhere. It was intense. My squad leader, Hachinka, she got it in the neck—a blaster shot hit her and the spray caught me in the face and—" He has to take a second. She lets him. It's good drama. The cam droid has a high enough resolution, too, that it'll capture and confirm what Khadur said: In his face she sees the flecks of dry blood that belonged to his leader. "We got her out of there and she's still holding on. We lost a lot of good men and women, but we did it. We took the ridge."

She holds up a finger and as the cam droid pivots toward her she instructs it: "Mark it. Run segment: 'Govneh Ridge footage.'" She already edited together a package of clips from last night—the cam droid will auto-splice it into this interview and send when they uplink to the HoloNet servers. Khadur seems confused as to what's happening, but she just smiles as reassuringly as she can. Tracene gives the droid a second as it runs through a catalog of beeps, then continues. "Private Khadur, can you tell me where we are and what you believe happened here?"

His tongue licks his lips—it makes a raspy sound—and he says, "This is an Ubdurian city. A merchant city. Binjai-Tin. A mostly Ubdurian population. The Empire, they came in here and—" His voice cracks. "They slaughtered everybody. These people weren't soldiers.

They were already . . . under the boot, you know? Weren't allowed to
carry blasters. Had to give a percentage of all earnings to the Empire.
And what did it get them? This. A *massacre*." The Kupohan soldier
flares his many nostrils.

Tracene sees that he's at the edge of breaking. It's not his fault. She
decides that this is good enough—the footage will speak for itself and
anything else he has to say won't come close to the impact in the way
he said that last word. *Massacre*. She tells him he can go, and thanks
him.

As he starts to walk away, Lug steps in front of the Kupohan and
gives him an awkward hug. The Trandoshan isn't good at affection,
really—the "hug" is stiff and uncomfortable and has all the warmth of
a protocol droid romancing a tree stump, but she supposes it's the
thought that counts. Then Lug hands the man a small token: a tooth
broken off a zlagfiend, which she understands is some kind of . . .
many-mouthed, dagger-fanged hell-predator? Lug killed one when he
was a boy, still hunting for his pack. He kept the teeth, of which there
were many. Lug says to Khadur, as he says to all the soldiers with
whom they speak, "It's good luck. Take it. I tied it to a length of gut-
cord so you can wear it around your neck or wrist or . . . Just take it."

Khadur nods, then clasps Lug's hand before walking off.

"You're nice the way you do that," she says, a wry smile on her face.

Lug shrugs and offers a growl-hiss. "Mnuh. They have it hard
enough." He almost looks sheepish about it.

She laughs. "All right. We need to get an uplink on the highest
point." She gestures toward a guild tower—it's half collapsed, but even
broken it's still pretty tall. "Get the beam-com set up there."

"That's high."

"And you can climb."

Another disappointed hiss. "Fine, fine, yeah, yeah."

He turns, starts walking—no spring in his step, of course, because
Lug has two speeds: slow, and slower—and she turns to look back at
the gathering soldiers coming into the city square. Setting up tents

and generators. A gonk droid meanders about. Two soldiers splice a pair of cables together with a shower of blue electricity.

Then their eyes turn heavenward. Panic registers on their faces.

Before she can turn, Tracene hears the sudden sound—

TIE fighters. Twin engines shrieking.

She turns to look—and sure enough, a dozen of them framed against the purple sky. Coming in, and coming in *fast*. Tracene expects the obvious: lasers cutting across the city, digging furrows in the cobble-rock, tearing through soldiers and maybe even her if she's not lucky.

But no lasers.

And yet, the TIEs keep coming.

She turns, screams for everyone to get back—they're setting up weapons and turrets but it won't matter. Tracene grabs the cam droid and tucks it under her arm, running like hell toward Lug. Yelling for him to run, too, now, fast, *go, go, go—*

Wham. The first TIE fighter hits the ground about 150 meters away. It plows into the wall surrounding the Binjai-Tin city square, and a massive fireball belches into the air—stone and scrap rain down around her and the ground shakes like it's throttled by a quake.

It's the first, but it's not the last. The Imperial starfighters punch into the city, one after the next. Suiciders. *Wham. Wham. Wham.* The ground shakes so hard she loses her footing—the cam droid tumbles away, its lens cracking. She hears screams and sees the space above smear behind a gauzy haze of superheated air. And then she closes her eyes, her ears ringing.

It keeps going—until it goes no more.

In the darkness behind her eyes all she can do is think: *How desperate they must be to send these pilots on a suicide mission.* Because that's what this is. TIE fighters flung to the surface? Each a weapon unto itself?

Those bastards.

She tastes dirt and blood. Tracene has no idea how many TIE fighters hit or how long it took. With a groan she lifts herself up on wobbly arms. Where the soldiers were entering the square is now a TIE interceptor, smashed into the ground, fire crackling and circuits popping. Bodies lie around. Others are alive, running for cover, weeping, or mobilizing in case it means incoming troops. She sees Khadur not far away, standing in the middle of it all. Dizzy and bewildered. One of his arms is missing. Sheared off, it seems, from a piece of fighter debris stuck in the ground nearby.

He waves at her. Such a strange gesture.

But in her short time out here, she knows that trauma will do that to you. It'll leave you spinning like a top.

In that waving hand of Khadur's is a fang dangling on a leathery cord.

Lug.

She turns toward her cam operator—

No.

No.

Where he stood is a wing panel from one of the TIEs. Bent up and smashed into the ground. Tracene cries out and runs toward it—if anyone can survive something like that, it'll be Lug. Trandoshans are built like steel rebar swaddled in scale armor. She once watched him head-butt a jukebox in half because it wouldn't play his song. Didn't make a mark on him.

But there, she sees an arm—*his* arm—splayed out across the broken stone. She sees his face, too, Lug's head half crushed underneath the metal. Tracene hurries over on her hands and knees, calling his name, that name dissolving on her lips into a blubbering gush. His eyes are open but empty. Blood runs from his mouth. He's gone.

She weeps for a time. How long, she doesn't know. Long enough that night starts to creep in, like a thief. Someone comes over, checks on her, and she shoos them away with a swipe of her nails.

Eventually, she stands and feels the cold reality settle into her veins. Then she does what she does best: She goes, picks up the cam droid, hits it a few times until it's working, then she brings it back to Lug's body.

She crouches down, turns on the cam, and speaks into it, trying very hard not to cry:

"This is Tracene Kane, HoloNet news reporter embedded with the New Republic Thirty-First. And I'd like to tell you about a friend of mine. A friend the Empire just stole from me."

CHAPTER TWENTY-FOUR

Ashmead's Lock goes dead.

All his cams, all his connections, they go dark in perfect simultaneity. The feed is gone. The prison is liberated.

Admiral Rax smiles.

It is time.

"Your ribs," Jas tells Norra. "They're broken."

Norra struggles to breathe. "Am I going to be all right?"

"Eventually. Doesn't feel like they punctured the lung—though I'm betting it feels that way to *you*." Jas manifests a rare smile. "I've been there, Wexley, more times than I can count. You'll make it through."

All around them, pocket lights spear through the darkness of the now derelict Ashmead's Lock. One by one, her crew rescues the prisoners from their docks. It's literally *dozens.* Maybe even a hundred or

more. Many of them are dressed in the uniforms of the Rebel
Alliance—officers and pilots and doctors from the days before the
second Death Star fell. Some even before the first one blew thanks to
the farm boy from Tatooine.

Bodies shuffle past. Weak and confused. They all get the same
instructions—head outside and wait. Oh, and don't stray. Because
who knows what waits out there in the dread Kashyyyk forest?

Norra grunts, winces, and tries to stand.

"Sit down," Jas says.

"You're not a doctor. I want to help."

"You can help by sitting down."

"Would *you* stay seated?"

In the half darkness, she sees Jas's shoulders shrug. "No."

"And neither will I. So help me up already."

The bounty hunter does as asked.

All around, the shadows of droid carcasses surround them. Once
the power cut out, they all slumped and fell like okari junk-puppets
with their dancing wires cut. Clatter and collapse.

"We find Sinjir and Jom yet?" Norra asks.

"Jom's outside, helping keep people together. Sinjir, we haven't—"

From somewhere in the darkness, an all-too-familiar voice reaches
their ears. The voice is hoarse but clear. "Everything tastes like licking
a blasted battery. Someone *please* come get me."

Sinjir.

Jas retreats into the darkness, then returns with the ex-Imperial. In
the glow of Jas's pocket light, Sinjir looks like he just woke up from a
weeklong bender: hair amuss, the whites of his eyes red, the skin
around gone bruise-dark. He is licking his lips and making a wrung-
washrag face.

He nods. "Norra. Been a while. You end up in one of those . . .
pods?"

"Yes. Well. Almost?"

"Not restful at all. Would not recommend." He leans in between both Jas and Norra and in a low voice asks: "Either of you fine up-standing New Republic citizens happen to bring a jorum of skee with you? A nip of korva? I'm feeling a bit *dry* over here."

"Anyone ever tell you you have a drinking problem?" Jas asks.

"My only problem is I'm not drinking."

She shakes her head. "Go help Temmin and Solo get more of the prisoners free. I'll go with you." Jas turns to her. "Norra, *you* take it easy—"

"I'll go help the prisoners outside. Make sure they stay close." Jas starts to protest, but she cuts her off: "I need to stay busy. Need to keep focused." The way her mind was going in that dock, it feels like she's on stable ground but too close to a rain-slick edge—it wouldn't take much to tumble down again into the darkness of those terrible thoughts. "Okay?"

Jas sighs and nods.

Norra grabs the light off her belt and makes her way outside.

Out there, the dead forest is filled with life. Prisoners. *Rebels.* A Rodian in a flight suit stands staring off at nothing. A woman ties the sleeves of a cold-weather coat around her middle. A Sullustan in blue Dantooinian robes leans for support against a pudgy old Corellian in a tattered rebel army jumpsuit. Norra limps along, shaking hands and clasping arms, offering words of wheezy encouragement—all the while trying not to cough, because coughing just feels like she's being punched with pistoning fists. She tries to share the good news with them that they're free, that they can go home soon, that the Rebel Alliance has become the New Republic—

"Is he out here?"

Solo comes out of the prison ship with the fury of a storm. He steps into the middle of the crowd, not far from Norra. "Yeah, yeah, hi, yeah," he says to those gathered. "I'm looking for a big guy. Hairy as anything. Wookiee. Name of Chewbacca." Desperation shines on his face like a beacon. He spies Norra. "Norra. Where is he? He's . . . he's not in there—"

"Han, I'm sorry . . ."

"Don't say sorry, just find him!"

The panic on his face is clear. And she feels it, too. Rescuing all these prisoners is a victory for the New Republic—but it's an accidental one. For Solo, the only thing that matters is paying what he owes.

And that means finding his friend.

Just then—

A gurgling roar cuts the air.

Solo spins around. There, coming out of the ship—alongside her son—is the massive walking fur-beast. The Wookiee, Chewbacca.

"Chewie!" Solo calls, and laughs as he breaks into a run. The Wookiee looks bedraggled and beaten down, but that doesn't diminish Chewbacca's enthusiasm. The Wookiee tilts his head back and ululates a loud, joyful growl, then wraps his impossible arms around the smuggler. Solo looks like a child snatched up by an eager parent—for a moment his whole body lifts up off the ground, his legs kicking as the Wookiee purrs and barks.

"I messed up, pal," Solo gasps as the Wookiee sets him back down. The Wookiee yips and barks. "No, no, I gotta own this one, big guy. I shoulda been there with you. But we'll make it right. I promise." Then, a moment as the Wookiee looks around. His body goes slack like he's taking it all in. Everyone goes silent.

The *Falcon*'s copilot utters a low growl.

Solo nods. "Yeah. You're home, Chewie."

The Wookiee stands there, stock-still and dead silent as he stares up at the trees. As if he's just realizing where he is. He makes no movement and utters no sound, as if nothing could convey what he's really feeling. Everyone waits to see what he'll do, but Chewbacca does nothing.

More Wookiees emerge behind Temmin. "Found another chamber of prisoners in the back. I think they're with you, Solo."

"Thanks, kid. Thanks."

Those Wookiees join with Chewie and together they stand with one another, staring up into the darkness of their damaged world.

Norra watches it all. The tears that warm the corners of her eyes are ones she tells herself belong to the pain in her side and not the one in her heart. She steps forward, intending to go to her son, hug him, ask him about Bones—but then behind her, someone says her name.

"Norra? Is that . . . is that you?"

Her knees go weak. She almost falls. Temmin rushes to her, helps her before she falls. That voice . . .

She turns to see if it really could be him.

It couldn't be—after all this time—

"Brentin," she says.

He's standing right there. Surely just a phantom. He's thinner, older, his skin pallid and his eyes bloodshot. But it's still him. Temmin's voice is small at first when he says: "Dad?"

Which means Temmin sees him, too.

He's not a phantom at all.

Brentin is real. Her husband is alive. And he's standing right there.

CHAPTER TWENTY-FIVE

On the bridge of *Home One*, the Mon Calamari cheer. Out there in the expanse of space, the wreckage of ships floats above Kuat—Imperial ships, mostly, though the Republic lost some of its own over the last several weeks.

The bombing campaign against the shipyards and supply bases of Kuat is complete. The sector governor—Moff Pollus Maksim—and the guild head of the Kuat Drive Yards have surrendered. The scopes are clear with no further intrusions expected by the Empire.

It has been a long, protracted fight.

And now it's over.

"Congratulations, Admiral," Leia says to Ackbar—she is not physically present, but she stands there as a holographic communication: an avatar summoned by the Mon Calamari. "You and Commodore Agate have won the day for the New Republic." With a plucky smile she adds: "Again."

Ackbar, though, is not one to cheer. Leia knows that he shares in the optimism of his fellow officers, nodding and smiling along. He wouldn't dare darken their light with the shadow of cynicism and worry. Just the same, he remains steadfast in reminding everyone that every battle has its costs. The battle for Kuat Drive Yards is no different.

Next to Leia, the other hologram—this one of Commodore Kyrsta Agate—nods and smiles stiffly. "I'm glad we accomplished something today," the commodore says. "Taking weapons out of the Empire's hands was a worthy goal and one I'm glad the Senate supported."

Battles with the Senate, Leia thinks. She knows that this is the nature of democracy and she welcomes that struggle. Just the same, this will be a chaotic time, and though it is the soldiers who experience the true trauma, the galaxy's citizens are war-weary. Theirs is a deeper, more sustained trauma—a fear and suspicion embedded like a splinter under the skin. This time with the Senate will be a tumult of indecision. They're understandably gun-shy. *And,* Leia knows, *this is why Kashyyyk remains enslaved.*

Through the viewscreen the front, hatchet end of the *Starhawk* battleship cleaves its way through the open space above Kuat. A considerable ship, the *Starhawk,* and one that belongs exclusively to the New Republic forces. Getting the vote from the Senate to approve the scrapping of Imperial craft in order to build new ships, droids, and weapons was its own battle that may have been harder fought than the orbit-to-ground battle here at Kuat. A not-inconsiderable number of the current senators still remember when Palpatine formed the Empire out of the ashes of a Republic they didn't even know was burning. He quickly commissioned ships, too, to serve his new military order. Their fear is born of good reason.

It is a credit to Mon Mothma that she was able to marshal the votes—despite her own doubts about creating new weapons of war.

Kyrsta Agate, for her part, has mitigated her accomplishment today with a heavy brow. It's one of the reasons both Leia and Ackbar like her so much: Agate understands that the costs of war are heavy even in victory. The balance on that bill is not easily paid off—and it shows in the suffering of soldiers decades after fighting ends. It manifests as political fear. It is demonstrated by criminals, terrorists, and other sympathizers. Only peace—protracted peace, *true* peace!—balances those books.

Just the same, Leia wants both the admiral and the commodore to feel proud.

"The shipyards at Kuat were a vital resource for the Galactic Empire, and their loss will be keenly felt," Leia says. "We have hamstrung the production of new fighters and capital ships. Further, we can turn these resources around and use them as our own."

Agate smirks. "I know all this, Princess Leia. But I appreciate what you're trying to do."

"Take the victory and enjoy it, Commodore. You too, Admiral."

Ackbar harrumphs. "I will. But I want to keep my eye on what matters most: ending this conflict. Nobody wins a war, Leia. Best we can do is find a way to stop fighting."

"In that, Admiral, we are agreed."

Just then, a new communiqué incoming—Ackbar nods to Comm Officer Toktar, and she puts the visual through.

Another hologram appears: Chancellor Mon Mothma.

"Chancellor," Ackbar says, giving a deferential nod. "I did not expect to hear from you so soon. Is today not the Senate budgetary proceeding?"

"It is." Even in hologram, the chancellor looks weary. This is taking a lot out of her. It's taking a lot out of them all. Leia notices a moment when Mon Mothma's gaze flicks toward her. What is that there? What forms the backbone of that hesitation? Suspicion? Irritation? As fast it came, it's gone again, and Leia wonders if she's just imagining things. Mon Mothma, anxious, says: "There is another matter. Something pressing. We have received a communication request from the Operator."

The Operator—the shadowy operative from deep within the Empire who has periodically appeared in order to direct the New Republic to Imperial vulnerabilities. Leia has never properly trusted that source. After all, the destruction of the second Death Star was born of a ruse concocted by Palpatine—one that perhaps should have been more easily seen. This, though, feels different. It has gone on too long. The Operator's intel has afforded them a dozen victories already, and it's hard to imagine exactly how this could be a deception—it would have to be a very long confidence game. And even then, to what end? Why would the Empire hobble itself?

They have all come, however reluctantly, to trust the source.

But it's been some time since the Operator has revealed himself. Since Akiva, as a matter of fact. Mumblings inside the New Republic have pondered at the fate of that mysterious agent. Was he caught? Killed? Did he flee?

Who was he, after all of that?

"Has the Operator set a time for this communication?" Ackbar asks.

"Now, actually," the chancellor answers.

Hm. "So be it." To his comm officer, he says: "Toktar, please, if you will: Open a channel. Old Alliance frequency Zeta Zeta nine."

A new holographic image shimmers into view.

And it is *not* the Operator.

"Grand Admiral Ackbar," says the vision of Rae Sloane.

On her end, Leia feels everything clench up. The Operator is gone. The Empire has surely discovered the traitor. The appearance of Sloane—one of the heads of the Imperial remnants, the *strongest* remnant if their intel is accurate—only confirms it.

"*Grand admiral* is an Imperial ranking," the Mon Cala says. "I, like you once did, identify as *fleet admiral*—but you seem to have taken the title 'Grand Admiral' for yourself."

Sloane stiffens and shrugs. "No one above to promote me, I'm afraid, Admiral. In this new order one must take what one deserves."

"Why do you darken our door today?" Mon Mothma asks.

"I come to reveal myself."

"Reveal yourself? I can't say I understand—"

"I am the Operator."

No, Leia thinks. *It couldn't be.* This woman has been her counterpart, in a way—the two of them operating as a voice speaking to the wider galaxy. Each trying to secure fresh footing among the citizens. Each speaking for her people—Leia for the resurgent Republic, Sloane for the dwindling Empire. And so it seems impossible to believe.

The others don't believe it, either. Agate says: "That curtain is all too thin, Admiral Sloane. It's easy to see the lie."

"I'm sorry, who are you again?" Sloane asks.

"Commodore Agate."

"Ah. Yes. The one who led the charge on Kuat. A convincing victory and deserving of respectful congratulations, Commodore."

Agate isn't having any of it. "You were on Akiva. You were part of that secret cabal—and the Operator turned us onto it and against it. That put *your* life in danger. You cannot be the Operator. It makes no sense."

"I gave you targets," Sloane says, "in order to strengthen my position within the Empire. The events on Akiva allowed me to seize control. Relatively speaking. All the targets, you will find, stood in opposition to my ascent." Leia mentally tallies their victories performed in service to the Operator. She wonders: Could Sloane be right? Leia wondered what exactly the Empire would have to gain by sacrificing parts of itself, and there, so clear they should've seen it, was the answer: *the elimination of competition.*

"Why tell us any of this?" Leia challenges. "More likely you discovered the identity of the Operator and had him or her executed."

"Ah. Leia. So we meet—or as close to it as we can muster. It is an honor to meet you. Genuinely. You have done so much. Amazing how so much of the galaxy has changed based on the actions of one Alderaanian princess."

"I am only as good as those who surround me," Leia says. "Now answer the accusation: You killed the Operator and are lying to us."

"No. I'm using the Operator's channel because we are losing this war, Princess. Your victory at Kuat demonstrates that neatly. And I'm tired of losing. I'm tired of all of this, to be frank. It is time to negotiate."

"Surrender?" the chancellor asks.

"Don't be hasty," Sloane chides. "I offer you surrender and the Empire takes my head. They'd probably send it to you packed into the nose cone of a thermoclastic missile. It is time for peace talks."

Ackbar's chin tendrils curl inward upon themselves. He must be feeling what Leia is. Her own instincts light up like an alarm: Something's off kilter here. Sloane is playing with them.

And yet the loss of Kuat *is* significant. A major wound.

The Empire would certainly want to stanch the bleeding . . .

But what should the New Republic do in response? Allow them time to tend to their injuries—an act of compassion against an Empire that has demonstrated none? Or press the advantage, grinding them into the dirt? Leading to more lives lost, more instability, more madness across the galaxy? Giving them a place in the future of the galaxy allows for some measure of constancy and peace . . . and here, Ackbar's words haunt her: *Nobody wins a war. Best we can do is to find a way to stop fighting.*

This could be that. It could be an opportunity.

Or it could be a grievous mistake.

"We will need to speak about this and then put it to the Senate," Mon Mothma says.

"I understand. Palpatine did away with the Senate because it cooled the engines of progress, but his way has not been proven effective. He is gone and you remain, so here we are. Talk to your people. I would suggest having the peace talks on your world with minimal guard. I am offering that as a concession of trust."

"So noted, Admiral Sloane. Thank you."

"Good day. And congratulations again to you all. I am a warrior before I am anything else, and what you have accomplished is impressive. I hope to hear from you in time. Use this channel and I will respond."

And with that, her hologram blinks out.

It leaves behind a considerable vacuum. The four of them are silent—the others are surely like Leia in that they are bewildered and bemused by what just transpired. Could this be real? And if it is, then what?

"I will convene an emergency session of the Senate," the chancellor says. "Let's hope this is something. It may be a way forward to peace. May the Force be with you."

When the chancellor is gone, Leia says to Agate and Ackbar: "May the Force be with us all. I fear we are going to need it."

CHAPTER TWENTY-SIX

The quiet of Kashyyyk is unsettling. Nothing is here. No life. No insects buzzing. No rustle of underbrush as creatures pick through sticks and leaves. In contrast, the jungles of Akiva are alive, *too* alive—Norra remembers how the canyons of Akar were home to hooting ateles and squawking clever-birds and hissing bladder-bugs. The cacophony of the rain forest was almost deafening—louder at night than it was in the day.

This is not that. It's a dead channel. A null frequency.

At least here, in this small section of the planet, the Empire has killed everything. And Norra sits, staring off into the silence. Wishing for a moment she had a little jaqhad—leaf-chew. Muddle the black leaves and pink petals of the jaqhad flower, then chew it to make yourself awake, alive, aware. An Akivan tradition.

It would make her ribs feel better.

It would make *everything* feel better.

Right now, not far behind her, the rest of her crew is helping bring the rest of the captives out of the prison ship, preparing their egress from the planet's surface. Brentin, her husband, is with Temmin—last she left them, they were both on the *Halo* looking over the pieces of Bones, who had been ultimately torn limb from limb. The droid is still functioning, but can't seem to speak—he can only broadcast garbled, mechanical static blasts.

She hears someone coming up behind her. A glance over her shoulder reveals Han Solo.

"Hey," he says.

"You did it. You found him."

"*We* did it. You were right. I couldn't have done it without your help."

"You going soft on me?" she asks.

"No, but I'm in a good mood. Just go with it." He comes up alongside and looks out with her. He's got that aw-shucks sheepishness about him, suddenly. Hands in pockets. Waiting to say something but not really able to say it out loud. "So, ahhh, you know. Thanks."

Norra doesn't have much to say in return, and talking only makes her two shattered ribs—now swaddled in a hasty wrapping of bonding tape courtesy of the oh-so-compassionate Jas Emari—feel like they're stabbing her. So instead she just nods and keeps on staring out.

"That really your husband back there?"

"It is."

"Then we both have cause to celebrate."

"Absolutely."

But he must detect the tremor in her voice. "Why aren't you with him? You're out here, instead."

"I wanted him to have time with my son."

"Sure, sure. Nothing more to it than that, huh?" He's poking around, feeling her out. "Nothing on your mind?"

I failed Brentin.

I found him here only by accident.

It's been so long.

Everything is changed. I've changed. Temmin has changed.

The whole galaxy *has changed.*

But Brentin hasn't.

"No," she lies. "Nothing." She feels like a failure. A traitor—and here, her mind flits to Wedge, and that only deepens her sense of treachery. It's not that she doesn't love Brentin. She does. And will. He is her husband and the father of her child and—she can't face him. Not easily. Not now.

"I got a kid on the way," Solo says suddenly.

"I . . . yes. I suspected."

He kicks at a stick. "I should be there. I should be there *now*. For Leia. For that kid. But I got this . . . *thing* hanging over me. This thing I gotta do. I'll never be all the way there long as it isn't done. I'll never be *me*. I can't be a good father until . . ." He curls his hand and presses a knuckle into the tree—not a punch, but hard enough that the bones in his fingers crack and pop. "I'm just saying, sometimes you have to do what you have to do."

"You're not leaving, are you?"

"Am I that transparent?"

"As clear and as tough as a sheet of blast glass."

"You take the *Falcon*. It's the fastest ship in the galaxy, and we got just shy of a hundred prisoners who need medical attention. It'll be a tight fit, a real cattle car, but you'll manage. Plus, some of those prisoners are staying here with me and Chewie."

"The refugees?"

"Yeah, and a couple other poor undesirables who got swept up by that Star Destroyer. See what kind of damage we can do."

Norra stares off into the dead forest. "Looks like the Empire already did its damage."

"It isn't all like this. Right now we're at the edge of the Shadowlands. Closer to the cities, that's where you find the camps, the mines, the labs. That's where you find the Empire."

"You're going to liberate it all by yourself?"

"Or die trying."

"Leia? And your child? How will they feel about that?"

He scratches at the back of his head. "I don't know. They'll hate me, probably. But maybe in time they'll get it. They'll see I had to do this."

"Better come back alive, then."

"Guess I'd better."

Norra grimaces as she reaches out with her hand. Solo takes it, shakes it. "It's been an honor," she says.

"Go be with your family. Take them home, Norra Wexley."

"Thanks, Solo. Good luck here."

"Luck has saved my tail before. Let's hope that trend holds."

Not long after, Norra gathers the whole crew.

Everyone except Temmin. He's with Brentin, still. As it should be. And she doesn't want to give him this choice.

The darkness here on Kashyyyk is lightening now—a gray, gauzy light from the sun in this system. Fingers of that light shine through the trees and the mist, and Norra steps into a beam of it and tells them all what's happening. She explains that Solo is staying behind.

"A fool's crusade," Sinjir mutters. Then, louder: "An idiot's parade!"

"I think some of you should stay with him," Norra says.

"I'll stay," Jas says with zero hesitation.

"What?" Jom asks.

"*What?*" Sinjir echoes.

Jas shrugs. "We took out Gedde, but we didn't free any of Slussen Canker's slaves. That didn't sit right with me. We can do differently here."

"This is a whole fragging planet," Jom says. "We're going to free it? Ourselves? We're good, Emari, but we're not *that* good."

"Besides," Sinjir says. "I don't think there'll be a payout for this."

"I can usually wring a few credits out of any situation. And maybe *this* payout isn't about money. We helped free Akiva. That felt good.

Sinjir, how did it feel almost sticking a sharpened antenna into Aram's ear?"

Norra watches—the ex-Imperial starts to answer, but instead just looks down at his feet.

"You shouldn't feel bad about it," Jas says. "You did a bad thing because you had to, because sometimes you have to do bad in service of good. But once, just once, I want to do something really good. Good even though it's stupid. Good because it's *right*."

Sinjir makes a faux-gagging sound. "Oh, yuck. Jas, no."

"Sinjir, yes."

"Fine," he says, rolling his eyes. "Blah blah blah I crave purpose and recompense for my crimes and et cetera, et cetera. I'll stay, too. Besides, this is an Imperial-governed planet. Maybe news of my treachery has not yet reached these forested coasts and I can press that advantage."

"You've all gone batty," Jom says. But then he sighs and throws up his hands. "But I've already gone off the map on this one. Might as well stick around a little while longer, see what kind of damage we can do here to the Imperial war machine. Soldier is as a soldier does and all that."

Norra nods and smiles. It's what she hoped would happen.

"How about you?" Jas asks Norra.

"I'm taking my family and the captives—along with my injured self—home. But I'll be thinking about you, and I'll see if I can send help."

Jas nods and steps up to Norra. "Stay safe, Norra."

"Be good, Jas."

"A little good. But not too good."

She says her goodbyes, too, with Sinjir and Jom. It hits her, suddenly—the overwhelming feeling that she might not see these people again. Her darkest thought is also the loudest: Staying behind and trying to liberate Kashyyyk is a suicide mission.

CHAPTER TWENTY-SEVEN

Everything's so dizzying, and it's hard to cut through the pain in her side and see her way through to what has happened, but one shining moment is bright enough to manage: Norra's sitting there in the pilot's seat of the *Falcon* feeling like a stranger in someone else's house. Her son is next to her, acting as copilot. And then, Brentin comes up behind them.

He kisses the top of his son's head.

He kisses Norra's cheek.

He leans on them both—one hand on her shoulder, another on Temmin's shoulder—and as Norra brings the *Falcon* out of hyperspace, Chandrila rushing into view, he laughs a little.

"It's amazing," he says.

"Amazing?" she asks, a little cheekily.

"Things have changed. And I hate that I missed it. But look at the two of you! Norra, you're a *pilot*. Temmin, you are, too. The Rebel Alliance *won* and . . . I'm not happy I missed all that, but I'm happy to see what you both became." His voice shakes when he says, "I feel like I woke up from sleep and the galaxy moved on without me."

"We didn't move on," Temmin says.

Norra rubs the top of her husband's hand. That hand is trembling just so. "Tem's right. You were missing from us, but now we're a family again and nothing can change that," she says, convincing even herself. "Things will feel weird for a while but that's okay. We'll get past it. For now, though, can you check on everyone back there? Let them know we'll soon be clear to land?"

"I will," he says, and then adds: "I love you guys."

"We love you, too," Temmin says.

As Brentin heads back, Norra and her son exchange looks. She remarks to herself just how *happy* the boy looks. In fact, she can't remember the last time she's seen that look on his face. He's beaming, bright as a sun.

"Let's go home," Temmin says.

Norra transmits clearance codes to Chandrila tower control.

The *Falcon* descends.

The ship is crammed full of people. Temmin works his way through the back of the craft, talking to them all as he passes. "You're free from the Empire," he tells an Ithorian woman pressed into the back corner. She murmurs gratitude at him. "We're landing now," he says to a young Rodian whose face is marred with a meshwork of scars. "It's gonna be okay," he assures a barrel-bellied man in rebel army raiment.

At the back of the ship, through the throng of bodies, Temmin finds his father doing the same thing. Assuring the others. Holding their hands. Embracing them. Some weep. Some laugh. Excitement is present like a static charge in the air.

"Dad," Temmin says.

"Son," Brentin says.

"MASTER TEMMIN'S FATHER," Mister Bones says, suddenly interjecting himself between the two. He reaches out with two claw arms and mashes father and son together. Their heads bonk. "THIS PRECIOUS MOMENT MUST BE SEALED BY A HUG: A LOVING YET VIOLENT ENTANGLEMENT OF BODIES WHEREIN ONE PERSON GRABS ANOTHER WITH GREAT FORCE AND SQUEEZES, BUT NOT SO HARD THAT THEIR EYES RUPTURE FROM THEIR—"

"Bones," Temmin says sharply. "Shh."

"ROGER-ROGER."

Brentin stares on with goggling eyes. "The old B1. You repaired him already?"

"Yep."

"Just with the supplies from the *Falcon*?"

Temmin hears some awe in his father's voice.

"Yeah."

"You take after me."

Temmin grins big. "Yeah."

A crowd has gathered on the landing platform as the *Millennium Falcon* swoops in low, easing downward.

News traveled fast and wide: Not only is Han Solo's ship returning, but it's bringing with it a bevy of prisoners, many of whom haven't been seen since the earliest days of the Rebel Alliance. Some family members have gathered, as have others from that era who are eager to see if they can welcome the return of friends, comrades, and loved ones.

Those gathered cheer and whoop.

Two of those gathered are about to be disappointed. They will arguably be the *only* two truly disappointed—and each will feel this disappointment keenly, and starkly in contrast with what must be an otherwise triumphant, happy-making day.

Those two are Leia Organa and Wedge Antilles.

Wedge stands there with flowers. Nothing too big or ostentatious— the strange little woman at the Hanna City greenhouse tried to get him to carry a bouquet as big as his chest and full of all the colors of the rainbow, but he said that wasn't Norra's style. Instead, he went with something understated. Simple, but elegant: six sun-dew flowers. Beautiful, yes. But they last. Firm stems and resilient petals. They don't wilt. They smell beautiful.

And they're as golden to him as Norra is.

Leia, for her part, has brought no gift but herself. She beams, her cheeks flushed with excitement. The *Falcon* is returning.

And with it, her husband must surely be returning, too.

"This is a good day," she tells Wedge over the din of the crowd.

"It sure is," he answers.

The *Falcon* eases down onto the platform, rocking on its landing gear. The plank descends, and through the hiss of steam come the freed captives. Dozens of them, each meeting guards as they come off, guards who usher them through a receiving line where they meet Ackbar and Mon Mothma. They aren't forced to dwell; they're directed to a series of transports lined up at the edge of the platform. Transports that will take them to the Senate Plaza, where the chancellor has food and a medical tent and officers waiting to perform interviews of those returning.

The captives keep coming, off-loading one after the other.

Leia must know that Han and Chewie will be among the last off.

Wedge knows this, too, about Norra.

And then, Norra *does* step off the ship—Temmin just ahead of her, and the clanking droid Bones just ahead of him. Temmin is happy, happier than Wedge has seen the kid. He's about to call to the boy, about to say, *Hey, Snap, over here,* but then he sees the man next to Norra.

He doesn't know who the man is, but . . .

The man has his arm around Norra.

He kisses her cheek.

She kisses his lips.

It clicks into place pretty quick—clicking like a thermal detonator set to blow. And blow, it does. Right inside Wedge's chest. The realization that Norra found her husband robs his lungs of air.

He looks to Leia, and he sees her searching face. And he watches the moment, too, when Norra and her husband are last off, and the *Falcon* closes up after nobody else gets off.

"He didn't come home," Leia says.

"I know," Wedge answers. "I'm sorry."

"He's still out there."

"I'm sure Han is all right—"

"I'm sure he is, too. I trust him." But the way she says it, Wedge isn't so sure. "I have to talk to Norra, though. I have to find out what happened."

"Maybe give her just a little time. It looks like she brought home someone special to her."

Leia smiles despite her certain disappointment. "It does, at that."

CHAPTER TWENTY-EIGHT

With the *Halo*, Jas got them out of what the Wookiees called the Black Forest—an area of the world that had long been dead. Dead for millennia, they said, a place poisoned by "something real bad happening here. Something that left a darkness. Like an imprint in wet concrete." At least, that's how Solo translated it. Jom doesn't speak Shyriiwook, so that means relying on the smuggler as the go-between.

Working with Solo on this has been interesting. Chewbacca the Wookiee is the man's copilot. His *sidekick,* of a sort. At least, that's how Jom had always heard it. The two were inseparable, but Solo was the pilot and Chewie was the copilot and so would it always be.

But here on Kashyyyk, the roles are reversed.

Chewie's in charge. He leads the way.

And the real surprise is, Solo follows. He lets the Wookiee set the course. He offers insight, but it's deferential. And if anybody says boo to Chewie's ideas, Solo's first on the line to get snappy about it.

Once Jas got them out of the Black Forest, Chewie had the ship fly low to the ground along a white-rapids river that had carved a channel between massive trees. Solo said that he and Chewie had been collecting intel on Kashyyyk for *years*. Jom protested, said that by now the data was probably out of date and the on-the-ground intel was more important. Solo bit back: "No kidding, commando. But what we got is good, and unless you got better, I suggest you shut your mustache hole."

Sinjir chuckled and said: "Mustache hole. I'll have to write that one down."

"Quiet, Sinjir," Jom said.

Jas just snickered from the pilot's seat.

(Which, Jom admits now, hurt him more than he expected.)

The river roared down over a tumble of broken trees, down into a dammed-up reservoir ringed by shattered trees. Chewie had Jas bring the *Halo* up over that waterfall and park it atop on a wroshyr branch— right where the branch met the tree. Jom didn't think the galaxy *had* trees big enough for the branches to support a whole ship, but he's happy to be proven wrong. Together, they all go out along the branch— there exists plenty of space to walk, though vertigo still plucks at Jom's strings and he can't help but wonder how long it would take to hit the ground if you fell.

Solo goes on to explain Chewie's plan: "This is a big planet and best anybody can tell, the Imperial occupation is dug in like a bloodworm— maybe dug in *harder* given the shoddy state of affairs after the Death Star went boom. But Chewie's got an idea, don't you, buddy?"

The Wookiee nods and growl-barks a reply. The one-armed Wookiee, Greybok, gestures with his remaining hand in apparent agreement.

"We can't free this planet by our lonesome," Han says, "much as we'd like to. We've been lucky in that regard before, but this time, no go."

Chewie grumbles.

"That's right," Solo says. "We need an army."

Jas leans in. "I work lean. I don't work with armies."

"Too bad," Solo says.

"Give us a target. Find us the dragon's head and we'll cut it off and watch the planet fall."

"Won't be that easy. Sure, the planet's under the governance of one man: Lozen Tolruck. But he's got three Star Destroyers up there and intel says he's hidden away in an island fortress. He's a target, though, because he's the one in charge of the inhibitor chips."

"What?" Jom asks.

"Every Wookiee on this planet has a chip stuck in their heads. Keeps 'em docile—anytime they act out, the chips fry them with pain until they fall back in line or die. We take out the chips, we give the Wookiees their minds back. But they'll still be locked away in settlements. We kill the control chips and liberate just one big settlement and we have the army we need to free the rest. To do that, we need more information."

Sinjir cracks his knuckles and winks. "I can handle that part."

"You still need to start somewhere," Jom says.

"There," Solo says, pointing down past the massive dam and reservoir. Tucked between two fallen trees is a command installation: an Imperial cinder block plunked down into the rich, loamy soil.

Jom grabs a pair of quadnocs and focuses in.

As he does, Solo keeps talking.

"That command station is going to have computers and officers. And that means *intel*. They can tell us where Tolruck's settlement is. They can point us to the most vulnerable settlement. But that means we gotta go in hot. We take the *Halo*, fly in fast with the cannons blazing—"

"Slow up," Jom interrupts. He pulls the quadnocs away from his eyes and says: "I see *four* ground-to-sky turbolasers down there. You fly the *Halo* in and she'll get blasted into cinders."

"*Kavis-tha*," Jas says, cursing at him. She spits on the ground. "You saying I can't handle my own ship? I'll stay clear of those lasers easy, Barell. You haven't seen half of what I can do."

"Fine. Let's say you manage." He lifts his chin in defiance. "They'll still see you coming a kilometer away. That gives them plenty of time to mount a proper defense or even escape. We can't see on the other side of that station. They might have a couple of chicken walkers or an escape shuttle waiting."

"Oh, you have a better idea?" she challenges.

"Slaggin' right I do. Send me down. On the ground. Two-prong approach: I take a couple of these hairballs—"

"Watch it," Solo says.

"Sorry. I take a couple of these *noble warriors,* and we sneak in and hit 'em hard. We shut down whatever defenses we can, and *only then* do the rest of you come blasting in with the *Halo.*"

"I like it," Solo says. "You can take out those turbolasers."

"That's the plan."

Jas grabs his arm. "Can I talk to you for a second?"

"Sure thing, Emari."

She pulls him back toward the *Halo* and shoves him behind one of the tilted turbines. "What do you think you're doing?"

"My part," he answers.

"Don't play the hero."

"I'm not a hero. I'm a soldier. A workhorse."

"A soldier who left his command for—well, we know why."

"Do we?"

She scowls. "We do. You left for me."

"Don't get so full of yourself."

"You chased me like a puppy dog to Irudiru."

"*Hey,*" he says, rebuffing her. He stabs his finger in the center of her chest. "I wanted to do my part and find Solo."

She grabs his finger and twists. "Great. You found him. Did you then run back to Chandrila with him in a bag?" She lets go and he pulls away. "No. You stayed on. Like that lost puppy."

"You're a brat."

"And you're a thug."

He shrugs. "I'm a thug who's here. I'm a thug who can fight. Don't question my motivations."

She stomps off. "Fine. Do what you want, Barell."

"Fun's over, I guess!" he calls after her.

The commando lingers behind, fuming.

She *is* a brat.

What's worse, she's not wrong. He *did* follow her to Irudiru because damnit, he likes her. And that makes him feel exactly like the lost puppy she thinks he is. Imagining her taking the *Halo* and getting chewed apart by those turbolasers . . .

He shakes it off.

Time to rejoin the others. Time to do the work. Time to *fight*.

PART FIVE

CHAPTER TWENTY-NINE

It has been a month.

Nothing has changed.

Everything has changed.

Wedge Antilles crosses the white macadam of the spaceport, walking toward a fat-bellied shuttle at the far end. Ahead of him, the wind carries sachi blossoms—petals caught on the breeze, looking like canary moths flitting about the air. His leg is getting better. He no longer needs the cane. The limp is still there, haunting him like a spirit who refuses the exorcism from his bones, but slowly, surely, he's getting up to speed.

Ahead, a Pantoran man with bristle-brush muttonchops polishes the flat chrome plating on the shuttle's fore.

As Wedge approaches, the man turns, then offers a hasty salute.

"Captain," the Pantoran says.

"At ease, pilot," Wedge says.

"Technician, actually. Name's Shilmar Iggson," the Pantoran says. "Help you with something?"

"I'm looking for—"

From behind the shuttle's folded wing pokes a face—one smudged with streaks of dark grease. Wedge almost doesn't recognize her.

"Captain," Norra says. She slides under the wing, her knees on a repulsor creeper. She kicks the platform and it floats away. As Norra stands, she wipes her hands with a rag.

"Captain?" Wedge asks. "Norra, come on, we're friends."

"Oh. Yeah, no, of course, I just—" She offers an awkward smile. "Hey, Wedge. It's good to see you again."

She moves to shake his hand and he moves in for a hug and neither actually happens. There's that awkward moment where his arms are open and her hand is hanging out in midair. They laugh nervously and retreat.

"So," he says, admiring the shuttle. "You're a pilot again?"

"I am. I work for the Senate. Sometimes they, well. They need rides. Later today I'm taking the, let's see if I get this right, the 'Special Senator Council on Galactic De-Escalation Strategies.' Or is it the 'Senate Special Council?' I can't remember. Either way, they're heading out to Lake Andrasha to convene another meeting."

"The peace talks are coming up in a few days."

"And the big celebration."

"Right, right." Wedge has been on special security detail for that event. The liberation of the captives of Kashyyyk was a boost in the arm when it came to morale. Some of those prisoners were high-ranking folks from the Rebel Alliance. Many were heroes and liberators in their own right, and freeing them—well, it was decided that such an event demanded a proper celebration.

Liberation Day, the Senate voted to call it. The chancellor's idea.

And the peace talks will dovetail with that event. Wedge isn't much of a politician, but even he can see the play there—peace talks with the Empire are viewed with a great deal of suspicion. He feels it, too. Imperial oppression has fomented a great deal of bad blood over the many years, and those in the New Republic aren't necessarily keen to give the enemy room to move. Having Grand Admiral Sloane here only stirs up that blood—hell, just thinking of her name makes Wedge's body ache with the memory of what they did to him there in the satrap's palace on Akiva. That woman deserves no measure of compassion—no *moment* of kindness. Give her that moment and he believes she'll use it to flash a knife and cut their throats.

Then again, he might be *just a little bit* prejudiced. Which is why he's staying out of it. Either way, a big celebration like Liberation Day will go a long way to cool the hot blood over the peace talks.

"It's been a while," Norra says.

"Yeah. It has. Sorry about that. It's just been—well, you know."

"Everything's hectic."

"Everything's moving fast right now. Lightspeed fast."

Human emotions are basically a pack of tooka-cats chasing shadows, Wedge decides. He is happy that Norra has her husband. And yet . . .

And yet.

"So," Norra asks. "What's up? Everything okay?"

He dithers a bit before saying: "I don't think it is."

"What? What's wrong?"

"It's about Temmin, Norra."

Clang, clang, clang.

Temmin knocks the last spring-bolt into place with the handle of the coil-driver, then flips it around and gives the skull one . . . last . . . *twist.*

It buzzes and clicks into place.

The red eyes flicker, then strobe, then stay lit.

Bones's narrow, vulpine head looks left, looks right, then finally his eyes telescope and focus on Temmin.

"HELLO, MASTER TEMMIN."

"Bones!" He grabs the droid and presses his forehead against the flat of the droid's cold metal head. "Glad you're back, buddy."

"I AM GLAD TO HAVE NO ASTROMECH PARTS."

"I know."

"ASTROMECHS ARE MEDDLING, WEAK THINGS THAT RE-MIND ME OF TRASH RECEPTACLES OR REPOSITORIES FOR HUMAN WASTE FLUIDS. THEY ARE NEARLY AS USELESS AS PROTOCOL DROIDS, WHO SERVE NO FUNCTION AT ALL EX-CEPT TO TALK, TALK, TALK, TALK, TALK, TALK—"

"Okay, okay." Temmin laughs. "I get it, pull back on the flight stick, killer." He makes a mental note: *Tweak Bones's personality matrix.* Something must've gotten knocked around in there—the B1's not usually this chatty. "How are you feeling?"

"I APPEAR TO HAVE BEEN MODIFIED AGAIN."

"Yeah. Mostly just cosmetic." The B1's torso got dented in and torn up enough by those drones back on Kashyyyk that Temmin decided to lean into the skeletal look and just cut out those dents entirely. Now Bones's torso looks more like a human rib cage. Albeit with more . . . spiky bits.

He thought about putting one of those droid arms onto Bones—those whipcord limbs were pretty primo. Sophisticated stuff.

His father said he could maybe help, but then . . .

"YOU SEEM STRUCK WITH A MOMENT OF GRIEF, MASTER TEMMIN. PLEASE IDENTIFY THE SOURCE OF THIS GRIEF AND I WILL TEAR IT APART AS IF IT WERE AN UNSUSPECT-ING BUG."

"I'm good, Bones, I'm fine. Happy to have Dad home."

"THAT'S NICE. BUT IT DOES NOT EXPLAIN THE UPSET YOU ARE DEMONSTRATING ON YOUR FACE. YOUR GRIEF AND WORRY HAVE BEEN ONGOING. EXPLAIN, PLEASE."

What can he say?

Things were good. Brentin came home. Mom seemed happy. Tem-min was happy. They did things together. They went to the zoo out on Sarini Island, watched the pangorins in their grottoes and the scut-tling caw-crabs splashing about their enclosures and Dad laughed at the ooking uralangs. They ate dinner every night. Dad even cooked, trying to navigate his way through the strange Chandrilan herbs and spices. Mom and he stayed up late for the first several nights, laughing long into morning.

But then something changed . . .

Somewhere in the apartment, Temmin hears the sound—the clatter of utensils on a dish, the hum of the protein cycler, the splash of the spigots.

"Stay here, Bones," Temmin says, then heads into the kitchen.

It's his father.

That still amazes him. His *father*. Ripped from his life years ago—dragged out of the house in the middle of the night by Imperial forces. It should be amazing. And Temmin combats that thought by telling himself, *It is amazing, you're just too selfish to realize it.*

But after those first couple of weeks, Dad hasn't been the same. It's like he's not *all there*. He's still Brentin Wexley. Still sometimes wears that winning smile. Still is good with tools. Still snaps his fingers like Temmin does when he's thinking, and he's fast with a joke now and again. But . . .

He usually walks with an easy, effortless lean. Like he doesn't have a care in the world. And music—Dad always loved music. Temmin even went out to a junk shop (which are few and far between here on Chandrila, as the people view junk as junk and not as the treasure Temmin sees it can be) and brought home a small valachord. Dad poked the keys a few times.

Hasn't touched it since.

The doctors and therapists said this was all normal. Nobody really knows what his mind went through. Far as Brentin Wexley recalls, it seems like he was in stasis for most of those years—held fast in those cradles and used to power the rest of the prison ship's security protocols. Mom said that the chems they pumped into her made her feel anxious and afraid—and that was just after a few minutes.

Who knows what Dad went through having that cocktail churning through him for years? Might've been an endless nightmare.

Still. Dad's back but he's not . . . *back.*

And that sucks.

"Tem," Dad says. "Hey, kiddo."

"Dad. Hey."

"You okay?"

"Fine. I just . . . I thought you were supposed to help me today."

"Help you? I . . ." Then his face twists up like a wrung rag. "With the droid. Your B1. Right, yeah. I'm sorry, Tem. I've just been distracted."

"Where were you?"

"I took a walk."

He does that, now. He takes walks. Lots of them. Morning, midday, even in the middle of the night. The one therapist, Doctor Chavani, said that was normal, too. Said a lot of stuff might've built up in his mind over the years and this might be his way of shaking it out. Everyone assumed he was dead and now he's not—he's risen, effectively, from the grave like a glow-wight from the old Meteor Horror serials.

"I can take a walk with you sometime."

"No," Brentin says. "I think I like to be alone on those walks."

"You think?"

"Everything's not real clear right now, kiddo."

"Oh. Okay. Yeah. You and Mom all right?"

"Sure." But the way he says it, he knows they're not. Temmin's seen that for himself. There's a distance there. And it's growing wider.

And, he decides, it's all Norra's fault.

"He's mad at me," Norra says. She takes out her thermal carafe and pops the two disks out of the lid—disks that with a flick of her finger become two small telescoping cups. She and Wedge retired to a small table around the back of the shuttle hangar—a place where some of the pilots, techs, and mechs eat meals on the job. She pours him a cup of chava chava: a hot brew from the root of the same name. It's no jaqhad leaf-chew, but it'll do.

Wedge sighs. "I got that feeling."

"We're not really talking much now."

"Why? Is it you and Brentin?"

"Me and Brentin are fine. We're fine. Everything's fine." She hears the stiffness in her voice. It's like she's got this cough in her chest and she's trying not to let it out but it tickles and scratches and hurts and—"Oh, damnit, it's not fine! It's not fine *at all*. Temmin's right to be mad at me. His father comes home and he's not *present*, like, in his eyes? He's not there with us all the time. He's somewhere else even when he's sitting right across from me."

"Most of the captives are like that a little bit. I heard they were anesthetized, but . . . they had nightmares."

"That's right. Brentin probably underwent *years* of nightmares. And so the way he's acting is normal. It's *more* than normal. I . . . I . . . it's not his fault, and yet I can't get close. It's like he's just not Brentin anymore." *And you're just not Norra anymore, either.* "I blame myself. He'll get there. I have to be patient. I have to be nice and smile and just shut my fool mouth because *he'll get there.*"

Wedge's hand finds her own. Their fingers enmesh.

It's warm and it's comforting and—

She yanks it away.

"I'm married."

"I know. I know! I didn't mean—"

"I know you didn't, I just mean—"

"Of course."

"Yeah."

"Sorry."

"Don't apologize," she says. *It felt good and I want you to take my hand again* and she grits her teeth while working to banish that thought. "Just—tell me what's wrong with my son."

"Nothing's wrong. He's actually scheduled to be on reserve for Liberation Day . . ."

"But?"

"But he's missed too much training."

She pinches her brow. "Which means he can't actually be on deck."

"Right."

"He's having a hard go of it right now. His father coming home has been all he's ever wanted, but the reality of that is far less than the magic we all expected." She takes a long pull of the chava. "I'll tell him. About Liberation Day."

"You're sure? I can tell him."

"He's already mad at me. I might as well."

"Thanks."

They sit there for a while, each wreathed in steam from the cups. She says, finally, "Any word from Kashyyyk?"

"None."

"It's been a month, Wedge."

"I know."

"Leia must be losing her mind."

"She is. Trust me, she is."

The Eleutherian Plaza outside the Senate Building is abuzz with activity—all of it conducted by the masterful hand of Chancellor Mon Mothma and her advisers. She wields people like instruments, creating harmony and rhythm out of sheer noise. It is a thing to watch.

Unless, of course, you are one of her discarded instruments.

That is how Leia feels. But even if she is no longer contributing to the song . . . she can still bring noise, can't she?

She strides up through the center of the plaza. She's showing now. No way to hide it. No way to avoid the whispers, either—rumors of the child born of a smuggler and a princess, a smuggler who fled, a princess who stayed. Leia does not care about those whispers. She *cannot*.

As Mon directs Senate Guards, telling them where to stand—simultaneously fielding questions about the illuminations display that will fill the night sky after Liberation Day with an unparalleled show of lights and fire—Leia walks right up to stand in front of her. Forget protocol. Decorum is a thing of the past, a thing that Leia has buried deeply. Besides: Mon is a friend. Isn't she?

"Leia," Mon says. In that voice, Leia detects the competing emotions of warmth and irritation. The chancellor is pleased to see her while annoyed by her interruption. "As you can see, I'm a bit busy—"

"Yes, I'm busy, too. Busy worrying about my husband and his team and the *entire world* of Wookiees slowly being ground to dust in the crushing fist of the still-existent Empire. Mon, please."

Leia has been driven ceaselessly to find a solution to this crisis ever since that day the *Millennium Falcon* landed here in Chandrila—and her husband failed to meet her. Norra and the others rescued prisoners, but Han stayed behind. *Something he had to do,* Norra said.

Her jaw clenches at that.

Leia tried marshaling the votes needed to send aid and troops to Kashyyyk, but of course the Senate is full of representatives whose own worlds need that aid and, sometimes, the military presence, too. The vote was close, but not close enough—the measure will not return until the next cycle, and by then it will be far too late.

After that, she tried interfacing with Admiral Ackbar directly—Ackbar agreed that it was time to do something about Kashyyyk, and together they pondered the options. He considered sending a small SpecForces team to the surface in order to help locate and assist Han's team . . .

Mon Mothma blocked that effort. Like slamming down a giant wall of ice between Leia and her goal.

At the time, Mon said it would be "inexcusable" to stir mud into the water after Sloane came to them with the offer of peace talks. The galaxy, she said, was momentarily at peace—a tense, unpleasant peace, perhaps, but one where all was quiet on the galactic front. It was a much-needed respite from the weariness of war, and to make *any* formal, official incursion against Kashyyyk at this point could reawaken those troubles.

That, the chancellor made clear, was not an option.

And the Senate backed her up.

"Leia, please. If you give me a few hours—"

"Mon. Stop. Listen to me. I won't negotiate on this."

Mon leans in and whispers: "I understand you're upset—"

"Understand *this*," Leia says, her voice louder than a whisper. "You need me. I'm still the face of this Republic. Don't make me walk away from that."

Mon stiffens. "You'd really do that? You'd injure the New Republic over this?"

"I would burn down the whole galaxy if I thought it was right."

Mon sighs and forces a smile. "I do know that." The chancellor nods to everyone gathered. "Take a short break. I'll be back."

The chancellor secures Leia's elbow and the two of them walk to the far side of the plaza. Nearby, a trio of whiskered vole-kites scurry about, searching for crumbs with scrabbling paws. Startled, the little animals take flight in a flurry of furry feathers.

"You have my attention," Mon says. "I wish you'd found a nicer way to secure it, but here we are."

"We are friends. Aren't we?"

"I expect and hope we still are. I know this is about Kashyyyk and— believe me when I tell you, my hands here are tied. Things are *different* now. In the days of the Alliance, we did what we could—and sometimes that meant individuals making snap decisions for the whole. But this is no longer an insurgency. We aren't in hiding. We don't operate in cells or in ragtag bases strewn across the galaxy. All eyes are on us, all hands are joined. We are united, and *in* that unity we are beholden to the whole, to the machine of government, which is slow, yes, but effective—"

"Effective at what, exactly? Indolence? Concession?"

"*Compromise.*"

"Such cold logic and all while worlds die. What is our compromise on Kashyyyk? Because it seems to me there that no such compromise has manifested, not a compromise that the Wookiees would understand—"

Mon takes her hand and clasps it tight. "Kashyyyk is one world among the *thousands* we are trying to reach—and thousands more beyond that to come. Please see beyond your entanglements with Han and see that this is more than just one man."

"Yes, you're right. It is! It is about *millions* of Wookiees—many of whom are already dead because nobody came to help them. Chewbacca is a friend and a protector. He is *family*. And I owe him just as Han owes him." Awareness blooms inside her, fierce as a plume of fire. She understands why Han is out there. He's not running away from her or from the child. He's running *toward* something. That's what Norra meant—he has something left to do. Something that can't remain undone before he starts his own family.

"I've been thinking," Mon says, "and what Han is doing may be the right way to go about it. On worlds where the Empire still holds sway—or where criminal syndicates fill that void—individual resistance movements may rise up and serve as small rebellions all their own. Just like what happened on Akiva. We cannot officially support them but we may be able to find ways through back channels to offer aid."

Leia scoffs. "Back channels? That's what we've earned?"

"As I told you before, I will also put this on the table with Admiral Sloane during our peace talks. I will ask that the liberation of Kashyyyk be a condition of peace—"

"You want to negotiate something that is non-negotiable," Leia hisses. She holds up two hands, palms flat up. "Over here is the right thing, the *good* thing. On the other side is the wrong path. The evil path. We have long fought to be good. To be heroes! But now? You want to negotiate in this middle space. You want to dither about in the gray."

"It's not as simple as good and evil, Leia."

"It is to me!—" Leia turns toward the door. "I'm not getting anywhere. I . . . have to go, Mon. I thought I could try, but I can see it's futile."

"Wait. Liberation Day is almost here. I need you by my side—the face of solidarity. Unity, as I said."

"We have no unity on this. You will go at this alone."

"It's not me who's alone, Leia."

A twist of the blade. Leia attacks right back:

"I'd rather be alone than with you, *Chancellor*."

With that, she storms off, certain now what she must do.

Norra finds her son standing alone in the kitchen. He's eating a pakarna bowl—a kind of noodle concoction. A Chandrilan dish. Herbaceous and spicy. He twirls noodles onto a fork and shoves them unceremoniously into his mouth, sauce dribbling on his chin as Bones stares, rapt.

The boy barely acknowledges her as she comes in the door.

"Hi," she says.

He doesn't respond. Just a mopey nod is all she gets.

"Where's your father?"

"What do *you* care?"

"Okay. I probably deserve that."

Temmin shrugs. "Yeah. Well. He's out. Again. On one of his walks."

"He just needs to clear his head, honey."

"What he needs is to get away from *you*."

That raises her hackles. She doesn't want it to. Norra wants to lean into this, to take her licks if they're earned—but fast, too fast, she's biting back at him: "Watch the attitude, Tem. We're all going through something. This is going to get tougher before it gets easier. Your father has been away a long time—"

"Because he was captured. What was your excuse?"

"I was—"

"Trying to find him? How'd that work out for you?"

She ignores that. Or tries to. "Your father's been a little strange because of what they did to him on that ship."

"He's been strange because you've been strange with him."

He's right. She has. They eat dinner mostly in silence. The first week they slept in the same bed, but since then he's been falling asleep on the settee in the family room. They barely talk now. What should they talk about? The state of the galaxy? The upcoming peace talks with the people who put him in prison, the ones he fought against for years? Would they speak of his nightmares? Her time with the Alliance?

She's tried, in private moments, to probe at the edges of that, to tease out what he thinks of her following in his footsteps, but mostly he just seems distracted. It's something she's seen with other pilots and soldiers in the war—they've been trauma-blasted to oblivion. Ripped asunder, until they're just tattered scraps of who they once were.

Is that Brentin, now? Just tattered scraps?

Can he be stitched back together? Can their marriage?

Temmin flings his noodle bowl into the sink, half eaten. Bones cranes his neck and looks down at it.

"I WILL CLEAN THAT UP," the droid chimes.

"No," Temmin says, hooking a finger around one of the robot's newly forged ribs. "Let's go somewhere else."

She catches his arm. "Wedge spoke to me. You've been missing training."

"So?"

"*So,* it means you can't participate in Liberation Day patrols."

He shrugs like it doesn't matter, even though the shrug is so aggressive, it *has* to matter. "Whatever. Great. Liberation Day is dumb anyway. Peace talks with that monster, Sloane? We freed some prisoners. Whoopee. They're not even giving us medals."

"Temmin—"

"No, you know what? It's fine. It's great. I'm gonna follow Dad's lead and go for a long walk. *Alone.* Come on, Bones."

"IF I GO, THEN YOU WON'T BE ALONE."

"I said, *come on.*"

"ROGER-ROGER."

Norra is left by herself. Her eyes burning with tears. Her mind suddenly flies not to her husband, not to her son or Wedge, but to the team she left behind on Kashyyyk. She hopes they're okay.

CHAPTER THIRTY

Lozen Tolruck, Grand Moff of Kashyyyk, is hunting.

A visor sits strapped to his round face, and on each side small electro-stim pads are affixed to his temples. Through the visor, he sees—and controls—a small assassin probe. The probe was a droid, once, though one of his techs removed the thing's personality matrix and turned it into something that Tolruck could control from afar. It's a mean little thing, that probe. Small enough to be tucked under one's arm. Fast as an arrow. Nimble, too, with perfect movement in every direction. It possesses a chroma-coat of shimmer-paint, allowing it to appear as if it blends in with the rest of its environment—providing it with powerful camouflage.

It is a wonderful device. In theory.

Lozen Tolruck despises it.

Through the visor he sees his prey—one of the Wookiees they've been training. This one is Subject 478-98, though Tolruck likes to give them nicknames. Makes it more personal. This one he calls Blackstripe, because of the single black stripe that bisects the center of the beast's face.

Blackstripe runs and Blackstripe climbs, but it matters little. The assassin probe is fast. It has thermal imaging and motion detection. It sees all and can pursue with swift efficacy. The beast scrambles up one of the massive wroshyr trees in the Garden Preserve, and it ducks through branches and swings under spongy zha-raratha vines and scrambles around clusters of blood-red needle blossoms. Blackstripe climbs and climbs.

And soon, the beast sees its hunter.

It roars. Tolruck flinches as the beast's paw swipes across his vision. The probe flinches, too, darting backward; the clumsy swat fails to connect.

Tolruck merely thinks about what he wants to do and the assassin probe does it. It barely needs to be a conscious thought. He blinks and the probe extends a telescoping barrel and then—

Kiff, kiff.

Two toxo-darts stick in the beast's chest. The poison is fast acting, and the Wookiee *should* fall, but he doesn't. He is robust. They trained him too well, it seems. Clumsily, the creature continues his ascent of the tree, moaning and gurgling as he leaps inelegantly from branch to branch . . .

Fine. Anger seizes Tolruck. He roars the way the Wookiees roar—even though the beast will never hear that sound, given that the damn thing is over sixty kilometers away—and then he launches the assassin probe right at the wretched monster. Soon as it hits, he signals the elimination code—

And the probe self-destructs.

That will kill the awful thing. Blackstripe will be dead—a hole blown in the beast's back. Maybe it would even have split the monster in half.

The visor goes dark. Tolruck rips it off his face with a growl. He dashes it to the ground and steps on it as if it is an offensive pest.

There, in front of him, stands his attaché: Odair Bel-Opis. A capable man, Odair. Organized. Merciless. Corellian. He is a brutal killer, yes, but also trustworthy—he has no designs on Tolruck's position. Odair is as necessary and as simple as a club held firm in one's hand.

"This *thing*," Tolruck growls, toeing the broken control visor, "is worthless to me. This isn't hunting, Odair. It's *voyeuristic*. I want to *be* there. I want to smell those ragged beasts. I want to hear their growls and their rasping breath. I want to chase them and be chased. That is the hunt. Not . . . whatever *this* is."

He paces around the room like the whirling winds of one of Kashyyyk's dreadful mrawzim storms—he runs his hands along the gnarled, knotted logs that make up the walls of his circular chamber. His thumb tracks across a line of sticky sap and he brings it to his lips. He sucks that thumb the way a baby would. It gives him chills and he shudders. A wave of pleasure washes over him. The sap—hragathir, the Wookiees call it—becomes narcotic over time, after the wood is culled from the tree.

He flops down in his chair: a massive skeletal thing formed of dark, dead wood. The many-pronged antlers of the arrawtha-dyr frame him as he slumps and slouches, pulling aside the fabric of his robe (made from the dyr's own pelt) to scratch the expanse of pale, exposed belly.

Scritch, scritch, scritch.

"You may speak if you have words," Tolruck slurs.

"I will tell the techs that a new probe is necessary."

"No. I want to go *out*. I want to *hunt*. Proper-like."

"It is too dangerous right now."

"Bah." He sweeps his arm across the air. "This is no revolt. The Wookiees remain in our control. It's an insurgent cell—a little cancerous shadow clinging to our operation here. No more than a blood-bug. Let's squash the *rathhakkhan* thing and be done with it. They can't hurt me."

"They have been attacking vital targets. And you are our most vital."

With that, he won't argue. He is lord of this world. The Empire has abandoned him. He is grand moff only in name. In truth, he is warlord. He is emperor. No—

He is *god*.

An entire world and its feral species exist under his sway.

What glorious power.

He hated this place for so long. But now it's a part of him. Its dirt is under his nails. He *stinks* like it. And that stink? He likes it. He hasn't bathed in weeks. He's even taken to eating some of those wrosha-grubs whole and uncooked—fat, plump worms whose skin pops when you bite them, their guts evacuating their rubbery bodies and slicking his tongue. He wishes he had some now, even though he just ate not long ago.

He burps into his fist. His head lolls back. "I refuse to be cowed, Odair. I will hunt these mongrels myself. We've already caught one of them. Maybe we can use him as bait. Get me my rifle—"

"There's something else, Governor."

"Out with it, then."

"We have a visitor."

"Who?"

"An Imperial. One of Admiral Sloane's people."

That makes him sit up. Perhaps they have finally remembered him. Perhaps they hope to include him and his throneworld in *their* Empire.

But then, that gives him pause. Does he want to join them? Does he care for their token advances, their crumbs flicked into his waiting mouth—they will expect him to be gracious, but they have abandoned him here.

He can do better on his own.

Best to let this Imperial stew. Besides, Commandant Sardo has been pleading for a meeting now for some time. He'll take the call, and that'll give Sloane's lackey plenty of time to sit and simmer in regret. Then he'll meet with her man, finally, and when he does, he can send Sloane back a present—her man's head in a footlocker.

The Wookiees built many of their cities in and around the massive, skytower-like wroshyr trees—trees whose trunks are of an unimaginable circumference, big enough that to walk around the base of one could take you half a day. The trees turn and twist around one another, as if frozen in a mad dance—this, a competition for the boughs of each wroshyr to crest the upper atmosphere ahead of the one next to it.

Each tree, forever seeking the sun.

The sun, now, is veiled behind bands of dark cloud and ash. Spears of light stab through that darkness, but even then, the light is pale and thin. It feels insubstantial. It fails to bring warmth or even much illumination.

What it does illuminate is that the Wookiee city of Awrathakka is in ruins. The city once climbed the tree, as many of the cities do—following the bends and turns of the trunk. The life of the Wookiees was bound to the life of the tree. They tended to it. And in turn, it gave them shelter and food and all of their existence. Their symbiosis was honored as a bond both sacred and biological. But now, most of the city has been gouged from the bark. Pieces hang. The wood is burned in places, and so are the structures that were once affixed to—or grown into—the tree. The bond is broken.

It was once a city of gardens.

Now it is only a city of ghosts.

The Wookiees who dwelled there, though, are still near.

Far below, down through the layers of mist, is Imperial Work Settlement #121, aka Camp Sardo, after the man who runs the settlement, Commandant Theodane Sardo. It is one of many such settlements on the surface of Kashyyyk—all are built on the ground, for the Empire cares little to try to navigate the confusing topography of the wroshyrs.

Camp Sardo is also the largest of these settlements.

It is home to over fifty thousand Wookiees.

They work in varying capacities. They dig up the roots of the tree—the roots are softer than the tree itself, and it is easier to make use of the wood there. They also mine the fungal nodes that cling to those roots: Mineral deposits form, attracting fungus to feed on those deposits. And once a node is mature, the fungus can be scraped away; within is wroshite—a hard, flinty crystal the color of gun-steel. Good for focusing Imperial beam weapons. And worth a helmet-load of credits on the black market.

The Wookiees also grow food.

They fight for entertainment.

They are forced to breed.

They are subject to various chemical and medical tests.

And they do not revolt. They do not resist. Because if they do, the chips in their heads will end them. Or better yet, end their families—that is a trick it took the Empire too long to learn. A Wookiee will only fight so hard for herself. But they are slaves to their own bloodlines, and family is everything. Got a ruthless, undomesticated, willful Wookiee on your hands? Threaten those of her pack and she becomes as pliable as warm dough.

Still. Sometimes the Wookiees starve or are worked too hard, and when that happens, they are thrown into one of the carcass trenches and burned. Sardo brings in one new Wookiee for every other that falls.

"Productivity is everything," Sardo says over hologram. Tolruck grunts. The man is a sycophant. Which is fine; Tolruck needs men like Sardo, men willing to bow and scrape and lick boot. Just the same, it's disgusting to witness. Though Sardo is a great distance away in his camp (that man would never be invited within the walls of Lozen Tolruck's island fortress), his obsequiousness bleeds through. "The Empire may have left us behind, but you remain, and in your name we seek to improve our margins. I've been trying to think of new ways to use the Wookiees . . ."

Sardo goes on and on, explaining how the Empire has stopped bringing Wookiees offworld—it used to be that they would ship them away from the planet by the thousands for work (after all, it was Wookiees who helped build much of the Imperial war machine). "But since that has ended, the breeding programs have become problematic. We have a surplus of slave labor—but what to do with it?" That is the conundrum Sardo puzzles over just now. "Could the Wookiees be farmed for their meat? Presently it's stringy and tough, but maybe if they could be fattened up, or modified in some way—crossbred with another species, perhaps, like the Talz." (Tolruck does not hate this idea. The Talz are delicious.)

Just then, the holo of Sardo flinches.

Tolruck asks: "What is it?"

"I . . . we've lost a turret is all. In the trees." Tolruck snorts. What's in the trees above Sardo? He glances at the map on the wall. An old Wookiee city, isn't it? Awrathakka. Hm. "Probably nothing."

Probably nothing, indeed.

Tolruck says, "Check on it anyway. Do not be lazy, Commandant. Control your environment. Do not disappoint me."

Sardo nods furiously. "I will. Of course. Thank you, sir."

Tolruck nods back and ends the holo. He sighs. He looks to Odair: "I suppose it is time we see what Sloane's fool wishes of me."

In the ghost city of Awrathakka, a single ship eases in for a landing in the safety of a dead turret's shadow.

It is an SS-54 gunship—or, rather, "light freighter."

Its designation: the *Halo.*

Lozen takes his time walking through the fortress. Fur-matted Wookiees and corroded droids work as he passes—many cutting thick planks of *wroshyr* wood to fortify the stronghold. That wood is damn near supernatural in terms of the protections it affords. It refuses to burn. It can take hits from a turbolaser and suffer only a little charring and splintering. Of course, that means cutting the stuff takes proton-teeth saw-blades. And even those break in contest with the wood—many a Wookiee has had his head split in half like a tongo nut by one snapping in mid-spin.

The Wookiees do not look at him as he passes. They have been trained not to turn their animal gaze toward him. And the inhibitor chips bolted to the backs of their skulls ensure that any violation results in varying levels of misery (escalating of course until paralysis and then death).

His feet splash in puddles as he walks from level to level, down one set of steps to another. Around a wooden walkway, across a planking of sheet metal, through a longhouse of painted forest troopers readying their blaster rifles for target practice.

Out here, the air smells of ash and char and burning hair. Clouds turn and twirl overhead—gray and dead as a diseased lung.

There, ahead, waiting at the bottom of the rusted metal steps:

The visitor. Classic stiff-backed Imperial posture. Chin up, nose down, hands behind the back. The uniform shows a naval banding. Just a lieutenant. A man of little significance.

That man offers a wan smile that lifts a mustache far too sculpted for this brutish world. Lozen's own beard is unkempt, unruly—a wild thatch-scrub growing from his cheeks and jowls. Even Odair's face is a patchy rug of dark stubble. Mad men for a mad place.

The Imperial salutes, then offers a hand.

"Lieutenant Jorrin Turnbull," the man says.

Lozen does not take the man's hand or offer much acknowledgment at all. He does little more than twist his face into a dissatisfied scowl. "Sloane sent you, I'm told."

"That is correct, sir."

"*Why?*"

"She understands you're having some, ah, problems."

"And the Empire wants to help."

"We are all the Empire, sir."

"Are we?" Lozen growls, then steps up to the man. Odair closes in, too—he is strung tight like a bow cable, ready for anything. The warlord gets into the lieutenant's face and bares his teeth. The man is small and Lozen is large—he's let himself gain size over the last many years, filling himself with bulk. Fat and muscle wreathing his bones. His beard is long, yes, but his hair is pulled back in a knotty snarl. He is everything this tall, thin man is not. "You have abandoned us. Gone is our resupply. Our slave stock is building up and nobody is taking them off our hands—we'll have to cut breeding lines before too long. We've seen no changing of the guard, no passing the baton for our ships or our craft or our officers. It is as if we are forgotten. But we remember. And we survive."

The man looks nervous now. As he should. He may die before this day is done. "Grand Admiral Sloane surely begs your forgiveness in this regard—as you may know, the Empire has fractured since the Emperor's death—"

"The Emperor is alive," Lozen seethes. It is a lie. He knows it to be one. And yet it's one he props up. The story he tells his men and women here is simple, because simple is effective: The Empire has been robbed from its Emperor, and one day he will reclaim it. Until then, they are on their own. It gives his soldiers a future. It gives them an end. It whispers of victory.

"Yes. Of course." The Imperial visibly swallows. He knows now that the rope coils around his neck and tightens ineluctably. "Just the same, Sloane is extending a hand. You are menaced by terrorists?"

Lozen's eyes narrow into fat-pinched slits. "Yes."

"We know who they are. Ah, we think. They came to this world with a stolen code from an Imperial prison-maker."

"Golas Aram."

"That is correct."

"Never trust a Siniteen. A brain that large contains a multitude of treacheries."

"That holds true here. The terrorists arrived with those codes and under the false blessing of Admiral Sloane."

Lozen leans in. "Who are they?"

"Imperial hunters sent by the New Republic. Led by a known scum-raker: the criminal Han Solo. Now a general in their ranks."

Lozen nods. That makes sense. "Interesting. The one we have hasn't talked. Would not let a single word slip past his vile rebel lips no matter how much we hurt him."

"Do you still have him? Is he alive, the prisoner?"

The governor snorts. "He is." He holds up a finger and loops it in a lasso gesture. "Bring me the captive, Odair."

His attaché goes away and returns shortly with a short cage on grav-pads. Odair nudges it along with his knee—the cage is too short for a human. It's an iron kennel meant for one of Lozen's strega—a blunt-beaked harrier bird. Big as a dog and a powerful hunter. Trainable, too. With the right . . . motivation. But this cage contains no such bird.

Rather, it contains a man.

This man belongs here. His eyes are wild like the forests of this place. He is rangy and savage—an undomesticated cur.

The Imperial stoops to look. His face tightens as he sees. "This one, he's missing an eye."

"We loosened that eye thinking it would loosen his tongue." Lozen growls mucus up out of his throat and into his mouth and chews on it. "It did not." He spits the phlegm against the ground: *spat.*

"Well. Your methods are your own. I could use a tour of your . . ."

Just then, someone hands something to Odair. A holoscreen. Odair's gaze flits to the Imperial, then to the screen, then to Lozen.

"Governor, you should see this."

Odair sidles over and hands him the holoscreen.

On the screen: a series of WANTED posters. This, he realizes, is the team of Imperial hunters that is plaguing him and his domain. He sees the man that is kept in the cage: a commando, looks like. Jom Barell is his name.

Thing is, he recognizes another face on there, too.

Sinjir Rath Velus.

It is the face of the Imperial in front of him. Oh, sure, the man has endeavored to change a little about himself: hair a bit longer, and not to mention that overgroomed caterpillar crawling on his upper lip.

But that, without a doubt, is not Jorrin Turnbull. (If such a man even exists.) He is an intruder. He is prey.

Lozen feels his blood go hot. What a wondrous reversal: This man thought he could hunt the governor, but now this fool has gotten himself caught in a bind. And he senses it, too. Some prey is too dumb to know, but the best prey—the kind you want to hunt for the challenge it presents—can sense when the wind has changed, when a predator stalks the wild.

The man tenses—his gaze flits because he's looking for a weapon or an exit or any advantage he can manage.

But he's too slow.

Lozen has a knife in his hand: a kishakk blade. A Wookiee weapon; the name translates roughly to "bramble thorn." The beasts use them for eating—they pry open the shells of various crustaceans and bugs. But Lozen has found the blades to be elegantly balanced. So balanced, in fact . . .

He throws it. The traitor turns to flee—

The blade lands true. It sticks in the back of the man's calf, crippling his leg. His prey—Sinjir whatever-his-name-is—falls forward, catching himself with open palms. His foe howls like a wounded dyr.

"Bring him to me," Lozen barks to Odair.

His attaché complies.

Burned bone chimes *tink* and *tonk* in the unstill air. As Jas sets up her rifle, snapping the scope on, one of the crew behind her—Greybok, the one-armed Wookiee—bumps something and it rolls past her.

A toy. A child's toy. It's a wooden saurian with wheels instead of legs, and as it rolls, its jaw squeaks open and closed.

She wonders how long it's been since a Wookiee youngling has played with it. That youngling might now be older. Or dead.

A shadow falls over her. Chewbacca stands, staring out into the mist. He looks up, too. Like he's equal parts sad and afraid.

He chuffs and barks.

Solo hunkers down next to her. "We'll keep our eyes peeled."

"What'd he say?" she asks him.

"You don't wanna know."

She screws the thermal imaging module onto the side of the scope. "I'm a big girl. I can handle it."

"He said to watch out for spiders."

"Spiders don't frighten me." She thinks: They sure frighten Sinjir, though. Even a teeny-tiny house spider running across the floor will have him freeze in place, saying a prayer to a hundred gods he doesn't believe in. It occurs to her suddenly: She misses Sinjir.

Solo leans in. "Spiders don't frighten you because most spiders are no bigger than your hand. These spiders, webweavers? Big as you and me."

"That's horrifying."

"What's more horrifying is what they do to you."

She blinks. "You're right. I don't want to know."

"The Wookiees eat 'em. Chewie says they're, well, chewy."

Chewie yips in agreement.

Just the same, she looks over her shoulder, half expecting to see some massive scuttling thing coming up fast. But all she sees back there is the *Halo* and the team they brought on board: a ragtag crew of battle-hardened Wookiee refugees, plus a smattering of smugglers. That includes two of Greybok's friends: Hatchet and Palabar. It's Palabar who helped them conceive of this plan. The Quarren is utter poo-doo in a fight—even the whisper of threat leaves him cowering and praying. But he's tech-savvy and smart when he can see past his own fear.

The crew is doing what they're supposed to—anchoring massive eyebolts into the wood with pneumo-hammers. The wood resists, but the Wookiees know the weak spots. Once the eyebolts are in, they start threading through the jump-cables. Everything is going according to plan.

Her mind drifts back to Sinjir . . . and Jom, and she feels suddenly less relaxed. But there's no time for that distraction. Everyone has to do their part.

Her, included.

Jas leans in and tucks the scope against her eye.

It's comfortable. Sitting behind a gun is always comfortable for her. That probably says something unhealthy about her, but she doesn't care.

Solo flips the thermal imaging switch. "Thanks," she says, as the dead mist below suddenly flares with colors and contours.

There: Camp Sardo. Far below. The shape of a lumbering thing roams into view—an AT-AT walker slowly stomping along the perimeter. From up here, she can't even feel the vibrations of its feet, that's how high they are.

She sees the great blob of life down there: Wookiees and forest troopers and the officers who belong to Lozen Tolruck's demonic regime.

"You see it?" Solo asks.

"Not yet."

"Here, gimme the rifle."

"I *have* it," she whispers. "Patience, Solo."

He yanks back his hand as if bitten. "Hey, all right, all right. But put a little thrust in it, willya?" He looks up at Chewie. "How we doing, Chewie?"

Chewbacca rumbles a reply.

"Inhibitor frequency is still up," Solo says. "But it could be down any minute. C'mon, Emari. Find the damn—"

"I found it," she says.

The shield generator gives off its own heat signature. And it's one of the taller structures in Camp Sardo—a dodecahedral tower on four steel posts. It controls the field that surrounds the camp: a field that Imperials can pass through without harm, but any chip that passes through it will detonate. Meaning, if a Wookiee waltzes through the field—*boom*. Unfortunately, it's an entirely separate mechanism from the inhibitor frequency.

Which means it has to go separately.

But it can't go too early—they blow that field too early, and they'll set off alarms. That could compromise their plan.

"I hope your pair can handle this," Solo growls.

"Sinjir has it handled."

"The commando, your boy toy there, he wasn't supposed to get captured."

She hesitates. *I hope he's all right.* "He also saved our hides and let us get away from that ambush. A fact I hope you appreciate."

"Yeah, yeah." He shifts impatiently. "And that explosive slug of yours will take that whole thing down? You sure about that?"

"It will," she growls through clamped teeth.

"Longer we sit up here, the bigger the target on our backs."

She gives him a look. "You need to trust us."

"Yeah, yeah, relax. I trust Sinjir. I'm just on edge. And I . . . trust you enough to take the shot when the frequency goes dead."

"Me?" She smirks. "I thought you were Mister Crackshot around here. The scoundrel with the luck of the Force on his side."

"Here, how about this? We tell the world that I'm a better shot with a blaster, and you're a better shot with a rifle. We'll call it a draw."

She nods, says "That's fair."

She likes Solo, after all this. Even with his boyish impatience. He gives off a vibe that floats somewhere between a sharp-tongued cad and a dim-witted oaf, but at the end of the day, there's something genuinely good about him. She likes to hope he sees the same in her.

"All right," he says. "Stay frosty, just in case we—"

The mist around them lights up with a single laser spearing the air.

"—get company," he finishes, and then pivots on his heel with one blaster already up and in his hand. He yells to Jas: "Stay here with Chewie. Get ready for the shot! We'll hold 'em off!"

Coming up out of the mist behind them—and above, and below

them—forest troopers in camouflaged armor. Everything lights up with the exchange of blasterfire, and Jas hunkers down, jaw tight, trying not to die.

Jom Barell is in his cage. His one eye, gone. And the men responsible are out there right now, about ready to kill Sinjir Rath Velus.

He didn't recognize his crewmate at first. Having one eye didn't help, but Sinjir disappeared into the role of some needy bureaucrat. Tolruck bought it, too. That ex-Imperial is good at his job.

Jom Barell appreciates those who are good at their jobs.

Right now, though, Sinjir is also about to be good at getting his hind end handed to him by Lozen Tolruck's brute, Odair. Jom bangs against the cage, growling like an animal, his voice like two stones grinding together. "Get up! Get up, Rath Velus, you bloody sack of meat!"

Odair advances—

Sinjir moves fast, rolling over and pinwheeling a kick with his good leg. Odair doesn't see it coming; the kick knocks him down to the ground.

Others gather around—men of Tolruck's with mud on their cheeks and callused hands, women with leering stares hungry for violence. Fights erupt here in the fortress from time to time. Sometimes they even make Jom fight—usually with one hand tied behind his back because even half blind he still put his attackers in the dirt. All around, Tolruck's people hoot and call with the atavistic urgings of a primitive species.

The two men scrap. Odair crashes an elbow against Sinjir's collarbone. But Sinjir bends back and fetches the blade from his own leg—it squishes and squirts a line of blood as he claims the knife as his own. It's an opportunity, though, and Odair takes it, dropping a fist into his foe's gut—again and again it falls like the head of a hammer, wham, wham.

It goes on like this for a while. The two men pummeling each other.

The knife passing between them, the blade never drawing any more blood. Tolruck watches with eagerness, picking his teeth with a chipped thumbnail. Jom watches Tolruck. He thinks, *Soon as I'm out of here, you're a dead man, Tolruck.* He's dreamed of taking the man's eye as vengeance for his own. When he was captured, the crew had been running the same two-prong approach that they started that day with the command station on the other side of Kashyyyk: Jom and his ground team did their commando recon business, in this case trying to secure a shuttle platform in order to grab an Imperial ride that would get them safely out to Tolruck's island. But they were ambushed—turns out, they'd pulled the same trick too many times and gotten cozy with it. So did the local Imperials. Jom's team of Wookiees got away, but he wasn't so lucky. They captured him and brought him here.

And that's where they cut out his eye.

Suddenly, Tolruck applauds—Jom looks and sees Odair finally get behind Sinjir. The brute pulls his arm tight around Rath Velus's throat. Eyes bulge. Tongue wags. *C'mon, Sinjir. Give 'em hell. Fight. Fight!*

The knife drops from the Sinjir's hand and clatters to the ground.

And with that, it's done.

The crowd cheers. Jom slumps against the cage. His one chance at freedom, over. They shouldn't have sent Sinjir.

Odair spits out a pair of teeth, then drags the ex-Imperial over by his heel. Panting, he says: "Here he is, Governor."

Sinjir rolls over. Jom winces; the man's a bloody, bruise-dark mess. The side of his face is swelling up like a balloon. His nose might be broken, and blood spackles that twisted mustache.

Sinjir licks his lips. "I'll be fine in a second. Then we can go for—" He grimaces and grunts. "Round two."

Tolruck lords over him, scratching his belly. "Why would you come here? Into the heart of it. Into my *lair.* Do you think me prey?"

"Not at all. Just looking to borrow a cup of sugar, love."

"You came for your friend, then. The one-eyed man."

"No, not that, either. Actually, I came for your—" Here he coughs so hard it sounds like he might shatter a rib doing it. "Your control module."

A lantern of hope alights inside Jom's chest.

At that, Tolruck barks laughter. The control module is how they program and control the chips in each of the Wookiees. It controls literally hundreds of thousands of chips. Jom's seen it. It's old tech, practically Clone Wars era. Tolruck probably barely understands how it works.

"You *idiot*. I would never have let you get near that, no matter who you claimed to be. The control module remains in *my* control only."

"And yet—" More coughing. "It doesn't."

He frowns. "You are a sad, delusional little man."

"Probably. But not about this, I'm afraid." Sinjir sits up. One eye now is sealed shut behind a tomb of swollen flesh. "See, you checked me for weapons at the door, but you did not check my *boots*. I've got a hyperwave transceiver spike hidden in my heel—and, so sorry, your precious console is of the *transmitting* variety. Totally wireless. An old security flaw, but one that remains mostly uncorrected across the Empire. I should know."

"You . . . you didn't . . . you *couldn't* have . . ."

"I didn't need to be at the console to hack it. I just needed to be *near* it. Oh, of course, I also needed enough time for the remote hack to work. Which, I think you've given me enough just . . . about . . . *now*."

The datapad in Tolruck's left hand begins to flash red.

The alarm.

Now it's Jom's turn to bellow with laughter. He bangs his heels against the cage, cackling madly.

To Odair, Tolruck screams, "Kill the intruder. *Kill him!*"

A laser lances through the air and Jas hears it hit flesh—*bazzt!*—and next to her, one of the Wookiees, Harrgun, topples off the platform. His body tumbles down into the mist, massive tree-trunk arms pinwheeling.

Every centimeter of Jas wants to get up and take the fight to the troopers. They're surrounded now on damn near every side—they've got troopers behind them. And a LAIT—a low-altitude Imperial transport—keeps making flybys, the troopers within firing on them as they pass. On the latest pass, Chewie takes aim with a bowcaster and the air sizzles as he clips one of the forest troopers right in the visor. The visor shatters and the body rolls out of the transport, falling through the air and joining Harrgun in death.

But Jas can't get up. She has her shot lined up.

All she needs is—

Chewie roars.

The inhibitor frequency is dead.

The chips are off planetwide.

The revolt begins here and now with the pull of her trigger.

Her finger twitches and the slugthrower bucks against her shoulder.

Bang.

Above Camp Sardo, a thunderclap explosion. Fire rains down in streams and bits of the shield generator slam against the ground, crushing troopers underneath. Metal burns. Smoke rises. Around old Awrathakka, the mist pulses with what looks like red lightning.

The shield is down.

All around, Wookiees climb the towers, crawling on top of buildings, swarming over their troopers. A trio of them offer thunderous roars as they wrench a turret out of its mooring. Not far away, two Wookiees grab for one of the forest trooper guards—each takes an end and they twist. The trooper's spine snaps as his body corkscrews.

They rage. Fur and fangs and swiping limbs. Men screaming. In the distance, something explodes. Fire jets into the air.

The beasts ululate.

They are free. Fire blooms like a flower in the mist as the shield generator goes down. Around Jas, the Wookiees roar and raise their arms and weapons in triumph—a small moment of victory before the next phase begins.

Already Han is clipping himself onto one of the cables. He throws an anchor line to Chewie, who loops the cable around him and hooks it into his belt.

"You good?" Han says to Jas—flinching as a laser bolt cooks the air behind his head. He growls and returns fire. A trooper scream cuts through the mist and she sees a shape fall.

"I'm good."

"We're almost there," he says, his hand on her shoulder. "See you on the other side of this, Emari."

"Good working with you, Solo."

To Chewie, he says: "C'mon, pal. Let's go steal us an Imperial walker." Then he and Chewbacca take a running leap off the platform.

Vzzzzzz!

The two figures disappear over the edge.

And then the other Wookiees join them. One by one they leap bodily off the end of the platform, arms and legs splayed out as they dive through the mist toward the vile Camp Sardo. Cables trailing like umbilical cords.

That leaves her with her command crew: Greybok, Hatchet, and Palabar. Three ex-prisoners from Sevarcos who joined Solo's mission on a fluke—Hatchet claims he doesn't want to be here, keeps saying things like, *I wanted to get away from prison planets, not take a vacation on one,* but then Greybok silences him with violent, one-armed shaking. Palabar mostly just quivers and peeks out from behind his hands.

They're the dregs of this team. Good thing Jas likes the dregs.

Already, they're waving her toward the *Halo*. A pair of forest troopers comes up a long spiraling ramp—one is already on her, so she cracks him hard enough with the butt of her gun that his helmet spins. The other gets a point-blank shot to the chest plate. It splits in half and he goes down, his armor shattered and smoldering as he twitches.

Hatchet waves her onto the *Halo*.

"This is all going too good," he says. "It's gonna balance out the other way, Zabrak, just you watch. Can't go nice forever."

"Shut up and man the guns," she tells him, then hops in the *Halo* and kicks the thrusters into gear. They thunder to life and the ship lifts into the air. Time to go rescue her friends.

Everything is pulsing like a pounding heart. Sinjir gags as the man's hands wrap around his throat. Tolruck's attaché glares down with bloodshot eyes, a mad grin spreading across his face like a pool of spilling oil set aflame. Sinjir's hand swats uselessly at the man, then paws along the ground, feeling for the knife—a knife he knows can't be too far away.

There. He has it—his fingers tickling the base of the hilt, and as darkness sucks at the edges of his vision he tries to pull it close, closer . . .

A miscalculation. It spins out of his reach.

Then, a shadow falls over him. Death, he decides. It is the specter of the end coming to claim him.

He has part of it right. It is death, yes.

But it hasn't come for him.

One of the Wookiees brings the flat end of a circular saw-blade against the side of Odair's head. *Whonnnng.* Odair cries out and tumbles to the side. The Wookiee takes one stride, straddling the man.

Then he flings the saw-blade to the side and reaches to grab the man's arms. The freed slave begins to pull, pull, pull—

Odair screams. Then comes the sound like branches breaking.

It is a sound that fails to disturb him, for he knows its ilk well. The sounds of pain were once his song.

No time to think about that now.

Now: It is time to move.

He scrambles onto his hands and knees, only now regarding the chaos around him: Troopers are storming onto the scene, firing blasters. But the Wookiees, now freed, are not easily cowed by that—they roar and rage and rush Tolruck's men. A trooper flies through the air over Sinjir's head, arms pinwheeling as he hits the log walls with a dull crunch.

The knife. Sinjir's hand finds it, and he finally gets back onto his feet—unsteadily, for his entire body feels like it's been passed through the gastrointestinal tract of a gundark—and he dives toward Jom's cage.

He uses the knife to pick the lock.

Jom, for his part, watches silently. Chest heaving.

A moment of sympathy plucks at Sinjir's strings—the man really is missing an eye. His left. And it was removed without elegance. The socket is just a ragged pucker, a crass asterisk of ill-stitched skin. No signs of infection, at least. That's something.

The lock springs. The cage pops open.

Barell grunts. "I don't feel so good."

"You don't *look* so good, either. If you take my meaning." Sinjir winks and points to one of his eyes.

"Are you drunk?"

"Regrettably, no."

It's like something clicks in Jom's head. He grabs Sinjir by the arm and pulls him forward. "Come on, Rath Velus. Let's go find Tolruck and make him eat that knife."

"No," Sinjir says. "We have to go, Jom. Jas is coming." Or she should be. If everything else is going according to plan . . .

The commando pulls him close even as violence unfolds around them. "That man? He took my eye, Sinjir. Cut it out of my head while he was . . . high as a wind turbine, drunk on some kind of tree sap. Then? He threw my eye into a campfire. I heard it pop and sizzle. He has to pay for all his crimes. The ones against me. The ones against these Wookiees."

"You're angry."

"I have gone beyond the margins of angry."

Sinjir looks around. Tolruck is nowhere to be found. The deranged governor has fled the scene. Sinjir knows how this works—Jom will go and do this no matter what he says.

The question now is whether or not Sinjir will join him.

And that, of course, is no question at all. Debts must be paid.

"Tolruck awaits," Sinjir says, grimacing. "Shall we?"

It's like a giant thermal detonator primed and gone pop—

Beneath the *Halo*, Jas sees that freedom has come to Kashyyyk. Wookiees, immediately free of the inhibitor field that suppressed their minds from the chips embedded in the backs of their heads, are raging. They scale the towers of Camp Sardo. They rip at tents. They swarm over AT-ST chicken walkers, tipping them over so they crash against the ground. The forest troopers flee as Wookiees claim blasters, mount turrets, and begin to overwhelm their captors. They outnumber the Imperials by ten to one, easy.

It won't be like this everywhere. Not yet. Many of the settlements are still contained by suppression fields—the Wookiees there are still imprisoned. But with their chips cooked, they will be able to push back and claim their prisons for themselves. And not every Wookiee is in a settlement.

The revolt has begun.

Greybok grumbles.

Hatchet leans in toward Jas, his shriveled Weequay face wearing a dubious mask. "He says the planet has had its revolutions before, you know."

"This one will stick," she says. She *hopes*.

"It better."

Palabar points. There, as she swoops the *Halo* low over the action, firing at troopers who are mounting guns on turrets, she sees the towering shape of the AT-AT walker ahead. The top of its cockpit is cracked open, and a familiar Wookiee is flinging the driver off into the air.

Chewie waves. Solo gives her a salute from below as he slides into the opening. The refugees—Kirratha and the others—walk on the back of the AT-AT like conquering doom-riders.

The *Halo* burns sky as it blasts forward.

Soon the settlement of Camp Sardo is aft. Jas weaves the ship through the wroshyr trees—ahead, a pair of LAITs come blasting through the mist, and Hatchet surprises them with a rain of red lasers. One transport's wing peels away—and it clips the second transport. Both spin down through the mist. The fog pulses with twin explosions.

Ahead, the mist thins. And one of Kashyyyk's coastlines emerges—a dark sea, the whitecapped tides cutting lines across the water. Beyond that, the *Halo*'s scopes show a rocky island. That's Tolruck's fortress, a massive log-walled monstrosity built on the cusp of a long-dead volcano.

"Shall we soften them up before we set her down?" Hatchet asks.

She shrugs. "Why not? Light it up."

Hatchet grins and fires up the weapons system. He cackles.

"It's over," Lozen Tolruck slurs. "The hunt has ended."

The warlord sits in his throne, slumping forward. Sap is sticky around his fingers and his lips. Jom has the thorn-knife in his hand, and he has the urging of a storm in him, but Sinjir stays him with a gentle gesture.

"Wait," he says.

"Sinjir—"

To the governor, Sinjir says: "You are coming with us."

"Sinjir—"

"This is what we do, Jom. We hunt the Imperials. We capture them and take them. He's taking a ride with us." He presses a hand against Jom's chest. "We're not killers."

How strange that sounds, coming out of his mouth. Hm.

Jom's one good eye closes. His chest rises and falls—the heaving breath of a man trying to contain his fury. That eye opens again. "Fine. Lozen Tolruck, you're under arrest by authority of the New Republic."

"It doesn't matter," Tolruck says, bubbles fizzing at his lips. His eyes search the space around them, but they don't seem to focus. "We're all dead. You and you and all the Wookiees and even me. All. Dead."

"What?" Sinjir asks. "Speak sense, you slobbering blob."

"If I can't have this world, then nobody can. Not the New Republic. Not the Wookiees. Certainly not the *Empire*."

The ground shudders.

"What was that?" Jom asks.

Another boom.

"Orbital bombardment," Tolruck says with a sloppy grin. Those two words, drawn out drunkenly. "Annihilation from the stars. Or rather, from the Star Destroyers. I sent the code. Nothing is to survive."

Sinjir whispers to Jom: "We have to move. Now."

"But he—"

"Leave him. I know when a man is broken."

Jom concedes. The two of them peel away, fleeing Tolruck's chambers. The man's gabbling laugh follows them as they go.

A triumvirate of Star Destroyers floats in the slate-gray sky—gauzy shapes hanging there above Kashyyyk like executioner blades.

And destruction rains from those ships as they earn their name.

Death comes in streaking flame and shrieking light. It comes from the shuddering batteries of turbolasers. It comes from the bellies of the beasts, dropped as propulsion bombs. It is clumsy and brutal—an act of killing like spraying a hive of wasps with a flamethrower. Imprecise, yes.

But over time, effective.

Jas steps out the side door of the *Halo* and takes a moment to watch as the ships—far off for now—fire on the planet below with their massive, world-scouring weapons. The ground shakes just slightly even here.

Soon, she knows, the ships will come this way.

Centimeters from her head, a laser bolt *thwacks* against the side of her ship. She flinches as it brings her back into the moment. They landed the *Halo* smack dab in the center of the fortress, taking out a couple of bolt-throwers and the troopers operating them as it found its landing zone. Now, as troopers rush to greet them with screaming blasters, all they can do is hold off the swarms of Tolruck's men, hoping like hell that Sinjir and Jom show.

Hatchet is by her side now, and he's got Jom's heavy cannon—a BlasTech DSK loaded with steel-melting dragonsfire cells. The Weequay refugee bellows and hoots, spraying the incoming troopers with green fire.

A shaggy shape darts forward off to the side—it's Greybok. A blade gleams in his lone hand: She sees the scythe-like swoop of a ryyk blade. He howls some battle cry in the Shyriiwook tongue and begins slicing and dicing troopers like they're nothing but paper to be cut into dolls. Bits of armor fling and fly. A helmet tumbles to the ground, its head still in it.

"Greybok is having a good time!" Hatchet yells over the din.

"Just look for the others," she answers.

Come on, come on, where are you?

In the distance, the three Star Destroyers begin to drift apart—each likely going on a separate bombardment course. It'll take a long while to bomb this world into submission with just three of those ships, but in the meantime the death they cause will be unparalleled.

And who, truly, will stop them?

An ill feeling leaches at her guts: Their success in liberating this planet will do them no good if the result is blowing it all to hell.

"There!" Hatchet growls, and lays down covering fire as Sinjir and Jom come bolting out through a wooden archway—behind them, forest troopers storm after in close pursuit. Jas reaches on her belt, pulls a detonator, primes it, and pitches it.

The orb flies, beeping as it goes.

It lands at the feet of the troopers.

Gotcha, she thinks.

It's fire and spinning bodies as the detonator goes off—the wave of concussion almost lifting Sinjir and Jom off their feet. But the two stagger and keep hurtling forward. As they reach the *Halo*, Jas helps them aboard.

"Hello, honey, I'm home," Sinjir says, giving her a wink. "I found this poor orphan, and I thought we could adopt him."

"Emari," Jom says, giving her a nod.

"Your eye," she says. It's . . . gone. Her hand moves to his cheek, fingers searching out the crude stitching.

"Didn't think I could get any prettier, did you? Proved you wrong again." He leans in, gives her a peck. "Let's get this bird flying before hell rains down on us from those Star Destroyers, eh?"

Tolruck sits, laughing at nothing. He is barely aware of the shape standing before him. His eyes, blurry, strain to focus.

Ah. A Wookiee.

He knows this one. Subject 6391-A, designation: Cracktooth. She once tried to bite her way through shackles, which broke most of her teeth. She learned the hard way that escape was not an option—and since then, she's been one of the most docile beasts in all of Tolruck's fortress. He uses her for more delicate matters—gardening, cleaning, putting up tents. She's often nearby and she never turns her gaze to him. Cracktooth is very respectful. *Very respectful.*

She reaches in, her hands closing around his neck.

Grrk!

Cracktooth bares her yellow teeth.

She snaps his neck like a bird bone.

So ends Lozen Tolruck.

INTERLUDE

DARROPOLIS, HOSNIAN PRIME

"All right, Mister Hetkins, lean forward and step down," Doctor Arsad says. "*Gently,* gently, left leg first," she adds.

Dade screws up his face and eases forward off the bed.

He does as she says: left leg first.

As for the second leg, well. That one's *gone.* Blown clean off back in the thicket of Endor. He and his team were doing cleanup in the weeks after the Death Star's destruction, tracking down ragtag Imperial battalions that never made it off the surface of the Sanctuary Moon. All it took was one—*one!*—scout trooper. A scout trooper with a box of thermal detonators and the willingness to use them. Then—

Boom. A crater in the ground vomited fresh dirt. It rained down around him as he fell, clutching the spot where the right leg below his knee once was. Then darkness took him. Thankfully, triage saved his life.

(If not the leg.)

And now he's here. At a New Republic vet hospital on Hosnian Prime.

Living the dream, he thinks.

"Go on," Arsad says. She's an older woman, with lines drawn in her skin—deep enough they're like a knife carving a name into dark wood.

"Yeah, yeah," he says, and eases forward.

The prosthetic foot clicks against the ground, and awareness blooms in the sole of the metal foot. It isn't his flesh and blood; he can *feel* it connect with the floor. It doesn't feel the same as the other foot. This is cold and electric.

He hates it.

His new toes drum impatiently, even angrily, on the floor as Arsad asks him to hold still. Nearby, an FX-7 droid's dozen spindly limbs furiously tap buttons on a diagnostic machine while also measuring and examining a scrolling holographic readout beamed above. The droid whirs and beeps.

She has him stand. Then walk. Then sit again, then stand again. Flex and stretch. Move and pivot. The droid continues to work diagnostics.

"Things look fine here," Doctor Arsad says.

"Thanks, Doc. Guess I'm good to go." He stretches the leg out, and the crass facsimile of a half leg hangs there like a curse. It shines. Red wires braid up through its pistons and screws. *I'm less than who I was before,* he thinks—an idle thought that causes anger to surge inside him like an eruption of hot lava. It's hard to swallow and force a smile, but he manages.

"Not just yet," Arsad says. "The leg is fine. But how are *you*?"

"Like you said. Leg is fine. So I'm fine."

But the way she looks at him is almost like she's looking *through* him. Or, rather, seeing through his smokescreen. "Any bad dreams?"

"Nope," he lies. He doesn't flinch at remembering the one from just last night—trapped in trees falling all around him, hopping around on one bloody leg, the last man alive on a forest moon full of Imperi-als.

"So you're sleeping okay?"

"Like a purring nexu." Another lie.

"And no mood problems?"

I definitely didn't kick a potted plant to death yesterday with my one good leg. That poor little kaduki plant. All those crushed flowers, all that spilled dirt. "Not that I can see."

"Suicidal thoughts?"

"Zero." That, at least, is not a lie. He wants to live. He's just not par-ticularly *happy* about it.

The FX-7 warbles and buzzes. Arsad nods.

"The droid suggests you are not being *entirely* truthful."

His eyes pinch shut. Droid traitor! He should've known that being hooked up to that thing gave a lot more bio- and psycho-feedback than he figured on. "Listen, Doc, I'm fine. I'm *good.* Okay? I got my leg, I'll learn to use it, no problem. As for the rest, I knew what I was signing up for. I didn't decide to go toe-to-toe with the Empire thinking it would be like riding the grav-rails at Domino Park. I knew what could happen. I'm alive and I'll take that as a blessing, thank the Force."

"And *yet,*" Arsad says, leaning in and watching him with those kind eyes. "Republic protocol demands I not let you leave without some help."

"Don't need help. Leaving is help enough." *Been in this hospital for two months now.*

She hits the button and the auto-blinds rise, letting light in from the hospital courtyard. Outside, Alliance vets sit on benches or move about on hoverchairs, many tended to by FX droids. Beyond that are the crystal dunes on the outskirts of the city, on which sit dome-style Hosnian homes. "There we go. Let a little light in. We all need light."

"That feels like a precursor to something."

"I have two prescriptions for you. First is that you return here every month for group therapy—other combat veterans gather here and talk about what they've seen and what they're feeling. It helps."

He laughs, though it isn't a happy sound. "Doc, I wasn't planning on sticking around. I was thinking of going back to the NR, doing another tour—maybe something in the Outer Rim, I dunno."

Now it's *her* turn to laugh. "Oh, Dade. No. Your time at war is done. For you, it's peacetime. If you let it be. Now, if you want to leave Hosnian Prime, we can set you up with a therapy group on other worlds. Chandrila. Corellia. The light of the Republic reaches new worlds every day now."

"I . . ." He bites his lip. "Okay, fine. I'll talk to a bunch of scarred-up old battle idiots like me. Are we good?"

"As I said, there is a second thing. Wait here, please." As if he's going to just get up and run laps.

A mischievous twinkle shines in her eye as she leaves. Dade sits there for a while, tapping his new metal toes on the floor—*cl-cl-click, cl-cl-click*—when she returns to the room.

A droid follows close behind.

This droid is unlike one he's ever seen before. It's got a clunky, squarish head, but it rolls around slowly on a blue-and-gold ball-shaped body. Smaller than your standard astro-droid—this one only sits about knee-high. It warbles and blurps at him, focusing a pair of ocular lenses on him as it juggles its own head, which sits improbably upon its body like a box balanced poorly on a child's ball. The droid tries to stay balanced as its head dips dangerously to the side.

"What is this?" he asks.

"It's a droid, Dade."

"Yeah, Doc, I see that, but *why* is there a droid here?"

"This is QT-9. He is *your* droid."

Dade arches an eyebrow so high he's pretty sure it hovers a few centimeters above his head. "I don't recall owning a droid."

"Think of it as *renting* one, except for free. QT-9 is a prototype therapy droid."

"I don't want a whatever-that-is."

Arsad smirks. "I *could* put you in for a therapy Ewok, instead. Some of the native Endor creatures have agreed to travel offworld to help veterans like you recuperate. As a manner of recompense for saving their home."

"Oh, yeah, I don't want one of those. They smell horrible."

"Good news, then. The droid smells clean as new metal. In part because it *is* new—with the Empire falling, opportunity arises across the galaxy for new technologies. Droids included. This one is designed to be friendly and familiar. Like a pet."

The droid rocks back and forth, purring.

He sighs. "I have to take the droid? For real?"

"And come to meetings."

"Doc, you're killing me."

"I think you mean, *Doc, you're saving my life.*"

"If you say so."

She holds his hand and clasps it tight. "I do say so, Mister Hetkins, I do. Congratulations on your new foot, your new droid, and your new lease on life. The galaxy is yours to conquer."

"Thanks for your help. *I guess.*"

Doctor Arsad hugs him, then leaves him alone with the droid. Dade stretches and groans as he stands fully. Again he feels the floor up through his clearly fake foot. Nearby is the silicaform sleeve (aka skin sock) that she told him he could pull over it if he wanted to. But honestly, he'd rather just have a weird metal foot. Why pretend? He leaves it behind.

QT-9 makes a string of trill-beeps at him. He just shakes his head and says, "Come on, you roly-poly pain-in-my-ass. Let's go home."

(Wherever *that* is.)

The droid squeals with robot delight as it trails behind.

CHAPTER THIRTY-ONE

Dreams.

Leia knows she's just dreaming. She recognizes them for the illusion that they are. But they trouble her just the same, threading in and out of her sleep. Phantasms pursue her. She dreams of Han, dead in the snow. She dreams of poor Chewie in a cage somewhere. She dreams of herself on a table, dying as her child—no, children—are born. Then comes a vision of Luke, lost among the stars, searching for something and failing, never returning. She dreams of being lost in a forest, and then of being lost inside the Death Star—she and Luke and Han are fleeing stormtroopers, trying desperately to get back to the *Falcon* after Obi-Wan powers down the tractor beam controls, but now she knows the dread truth: He failed, he *died,* and the ship is still anchored there, and even if they could find their way out of the tangle of passages, they'll never escape . . .

Her stomach twists. Not an alarming pain, but a kick from the child inside her. *Oof.* She has to sit up. Her brow is slick with sweat.

The bed beneath her is, too. Her hand moves to her belly and feels the shape there, shifting and stirring. He's hungry. Which means she's hungry, too.

But then, a shape in the doorway.

It's T-2L0, one of her attendant protocol droids.

"Your Highness," the droid says. "I know that it's late—"

"It's late, Ello."

"Yes, Your Highness. I believe I noted that? Well. You have a visitor."

"At this hour?"

The droid nods. "It is a man named Conder Kyl," she explains. "He said you would want to—"

The slicer. "Let him in, Ello. I'll be out in a moment."

Leia takes a moment to center herself. She puts on a robe and washes her face, then heads out to meet her guest.

Conder Kyl is scruffy, but in a particularly *groomed* way—it seems a controlled chaos. His clothing is modern, very modern even by Chandrilan styles—a long dark vest with exposed arms and narrow-leg leather pants. He stands as she enters.

"General Leia," he says.

"That word makes you nervous. General."

"It's just—I'm not military."

"I know. I hired you, remember?"

An embarrassed smile as he says, "Yes, of course, Your Highness."

It's funny, meeting like this, late at night. In secret. Reminds her of the rebel days. Except now she's hiding from her own government.

"You have news?"

"I do." He sets up a small tripod in the center of the table, its metal legs clicking into place. The holoprojector immediately casts an image of the Wookiee planet, Kashyyyk. "The probe droid recorded this."

Information on Kashyyyk has been incredibly hard to come by. It is a walled, protected world. The Empire has it in a chokehold. But she hoped a small probe droid could escape their sweeps, and so she hired Conder—a friend, she understands, of Norra—to build a probe designed for stealth and capable of slicing into Imperial frequencies and, further, recording *something* to give her a sense of what's going on there. Most of its data has been orbital and atmospheric, though it has a long-range sensor-cam that can take satellite images from above.

She watches the three-dimensional scene unfold. It flickers blue as three Star Destroyers move together, and begin—

"Oh," she says, her hand flying to her face. Orbital strikes. They're going to bomb the planet into submission. But why?

Conder must anticipate that question coming, because he turns off the image, then plays an audio file. "The probe intercepted this burst of comm traffic from the surface. Lozen Tolruck sent it—I don't know why he failed to encrypt it, but the droid was able to pick it up."

The man's voice appears from the projector, accompanied by a visualization of the spikes and dips of the sound waves—

"The terrorists have won, Admiral Orlan. The inhibitors are down. The animals are . . ." His voice slurs when he says this next bit. "*Escaping the zoo.* Bomb it all. Burn it to a cinder. Uploading authorizuh . . . authorization code now. Begin orbital campaign."

The voice cuts out.

She takes a moment to process.

Han did it.

He must have. If anyone could cause an overreaction like *bomb the whole planet into bits,* it'd be him.

But now what? An orbital bombardment will be a nasty, protracted campaign. It won't stop until most of that world is dead. And that means Han and the others cannot escape. They could *die* there.

This is it. This has to stop now.

The course of action she decided upon after her meeting with Mon Mothma can no longer wait until after Liberation Day. Even though the celebration is tomorrow, every moment counts. She must not waste them.

"Thank you," she says. "I'll have the credits transferred to your account immediately."

"Nah," he says, waving it off. "Let's call this one a freebie."

"I owe you credits, Conder."

"Slate's clean. You can pay next time."

"Thank you."

"Mind if I ask: What are you going to do, Your Highness?"

"I am going to do what every wife must do now and again," she says. "I am going to go rescue my husband."

Grand Admiral Sloane cannot sleep.

Tomorrow is the first day of the peace talks. Worry threatens to eat her up from the inside like beetles chewing the rotten middle of an old tree. She knows her role in the peace talks, and that role is *not* to reach any kind of accord with the conspirators of the New Republic, but rather to distract them from the attack that's coming—and then to help marshal that attack from the ground. Rax said to her: "You will be a hero. It will cement your role as Emperor—or whatever you wish to call yourself. The galaxy will see you on all the screens. The Holo-Net will broadcast your valor."

She asked him, *But won't I be in danger?* It seems strange, after all, to put someone of her value right in the heart of battle. She reminded him that Palpatine was notoriously reclusive. Rarely did he appear unless he already controlled the environment he was entering.

"We will control the environment," Rax said. "You'll see. You won't be in meaningful danger. They won't kill you. Besides, the attack will give you plenty of opportunity to make your way clear."

This could be a trap. Or one of his *tests*.

Even if it is, the chance to attack Chandrila—it's tantalizing. It would grant them dominance. They would show their military might to the galaxy once more. Revealing the secret fleets hiding in the various nebulae . . .

That thought brings chills of delight.

For now, though, she needs her sleep.

She tries listening to some potboiler phono-play about a droid detective with an artificial intelligence inside his head named ADAM, but the droid is not really a detective but rather, an assassin? She tries connecting with it, but her mind keeps wandering. Then she gets up and paces her chamber, pulling up a galactic star map to behold the present state of Imperial assets—that, however, only depresses her. They've lost so much, so fast. Kuat is gone. G5-623 is falling—though Rax purposefully let that one loose, and she's quietly pleased to see it go. Slavery has never been part of the perfect Empire that lives inside her head. It may have been necessary for a time, but now the galaxy should be made to see the Empire's glory—and you can't teach them of its splendor through slavery. Slavery is not strength; it is weakness. Citizens should serve the Empire because it is right to do so. Why would any choose otherwise?

All of this is just a distraction, too.

Sleep. I need to sleep. I need to be fresh and ready and aware.

Instead, she puts on one of Rax's favorite operas: *The Cantata of Cora Vessora*. This version that he gave her has no words, only music.

At first, she finds it as distracting as everything else—music to her is just noise. Meaningless piffle meant to lull idiots to sleep.

But soon she realizes that she, too, is lulled by it. The strings and the drums. The hisses and the thrum. Her eyelids flutter. Her mind goes blank.

Perhaps I am just such an idiot.

The music draws her into it. Like a gentle wave carrying her away from shore, out to sea. It haunts her with its ethereal beauty.

It does not give her cause to sleep. But it lets her rest her mind for a while. Maybe she should trust Rax more often. Tomorrow is a big day. She will know soon enough if that trust is deserved—

Or if she has been a fool.

They work together long after dark. Temmin and Brentin, and Tem pretends that it's just like it used to be. Nothing different. Everything the same. But when he asks for the arc-driver for the fourth time, and Brentin just stares off at an unfixed point, Temmin has to admit:

Things are broken.

In front of them on the workbench is the valachord Tem bought—he had the bright idea to make it self-playing, so that Dad could enjoy the music without feeling pressured to play it himself. And Brentin agreed, to Temmin's surprise—but all the while, his father's been disconnected from it all. Like he's only partly here.

"Dad, is something wrong?"

"Nothing," Brentin says. The smile on his face is small and forced. "I'm just tired. It's been a long day."

"Oh. O . . . kay."

Brentin stands up suddenly. "I'm . . . going to take a walk."

Sure. Of course he is. All these walks of his.

Dad leaves.

And Temmin follows. As Brentin winds his way through Hanna City, so too does Temmin. It's almost time here in the capital—the tents are set up, as are the food stalls and the generators. The celebration of Liberation Day starts in the morning with a parade, and then Sloane arrives. Peace talks go on while Liberation Day events are ongoing—*distracting* people, Temmin thinks. Giving them a show while that monster Sloane tries to talk her way out of a war crimes trial. It makes him angry that they're giving her any time at all to plead her case. (Temmin has a lot of anger these days.) He follows his father out of the residential district, down through the gardens and the theaters, through the now quiet Old Hannatown Market, past the pakarna stands down by the sea. That's where Temmin loses him—he turns the corner and, poof, Brentin is gone. He wishes suddenly that he hadn't told Bones to stay back at the apartment. The droid could run a scan looking for Dad's life-signature—

Wait. There. He sees a shape gone off the Barbican Road and down onto the pebbled beach toward the water. Temmin hurries after.

The wind turns and comes up over the sea—its fingers ruffle Temmin's hair. It brings with it the smell of fish—he realizes now that down there are the docks, and by the docks is the fishery. There, droids process the day's catches, hauling in skor-fin and marmal-fish, star-legs and pearlshells. Right now, the fishery is quiet and dark. The piers beyond extend out into the sea like long, dark shadows. At the end of one, he sees Brentin.

And Brentin is not alone.

But who is the other person? Just some angler, maybe. The old salts who used to make a living bringing in the day's catch—before it was all automated—still like to sit out there before the sun is up. Brentin just ran into one and there they stand, having a conversation. Right? It makes sense.

Temmin gets closer.

And yet, he stays quiet. He tells himself that's just so he doesn't startle them, but all the same, it's hard to ignore the doubt creeping into the back of his mind like a sneaking thief looking to steal trust away one bit at a time.

He ducks around the side of the fishery. In through the windows, he sees the skeletal shadows of the droids powered down for the night, standing over the conveyor lines like frozen sentinels. Now he's glad he didn't bring Bones—if Bones is bad at one thing, it's keeping quiet.

Temmin darts along the far side of the fishery, coming up at the edge of the docks. He ducks behind a small mountain of fish crates.

Now he can see more in the moonlight.

Dad is standing there with—

A guardsman. Chandrilan. Doesn't Temmin recognize him?

He realizes that indeed he does. The man was the one guarding Yupe Tashu's cell. There's that same cresting wave of blond hair. And he can't see it from here, but he bets the man also has a chin scar and pale eyes.

Stupid, Temmin thinks. Dad's just talking to a guard. Maybe about tomorrow: Mom and Dad are both scheduled to be there on the dais for Liberation Day, alongside the chancellor and Leia and most of the other returned captives. Surely it relates to the events to come.

And he was worried! Dumb, dumb, dumb.

Temmin stands up and jogs down the pier, waving. "Dad. Hey!"

The two men turn toward him.

It's then he gets that bad old feeling. Something's wrong. Brentin doesn't wave. The guardsman braces with tension.

"Tem," Brentin says.

Temmin slows his jog, and then walks slowly.

"Dad, I don't . . . I just wanted to say hi and get away from Mom."

The guardsman scowls. "Deal with this, or I will."

Brentin nods.

Temmin is about to ask: *Deal with what?*

But he never gets the chance.

His father wheels on him, a blaster in his hand.

Brentin pulls the trigger.

CHAPTER THIRTY-TWO

Everything shakes and rumbles. Kashyyyk is caught in the throes of tectonic spasms—above their heads, the packed-dirt ceiling gives way one stream of soil at a time. Clumps of moss fall and the massive twisting roots around them writhe just so, like serpents stirred from a restive sleep.

Jas waits, back pressed against the tunnel wall, as Wookiees pass her in droves. They shuffle past, growling and ululating to one another. She cannot parse their tongue—Shyriiwook is a guttural, glottal language that when you listen very closely has a bewildering complexity. She may not know what they're saying, but she can hear *how* they sound.

They sound just as she herself feels:

Worried, anxious, and sad.

They're so close.

So close. Right up against the edge of freeing a world and a species. Of doing the right thing for the right reasons.

And yet—

For all their efforts, it has led to this. The Empire—if those ships above even claim to be that, anymore—is now attempting to bomb this planet to oblivion. Already she knows how this will go: Many of the newly freed Wookiees are only peripherally free. Most are still trapped in settlements. Which means killing them will be as easy as firing a blaster into a bucket of frogs.

Here, at least, they have the excavated root systems of the wroshyr tree above Camp Sardo. Together they had time—precious little but just enough—to get most of the freed Wookiees underground before one of the Destroyers appeared in the sky above to hammer them into mud, blood, splinters, and fur.

Jas thinks: *I should've stuck to bounty hunting.* All this trying to do the right thing isn't her speed. Nobody should've let her have this responsibility. It overwhelms her. It feels like a crushing weight on her shoulders, pushing, pressing, *grinding* her down into a greasy paste.

The Wookiees are dying. Jom has lost an eye—and maybe more than that when all this is over. They've failed.

Someone jostles into her—it's Solo. The half dark of the root tunnel makes it hard to see.

"Solo," she says, and she hears the frantic sound in her voice and she fears she's about to start blathering and, yes, indeed, it turns out she is: "We screwed this all up. This job was too big for us. We're just bugs under their feet now. You and me, we're scum, a couple of lowlifes who tried to turn away from what we are—just a smuggler and a bounty hunter and—"

"Hey," he says.

"And all we did was step on the dragon's tail and now it's turning around to bite—"

"*Hey.* Take it down a notch. We ain't out of this yet. You're tired, Emari, and you haven't had enough to eat. I get it. But I need you clear for this next part."

"Next part?"

"That's right. You and me, we are a couple of lowlifes. So we're gonna act the way the galaxy made us: like a smuggler and a bounty hunter."

"I don't follow you."

He grins. "I got a plan."

"It's not a real plan, is it?"

"Not a *complete* one. But yeah, it's a plan. Mostly."

"So, what is this 'plan'?"

"What are we good at, you and me?"

She frowns. "Lying. Cheating. Stealing." The last one, she hesitates to say because it is a truth she doesn't want to admit. Finally, she lets it slip: "Killing."

"Bull's-eye. So—we lie, cheat, and steal."

"And that last part? Killing?"

"Well, let's see if we do the first three right, and we go from there."

Then Han tells her his plan.

It's not a perfect plan. It's damn sure not a *complete* plan.

But maybe, just maybe, it'll work.

CHAPTER THIRTY-THREE

Across the hangar awaits a woman so tall and so blond they could use her as a coastal beacon here on Chandrila. Leia hurries toward her, a gray robe pulled tight with a hood over her head so her face is hidden.

"You can take the hood off," the woman says. "We're alone."

Leia draws back the hood.

She can't help but smile. "Evaan Verlaine," she says.

"Hello, Last Princess of Alderaan."

"I don't go by that anymore."

Evaan tilts her head and gives Leia a bemused look. "To me, it's who you are. You carry the torch for our world. For our home. Don't ever set it down."

"I know. And I do. It's actually why I'm here today."

Evaan Verlaine has been a friend and a cohort—and occasionally a co-conspirator—of Leia's since not long after the Death Star took their homeworld from them. Verlaine helped lead the charge to bring the diaspora of Alderaan refugees together. She's been vital in that effort, and as a result Leia hasn't seen much of her in a few years. (To her shame.)

The pilot knows Leia well enough. Evaan plants her fists on her hips and gives a playfully distrustful look. "I see that gleam in your eyes."

"What gleam would that be?"

"You're about to go rogue."

It wouldn't be the first time, but Leia plays coy. "Me? Never."

"Please, Leia. I hear people whisper, *I don't know what Her Highness sees in that scoundrel*. And I always respond: She's a lot more scoundrel than you think. Maybe even more than he is. So, spit it out: What do you need from me?"

"I need a pilot."

Evaan smirks. "I assumed that much. I didn't think you wanted droid repair. And where would this pilot take you?"

"To the Kashyyyk system."

That gives Evaan pause. "That is under Imperial control."

"Yes, I realize. And you're free to say no—I understand you have duties here in the New Republic now, and I also understand that with Liberation Day ramping up in . . . well, a few hours, you may be needed. But say so now, because I need to be off Chandrila before it all begins."

"I am a pilot for the New Republic, yes. But I am an Alderaanian first and a Republic pilot second. You command me and I will comply, Princess."

"I won't command you. I'm asking as a friend."

"And I'm saying yes as a friend *and* a loyal subject. But as a friend and a loyal subject, I feel the need to utter the disclaimer: This is likely to be dangerous, and it's surely foolish, and we could instead *not* go to Kashyyyk and stay here and watch the festivities unfold." Leia's about to speak, but Evaan gives her little chance. "And yet, I know you, and I know you wouldn't ask me without a very good reason, so—the cruiser's in the next hangar. You ready to go? Of course you are. Let's go flying, Your Highness."

"Actually," Leia says, "we're not going to take the cruiser."

"Do you have a ship in mind?"

She grins. "I do. And we won't be alone out there. At least, I hope not. Now let's go steal the *Millennium Falcon*."

INTERLUDE

RYLOTH

The garrison is a dead place.

Yendor and the others come up out of the caves spoiling for a fight—as Dardama says, *Stocked, locked, time to shock.* There's half a dozen of the Twi'lek soldiers, each armed to the teeth with blaster rifles, detonators, and kurr-claw knives. They know opposition will be fierce up here. Even this small garrison has a trio of AT-STs and a squadron of well-armed troopers. The goal isn't to wipe them out, but to do some damage. Take out a chicken walker, maybe. Knock over a few bucketheads. Then retreat to the caves once more. The Imperial probe droids can't navigate the tangled spaces beneath the surface very well, and if they were lucky enough to draw the stormtroopers down into the caverns, the rebel traps would make short work of the those trespassers.

And yet, when they get there—

The garrison is abandoned.

In the distance, the wind howls through the red rock towers.

"I don't understand," Dardama says. "This is still Ryloth, yeah? We didn't come out on some other planet?"

Yendor says to her and the others, "Careful, this might still be some kind of trap." He lifts two fingers, signaling those with him to stick close and follow behind. Worry tingles in the tips of his head-tails—he's a pilot, he told them, not a soldier, and certainly not any kind of general. But they said he'd been to war. They said they needed him.

So, here he is.

He darts along the edge of the gray-walled garrison. Two of the three walkers are ahead and he flinches, ready for them to attack.

But the wind blows a stream of dust and dirt through the walker's legs. Up on top of it, a can-cell sits perched, wings twitching.

The walkers, too, are abandoned.

His demolition expert, Tormo, comes up, scratching at the space between his head-tails. "Uh. You want me to blow these, or—you know, because if you ask me, we take them. We use them ourselves."

"Take them," comes a rough voice.

It isn't one of their own. It's one of *them:* an Imperial. The Twi'leks wheel on the stormtrooper standing there at the garrison gate. His helmet is off, cradled under his hand. The armor on his left arm is peeled off, too, and that arm is swollen up underneath a swaddling of fluid-stained gauze. Even from here, Yendor can see the man is sick: sweat beading along his brow, his face red, his eyes and nose crusted with a white rime.

"Identify yourself," Yendor says.

"I'm LD-22 . . ." But his voice trails off. "Sod it. My name is Chorn." His arm goes slack and the helmet clatters. The sound is a surprise enough that Yendor almost fires on the man but thankfully, training keeps him from doing so. The others are in control, too, and don't shoot.

"You don't look so good, Chorn."

"I don't feel very good." With his head he gamely gestures toward his wrapped arm. "Got a scratch on the arm while out on patrol—

some of us had our armor off because it was damn hot that day and . . ." He sighs and slumps against the side of the gate. "Got infected."

"Where are your men?"

"Gone." He whistles like a rocket and points to the sky. "They left."

"Why?"

"Why stay? We're done. We lost."

"You abandoned your post?"

"I didn't." The man laughs, and then that laugh dissolves into a fit of racking coughs. "I would have, though, but I can't go far. I'm told most of the troops are gone. Or going."

The Twi'leks all share looks. *Could it be true?*

If it is true, that means their planet just regained its independence through an act of despair and cowardice. Not the way Yendor expected it to come, but he won't turn away such a gift no matter how inelegant the wrapping. One thing he knows for sure: War is a very strange animal.

"What will you do to me?" the man asks. "Can't take me with you. What's the point? You don't want to waste resources on me. This garrison is my grave—"

Yendor is about to tell the trooper that they *will* waste the resources—food, medical, whatever—if only to have someone to stand trial. But also because it's the compassionate thing to do. The *right* thing to do.

But then, a blaster shot sizzles the air and the man falls, dead.

Dardama lowers her rifle. "You heard him. The garrison is his grave."

Yendor thinks to chastise her, but maybe she's right. Maybe *that* was the most compassionate thing to do. Or maybe they just wanted to shoot at something today. Just to feel like they earned this victory.

Either way, it is what it is.

The planet, it seems, is theirs.

Later, back in the caves, as reports come in confirming that the garrisons are gone and that the Imperial reign of Ryloth is over, the old man Tekku Aylay said to Yendor as the other Twi'leks packed up their subterranean camps, "We are a free world now. Thanks to the Twi'lek resistance. Thanks to Cham Syndulla. And thanks to the likes of you, too."

"It seems so."

"We will need the Republic to help ensure that this never happens again. Which means we will need an ambassador to represent us."

"Who are you thinking, Tekku?"

Tekku just smiles.

"Oh, no," Yendor says.

"Oh, *yes.*"

CHAPTER THIRTY-FOUR

Grand Admiral Rae Sloane once ran away from home. She did this because her family was not wealthy, and because her world, Ganthel, was a way station to *other* worlds—richer worlds, greener worlds. So she did as many children wish to do (and some even accomplish): She escaped out her window while her parents slept and made her way to the nearest ship dock in the hope of sneaking on board a freighter and traveling the galaxy.

She, also as many children do, chickened out. But before she did, young Rae Sloane made it all the way to the ship dock, hiding between two crates of kelerium scheduled for shipment offworld. It was there she decided that this whole running-away thing was not really in her blood. And as she turned to go home, she found her escape from between the two containers blocked by a pair of thugs from a local gang: the Kotaska, spicers and slavers who wore metal masks cut into the shapes of skulls. The two men chuckled behind their skull plates and came for her—she ran the other way, and found that way blocked by two more of the Kotaska gang.

Sloane had no way out. They grabbed her and put a bag over her head. It was then she knew she was a goner. She would not run away. Rather, she would be stolen—abducted and carried off not to adventure or wealth but to a life of toil and, most likely, horror.

Thankfully, a nearby astromech saw what was happening and set himself off as an alarm: sirens and strobing lights that summoned the nearest dock constable to chase off the Kotaska. She was free, and the moment her heels hit steel, she bolted home. Her parents never found out. (Later, the Empire would come to Ganthel and clear out the scum on her world. That was when she first began to regard Imperial control as a heroic, necessary presence in an otherwise chaotic galaxy.)

Right now, as her command shuttle descends out of lightspeed, she feels the same feeling she felt then when caught between those crates.

I have no way out.

I am trapped.

I need to run.

Ahead sits the beautiful blue-green world of Chandrila. A world she fears suddenly will become her pretty, pretty tomb.

Chandrila is ringed by New Republic ships: ships born of the allegiance of worlds. Mon Cala cruisers, old Alderaanian frigates, Sullustan ring-ships, not to mention a trio of new battleships: Nadiri Starhawks. All these are craft representative of worlds spurned by the Empire.

The people on board those ships hate her.

She has no preternatural sense for it. Sloane does not possess the Force; she cannot *feel* the hate coming off them in waves. It is simply an estimate that they hate her. But why wouldn't they? She represents the blunt, brute fist of the Empire they despise. Their greatest desire, she imagines, would be to cut that fist off and leave it cooling on the floor at their feet.

They hate her and she does not know why their first response is not to immediately fire upon her with all their weapons. For this reason she already has her hyperspace drive sending fresh calculations back to the *Ravager*.

The shuttle's pilot, Ensign Damascus, says: "They are sending escorts. Stand by." Ahead, a quadrangle formation of starfighters—Y-wings—descends upon her. *Here they come,* she thinks. *Weapons hot.*

But they never fire.

Instead, they do as the pilot suggests:

They escort her down to the surface of Chandrila. For peace talks. Or, at least, the illusion of them.

Out the window of her apartment, Norra spies the ships streaking across the powder-blue sky above Hanna City. An Imperial shuttle sits alone in the midst of four Y-wings—

Sloane is on that ship.

Last she saw of Admiral Sloane, Norra was chasing Sloane's shuttle in a stolen TIE fighter. The TIE's cannons thinned the shuttle's shields until she scored a vital, direct hit, and then the shuttle detonated, catching Norra in the explosion. She survived that, to her surprise.

Apparently, Sloane did, too.

It takes a surprising amount of *sheer will* not to go darting out of her apartment and into the cockpit of whatever ship she can find to finish the job she began there in orbit above Akiva. Take down Sloane.

And yet, she doesn't.

Instead she quakes and she simmers and she wills herself to look away from the window and again at herself in the floor-length mirror—her standing there in her naval dress uniform. She didn't even know the New Republic *had* naval dress. This is a uniform that echoes her old pilot flight suit but in a formal way. It's stiff and itchy. She hates how she looks in it. She tried to tell them, *I'm not even with the New Republic anymore. I renounced that.* And they told her that would be a conversation for later. She received a handwritten invitation from the chancellor herself to come on stage with Brentin and

Temmin. That, in order to herald the celebration of Liberation Day—with her as one of the liberators, married to one of the liberated. The chancellor's note said at the bottom:

Yours is a crucial narrative, Norra Wexley. One we must tell to ourselves and to the Empire. We are lucky to have you. Will you join us?

Now, if only she actually had her son and her husband with her, maybe she could do what the chancellor wanted.

But they're nowhere to be—

Behind her, the door to the room slides open.

There stands Brentin. The light of the morning meets him through the window, and the doorway frames him in just such a way—

For a moment, he's *her* Brentin again. Boyish cheeks and wise eyes. A wry twist to his face. Hands stuffed in his pockets.

"Hey," she says, her voice quieter than she means.

"Hey," he says.

Then a cloud passes in front of the sun, and a shadow moves into the room and then he's gone. Returned is the Brentin of now: He's thinner, his eyes are set back more, and that wry twist becomes a dark line.

"I'm late," he says. And he is.

"Yes, you are. So is your son. Have you seen him?"

Brentin twitches at that—a fog seems to fall upon him. "I . . . no."

She has no time to try to shine a light through that muddle, and even if she did have the time, it might not matter. Brentin sometimes seems like he's dozens of parsecs away. Like he's still in that prison pod. All she can do now is lay out his clothes—a simple, formal white suit given to her by the chancellor's people—and help him get into it.

He seems to brighten for a moment. "I'm sure Temmin will join us."

"At the last minute, no doubt."

"He's so much older now," Brentin says as she hands him a pair of shined brown boots. As he buckles the tops, he adds, "I regret missing . . . all of that. Him growing up. You joining the Rebellion in my stead. Gods, the Rebellion isn't even a thing anymore." Then he looks up at her from the bed and his eyes are clear and bright but lined with trouble when he says: "I love you, and I'm sorry I missed all of it. Are we okay?"

She's frozen. Her mouth opens but no sound comes out of her. All this time she's been waiting for a moment just like this one. Some tiny glimmer of who he was. Some *semblance* of recognition regarding what came and then passed. And now, here it is. Laid out before her, as if on a serving tray, and all she can do is stare at it and gape. Her heart feels like an animal in a net. Her vision clouds from behind tears she quickly blinks away.

Then it all snaps into focus.

They're going to be okay.

She tells him as much, stroking his cheek. "We're going to be okay. We may not be now, but that's okay. Because we'll get there. All of us."

He offers a small smile and nods. "Okay. I believe you."

Norra stoops to kiss her husband. He's shaking just a little. Or maybe it's her shaking. Or both of them. The kiss is soft and slow. It isn't one of the romantic, passionate kisses of their youth—stolen under one of the market tents as rain pounded the ground and everyone huddled there to stay dry. It is a wiser, stranger, altogether more hesitant kiss. But it's all the sweeter, too.

"We have to go soon," she says, kissing him again—this time, more quickly. Just a peck.

"I'm sure Temmin will meet us there," he says, repeating himself from before. Almost mechanically so. Norra flinches at it, but it's probably nothing. She clutches his hand and gives it a squeeze.

"It would surprise me if he didn't."

Temmin kicks out again—his feet slam against the inside of the box. The crate rattles and the frame shakes, but the box is made of some kind of heavy, compressed wood. It's not budging. And it doesn't help that his whole body feels like it's been worked over by a drunken Besalisk boxer—four arms punching him like he's just some sack of kodari-rice. That stun blast hit him hard, left him hurting.

My father shot me.

What does that even mean? Why would he do that?

Temmin stays still, snaps his fingers idly as he tries to imagine why Brentin would do that to him. Maybe, just maybe, Dad did it because he was trying to protect his son. He didn't kill Temmin, after all. Maybe he knows something. Maybe he did a bad thing in service of a good thing . . .

Or maybe, it's not his father at all. Could it be someone else? Someone *masquerading* as Brentin Wexley?

Temmin almost hopes that's the case. It would make this easier.

Again he growls and renews his struggle against the box. *Bam, bam, bam.* The box shakes and shifts. But it's no good.

Something's wrong. Something's going on. Something—

Something is shaking.

Beneath him, a faint vibration rises.

Someone is coming.

"Hey!" he shouts, slamming his heel against the underside of the box's magna-sealed lid. "*Hey!* I'm in here! Help! Help!"

No more sounds. Quiet stretches out.

And then he hears a weapon warming up: the slow thrum to power. The box shakes, and sparks rain down on him. Temmin screams, covering his eyes with his forearm, scrunching up into himself as the top of the box is burned through with a bright vibroblade and flung aside . . .

"I HAVE DISCOVERED YOU," comes the mechanized warble of Mister Bones. "THIS WAS THE LONGEST AND MOST PRO-TRACTED GAME OF HIDE-AND-SEEK, MASTER TEMMIN. BUT AGAIN I AM THE VICTOR. SHALL WE PLAY AGAIN?"

Temmin springs up out of the box and hugs his skeletal droid. "It is so good to see you, Bones."

"IT IS GOOD TO SEE YOU HAPPY."

"I'm not happy. My father shot me."

"THAT IS UNFORTUNATE, MASTER TEMMIN. I WILL SCAT-TER HIS ATOMS IN RETURN."

"Not yet. First things first, we need to get to Mom."

"ROGER-ROGER. WE WILL FIND MASTER TEMMIN'S MOM."

"She needs to know that something is going on." *And I don't know what it is.* But Temmin aims to find out.

The door to the shuttle remains closed.

Sloane needs a moment.

Behind her she has four of her own people, and that's it. She has two Royal Guards—neither were Palpatine's original guards, but the menacing red cloaks and hood-helmets remain the same. She has the pilot, Ensign Karz Damascus. And she has her own attaché, Adea Rite.

Trusted, necessary Adea. So trusted and so necessary that Sloane almost didn't want her to come. Just in case.

Even now, she says to Adea: "This could be a setup."

"I don't believe that it is," Adea answers.

"Rax could be testing us."

"Rax is always testing. So let's pass his test."

Sloane scowls. "He may have sent us here to fail."

"What sense would that make? Then you would just tell the New Republic who he was. You could give up Imperial assets. Him putting you in their hands would be foolish if he believed this to be a danger."

She's right, of course. Sloane knows this. She's thought this out. Just the same, she fears what will happen. The tendons in her neck are pulled taut as a tow cable. Something isn't right. None of this is right.

You're just afraid. You're that girl again on Ganthel, surrounded by enemies. Don't run this time, Rae. This is the time to stand and fight.

"They might just take us into custody soon as we step off this shuttle," she says to Adea.

The girl nods. Her eyes show a glimmer of fear at that, too. "They might. But Admiral Rax believes them to be foolishly optimistic enough not to. Let us trust in his assessment just this once."

"Yes." What choice do they have, anyway? To the pilot, Sloane says, "Open the door, lower the ramp."

And he does. The door lifts. The ramp descends in twin plumes of steam—like the breath from a rancor's nostrils.

The brightness of the day reaches her eyes and she winces against it, shielding her face as she steps off. She expects a flurry of movement—guards coming for her, blasters up, staves crossing.

But instead, she steps forward and is met by Chancellor Mon Mothma. A tall woman with a wine-stem neck and hair the color of copper-stone. The chancellor dips her head. "Admiral Sloane. Thank you for this."

"Chancellor." She'll give that woman no more than that.

Behind Mothma is the rank and file: soldiers, guards, and of course various New Republic generals and admirals. Ackbar isn't here, to her surprise. Nor is the Alderaanian traitor, Leia Organa. She wonders why—then it hits her. They aren't here just in case this *is* a trap. If this shuttle were rigged to explode, then certainly—

Her chest tightens.

What if it *is* rigged?

It would take out the chancellor. And a wave of soldiers and officers. *And her.* It could be what Rax wanted all along. It could be—

No, no, no. That's absurd. She had the shuttle checked. And surely they did prelim scans before they let her land, too, looking for any kind of explosive residue or unusual chemical signatures.

"We have quite a day planned," the chancellor says, jostling Sloane out of her grim reverie. "We have a celebration ongoing, and then at dinnertime you and I will retire to begin our talks."

Sloane braces. "I did not come here to have a *party*, Chancellor. I would prefer to move straight to business."

"Your attaché said your presence here deserved pomp and circumstance as is the way of one sovereign entity greeting another."

Sloane shoots Adea a look. The girl made a mistake and she will be chastised for it. Now, however, is not the time. Instead, Sloane turns, forces a smile: "Yes. Perhaps she is right. We are all owed a moment of leisure. Thank you for hosting these talks, Chancellor. Shall we begin?"

CHAPTER THIRTY-FIVE

The transport eases in through the mouth of the hangar bay, settling into the belly of the Star Destroyer *Dominion*. Jorrin Turnbull—or, rather, Sinjir Rath Velus, once again borrowing the identity of an Imperial agent who died on the Endor moon—eases back on the throttle, his teeth gritting so hard he's afraid they might be ground to a fine white powder.

"This is a terrible plan," he says to Han Solo—Solo, who crouches down so as not to be seen. Han Solo, the jerk. The very handsome, very charismatic jerk. "And I hate you very much."

"Relax. This is going to work."

The transport thuds dully against the hangar bay—Sinjir isn't much of a pilot, and his landing is clumsier than a drunken dragonsnake the way it just sort of *flops* down. But nobody cares, blessedly, and in moments the ship is surrounded by a whole bloody battalion of stormtroopers. Oh, and what's this? Here comes Admiral Orlan himself.

Well, then. Orlan must be eager to collect his prize: the prize of the rebel hero, Han Solo.

In the back, behind the sealed door separating the cockpit of the transport from the hold, comes *the sound*. It's a sound Sinjir has been hearing during the whole flight from the surface of Kashyyyk—a susurrus of shifting and clicking. Each time he hears it, he flinches.

"You ready?" Solo asks.

"No. Not for this." He blanches. His guts feel like water. His skin prickles. "I should've known this was a bad plan as soon as you told me what 'captives' we'd be transporting. You're a dangerous man."

Solo shrugs.

Outside, a thumping. A stormtrooper pounding on the side of the transport. Over the comm, the voice of Lieutenant Yoff: "Open."

"Here goes," Solo says.

"Yes," Sinjir says grimly, then opens the door.

Sinjir winces and waits.

He flips the exterior hatch-port cam on, though he really doesn't want to see. But it's like looking at a speeder crash: It's hard to look away.

On the screen, Orlan seems confused at the lack of anything happening. (Though surely by now he's hearing *the sounds*. Those terrible sounds.) Instead of flinching away like a smart person, the fool actually *leans in*. It happens so fast, Orlan doesn't even get to scream.

He reels back, clutching his eyes as if something was flung into them. Hairs, Sinjir knows. Flung from the legs and thorax of the massive webweaver spider that now pounces on Orlan.

The spider is not alone: Others join it, leaping and scuttling forth, bristly legs pinning stormtroopers to the deck of the bay. Glistening chelicerae click and chitter as fangs emerge and punch holes clean through white armor. The screams of troopers dissolve into gargling bleats as they flail and fall. The spiders scuttle and shriek and pounce.

The admiral tries to run. Sinjir watches him out the front window of the shuttle. But Orlan, he's blinded. And the spider does not care to relinquish its prey. It knocks him down and—

Two fangs crunch through the officer's skull.

"Spiders," Sinjir grouses. "Why exactly are we using spiders, again?"

Solo shrugs. "Wookiees said it would work. Wasn't too much of a thing to secure this gaggle, and—well, look." He spreads his arms out to behold the bedlam. Stormtroopers fruitlessly fire their blasters as officers flee. Spiders fling themselves bodily against them. Screams and flailing ensue. "All right, this distraction won't last long. Let's do this."

He slides into the cockpit and mans the weapons controls. The sides of the shuttle bang as the laser cannons flanking the cockpit emerge.

Ahead, a pair of ship-sized turrets wait to take out any trespassing crafts. And next to them sit the hangar bay shield generators.

Han pulls the trigger once, twice, three times—

Red light screams above the bodies of the spider-pinned stormtroopers, and both the turrets and the shield generators explode in a rain of white light. Parts of them rain down in a clatter.

Sinjir signals to the comm:

"*Halo*, door's open. No need to knock."

"Come on," Solo says.

"I'm not going out there."

"Yes, you are."

"There are spiders out there. Not little spiders. Spiders as big as my grandmother. And while my grandmother was a fairly small woman, she was still considerably larger than *any other spider ever.*"

"They're occupied."

"Occupied?"

"Eating stormtroopers."

"Did I mention I hate you?"

"Maybe once or twice."

Sinjir growls, then gets up—they pop the door between the cockpit and the transport hold. His breath catches in his chest and won't release because *spiders, spiders, there are so many spiders.* Willing his legs to carry him outside the transport feels like a truly heroic act. Yet somehow he manages—and sure enough, there is one of those web-weavers.

It rises on its two hind legs. Its hairs bristle. Green ichor drips from fangs that pop free of its mouthparts like sprung traps.

Solo shoots it in the face.

Something squirts out of the top of its head and it drops, twitching.

Two more spiders come scurrying up behind it—Sinjir fumbles for his own blaster, but it doesn't matter. Spears of laser light rip into them as the roar of the *Halo*'s engines fill the bay. The gunship blasts forward, coming in close behind the transport, its turbines turning fast as it lands with a bone-jarring *bang*. In moments, the others are rushing off the *Halo*—Jas, Jom, and of course Chewbacca. Weapons drawn and already firing. Spiders bowl over, squirting fluid. Stormtroopers tumble and fall.

"Come on!" Solo waves them forward and whoops. "Let's steal ourselves a Star Destroyer."

Sinji stifles a groan.

"Don't worry." Han smirks. "I've done this before. What could go wrong?"

The logistics of this plan defy reality, Sinjir knows.

A Star Destroyer is home to thousands. This one is running light, admittedly, so its numbers are in the *hundreds*. But their one moment of arachnid distraction earns them precious little time—and piloting a Star Destroyer isn't exactly the same thing as weaving a gunship or a freighter through a nest of TIE fighters. Admittedly, Sinjir has never *piloted* a Star Destroyer, but he wagers it's a lot like trying to saddle and ride a stampeding trog-beast.

So, he's pretty sure this won't work. Though as they fight through the hallways and channels of the Destroyer, working their way toward the bridge of the ship, he starts to feel uncharacteristically *optimistic*. Fighting alongside Solo means some of the smuggler's trademark luck seems to rub off, like a curiously pleasant smell. Jas takes down troopers left and right with her slugthrower. Jom is altogether more brutal—he and the Wookiee get right in there, scrapping bodily with their foes, flinging white-armored incompetents left and right and often into one another.

And then, as if by miracle—or by the Force or whatever bizarre cosmic authority governs the weave and weft of the galaxy—they are on the bridge and Solo is waving around a pair of blasters saying:

"This is a robbery. We're going to need this Star Destroyer."

And for a moment, all looks bright and shining. The comm officers and ensigns start to stand, hands up. An older, paunchy officer with vice admiral bars on his chest hesitates before finally standing up.

Sinjir thinks: *My word, we've done it.*

But the thought of victory comes just a moment too early.

The door behind them blasts open—and more stormtroopers pour onto the bridge. The fight Sinjir thought was over suddenly follows them inside: Jom gets his blaster shot out of his hands and so lurches forward while swinging a fist, but the commando catches the end of a rifle to the throat and he falls. Jas replaces him—her rifle is too long to fire easily in such a tight fray, but she swings it like a club. Sinjir does his own work, too—he gets behind one trooper and stabs the flat of his hand just under the poor dolt's helmet. The tips of his fingers drive hard into the trooper's neck, and it has the expected result—the Imperial soldier's fingers fly open on reflex, and the rifle he's carrying clatters to the ground.

Ha ha, he thinks. *Our luck holds true once—*

A jarring hit from behind. Sinjir's teeth clack together over his tongue. He tastes blood and sees stars-going-supernova behind his eyes as he drops, face forward, onto the floor.

A stormtrooper steps over him and kicks him in the ribs. *Oof.*

Through blurry eyes, he sees troopers swarming Solo, taking his blaster. Chewie, too—and the Wookiee roars in protest.

It's over, he thinks.

He watches as the stormtroopers slam Solo against a console. A pair of troopers stun Chewie as the Wookiee storms forward. A boot finds Sinjir's neck and presses down.

Luck, it seems, is a finite resource, after all.

CHAPTER THIRTY-SIX

Liberation Day has begun.

Right now, a parade marches down the center of Hanna City—a line of musical clamor and bright colors. Holographic dancers march alongside a very real Chandrilan band: oompahs from bladderpipes, booms from the tumble-drums, the clapping of hands and the stomping of marching feet.

Even from where Wedge Antilles sits—up on a balcony overlooking the day's events—he hears it. He smells food, too: a dozen odors commingling in his nose thanks to food vendors scattered throughout the city. Durmic spice and chando peppers, vent-grilled blackbeaks and pickled blackbeak eggs, baked sour-tarts and crispy mallow-dainties.

He should be down there. Not eating or watching the parade. No. He should be *working*. Flying sorties. Keeping an eye on things. But they told him to *take it easy*. He helped plan, they said, so now it was time to relax and enjoy the day. And yet he can't. He wants to stay busy.

Wedge wants to do his damn job.

He winces as he pulls away from the balcony. His leg and hip ache. Less today than yesterday, though. That's something.

At his table, a blinking light indicates an incoming message.

He hobbles over, sets it to play.

Leia's face appears. It's a recorded message, not live.

As she speaks, his blood goes cold. Then it goes hot.

"Captain Antilles. I've gone and done something foolish. I've jumped ahead to a meeting point just outside the Kashyyyk system. I'm in the *Millennium Falcon* and have Evaan Verlaine as my copilot. We will soon make our way into Kashyyyk orbit. If we are alone, I expect that the Empire will win the day and take me as a prisoner. A very *important* prisoner, and one that would represent a great loss to the New Republic. Unless, of course, someone might want to intervene? I could use some company out here, Captain. Care to join us?"

And then her face shimmers and is gone.

Oh, Leia, what are you doing?

His heart pounds in his chest like a pulse cannon.

Wedge throws on his coat and grabs his cane.

Every free moment she has, Sloane gives Adea *the look*. The one that says, *this parade, this music, this noise and clamor—it's all your fault.* To her credit, Adea looks starkly chastened. As she should.

Meanwhile, Sloane is strapped in for this unpleasant ride. The Empire is no stranger to celebrations. Parades are a necessity to keep the populace docile. Yes, yes, citizens, eat your sweet treats and enjoy the show. But Imperial parades are *restrained* affairs. They put forth processions of officers and troopers. Bands play the known marches. *Suitable*, patriotic marches. Such celebrations are short and simple.

This, however, is a sloppy, egregious affair.

Right now, half-dressed acrobats are passing beneath Sloane's balcony seat—they're flipping and flopping about on poles, jumping back and forth from grav-bounce to grav-bounce, holographic streamers trailing behind. It is clownish and bizarre. Then, thrumming by on a hovering stage, comes a martial demonstration from the Mon Cala— admittedly impressive given that they are essentially an underwater race of squid people. Trailing after them is yet another band, this one playing the execrable ear-horror "music" of the Gabdorins.

Sitting to her right is the chancellor. Adea is to her left.

Her guards are present by the door—though the room is home to thrice as many New Republic soldiers.

"It's something, isn't it?" Mon Mothma says, and it occurs to Sloane—the woman really *means* it. She is earnest. Many politicians put forward false faces, and that rarely settles well with Sloane. But the chancellor's . . . *authenticity,* for lack of a better word, also unsettles her.

"It is. Something."

"Let's talk for a moment. I want to lay it all on the table before the official talks begin, before we have a scribe-of-record and the messy work of figuring out the parameters of our treaty."

I will lay it all out for you, Sloane thinks. *I believe your way of life is naïve. I fear you will bring chaos to the galaxy. I think the only messy work here will be cleaning up the dung heap you've built by conjuring this terrible vacuum of power. We kept order. You will keep only disarray.*

She speaks no such truth, of course.

Instead, Sloane simply says: "I would rather sit back and enjoy the show, if you don't mind." It's a lie. It's very difficult to enjoy Gabdorin music, which sounds not unlike a chorus of animals caught in various sharp-toothed traps struggling and failing to find freedom.

But the chancellor is persistent. "The show is part of it. The galaxy is a myriad, wonderful place. It is home to such wild miscellany. Present here is *individuality.* Something the Empire, I feel, has missed. If there is to be any kind of treaty, it is vital we preserve what makes life in this galaxy special. It is critical we preserve all of what you will see on display. All ways of existence. All the choices for all of us."

"Oh, absolutely," Sloane lies. Every molecule of her body is straining not to taunt the chancellor with the news that soon, an attack will
be incoming, and all the ships in the Empire's fleet will make short
work of this world—and that the New Republic will fall to its knees.
Individuality is a fine crusade if you're an idiot. Joining the collective
and supporting the greater good through Imperial control—that takes
true grit and real wisdom. She cannot say those things, so, instead, she
picks a different scab. "I don't see your Alderaanian princess here."

That scores a direct hit. The chancellor shifts uncomfortably in her
seat. "Leia is ill today, I'm afraid."

"A shame. I often feel that she and I were matched—by the fates, I
mean—against each other. She and I, dueling across the holo-waves. I
would have liked to have met her in person."

"Yes. She is the voice and the face of the New Republic."

"As I am of my Empire."

Just then the door behind them opens. A man stands there with
dark hair and a rust-red Republic flight suit. He leans on his cane and
then looks to Sloane—it takes their eyes meeting to realize who she's
even looking at.

Wedge Antilles.

He's the pilot she had laid out before her in the satrap's palace on
Akiva. The way he leans on his cane, she sees now that she truly broke
him. An odd worm of guilt crawls through her heart. He was just a
pawn in this game. She was, too, in a sense, and she regrets what happened to him.

The way he looks at her, he wishes his eyes were spears—each of
them piercing clean through her chest. He doesn't just want to kill her.
He wants to *end* her. She doesn't blame him. And at least that anger
tells her that she helped break his body, but not his spirit.

Good for him. Fool though he may be for serving the Republic.

The chancellor excuses herself and hurries over to him. They speak
in hushed tones. But the tension there is difficult to hide.

To Adea, Sloane whispers: "The chancellor appears rattled."

"She does, a little."

"Something that pilot said is upsetting her."

Mothma throws her a glance, then pulls the pilot back outside the room. Adea says, "I'm sure it's nothing."

"They may know something."

"They couldn't."

"Why?"

"Because they're not smart enough," Adea says.

Something about that sticks between Sloane's teeth. *Not smart enough.* She prides herself on being smart. The smartest in the room. But a trickle of doubt begins to creep into her mind—

She has little time to ruminate upon it, though, because the chancellor comes back into the room. Mothma is now off kilter, though she's straining not to show that to Sloane. "Apologies," the chancellor says.

"Is everything all right?"

"Of course. Why wouldn't it be?"

Gallius Rax watches the events in Hanna City.

He has no special access. He doesn't need it. The chancellor controls the HoloNet, now, and is broadcasting her Liberation Day across the waves.

It is quite the show. A demonstration from an arrogant bird: *Look how pretty my tail feathers are.*

The parade ends and slowly they clear the Senate Plaza. A stage is elevated from the stone—it rises not with any new technology but by men who dutifully crank old wooden handles, turning ancient stone gears. Chandrila is an old world. Modern tastes clash with a long history.

If they're bringing out the stage, then soon it will be time to fill it.

Which means it is also time to orchestrate the plan. He summons Grand Moff Randd to his chamber.

"Sir," Randd says, compliant and cold.

"Prepare the fleets to move on my command." Rax hands over a datapad. "When I give the say-so, direct them to these coordinates. All of them. Coordinate with Borrum, too. We'll need everyone on the ground there with everything we have. *Everything.*"

"But, sir, this isn't—"

"I know. Just do it."

"Does Sloane know?"

"She will. They all will. In fact, summon them. I wish to meet with my Shadow Council." He waves his hand. "Now go."

In the meantime, Rax turns his attention back to the events in Hanna City. It is time to watch his opera unfold.

CHAPTER THIRTY-SEVEN

I've failed.

Those two words race each other in the front of Han Solo's mind like a couple of podracers jockeying for position.

He came out here, leaving Leia and the New Republic, for one reason, and that was to do what nobody else wanted to do: *save Kashyyyk.* Leaving Leia behind like that was hell on him. But she understood. She knows what it is to have a cause bigger than yourself. If anybody gets it, Leia does.

I've failed.

Even as the gruff vice admiral commands stormtroopers to pick him up—which they do, handily—he plays through the list of failures. He trusted Imra, but she was bad news and he was too dumb to see it. The Empire snapped up Chewie, and Han got away. And then he was close, *so close,* to fixing it all: They fought their way across half a planet and took out Lozen Tolruck just in time for him to bomb the planet to splinters and mud. And, he reminds himself woefully, *Wookiee blood.*

It's all my fault.

The others are in shackles now: the bounty hunter, the commando, the ex-Imperial, and once again and worst of all, his copilot, Chewie. They were a good team. They did right by him. They did right by Chewie.

All of them are shoved forward, pressed against the wall. Solo included. Behind him, the vice admiral steps up. His breath smells like rot. The man stinks of sweat. *These Imperials have really let themselves go.*

The vice admiral growls in his ear: "My name is Vice Admiral Domm Korgale. You should get to know that name, villain. I'm going to be the one to deliver you into the Empire's embrace. You will make a most excellent bargaining chip at the table. You alone will buy me a seat."

"*Tooska chai mani,*" Solo says—a Huttese curse that's about the worst he can muster. Something about the man's mother and a Tusken Raider chief. "Don't you get it? You lost. You're not the other side in a war, fella. You're *criminals.*"

"Then as criminals, you won't mind if I spare you but execute your friends? Here and now?" Korgale twirls his fingers in the air, and the stormtroopers press blaster barrels against the backs of the heads of those pressed against the wall.

"It's been fun, everyone," Sinjir says, cheek smashed against the wall.

Jom and Jas stay silent, struggling futilely against their captors.

Chewie rumbles a low growl.

"I know, pal. We tried."

From across the room, one of the comm officers calls over: "Sir! We have an incoming ship dropping out of hyperspace—"

"What?" Korgale says. Then his voice lifts: "I asked for reinforcements. Perhaps now that Orlan is dead, they've listened."

"It's not one of ours. It's a freighter. Old Corellian make—"

Han's eyes jolt open. He looks to Chewie as she says the rest:

"A YT-1300."

He mouths the words to his copilot: *The* Falcon?

But who the hell is piloting it? Wexley?

"The craft is hailing us," the comm officer says.

"Put it through," Korgale says, "but then launch a contingent of TIE fighters. We must take no chances."

Over the comm comes a voice that lifts Han Solo's heart the same time as it sinks it:

"This is Leia Organa of the New Republic. You will stand down your ships or you will be destroyed."

Korgale's paunch shudders as he offers one stiff laugh. "One craft? She thinks she can take down three Star Destroyers with one rattle-trap freighter? Is she daft? Let the TIE fighters cut her to pieces. She's not even a pilot. She's a *politician*."

Han grins ear-to-ear. "You've never seen a politician like this be-fore." But in the back of his mind, he can't help but wonder:

How *does* she plan on doing this alone?

Evaan Verlaine gives her a look. No, not *a* look—but rather, *that* look. An all-too-familiar arched eyebrow and smug smirk and a gaze preg-nant with the question: *What have you gotten us into this time, Prin-cess?*

Leia isn't quite sure. For a moment, she feels overexposed: a tooth without its enamel, a ship without its armor, like she alone is dangling out in space on a tether. *Maybe this wasn't a very good idea . . .*

Dead ahead, the *Dominion* begins spitting TIE fighters into the black.

"Leia, we're about to have company," Evaan says. She doesn't mean the TIE fighters. Sensors indicate incoming ships.

A dozen stars behind the *Falcon* zoom close—stars that aren't stars at all. Ships. Starfighters. *X-wings.*

She actually flinches as they swoop down out of hyperspace and zip past the *Falcon* on all sides, their cannons flashing. A TIE fighter rockets forth going the other direction, fire belching from its top just before it implodes. Over Leia's comms comes the voice of Wedge Antilles:

"This is PhantomLeader," says Wedge Antilles. "Phantom Squadron's got your back, General Organa. Let's save the day and bring it home."

Korgale sucks in a small intake of breath: a moment of weakness that Solo detects. A moment of fear. Han likes that moment.

He likes the moment that comes next even better.

Because Korgale snarls, "A dozen X-wings and a crippled freighter is all they've brought? We have *three* Star Destroyers. Call the *Vitiator* and the *Neutralizer.* Time to eliminate this cloud of flies before—"

Another ship comes into view.

What follows is the moment Solo *truly* enjoys, as the vice admiral makes a tiny little whimper sound. Like vermin caught in a trap.

The comms come alive with the sound of Admiral Ackbar's voice: "This is New Republic Fleet Admiral Ackbar, commanding the Mon Cala cruiser *Home One.* Surrender or be destroyed."

Korgale paces. Nostrils flaring. Cheeks puffing out. He speaks to no one but himself as he runs through the motions: "We . . . we can't surrender. We must mount a vigorous defense. G5-623 is *our* world, and it's still three ships against their one—"

Chewbacca is apparently done with it. All of it. The Wookiee roars, swinging his head around and connecting with the helmet of the stormtrooper holding the hairy beast against the wall. The trooper cries out and tumbles to the floor and the Wookiee kicks away from the wall, charging toward Korgale. The other stormtroopers turn, rifles up.

They're gonna shoot Chewie.

Han gets underneath the trooper closest to him and slams the man up and forward—he careers into the next. Sinjir ducks and darts out with his foot, hooking it behind another Imperial's knee and dropping him. Jom and Jas take out the last together, each crushing the trooper between them—when he falls, they stomp and kick until he's still.

Chewie completes his trajectory.

He hits Korgale like a crashing ship.

The man bleats and falls. The Wookiee roars in triumph.

Outside, on the viewscreen, the X-wings swoop and pivot even as the *Vitiator* moves closer and the *Neutralizer* moves in beyond that. One of the Phantom Squadron ships is shredded by a trio of TIE fighters on its tail even as the *Falcon* cuts in and takes them out—a few seconds too late.

Solo knows that Korgale was right: They *do* have three Star Destroyers. The odds are still against them. It's like a long game of sabacc. When the chips are down and you have squat for cards, what can you do?

You even the odds.

And the way Han likes to even the odds is by cheating.

Jas, panting, stands next to him, her hair plastered down on her thorny head-horns. "What's our next move, Solo?"

"Won't be long before we've got stormtroopers all over this bridge," he says. "We need to take control of this bridge and lock it down, but first that means we gotta find a way to get these binders off—"

Chewie yawps, then bares his teeth as he wrenches his arms apart. The shackles snap like they were made of brittle candy instead of steel.

"That works," Solo says.

Chewie moves to help Solo and the others with their cuffs. Jom says, "I got the door," and then heads over to lock it down. Sinjir and Jas reapply the cuffs to the knocked-out stormtroopers. But one person is missing:

Korgale. He's nowhere on the bridge. That pig wriggled away.

No time to worry about that now.

"Let's figure out how to fly a Star Destroyer," Solo says, clapping his hands. "Time to properly even the odds. And somebody get on that comm, make sure those X-wings don't try to blow us up in the process!"

The battle rages for a time. Wedge's Phantom Squadron—comprised of a scattered remnant of washouts, burnouts, and capable freaks—deftly cuts apart the swarms of TIE fighters, though they lose a few. The *Falcon* flies true and soon Leia feels like the ship is a part of her. There are even moments when she can feel the battle unfolding around her in space—invisibly, as if all of it is a warm stream in which she has dipped her hand. The Force, she knows, is guiding her. A little bit, at least.

Luke will be happy.

Eventually, the compromised *Dominion* begins firing on the others, and the *Vitiator* breaks in half in a sharp knife slash of light before the vacuum of space crushes what remains.

"Your deranged plan worked," Evaan says, smirking.

"Then maybe it wasn't so deranged."

"Oh, no, it was full-bore moonbat, Princess. They always say it's Han who has the good luck, but I'm starting to think it's you."

The Force was with me today, she thinks. *But better yet, my friends were here.* And in this galaxy, maybe that's all one truly needs.

Ackbar's voice fills the air: "The *Vitiator* is down and we are receiving a full surrender from the crew of the *Neutralizer.*"

"Well done, Admiral. And thanks for coming when I called." Leia called him after she called Wedge. It was a gamble, of course; Ackbar could've stopped her. But he came. And because of that, she knows this will cost him. It will cost her, too, and Wedge as well. As it should. This happened outside politics. No vote made this happen. Nobody sanctioned putting these ships and these people at risk. Even Ackbar working with a skeleton crew on board his own ship and Wedge calling on a stable of forgotten pilots—many thought to be already out to pasture—won't pass easy muster with Mon Mothma. But that is a problem for Future Leia. Right now, the Leia of the Present is very pleased with herself.

And it's time to see her husband. She brings the *Falcon* in for an easy landing inside one of the *Dominion*'s hangar bays. A few stormtroopers offer casual resistance, fruitlessly firing their blasters.

The *Falcon*'s turrets make short work of them.

And with that, Evaan says, "I'll leave you to it. Give Han a kiss for me. Unless he still has that beard. Because really? Ugh."

Leia laughs. She steps off the ship.

The door at the end of the hangar bay whisks open.

A man stands framed by the light behind him. He steps forward, but she already knows who it is: It is her husband, Han Solo. One blaster in each hand. Suddenly, there's movement from the side as one of the stormtroopers clambers up over a crate, his rifle aimed right at her—

Solo's pistols flash fast and the trooper falls.

Han walks toward her. She leans against the *Falcon,* smiling.

"Your Worshipfulness," he yells, seeing her.

"Hello, scoundrel," she calls back in return.

"Making me walk the whole hangar, huh?"

"I like watching you walk."

"You okay?" he asks.

"I am now. I'm very angry at you," she says.

"Hey. I'm angry with *you.* Making me rescue you like this?"

Incredulous, she says, "You? Rescue me? This was *me* rescuing *you,* you hotheaded, thick-skulled ruffian."

He smirks.

"I love you."

She rolls her eyes. "Just kiss me already, you dolt."

He does. They swoop each other up in an embrace so tight, it feels to her that for a moment they are not only together, but they are one being that will never again be separate. As they pull away, his hand moves to her midriff and holds steady there. "How's our baby?"

"He's fine."

"He? Oh, he's a he now? I told you it'd be a boy. Didn't I? We're gonna need to think of a name for the little bandit—"

"Don't you dare say he's going to be a bandit. He'll be an angel."

"Nothing wrong with bandits."

"Nothing wrong with angels."

"Kiss me again," he says.

And she does.

CHAPTER THIRTY-EIGHT

Norra gazes out over a sea of people. Thousands of them have gathered here in the plaza to see Chancellor Mon Mothma speak and to hear the stories of those liberated from the prison on Kashyyyk. Next to Norra stands Brentin—she grabs for his hand and gives it a little squeeze, and finds his palm slick with sweat. He looks pale. He bites at his lip and stares out over the crowd, but not *at* the crowd—rather, he's gazing out at a fixed point in the precise middle of nowhere. She fears she looks the same. A host of emotions runs through her: anxiety at having to speak in front of a crowd, the certainty that when she does she will probably throw up all over her formal naval attire, and finally, worry over Temmin because he's still not here and that means he may truly be angry with her.

It's not just them on the stage. The chancellor has stepped out in front of dozens of those liberated from Golas Aram's strange prison ship. And other officials have come, too: senators, generals, admirals. She doesn't see Ackbar present, but she does see Commodore Agate, whose face wears that trademark pride and sorrow, both born of war. Norra thinks that she sees General Madine on the end—and next to him, the senator from Chandrila, Durm Harmodius.

Quite the company she's keeping (after all, she is a deserter).

If she looks over the sea of faces, the plaza is ringed in by the white clifflike buildings of the Hanna City center, and beyond that, the sea. Dead ahead is a series of dark lines: balconies, climbing the Old Gather-House like a ladder, all reserved for diplomats, senators, and other emissaries so they can view the day's celebrations.

At the very top, she sees the balcony reserved for the Imperial monster, Admiral Rae Sloane. Norra tries not to think about her. She tries not to think about any of it. Not that woman, not Temmin, not how she feels like she needs to run away before she pukes.

Mon Mothma steps up, flanked by her two advisers: the Togruta, Auxi Kray Korbin, and the Chandrilan man, Hostis Ij.

On each side and over the heads of the crowd float cam droids: holo-lenses extended, some snapping static shots with blue flashes, others capturing events as they unfold. Norra tries not to look at those.

Mon Mothma steps up to an old stone podium—it's chalky and white, crumbling around the edges but still surviving the ages.

"Hello, Chandrila. Hello, New Republic. And greetings to the galaxy beyond. I am Chancellor Mon Mothma—"

Applause erupts.

The applause roars, and Temmin yells over it to the guard blocking his way into the plaza: "I need to see my mom! She's on stage!"

Behind him, Mister Bones sways back and forth, impatient.

"Plaza's full," the guard says as the crowd dies down. "You are going to have to wait."

"I can't wait. This is *important*."

"I'm sure it is." Here, the guard steps forward, pushing Temmin back a little. "And even still, it's going to have to wait, kid."

"I'm not a—" *Never mind that.* "People may be in danger." That is an assessment he makes, though he doesn't really know that it's true. He *does* know that something is up, though. And danger is usually the outcome of this kind of mystery. *"Please."*

"Danger, huh?" The guard pulls a baton off his leg. Its white tip sparks blue. It's a shock-lance. He thrusts it toward Temmin—not to hit him, but to threaten him with it. "Step back, kid. Or I'll use—"

A whine of servomotors fills the air as Mister Bones dances forward, grabbing the guard's arm and twisting it upward—the shock-lance jabs hard under the man's golden helmet. The man cries out, stuttering, as he falls. His heels twitch and jump against the ground, though the rest of him is still.

"Uh-oh," Temmin says.

"THREAT TO MASTER TEMMIN NEUTRALIZED."

"At least you didn't kill him." From behind them, shouts reach Temmin's ears—and sure enough, here comes a trio of guards. Two with shock-lances, one with a blaster. "Come on, Bones!"

Mon Mothma speaks:

"—the citizens on this stage represent the best the galaxy has to offer. Many of them are the original architects of the Rebellion, an Alliance of right-minded, freedom-seeking worlds who wanted all of us liberated from the leash-and-collar of an Empire that subjugated countless systems, maintaining order through brute force and callous autocracy. That time is over and the Empire's edge has gone dull."

More applause.

Out there in the crowd, Norra sees movement. Her pilot's eye is trained to see such things: In the deep black of space, it's vital to know what light is a star and what is an enemy ship coming out of light-speed. Here, it's like seeing a tremor in the gathered throng: She can't quite make out what's happening, but she spies the jostled bodies and the turning heads.

The chancellor continues: "Slowly but surely, the Empire is being pushed back—planet by planet, system by system. Its time is dwindling, and where it crumbles, the New Republic rises from the ruin to collect the pieces and rebuild what they had damaged. And note that I say *damaged,* not *destroyed*—the Empire left us reeling, yes, but what they did was not permanent. The way is not shut. The path forward is clear and it is ours."

There. Someone is cutting through the crowd. She spies the golden helmets of the Senate Guard following after—

Wait. It's not some*one* cutting through the crowd.

It's two people.

One of them isn't a person. It's a droid. A droid she recognizes.

Mister Bones. Oh no. No, no, no. Not now. *Temmin, what have you done?* Now she sees him, too—the tousle of hair in a topknot. He looks to her. Their eyes meet. He's yelling something and waving his arms about, but it doesn't matter. The applause is thunderous again, a vibrant roar that swallows all other sound.

Sloane stares out over the balcony's edge, her elbows down, her chin resting on steepled fingers. The chancellor goes on and on. Freedom this, democracy that, never once acknowledging that the greatest threat the galaxy faces is not from Imperial order but from its absence.

All she can do is hope that the attack will soon commence. She knows Rax will be watching—this entire monkey show is being broadcast across the HoloNet. Her jaw tightens and she prays he has this under control.

Commence attack already, she wishes. As if her thoughts can be broadcast through time and through space. *The time is now.*

"We have lost many along the way, but today is not a look back at what we've sacrificed but a look forward to the future," Mon Mothma says. "A future that we now possess thanks to those liberated from the Imperial black-site prison: heroes like Garel's once-governor, Jonda Jae-

Talwar; the surgeon consul of Hosnian Prime, Plas Lelkot, who helped hide Imperial refugees in his own château; the radio operator Brentin Wexley from Akiva, who single-handedly transmitted our message across the Outer Rim and whose own wife, Norra, led the team to rescue him and all these others . . ."

Norra hears her name but it's a distant sound, a noise lost to the weight of deep water. All she can do is watch her son struggle against the tide of people. She snaps out of it and turns to Brentin to tell him—

But what she sees makes no sense. Brentin has his arm up and extended out.

In his hand is a small pistol: a three-shot hold-out blaster.

He points it right at Chancellor Mon Mothma.

Norra screams and grabs his arm, yanking it upward—

But it's too late.

The blaster fires.

No!

Temmin sees his own father draw something—a matte-black pistol, small and concealable. As he points it at the chancellor, Temmin sees that his father is not alone. All the liberated captives have them.

His mother sees it, too. She grabs for the gun—

It goes off just as someone tackles Temmin. Pain coruscates through him as one of the batons jabs hard into his side. His teeth clack and his tongue feels thick. For a few moments, his body seems like nothing more than a sack of meat, and the guard flips him over—

Bones grabs the guard and flings him backward like he's not much more than an old ratty poppet-doll.

Two more guards advance, and Bones meets them, blades out.

A flash of white cloth and the chancellor falls.

Norra twists Brentin's arm upward so that he can't fire another shot—and he spins to meet her. His face is a mask of horror. It's as if he can't believe what he just did. His mouth is open in a hopeless *oh*, eyes glistening with tears. He mouths, *I'm sorry*, then he drives a knee into her stomach—

"Brentin," she cries.

He slams the gun down on the back of her head and she drops.

Norra rolls over, groaning. The stage is chaos. She realizes now, only too late, how her husband is not alone in his act—the other captives also have pistols up and out, and they're firing at those gathered on stage and into the crowd. Searing bolts cross open space. Someone falls near her—one of the chancellor's own advisers, Hostis, drops hard on his side, a serpent of smoke rising from a cooked hole in his head. Norra strains to look around her. Brentin is nowhere. Panic is everywhere. One of the liberated steps in front of her—it's the first one the chancellor mentioned, Jonda Jae-Talwar, a tall woman with white hair. Her face is a mask of unrecognizable rage as she fires into the crowd.

Norra grabs the woman's leg and yanks hard. The traitor cries out and drops onto her back, the air blasting out of her lungs. It takes little effort to twist the pistol out of her grip—

On the woman's face, an odd moment of clarity passes in front like a cloud clearing away from the sun. She says something, something that's hard to hear over the sound of blasters and screams and thundering crowds. Something that might be, "What have I done?"

Norra doesn't know how to answer her.

The only answer she can supply is a straight fist to the woman's nose. Jae-Talwar's eyes flutter and she goes unconscious.

Norra gets up, then almost falls—a fresh starburst of pain radiates out from the base of her skull where Brentin hit her. Her vision goes double, then triple, then blurry once more. Ahead she sees a white crumpled shape: Mon Mothma, still on the ground. And ahead is Commodore Agate wrestling with one of the liberated, a Rodian man waving a pistol. Norra staggers toward them—

Flash. The pistol goes off. Agate's head snaps back. She screams, rocking hard against the podium as the Rodian man lifts the gun, aiming to finish the job. Norra now recognizes him as Esdo, once a senator's aide from Coruscant before ending up locked away in that prison ship—she rushes him, slamming him back. He falls. She kicks the gun away.

Agate is clutching at her face. Between the fingers, Norra sees the dark char and blistered skin. "Go," Agate hisses. "Get clear."

Norra nods. Ahead she sees the Togruta woman, Auxi, helping Mon Mothma up—*she's not dead,* Norra thinks. A small bit of good news on this dire, dread day. The chancellor's shoulder is wet with red.

Guards swarm the stage, firing stun blasts at the scattering liberated captives. Norra doesn't see Brentin anywhere.

She needs to find him. Now.

The epiphany that Sloane experiences is not one she expects, nor is it one she desires. As she watches the events unfold down below her balcony, she realizes grimly: *This is the attack Rax was planning.*

His fingerprints are all over it. How, she doesn't know. These rebels who returned from the prison have been . . . programmed in some way. Turned into traitors. Changed into killers.

It is genius.

And it disgusts her.

She says as much to Adea standing behind her even as Sloane cannot tear her eyes away from the chaos below. "This is not war," she says, her voice drawn out and ragged. "This is not *battle.* This is something else." *A test,* says a small voice inside her. "This is not how we conduct ourselves. This is how *they* do it. Insurgency and terror."

These were not the events Sloane figured she would witness today. Where are the ships? Where is her fleet, scouring Chandrila with sacred Imperial fire? But here it is, and deal with it, she must.

Mothma left her and Adea up here with a guard contingent: treating Sloane like an honored guest, but still taking precautions. Sloane turns. Five New Republic guards remain. And two of her own—the red-cloaked Royal Guardsmen stand silent and still.

Adea hovers nearby. Trembling just slightly.

To the two Royal Guards, Sloane gives a gentle nod.

The guards of the New Republic have no chance. Those picked to serve Palpatine and wear the elite red cloaks are blank soldiers filled only with the knowledge of how to defend and how to kill. A swoosh of their cloaks and a spin of the blades and in less than ten seconds, the bodies of the fallen Republic guards litter the floor.

Sloane tells those redcloaks: "Go. Clear the way and secure my ship. Adea and I will be along shortly thereafter."

They say nothing. They do not even offer a nod.

They simply do as commanded.

"We need a plan," Sloane says to Adea.

"As you said, the guards will clear the way—"

"*No*," Sloane says with a sharp rebuke. "A larger plan. This *aberration* of an attack must not become our dominant mode of doing business, Adea. We must deal with Rax quickly. *Mercilessly*. If he is given time, he will spin this as only he can. He will attempt to convince the others that it was sensible, a necessary evil."

"What if they do? Surely the New Republic will be left reeling—"

Sloane turns and again looks out over the balcony. Now she sees guards swarming the stage. The chancellor is up and disappearing in a circle of protectors. So, Mon Mothma is alive. Good. That woman must not die. She must kneel in fealty—that is the only fate Sloane will accept for the foolish chancellor.

"Don't be seduced by Rax," Sloane says, still watching below. Madness has seized the crowd beyond. "I was. Temporary idiocy on my part. I became complacent and now? *This* happened. We should've brought the fleet. We need to demonstrate martial ability. The Empire is a hammer striking down disorder, not a knife slipped between unsuspecting ribs. Rax must be arrested. And then executed. I will be the one to do it."

Adea says nothing.

The silence from her is deafening.

And then comes the second unwanted epiphany.

"Adea," Sloane says, turning toward her assistant. Her assistant stands there, one of the guards' own blaster rifles in her hand. Its barrel points right at Sloane's head. Adea isn't trembling anymore. She is firm-footed and sure of her actions. Sloane sighs. *Not her. Please, not her.* "I'm too late, aren't I? We were both fools, Adea."

"Rax is the way forward. The Empire must be willing to change. We must be willing to do anything to show the galaxy what it is to defy us."

"Don't point that weapon at me, Adea."

"This was a test. He wanted you to embrace it. To see things his way. It didn't have to be like this. You could have helped him rule. And I would be with you both, helping reshape the Empire and the galaxy beyond."

"I do not want the Empire reshaped by his hands. And I don't want you reshaped by him, either. We worked well together, you and I. You trusted in my vision. Didn't you?" Now, though, she understands. Adea has been betraying her all along, hasn't she? Giving intel on her to Rax. It's how he knew where she was on Coruscant. How he knew about her meeting with Mas Amedda. About *everything*. Maybe there's still hope. "Put that rifle down. I'll give you no more chances, Adea. Put. It. Down."

But Adea does no such thing.

She is resolute.

She is his.

So be it.

Sloane feints left, then moves right. Adea isn't combat-trained—the rifle follows Sloane's first movement and fires. The blaster bolt tears through the space where Sloane was moments before.

Sloane drives a fist into Adea's kidneys.

The girl cries out, tries to wheel on Sloane with the rifle—

Which is exactly the wrong thing to do. Sloane easily pivots the weapon out of the girl's hands and fires a bolt point-blank into her chest.

Adea's eyes go wide, and in them Sloane sees a young women she trusted. A woman she thought could've been her daughter in another lifetime.

Adea's lips work soundlessly.

She falls.

Sloane takes a moment.

And in that moment, rage surges through her like acid.

I am going to kill Gallius Rax.

Sloane leaves the room, rifle in her hand.

Brentin . . .

Norra fights against the crowd. They're panicked. They should be. She is, too. From somewhere, she hears someone weeping. Then more blasterfire. She tries to imagine what happened and what is happening even still, but she can't get her head around it—to see these captives held up on a well-deserved pedestal only to turn around and attack is incomprehensible.

Brentin . . .

Her husband is part of it. He tried to assassinate the chancellor. Who else would he have attacked if she hadn't stopped him?

And where did he go?

She has to find him.

To stop him, yes. But also to *understand* what happened. To look in his eyes once more and try to find out if the man who did this thing is still her husband—or if her husband is even there at all.

Brentin, why?

She fights her way across the plaza. Looking for her husband. But also looking for her son. Temmin knew. He tried to warn her.

Now where is he?

Get higher.

She's a pilot. She needs *height,* like a falcon scouting for prey. She pushes her way through to the Old Gather-House, then laps a couple of steps, almost running out of breath as she does. She sees a body in the hall—an Ottegan senator. Eyes as glassy and dead as a droid's. That means more captives were here, too, doesn't it? Of course they were. They weren't all on stage. Some of them were probably here. Watching. *Waiting.*

Norra moves on. Nothing to be done here.

She finds her way to one of the now empty terraces. The crowd has already started to disperse below, and the guards are locking down the plaza. Good. Hopefully they'll catch as many of these people as they can.

Someone needs to get answers.

And then, Norra sees him.

Brentin Wexley—to the far right of the plaza. He's crossing one of the skybridges, heading in the direction of the landing platforms.

Norra grits her teeth and moves in that direction.

"Stop."

Temmin stands behind his father as the man flees to the end of the skybridge—beyond, hundreds of landing platforms ring the far side of Hanna City, and beyond them waits the sea.

His father, pistol still in hand, freezes.

Temmin has no weapon. He's alone, too. Bones is gone, left back in the crowd to distract the guards so that Temmin could flee.

Slowly, Brentin turns around.

"Tem," Dad says. It sounds like Dad. His voice wavers.

"Mom was right. You aren't you."

"I am. But . . ." His father's words die on the vine before bearing fruit. He just stands there. Then he slowly raises the pistol. Almost as if he doesn't want to. As if something is lifting his arm—an invisible string tugging on his wrist. Or maybe Temmin is just imagining that. Maybe Dad *wants* to kill him. Either way, Temmin stands there. Chin up and out. Trying not to cry and failing miserably because he feels his cheeks tighten and his eyes go wet. He has no weapon to point, so instead he points an accusing finger.

"You killed people."

"Don't say that."

"You did. You're the Empire. Were you always? Was it all just a lie? Playing the good guy so we didn't know how bad you were?"

"No. *No!* I was . . . I never . . ."

"Shoot me. Go ahead. You shot me once."

The gun wavers.

Brentin fights against it. The struggle is plain on his face—like he's battling himself. The pistol shakes violently in his hand as the arm bends at the elbow, slowly pointing the gun . . .

At his own head.

"No!" Temmin cries, bolting hard across the open space. He leaps, tackling his father as the blaster goes off. The gun clatters against the empty bridge. Brentin stares up at him with empty eyes—

No, no, no, don't die—

Those eyes blink. The shot missed. Temmin got there in time and now, Brentin is alive.

His father cries out and pistons a fist into Temmin's stomach. He shoves the boy off him and then flees, leaving his son behind gasping for air and sobbing there on the skybridge. *Dad . . .*

The guard with a cresting wave of blond hair and a little scar on the bottom of his chin stands there, staring down. Yupe Tashu, once-adviser to Emperor Palpatine, looks up, his chin slick with his own spit.

"Hello, guard," Tashu says, mush-mouthed.

The guard drops the gate keeping Tashu imprisoned.

"Here to kill me?" Tashu asks, then his words dissolve into mad laughter. His laughter becomes coughing, his body racked with spasms until he's left curled into a ball. He gasps for air and then says: "I heard blasterfire."

"You heard correctly. But you are not a target."

"Then what am I?"

"A free man."

More laughter rises out of him, and more lung-spasms after. "The darkness has saved me. Long have I pleaded with it."

"You may go. There is a ship waiting. Docking Platform E-22."

"And the other guests? Shale and Crassus and Pandion?"

"Pandion died, you fool. And now the others have joined him."

Tashu stands on quaking bird legs. "You murdered them?"

"I did."

"Why?"

"Because I was told to. Just as I was told to free you."

"And who told you this, guard?"

"Our new emperor. You are to serve him now."

Tashu's lip quivers. Palpatine was his everything. To serve someone else feels treasonous beyond the pale. The void awaits those who betray Palpatine—that much has always been clear. *The void awaits traitors.*

"I only serve Palpatine."

"Emperor Rax serves Palpatine, too. Now go."

Tashu nods. "Yes. Yes. It makes sense. It's part of a plan, isn't it? A plan I couldn't see? Sidious always had a plan . . ."

He cackles one last time, then hurries past the guard lest the strange man change his mind at the last moment. *I am free at last.*

Blast it! Norra is lost. The Old Gather-House is a maze. She thought she could cut through the center and come out on the seaside facing the landing platforms, but this is an old building—some of it is new, yes, but much of it was where the first settlers on Chandrila gathered to sleep, to eat, to meet. They lived whole lives here, and this building was not all built at once but rather one strata at a time—and now, Norra is wandering its channels, sure she's doubling back on herself. Didn't she just see that light panel? That crack in the wall? That same painting of the first polis meeting?

She spins around, finds a door—she hasn't tried this one, yet, has she? Norra hits the panel next to it with the heel of her hand—

It shushes open.

And Norra nearly runs into somebody.

"*You*," Norra says.

"*You*," Admiral Sloane says.

Norra straight punches her in the face.

Sloane is rocked, but recovers quickly even as a line of blood crawls from her nose like a fleeing worm. The admiral licks at the blood, then brings up a blaster rifle, firing it—

But Norra rolls to the other side of the door even as the air around her heats up, laser bolts popping craters in the far wall.

This is it. This is her chance. All her anger and fear refines to a laser focus. Because *of course* Sloane is here. That monster did all of this. What Brentin did on stage was not his own action—it was Sloane. She's the puppet master pulling strings. A sudden sinkhole of regret opens up inside Norra's gut, because if she had just *done her job* and killed this woman when she had a chance, none of this would've happened.

At least she can finish what she started.

Sloane comes through the door, rifle out. Norra drives her knee under the blaster—and the barrel of it whips back and catches Sloane in the face. The woman blinks, then ducks low and hard charges into Norra. *Wham.* It's like getting hit by a grav-train. The movement carries her against the far wall and her skull snaps back into the mortar, blasting new fireworks behind her eyes. Again she sees Sloane point the rifle—

Norra catches the barrel with her hands and points it away. *Pop, pop, pop,* more bolts take chunks out of the wall. Dust streams and flecks of stone rain into her hair and her eyes. She has no focus and she feels dizzied, so all she can do is harness her anger and use brute force—

A loud, guttural cry is ripped out of her as Norra yanks the rifle from Sloane's grasp—it gives way with such force it falls from her own hands, spinning away on the stone floor. She lunges after it.

But she can't reach it. Sloane catches Norra's collar and pulls her back just as her fingers find the cold steel of the rifle barrel. The Imperial whirls Norra hard into the wall, then drives a flurry of hard punches into her side. One after another after another. Norra tries to fight against it, but she's not practiced at this, not at hand-to-hand, and this woman attacks with the tenacity of an orbital strike.

"I remember you," Sloane seethes. "You should be dead."

"So . . . should . . . *you*," Norra gasps, then whips her head to the side, ratcheting her skull against the other woman's chin. It gives her room to move, room to *breathe*, room to feel like she's not about to die.

She doesn't rest long.

Norra launches herself bodily at the woman. The Imperial meets her with fists up, absorbing every blow Norra throws, so instead Norra goes for the dirty play—she stabs out with a foot and catches the Imperial admiral in the knee. The leg goes backward and Sloane cries out—

Yet even that doesn't end it. *Whap.* Norra's head rocks and she tastes blood as her lip splits under an assaulting fist. Another hit closes her eye behind fast-swelling bruise-flesh. She throws her own clumsy fist and Sloane ducks it, pumping a return fist into Norra's gut.

Oof. She gags and staggers. Sloane grabs her by a hank of her ashen hair and bangs Norra's head into the wall once, twice, three times. *Wham, wham, wham.* Every time, she feels her brain rattle in her skull, sharp shocks of light flashing as her teeth clack and her tongue tastes fresh blood—

I'm losing. I'm dying. I failed.

"Stop right there!" a voice echoes down the hall. A woman's voice, and then the sound of blasterfire fills her ears. Norra drops, sliding against the wall as Sloane bolts and Senate Guards hurry after, firing their weapons.

———

Sloane curses under her breath. She wasted too much time scrapping with that pilot—that woman is meaningless, and yet she stopped to fight her? Why? Anger taunted her. *Distracted* her. Now she's on the run from guards in a building whose layout is labyrinthine. Her nose might be broken. One of her teeth is loose. Worst of all, she tried snatching the blaster rifle on the way past—but it spun out of her grip as the guards fired on her.

And then, out of the gloom comes one ray of light.

She heads through a door and finds her way forward—

A skybridge leads out to the landing platforms. The platforms fill the distance, topping tall towers along the shore. Beneath them wait sand and stone and sea. Leaving this planet won't be easy, and at this point she's sure there will be some kind of blockade in orbit—they'll be combing every mote of stardust for a sign of her. And if they capture her? They'll throw her in a lightless pit. She will never again see her Empire, and Rax will be left to kick it farther into hell. But she has to try. If she leaves now, she may be able to seize on the chaos—they'll still be looking for her *here*, not *there*.

She hurries across the skybridge, pulling off her Imperial gray jacket as she runs, revealing the white undershirt beneath. The wind takes the jacket as she reaches the end of the bridge. It flutters away.

A voice, then, carried on the wind.

Someone calls for her.

Adea?

A foolish moment as she turns and looks to see who it is—

It's that woman again. The damnable pilot. Norra something-or-other.

Norra has the rifle.

She fires.

Sloane turns to run as the first bolt flashes past her ear—she can hear the *hiss-crackle* as it goes by. The second digs a furrow out of the ground.

The third blast doesn't miss.

Her back arches as the shot takes her. Sloane spins like a child's top, the clouds above her, then the sea, and then she's falling off the skybridge—her arms out, her fingers searching the sky for something to hold but finding nothing at all. Darkness draws her down, down, down.

CHAPTER THIRTY-NINE

Morning comes to Kashyyyk.

Jas sits at the top of the world, her legs dangling off a platform, her feet swinging like a child's as she scoops some kind of goop out of a bowl with her bare hands and into her mouth. *A Wookiee breakfast,* Solo said. *Made of kabatha guts.* She asked him just what a "kabatha" was, and his response: *Don't ask, just eat.* So, she eats.

Jas is used to eating whatever she can get her hands on. The job being the job, it means she can't always get her mouth around a proper meal. Protein cubes, polystarch, veg-meat: Whatever she can eat, she eats. (Once she ate barnacles off the side of a hachi farmer's spelt silo.)

Behind her, Wookiees move and work and settle in. They waste no time, those big rugs. They climb the wroshyr like it's no feat at all—they dig their claws into the wood and move like lightning traveling up and down the bark. They jump from branches, they duck in and out of knotholes, they swing from one tree to the next. It's quite a thing to behold.

Once in a while she looks down to remind herself how far up she's come. The ground isn't even visible from here. It's hidden beneath the mist—mist that, right now, blazes with the fire of the morning sun.

She hears Solo—he's talking to Leia, to Chewie, and she considers getting up and joining them. Then someone plunks down next to her: Sinjir.

He scoots to the edge, then pulls back. "Mother of moons, why are you sitting here? And why are you eating . . . *that*?"

"Why do you still have that mustache?"

"I quite like it."

"It looks like an animal lay down to die on your lip."

"You're really too blunt for your own good, you know."

She winks, then keeps eating.

The ex-Imperial settles in next to her, though not so close that his legs drape over the edge. "You staying?" he asks her.

"Here? No."

The Wookiees have been liberated from their inhibitor chips, and the three Star Destroyers bombing the planet have been put out of commission—one destroyed utterly—but the Imperials here will still have some fight in them. Dozens of settlements dot the surface, and smaller outposts mark the margins. Even now, Chewbacca is prepping teams of Wookiees to survey the damage and the Imperial holdouts.

"Solo and Leia are staying for a time," Sinjir says.

"They're invested. I'm not. We did the job. Now the job is over."

"We did good, you know."

"I know."

"It *feels* good to have done good."

"I know that, too."

He leans in, eyes narrowed to suspicious lines. "So why do I get the sense that you're holding back on me?"

"I'm not holding anything back." But his scrutiny picks her apart, like a child plucking the legs off a beetle. "Fine, I'm holding something back."

"Spit it out."

"But I'm eating it," she says around a mouthful of goop.

"Not the *food,* the *secret* thing."

"Oh." She swallows. It's like pushing a clot of wet concrete down her throat. Jas smacks her lips a few times before saying: "I'm leaving."

"Leaving what?"

"The team. The crew. Whatever you call us."

"You're breaking up the band." He *tsks.*

"I am breaking up the band."

He sighs. "I was thinking about doing the same, honestly."

"Why?"

"Oh, you first, Emari."

"I have to get back to work."

"The job calls?"

"My debts call." *Not even* my *debts,* she thinks. Sugi's. And the deal with Rynscar haunts her, suddenly. *They'll want my head if I don't pay.* "I've been away from that for too long. I'll see if the NR has jobs. If not, someone will. It's a zoo out there and someone needs to catch the animals."

"If you'll still work for the NR, why not just stay with Norra?"

Jas shrugs. "She has her husband, her son. I feel like *if* she keeps doing what she's doing, then it'll be more of *this*—" She sweeps her arms to encompass not just the planet Kashyyyk but also what they did here: liberation with no cost to anyone but themselves. "And less of the get-paid-for-work business. If the NR won't have me—the scum and villainy of the world is still thick with rivalries. I'll get paid one way or the other."

"I'll miss you."

"Don't be mawkish. It doesn't suit you. Your turn. Why leave?"

"I . . . feel good about what we did."

"That's an odd answer."

"Well, I want to keep the feeling! I don't want to *complicate* it. If I stay with this fancy new government, eventually they're going to want me to do things I'm trying not to do. I am, quite frankly, tired of following orders."

"Fair." She arches an eyebrow. "What then? Travel the space lanes, having adventures? Settle down with your boy toy and a couple of purra-birds as pets?"

"Both? Neither?" Another sigh. "I really don't know."

"You are *takask wallask ti dan*. A man without a star."

"Oh, please. Some old saying. Go on now, tell me what it means."

"My aunt used to say it. She ran a crew of her own, and whenever she had to replace someone, or use someone for one purpose or another, she always said she looked for *takask wallask ti dan*—a man without a star. Someone without a home, without purpose."

"That's depressing."

"But is it true?"

He harrumphs, then idly twists his mustache. She bats his hand away from it and he frowns.

"You could come with me," she says. "Turns out, I could use a man without a star."

"I *would* make an excellent bounty hunter."

"Don't get cocky."

"That's like telling the rain not to fall." He puts his hands behind his head and lies back. "I would join you, but I don't think your calling is my calling, either. Maybe my calling is drunken-but-lovable rake. Impossibly handsome Chandrilan layabout. Charming house-husband, worthless but for his chiseled cheekbones and his whiplash wit."

"Try it on. See if it fits."

"I may." He sits back up. "Is this goodbye, then? Are you leaving right from here? Or can I expect a ride?"

"I'll head back to Chandrila. I'm sure everyone will be all . . ." She makes a face. "*Warm and fuzzy* in the aftermath of Liberation Day. So if you want one last ride in the *Halo*, I'm offering. We can tell Norra together."

"Thank you, magnanimous bounty hunter. What about *your* boy toy?" Sinjir gestures unsubtly with his head toward the commando, Jom Barell, working one platform away, helping pack up thermal detonators in a harness sling. "I think he came back to Irudiru for you and you alone. Broke rank and everything."

"We have to be done. We had fun. That has to be it. I need this bone to make a clean break. It'll heal faster that way." *For him, or for you?* she asks herself. She sneers. "I don't want some stray trailing after me. I don't owe him. He made his choices and now I'm making mine."

"I really will miss you."

"Fine. I will . . . miss you, too."

He leans his head on her shoulder.

He knows why she's come over, so he just gets it out of the way. Jom doesn't even finish bolting shut the detonator box and he says over his shoulder: "I know, you've come to let me down gently."

"I don't do anything gently," Jas says. He can't tell if her tone is playful or not.

He turns and grabs a leaf-fiber rag, wiping his hands on it before tucking its corner in his pocket. "I want to tell you first that you were right."

"I know."

"Do you even know about what?"

She shrugs. "I'm right about everything."

"Keep telling yourself that, Emari." He laughs. "No, you were right that I came to Irudiru chasing you. Then I came here and we fought. And they took me and they took my eye—"

"I don't owe you that. Don't put that on me."

He shakes his head. "I'm not. That's the point. I stayed because it's the right thing. I gave up my eye because it's the right thing." Jom leans in now—she sees that he's aged over this trip. Dark shadows cross his face. He looks weathered, like wind-whipped leather. But he grins just the same. "And you stayed because it's the right thing, too. You're a better person than you think, Jas Emari."

"Don't make me kill you, Jom."

"All this is me saying, I get it. We're done. It's good. I'm staying behind with the Wookiees. See if I can't help them."

"Good luck, Jom."

"You too. I'll see you later, bounty hunter."

Leia knows she should worry. After all, here she is on a world not her own, a world still with one leg in an Imperial trap, and she's pregnant. Her back hurts. She's hungry all the time. What if something goes wrong? She knows she should be worried, and yet she isn't. In fact, the only thing that worries her is just how little worry she has.

She feels good. *Happy,* even. She has Evaan standing by. She has Han. She has her baby boy growing inside her. The Wookiees have their world back—almost, at least. And she's here because she listened to Luke. He told her to let go. To let the Force flow through her. She did. She's here.

All is well.

Chewie comes up behind Han again, growling playfully as he gives her husband a big lung-crushing hug. Solo winces and pulls away, laughing. "You big lug, I know, I know, we did it." She's never seen Chewie so happy. He has family here. Family they intend to help him find. And then she wonders: Will he stay? Now that the Wookiee has his home, will he remain behind on Kashyyyk? Han seems to think so. He told her last night as they slept under the stars, *He has his family, and we'll have ours.* The Wookiee gurgles and lopes off toward Kirratha, where they're loading crates into a handful of stolen LAIT ships. Then they'll take them from city to city, settlement to settlement, assessing the Imperial presence as they go. Leia told Han that she could maybe call in the New Republic, and he said, proud as a cockbird, *We don't need them.*

Maybe, she thinks, he's right.

But then Wedge hobbles over, followed by Evaan. Evaan tells her, "Princess. You have to see this."

Wedge takes her to a transceiver and patches in a HoloNet feed.

It's then she watches the Liberation Day events unfold in Hanna City. The liberated rebels turning on their rescuers. The chancellor, shot. Others, too: Madine, Agate, Hostis Ij. Some still alive, others dead—the data coming in tells a confusing story with conflicting reports. Chaos has seized the capital, that much is clear. Leia's heart breaks as she watches. Further, she can't help but feel that if she had stayed . . . she might have been one of those dead. Or maybe she could've helped stop it. A choice too late to make, with consequences that will forever remain unseen.

Just the same: The Empire did this. That much, she knows.

A hand falls on her shoulder. Her husband's. He stands behind her, shell-shocked. "We just . . . we rescued those people. I . . . don't . . . understand." He visibly swallows. It's rare to see him rattled. This has done it.

"I have to go back."

It takes him a moment to find his focus. But soon he's looking at her with clear eyes. He nods and says, "I know."

"I don't want to. I want to stay here. With you. With Chewie."

"I know that, too. But I have to go, too. I have to come home."

"You could stay here. I'd understand. Help Chewie—"

"Chewie's got this. He and the others have hard work ahead of them. My part is over, Leia. I want to be by your side through this. Whatever . . . this is. And whoever did this? They'll pay."

"I'm going to go prep the *Falcon*," she says.

"I won't be far behind. I have to say goodbye, first."

She cups his cheek, then kisses him. Sadness shines in her eyes. Not sadness for her. But sadness for him. Because this will be hard for him. She knows that. He won't admit it. But saying goodbye might kill him.

Leia lets her hand linger on his face, and then she's gone, heading toward their ships with Wedge in tow.

———

Chewie is there with Kirratha, picking up crates that it would take three of Han to lift. The Wookiee is as strong as these trees. Sometimes it feels like he's damn near as tall, too.

It doesn't take long for his copilot to see him there. Chewie and he have always been in sync. Okay, sure, sometimes Chewie goes one way and Han goes another but they always meet on the other side of things and at the end of every day, what needs to get done damn well *gets done.* They're partners. Have been for most of the life that Han can (or cares to) remember.

Chewie grunts and growls.

"Ah, you're doing fine, you big lunk."

Another growl. This one, a question.

"I, ahhh." Wow, this is harder than he thought. Han scuffs a heel and throws up his hands like he's folding at the sabacc table. "I thought this day would come later, Chewie, but something's happened and—"

The Wookiee steps up and nods, rumbling a soft response. Chewie understands. Even before Han says it, Chewie gets it. In sync yet again to no one's surprise. Chewie knows that Han has to go. And what's the first thing that the gargantuan hair-beast does? The Wookiee offers to come along right now. Han waves both hands and shakes his head as vigorously as he can, even waggling his finger up in his friend's shaggy face.

"No. *No!* You have to stay here. We fought like hell for this and now . . . this is yours. Okay? All yours. This is home. You got people here and I want you to find them. You hear me? That's my last demand. No arguments." Chewie rumbles but Han reiterates, more firmly this time: "I *said* no arguments. You be with your family. I have to go start mine."

A moment of silence stretches out between them and deep in the space between Han's heart and his gut he wants to seize on the desire that lives there—he wants to tell Chewie, *Just kidding, let's go, pal, get on board the ship and let's see what trouble we can cook up.* Then they'll race off together to Malastare or Warrin Station or back to that dusty Mos Eisley cantina to pick up some other wayward dust-farmer kid . . . and then when he gets home and his baby, his *son* is born, Chewie will be right there doing whatever needs doing because that's who Chewie is.

But he doesn't say any of that.

Chewie hugs him and purrs.

"I'll be back. We're not done, you and I. We'll see each other again. I'm gonna be a father and no way my kid won't have you in his life."

One more bark and yip as Chewie pets his head.

"Yeah, pal. I know." He sighs. "I love you, too."

CHAPTER FORTY

This is nowhere.

At least, not anywhere Sloane can identify.

Out there is the consumptive void of space. No planets, no space stations, no other ships. Nothing and nowhere.

The little cargo ship is the only thing out here. Sloane cuts the engines. It drifts. The ship could be her tomb, she realizes.

Every breath she pulls through her chest feels like she's inhaling broken glass. At least the bleeding has stopped. As she shifts in her seat, her pants peel away with a crackle as the tacky seal of dried blood breaks.

Survive. Fight. Get Rax.

She ponders opening a comm channel. In her head she conjures a message to Rax—a bitter threat that tells him she's coming for him, even though truly, she's dying here in the void. He will always be forced to look over his shoulder in case she might be sneaking up behind him with a whetted blade. It would be a wonderful curse to pass along. A small castigation sent preemptively from beyond the grave.

Her finger hovers over the button.

Sloane's mind is muddy. She thinks instead to go find medical help—certainly, she deserves survival. But where would she go? She fears the Empire has now fallen fully into the betrayer's hands. And anywhere else might earn her a one-way ticket back to Chandrila, because by now she suspects the word is out for her capture. She imagines her face up on a bunch of holoposters like a common criminal. What a crass indignity.

No. She has to wait. She sent out her message. She made her play. She can't get to the junk moon on her own, but someone else can . . .

Wait. The realization slowly comes to her that she is not alone on this ship. That is a mad, impossible thought. It is clearly her body dying—the toxins are running laps through her now. She's hallucinating. And yet, she feels someone's gaze boring into the back of her head.

Paranoid, she turns around.

A man is standing there. Pale. Mussed-up hair.

He has a blaster. A small, graphene blaster.

"Get off my ship," she murmurs, her words a smeary mess.

"You did this to me," the man says.

"Put you on a cargo ship in the middle of nowhere?" She barks a mirthless laugh. "Hardly. How did you get here?"

"I saw your uniform. I followed you. To get answers."

"Why announce yourself now?"

"Because I wanted to see what you were doing."

Her chin dips. "You won't find any answers from me."

"You turned me into a monster!"

Sloane blinks. He looks familiar. "*You* are one of *them*." She doesn't have to explain to him what that means—one of the captives-turned-murderers. A traitor made by the Empire. Not her Empire, though.

"Yes." The man trembles. "And you're going to pay for it."

"I'd rather not. Since it's not me that did this to you. The blame falls squarely on someone else's shoulders." Her words slur together. "I don't even know what happened there. I was set up, same as you."

"Not the same as me!" the man screams, and fires the blaster.

She doesn't flinch; her mind is slow, her body hurting, and the shot comes and goes before she even realizes what happened. The bolt scores the steel above her head. She blinks. "You *missed.*"

"If you didn't do this, *who did?*"

"A man named Gallius Rax. At least, that's the name he gives. You want whoever did this to you, go have at him." Her eyelids flutter as her chin dips. "Leave me in peace."

"You know him. You can help me."

"I look like I can help anybody? Can't even . . . help myself."

"You're hurt."

She rolls her eyes. "You don't say. Idiot."

The man seems personally upset by that. Thin-skinned, this one. "You haven't even touched the medkit under your seat."

"Medkit . . . what? Under the . . ." Her hand brutishly paws the space beneath her chair. Sure enough, she feels something. "Oh."

"Who's the idiot, now?" he chides.

"Pfft. Still can't save me. Got shot."

The stranger grumbles, then tucks the blaster in his waist before hunkering down and pulling out the kit. He pops it open with both thumbs and draws out something that looks like a wide-mouthed scatterblaster. Still grousing, he pulls out a wad of what looks like gray hull putty, shoving it unceremoniously into the mouth of the weapon.

"Hold still," he says. "This may hurt."

"What are you—"

He grabs her hard, crams the device right into her wound. The gun shudders—and then the pain hits like a comet. Hot and terrible, it burns her up from the inside and she can't breathe. All she can manage is a howling gasp as she doubles over, trying hard not to weep.

Unconsciousness takes her with its teeth.

Eventually, it lets her go again, and when she awakens, she's on the floor of the ship, on her side. A puddle of drool pools underneath her.

"Wha . . ."

"Bacta patch gun," the man says, sitting in the copilot's chair. "Healing web-epoxy. The Rebellion used it from time to time. We got covert training on how to stay alive to fight longer. The stuff is inside, mending what can be mended. Eventually you'll have to get to a real doctor. It isn't a perfect fix."

She feels like someone punched all her insides.

But she also feels clearer. And when she takes a breath . . .

It doesn't feel like needles stuck in her lung meat.

Well. That's something.

"Thank you. I suppose."

He points the blaster at her.

"Now take me to this . . . Rax."

"If only it were that easy. I can't just push one of these buttons and make him appear. He's not a hologram." Though really, he might as well be. "Getting to him will be a long con."

"Let's get started."

She shrugs. "It's not that easy. I'm waiting for information."

"I know. I heard you make the call. Who is Mercurial Swift?"

"Bounty hunter I work with sometimes. Tell me, though. What's your name?"

"It's . . ." The rebel hesitates. "Brentin."

"I'm Sloane."

They wait like that for a while. Talking here and there. Mostly just sitting in silence. Comes a point when she starts to fade out, and then when she startles awake, Brentin is right next to her. Damn near face-to-face.

She's about to grab for him, but he says:

"Incoming comm."

It's him. Mercurial. He appears above the dash, a blue ghost rising from nowhere. A cocky tilt to his stance.

"Sloane."

"Tell me," she hisses.

"You're pushy."

"I'm paying to be pushy."

"You know Imperial credits are damn near worthless, right? Might as well be plastochits traded during a game of pazaak."

Through her teeth she says, "Then I'll pay you back in favors. Ten favors. A hundred. A whole Star Destroyer packed to the *walls* with favors." And here she almost loses it, almost starts coughing, but she bites it back and holds her tongue. This stranger on board her ship has already seen her be weak. Mercurial will not be afforded the same luxury. "Now, did you get to Quantxi? Did you find the ship?"

The hologram hesitates. "I did."

"And?"

"Amedda was right. He had droids. I had a slicer take a look."

"Did you find anything on Rax? Anything at all?"

Mercurial nods. "I did."

"Tell me!"

"Infinite favors, you say?" He doesn't give her a chance to confirm. "Your friend is from a world in the Western Reaches. Right at the edge of Unknown Space. Jakku. I'll uplink the coordinates."

The drive console *dings*. A map shows on the screen charting the hyperspace path through to Jakku. It's all she needs, so she finishes up with, "Good. I owe you." Then she ends the transmission.

She sets a course for Jakku.

The *Ravager* launches through hyperspace.

Those gathered around the table with Gallius Rax at its head know where the Super Star Destroyer is headed, and as yet, none of them are quite sure why. They give each other furtive looks: Obdur looks to Hux, Hux looks to Borrum. Only Randd keeps his eyes forward; a sign of civility, loyalty, and fear.

Rax appreciates that.

"By now you know that our precious Grand Admiral is lost to us," Rax says. He shakes his head and clucks his tongue. "We will of course make every effort to get her back from the clutches of the New Republic, should we discover that she is alive. Thankfully, she is well-trained in resisting interrogation. We have no expectation that she will give up the location of the fleet. She will be true to us."

It's Hux that speaks. He's agitated when he says: "She knew? She knew what would happen? Are you saying Grand Admiral Sloane was in on it all?"

"Of course. I only advised her on this plan, but the plan was hers all along. Hers is an incisive mind. And the loss of that mind leaves us in the lurch, doesn't it?"

Together, the men nod.

"As such, it is vital we preserve her vision of the Empire. And we need to preserve her leadership and the vision that directed her leadership." Rax pauses, letting his words hang in the air.

"Are you claiming the mantle of Emperor?" Borrum asks.

Rax *hm*s. "I think not. I am not worthy."

"Grand Admiral, then."

"No. I am far too humble for such mighty titles. As I am the adviser to this group and to the Empire at large, I shall take for myself the title of Counselor to the Empire, serving as an interstitial leader only until Grand Admiral Sloane returns to us."

"This is unprecedented," Borrum blusters. Of course the old man would be the one to protest. Age brings stubbornness. Age diminishes vision. "Counselor is not a title in our record and it leaves us effectively leaderless—"

"Our record must evolve, much as the Empire must evolve," Rax says sharply—too sharply, he fears. He must maintain the illusion. He must lead his men to the conclusion he seeks, not the conclusion they want or expect. "Again, I expect this to be a temporary title."

Borrum again: "As temporary as the Emperor's title when he ceased to be Chancellor of a lost Republic?"

At that, Rax smirks. "Perhaps."

"And why Jakku?" The general is pressing his luck. "Jakku is a wasteland. It has no strategic value to us. No resources, no populace to enslave, it has—"

"It will be our proving ground," Rax says. "We will test ourselves on Jakku. And we will do so far from the eyes of the galaxy, far from the eyes of Mon Mothma and her sycophants. And when the time is right, when we have whetted ourselves to a vicious point, we will strike once again. The Senate is injured. The Republic is wounded. We will go in for the kill, but it is too soon and we are too weak."

In their eyes, the firelight of uncertainty and fear. That is fine. He needs them only so long. All of them but Hux. Hux will be necessary.

CHAPTER FORTY-ONE

The aftermath of Liberation Day is like a slow concussive wave. It ripples through the New Republic in the weeks after the assassinations.

It has only been a few days, but this is what they know:

Grand Admiral Sloane is gone. She fell off the skybridge, but then landed on another—all that they found of her was a streak of blood and, later, her jacket all the way down on the shoreline, caught in some fisher-droid's net.

The theory on Sloane is that she escaped in a small cargo ship—a Chandrilan HHG-42 Bulkstar docked close to where she fell. It took off not long after Norra and the Imperial finished their fight. The final clue is that the ship never made it to any of the Chandrilan colonies. It escaped through the blockade above the planet, seizing the chaos and its cleared colony codes as a likely opportunity.

Brentin is gone, too. Where, none can say. They have not found him. Not alive. Not dead. He is a ghost, once more banished to the void.

Many are dead.

Those liberated from Ashmead's Lock had weapons—small concealable graphene blasters that remained shielded from detection. Those pistols held only a handful of shots, but each was lethal. It seems that the dissemination of the pistols comes down to the efforts of a single guardsman: a man with blond hair and a little scar, a Chandrilan man named Windom Traducier.

With those weapons, the turned captives fired into the crowd. Citizens were injured and murdered.

They killed members of the New Republic government, too. Madine is rumored to be dead. So is Hostis Ij. As are senators, diplomats, and military higher-ups. Agate is alive, but her face requires reconstructive surgery. The chancellor is alive, too—her injury is serious, but she's awake and aware. The doctors expect her to make a full recovery, though every day she's injured is another day the New Republic looks weak and its future uncertain.

Norra was told she will receive another medal for saving Mon Mothma's life. They said that her action against her own husband helped divert the blast meant for the chancellor. Norra ensured the blast only struck the New Republic leader in the shoulder, not in the chest or the head.

Norra does not want the medal.

No, she wants something else.

Temmin crashes the X-wing. It skims along the Silver Sea, going low to avoid sensor arrays—but he goes *too* low, and he's not paying attention to his proximity alarms. The tip of one of the S-foil wings dips into the sea, hissing and sending up a wave of spray—that spray cools the engines just as he's coming in way too fast. The starfighter's nose dips and twists, and next thing Temmin knows the ship is tumbling end-over-end, pieces breaking off, the cockpit cracking above him as the ship rolls into the water and sinks.

Everything goes dark.

Wedge drags him out of the simulator.

"Another ship down," Wedge says. The disappointment in his voice is as plain as it is on his face.

"Not like it's a *real* ship, since you'll only let me in the simulator," Temmin says, popping his knuckles nervously. He stomps off and sits down on the bench against the wall. The other line of simulators sits unused.

"I told you, Snap, we can't put you in a fighter right now."

"Because of who I am."

"It's not just that. Things are locked down right now, kid. The bureaucratic belt just got a little tighter, is all. If you score well on the simulator—and maybe don't crash your fighters every time—we can get you back in a ship before the next moon alignment."

"*Great.* My father tries to kill the chancellor and suddenly nobody trusts me." Temmin pauses. "Actually, when I say it out loud like that, it kinda makes sense?" He sighs. "Whatever."

"Things okay with your mother?"

The way Wedge is asking—the way he asks every *day,* in fact—makes Temmin think there's something going on he doesn't understand. It's now, *right now,* that he considers the possibility: Does Wedge Antilles have a thing for his mom? What the hell? That can't be right. He makes a face like he just licked a leaky battery. That's gross. *So* gross.

And yet . . .

At least Wedge isn't an Imperial assassin. So that's something.

Dad . . .

A familiar rage roars inside of Temmin like a firing engine. It won't stop. It won't leave him alone. He closes his eyes at night and there it is: anger at his father, a bottomless well. Brentin Wexley: supposed rebel hero turned, what, Imperial sympathizer? Drone and soldier for the evil Empire? They've been questioning the former prisoners—the ones turned into assassins—and it's like they're lost, confused, or stonewalling. Almost like they don't realize what they did. Temmin tries to hang on to that, clinging to the thought that maybe Brentin didn't know what he was doing . . .

Temmin's knuckles are already scabbed over from where he punched a locker a week ago. He wants to do it again and he almost hauls back and slams his fist into the wall. But with Wedge here, he has to restrain himself. So he does. Instead, he thinks about something else, something better. "I, uh, never said it, but good job with Kashyyyk."

"That wasn't me. That was Leia."

"I dunno. I heard you coming in there with Phantom Squadron was pretty slaggin' amazing. Wish I could've seen it." *Instead of being here and seeing my father up on that stage pointing a blaster at Mon Mothma.*

Wedge putting together Phantom Squadron like that—out of a bunch of washouts and weirdos—was a thing of genius. That's why Temmin wants to join.

"I did what Leia needed me to do. She led the way." And from what Temmin hears, it cost her political capital, too. Whatever *political capital* means. Wedge adds: "And hey, watch your mouth, will you? I don't want your mom thinking you're picking up that kind of language from me."

"Sure, *Dad,* whatever you say." He sighs. "I'll get the next flight right. Put me back in the sim. Right now. Let's do this." He's itching to do something. Get his mind off everything.

"You sure?"

Temmin is about to answer *hell yes,* but next to him on the bench, Wedge's holoscreen lights up. Temmin can see what it says:

It's a message from Norra.

His mother wants him to come home. ASAP. He arches an eyebrow to Wedge: "Do I have to?"

"Sorry, Snap. You'd better. Like I said, I don't want your mother mad at me. You can try the sim tomorrow. And hey, miracle of miracles, maybe you won't crash the fighter next time?"

"Yeah, yeah. I'll see you, Wedge."

Better get home, see what Mom wants.

The door to the interrogation room hisses open.

"Guardsman Windom Traducier."

The man looks up when his name is spoken. The shock of blond atop his head is mashed flat. He sneers in the half dark. "You."

Sinjir nods, then sits. "Me."

"The ex-Imperial loyalty officer has come to interrogate me," the traitorous guardsman says, lip still curled in a cold smirk. The man tries to lean back, but the cuffs bound to an eye-ring in the center of the table prevent him from moving too far. "Good luck."

Sinjir's nostrils flare with a long sigh.

A coldness has settled into his bones, his skin, his mind. When he and Jas learned the news of what had happened here in their absence, her response—as was the response of so many—was anger. Rage burning hot like a puddle of hyper-fuel spilled on the ground and set aflame. Sinjir's anger was not hot. It was cold. An icicle stuck into the meat of his heart. Perhaps what he felt could not even be best described as anger—rather, what he felt was disappointment. Disappointment that the galaxy confirmed for him its worst self. His deepest suspicions about how all things are broken and unfixable were suddenly given evidence.

But it clarified things for him, too.

Things about the galaxy. About the New Republic. And about where he really belongs and who he really is.

"I have not come to interrogate you," Sinjir says.

"Oh, really? The New Republic didn't send you?"

"They did not. I do not work for them. I paid the guard to let me in here. Interrogating you would do no one any good at this point. You've already given up what information you have. As I understand it, the New Republic security bureau did find your secret, second apartment, and *that* tells quite a story. They know that you distributed the weapons of assassination. They know that you planted a transponder on top of the Hanna City opera house, and that the transponder rebroadcast a scrambled Imperial signal to little inorganic bio-chips—undetectable slivers embedded in the brain stem of each of the Ashmead's Lock prisoners. They know that it was *you* who killed Jylia Shale and Arsin Crassus, and also that you helped Yupe Tashu escape." Sinjir leans forward and lowers his voice. "I'd ask you why, but I don't care. I don't care about any of this."

"Then why come at all? Why have me brought to this room? Don't you want to hear my reasons? Don't you want to hear how I believe the New Republic is a hobbling, crippled thing at the outset? How the Republic will allow chaos to take hold in the vacuum of control, how—"

"Shh," Sinjir says, thrusting a finger against his own lips. "You stupid little man. Let me tell you *my* reasons for being here. I no longer care about the state of the galaxy. I no longer give three damns about the Empire or the New Republic or whatever else comes rolling along when those both fade away. What I care about are the people I have in my life. I care about my friends." He shrugs and stands up. He moves to the corner of the room, where a cam remains fixed to the wall. As he speaks, he covers the cam with a small silken handkerchief. "I've never had friends before. I had no idea how that felt. It's rather . . . overwhelming. To *feel* for people like that? To *care* about them? It's almost disgusting, frankly. It's like I can't control it. But I don't want to control it. Not anymore. I'm all in."

"This is boring me. Would you get to the point?"

Sinjir sits back down. "Perhaps you're too insipid to understand what I'm getting at, so, let me lay it out for you, traitor." He enunciates the following words comically, as if he's speaking to a daft child whose brain is parasite-riddled: "You made my friends *sad*. And that makes me *mad*."

From behind, he pulls a vibroknife. Sinjir flicks it on. It hums.

The blade is small. But it is long enough.

The guardsman starts to protest—

Sinjir cuts that protest short as he plunges the thrumming blade deep into the man's sternum. Any words the guardsman planned on uttering are lost underneath a gassy, throat-clogged hiss.

When Sinjir retracts the blade, the guardsman slumps forward, dead.

With that done, he leaves the room.

Jas checks the board at the New Republic Security Bureau—everything here is in disarray, as it has been for weeks. The investigation into the assassination has taken priority, and that means the whole building is like a kicked-over redjacket hive. Doesn't help that the NRSB is completely nascent—hadn't been operating for a full month when the Liberation Day atrocity hit. They were unprepared. They *remain* unprepared.

The board is empty.

No jobs.

The officer behind the blast-glass tells her, "Focus has shifted. We're not looking for bounty hunters right now. Sorry, hon."

Jas gets it. She knew the day would come. Bounty hunters are thought to be scum. The Republic has a major public relations muck-up on its hands right now—already a number of systems on the verge of sending a senator to claim a Senate seat have withdrawn since Liberation Day. There's talk of moving the Senate from Chandrila to another, better-protected system. And already there's talk of an Independent Systems Alliance forming in the margins. Not Empire, but not Republic, either. Hiring bounty hunters will just make the New Republic look weak—even though Jas damn well knows that hiring bounty hunters is a very good way to *get things done.*

They don't need her? Fine. Someone will.

Time to head offworld, then. But where? Buccaneer's Den? Kanata's castle? Ord Mantell might be her best bet. She has contacts there—contacts who won't sell her out for the debts she owes. Of course, she's also heard of several smaller pirate states out there in the Outer Rim, taking advantage of the Empire's absence to establish a foothold. Hm.

She leaves the office and considers her options when her comm crackles. A familiar voice reaches her ears:

It's Norra. And she wants to see Jas.

Well, can't hurt.

"Norra Wexley has been trying to get ahold of you," Conder says as Sinjir enters their apartment.

"Mm."

"You all right?"

It's a loaded question. Conder knows that Sinjir is most certainly not all right. Whatever bliss the two of them possessed prior to Liberation Day has dissolved like a sand castle under siege by the sea. Stress has throttled them both. Conder's been off working freelance for the NRSB, doing whatever investigatory slicer work they have around—the work is plenty thanks to a recommendation from Leia herself. It also means they have him as the slicer trying to hack the little controller chips they found in the brain stems of each of the Ashmead's Lock assassins. That in an effort to figure out who made them and how they work. As such, Conder's barely been around. And Sinjir has *only* been around. Sitting here with naught to do but pace. And ponder. *And plot.*

So, when Conder asks that question, Sinjir wonders if it's wise to give the real answer. But he's tired of pretending otherwise.

"I am both better now than I was and worse," he says. What he does not say is: *I killed a man because he upset my friends.* Which only confirms for him what he's long-suspected and irresponsibly denied: Sinjir is not a good person. He is a bad man with a talent for bad things.

Conder comes over and takes Sinjir's hand.

Conder's hands are warm.

Sinjir's are cold.

"It'll be okay," Conder promises, but it is a promise he cannot know. He's sweet and optimistic. Translated: naïve as a wandering waif.

Sinjir decides in that moment. He leans forward and kisses Conder hard, and then tells him: "I am not the man for you, Conder Kyl. I am a moral weather vane spinning in this hurricane. You need a nicer breed of man than I." He thinks, *I love you, but that doesn't matter,* yet those words never make it to his lips. All he does is leave.

It feels almost normal, them meeting like this inside the *Moth.* It's Sinjir and Jas, Temmin and Mister Bones. They share hugs and small words, and though it's only been a few weeks since they've seen one another, it feels like it's been forever. So much has happened. So much has changed.

Norra cuts right to the heart of it:

"I regret dragging the rest of you away, too, and you're under no obligation to say yes to this—"

"Yes," Sinjir says rather abruptly.

Norra arches an eyebrow. "You don't even know what I'm asking."

"And I don't care. The answer is still yes."

Temmin claps Sinjir on the shoulder, grinning.

Jas hesitates. "I told you, Norra. I can't do this anymore. I have debts. It's time I deal with them before they deal with me."

"I know. And you can say no. But please understand: I'm only asking for one last mission."

"What is the mission?" Jas asks. "Who is our target? I assume that's what this is? Another hunt-and-find?"

Norra slides a small black disk across the table. She taps the side and a holoviz projects above it: the frozen image of Admiral Rae Sloane from the security cams on Liberation Day. The hologram rotates slowly.

All stare at it, wide-eyed.

"We've missed her twice now. That makes us responsible for what happened." Norra shuts her eyes and draws a deep breath. "No. It makes *me* responsible. But I don't think I can do this alone. I will if I have to—"

"You don't, so stop," Sinjir says.

Temmin adds: "If anybody knows where Dad is, it's her. I'm in."

"I ENJOY EVISCERATION," Bones offers ever-so-helpfully. "I TOO AM ALONG ON THIS FOOLISH ADVENTURE."

Jas rolls her eyes. "I'm guessing there's no money in this? A small ragtag crew of miscreants and deviants going after one of the highest-ranking Imperial figures cannot possibly be sanctioned by the New Republic, can it?"

"No," Norra says. "But . . ."

"You have my support," Leia says, stepping on board the ship. "Sorry I'm late, Norra." She steps up, hands unconsciously holding her growing belly. "The New Republic wouldn't touch this mission with a catch-pole. But I will. I have resources. I will use them to help you. Just the same, I cannot promise some grand payday, either. My actions at Kashyyyk have made me something of a political pariah. The New Republic is no longer offering bounties, and I don't have the political capital to make it so. But this is necessary work and I will do what I can to help you do it."

"There it is," Norra says. "We aim for the biggest star in all the sky. We capture her if possible."

"And if that's not possible?" Temmin asks.

Norra doesn't say. She doesn't have to say.

"Fine," Jas says. "I'm in, too. All right, crew. One last mission. Let's go catch ourselves an admiral."

CHAPTER FORTY-TWO

No wonder Sloane had no idea what the planet Jakku was. It lies at the margins of the Western Reaches, flung so far into the galaxy she's not really sure if they're even *in* the galaxy anymore. The system is close to Unknown Space—the uncharted end of the galaxy, beyond which lurk terrible nebula storms and gravity wells. Those who have tried to traverse the space outside the galaxy have never returned, though distorted, half-missing communications *have* come back—messages warning of geomagnetic anomalies and slashing plasma winds.

They take the cargo ship down to the ground. The world that awaits is a desolate, dead place. Sand and stone and bleach-scour skies. They set down not far from a rust-pan outpost near a wide-open salt plain.

She and Brentin walk.

Sloane grimaces and feels at her side—her hand comes away damp with fresh red. Just a few dabs of it. *I'll be fine,* she thinks. She hopes.

The sun scorches them. The air is dry as bone dust.

They head into the outpost, and she nods toward . . . well, it's not a cantina. It's too primitive to deserve that name. It's mostly a bar cobbled together out of soldered scrap underneath some bent and pitted roof. An unshaven man with a grease streak across his forehead stands behind the bar, pouring something chunky into a glass for a skull-headed alien whose species is unknown to her. The man turns toward her. "I don't know you."

"I don't know you, either," she says.

"*Na-tee wa-sha toh ja-lee ja-wah*," the skull-head says.

The man behind the bar shakes his head. "Yeah, I know, I'm not really from around here, either. Job's a job, Gazwin." To Sloane and Brentin he says: "I got Knockback Nectar if you want some. That'll be ten credits apiece or one quarter-portion from the Orkoon Hub."

"I don't want a drink."

"Then we don't have anything to talk about," the bartender says.

"What's your name?"

"Don't see how that's any of your business. But it's Ballast. Corwin Ballast. And you are?"

Sloane hesitates. She summons a name like a ghost: "Adea. Adea Rite."

"Great to meet you," he says, clearly not meaning it. "Again, I sell drinks here, so if that's not what you want . . ."

"This is a bar. Bars are usually excellent places to get information."

"Oh. You want information? Here's some: The planet you are on is called Jakku. Nothing is here. Everyone on this world is a ghost. If you're here, you might be a ghost, too. Anything more detailed than that, you'll have to wait till Ergel's on shift. I'm new-ish, so. Sorry."

"We're looking for someone."

"They're probably not here."

"Gallius Rax. Or Galli, or Rax or . . ."

"Yeah, lady, I don't know—"

But then, his words drift off as his gaze turns to the space above her head. Up, up, up. Suddenly, a long shadow falls over them—like a sword-shaped cloud passing in front of the sun. "No," he whispers.

Brentin gasps.

Sloane turns and she, too, gasps.

Up above, a Super Star Destroyer has come out of hyperspace, tearing the sky open like a slicing blade. *The Ravager,* she thinks. All around it, other ships begin to jump in one by one. Star Destroyers, mostly, manifesting out of nothing. Dozens of them. More than she commanded. Which can only mean: These are the hidden fleets. The ones concealed across the nebulae.

She came to Jakku looking for Gallius Rax.

It looks like Rax has come home. And he has brought the whole Empire—*her* Empire, and *her* ship—with him.

The bartender's face goes white as he says rather solemnly:

"War has come to Jakku."

EPILOGUE

THREE DECADES AGO

Galli is cold and hungry. He has hidden on this ship for long, too long. It seems to be leaching the heat from him. And his stomach growls so loud he's sure the whole galaxy can hear it. He tries to summon spit to his mouth in order to force it down and stop his stomach from rumbling. When that fails, he pinches the skin of his sallow, thin belly and pushes it in, in, in, until finally it goes quiet once more.

Time passes. The ship moves until it doesn't. Up and around and then back down again. Galli is tough. He will not weep. Even though he is alone and he is frightened. He tucks himself between boxes, making himself small. Small like a skittermouse.

Soon, a sound. Footsteps. Fabric dragging. *It's him,* he thinks: the man in the purple robe and the strange hat.

A voice from somewhere close.

"Boy. Show yourself."

That is not the voice of the man in the strange hat.

This voice has a crisp accent, but is guttural, drawn out—in it is a grim vibration that chills the boy's blood.

The boy swallows hard, then stands up and steps out from between the boxes. The voice beckons him: "Come."

It is a summoning. And in that single word is more than just a request—it has gravity to it. Like it's pulling him willfully closer.

The boy resists it. He plants his feet and presses his knees hard against the steel floor of the ship. Galli tightens his jaw.

The man makes a sound: a grunt of what may be amusement.

"I'll not ask again."

Menace presents in that sentence like a sword dangling just overhead. But this time, no compulsion pulls him. It is a request. A threatening one, but it is a request nevertheless, and so the boy steps forward, skirting alongside the boxes to face a man in robes, yes, but these are not the purple robes of the other one. These robes are black as night. Darker than the ship all around. The boy shuffles from side to side so that his front always faces the robed figure.

The man turns toward him. From under the hood, the boy gets a glimpse of an older face, pale as a moon and just as craggy. Lines lay drawn in the skin, like clay etched by a bent knife-blade. A smile stretches there. "Your name, boy?"

"Galli is what they call me." The boy licks his lips with his dry tongue. It makes a rasping sound. "Are you an anchorite?"

"Of a sort."

"Are you the Eremite come back?"

But that question, the man does not answer. Instead he says:

"You come from that world. Jakku."

"I do."

"This is my ship. The *Imperialis*. You are a stowaway."

"I . . . am."

"Brave little boy. Naughty and nasty, too. Good boys do not stow away on unfamiliar vessels. But I have little interest in goodness." The man leans in close. "Galli. I have a proposal for you. It is fortuitous that you should find me here. Would you like to hear my offer, boy?"

Galli is suddenly not sure he does want to hear it. *Stay strong, don't show him your fear,* he thinks. So he gives a hurried nod. "Yes. Sir."

"Your life is now in my hands." As if to demonstrate, he holds out a papery hand. His fingers make his hand look like an overturned spider. From nearby, a scattering of sand from where Galli had been sitting lifts off the ground, floating like a serpent made of particulate matter. The coiling sand floats to the middle of the man's hand and hovers there, until it collapses, forming a small pile in the center of his palm. Galli gasps as the man closes his fist over it. "Your preference in this regard matters greatly. I could end your life—and I would not blame you, being a young boy living in such a brutal wasteland as Jakku. Many on that world crave the luxury of death; I have felt their collective desire just as I can feel the cowardice that prevents them from fulfilling that desire. Or—would you like to hear the second choice?"

Another quick nod from the boy.

"The second choice is, I give you a new life. A better one. I give you a task that, if you manage, will lead you to greater things. Not something so mundane as a job, but a role. A *purpose.* I sense in you potential. A destiny. Most people have no destiny." He says this last sentence as if it disgusts him—as if those without a role to play in his game are just obstacles in the way. Piles of junk to be gone around. "They are useless. They are not actors on the stage but just props. Just decorations to be moved around, painted, knocked over. Do you know opera? No. Of course you don't. But we can fix that if you accept from me this new life. Will you, boy? Will you take the easy way—the road that leads to a quiet, immediate death? Or will you change your fortune? Here and now? Will you accept a new life?"

The choice is no choice at all. Galli knows death well; Jakku is death. Already at his young age the boy has seen many corpses out there in the dirt and the dust, skin gone tight and shiny like leather, hair gone brittle like the mane of a thissermount—one of the stump-legged riding beasts the anchorites ride. Death is a favor to many on Jakku.

But the boy has never sought it. Not even in his darkest moments. At least, he has not sought it for himself.

He says, "I want a new life. I don't want to be me anymore."

The man *hmm*s. "Good. Then I have your first task, young Galli. You will go back to Jakku. The spot there in the dirt where my droids were operating is precious. Not just to me, but to the galaxy at large." He sweeps his decrepit hand as if to the greater universe. "It is significant. It was significant a thousand years ago and it will be significant again. You will go back there and you will monitor my droids excavating the ground. Then I will send more droids and they will build something there below the ground. I want you to guard this space. Can you do that?"

"Guard it? I'm just a boy."

"Yes. But a resourceful boy, I wager."

"I am resourceful." He doesn't know if that's true, but what good is it saying the opposite? "I will guard it."

"Good. Keep others away. Do not let them taint this. Lead them astray. Kill them if you must. Can you do that? Of course you can. The better question is—*will* you do that?"

"I . . . I will."

"Then we may have a future together. For now, you go back. Go home. We will meet again one day."

"Thank you . . . whh . . . I don't know your name, sir."

A small smile. "We can be on a first-name basis, you and I. Galli, my name is Sheev. We will be friends. An Emperor must have friends, after all."

ABOUT THE AUTHOR

CHUCK WENDIG is a novelist, screenwriter, and game designer. He's the author of many novels, including *Blackbirds, Atlanta Burns, Zer0es,* and the YA Heartland series. He is co-writer of the short film *Pandemic* and the Emmy-nominated digital narrative *Collapsus.* He currently lives in the forests of Pennsyltucky with wife, son, and red dog.

terribleminds.com

@ChuckWendig

Find Chuck Wendig on Facebook

ABOUT THE TYPE

This book was set in Minion, a 1990 Adobe Originals typeface by Robert Slimbach (b. 1956). Minion is inspired by classical, old-style typefaces of the late Renaissance, a period of elegant, beautiful, and highly readable type designs. Created primarily for text setting, Minion combines the aesthetic and functional qualities that make text type highly readable with the versatility of digital technology.

Ru

KIM THÚY

Ru

Translated from the French by SHEILA FISCHMAN

Random House Canada

PUBLISHED BY RANDOM HOUSE CANADA

Copyright © 2009 Éditions Libre Expression
English Translation Copyright © 2012 Sheila Fischman
Published by arrangement with Groupe Librex, Montréal, Quebec, Canada

www.randomhouse.ca

LIBRARY AND ARCHIVES CANADA CATALOGUING IN PUBLICATION

Thúy, Kim
[Ru. English]
Ru / Kim Thuy ; translated by Sheila Fischman.

Also issued in electronic format.

ISBN 978-0-307-35970-4

1. Thúy, Kim. I. Fischman, Sheila II. Title.

PS8639.H89R813 2012   c848'.603   c2011-904061-1

Cover and book design by CS Richardson
Images: (winter landscape) Andrew Bret Wallis / Getty Images;
(dragon pattern) John Lock / Shutterstock.com

Printed and bound in the United States of America

10 9 8 7 6 5 4 3 2 1

In French, *ru* means a small stream and, figuratively, a flow, a discharge—of tears, of blood, of money. In Vietnamese, *ru* means a lullaby, to lull.

I came into the world during the Tet Offensive, in the early days of the Year of the Monkey, when the long chains of firecrackers draped in front of houses exploded polyphonically along with the sound of machine guns.

I first saw the light of day in Saigon, where firecrackers, fragmented into a thousand shreds, coloured the ground red like the petals of cherry blossoms or like the blood of the two million soldiers deployed and scattered throughout the villages and cities of a Vietnam that had been ripped in two.

I was born in the shadow of skies adorned with fireworks, decorated with garlands of light, shot through with rockets and missiles. The purpose of my birth was to replace lives that had been lost. My life's duty was to prolong that of my mother.

My name is Nguyễn An Tịnh, my mother's name is Nguyễn An Tĩnh. My name is simply a variation on hers because a single dot under the *i* differentiates, distinguishes, dissociates me from her. I was an extension of her, even in the meaning of my name. In Vietnamese, hers means "peaceful environment" and mine "peaceful interior." With those almost interchangeable names, my mother confirmed that I was the sequel to her, that I would continue her story.

The History of Vietnam, written with a capital H, thwarted my mother's plans. History flung the accents on our names into the water when it took us across the Gulf of Siam thirty years ago. It also stripped our names of their meaning, reducing them to sounds at once strange, and strange to the French language. In particular, when I was ten years old it ended my role as an extension of my mother.

Because of our exile, my children have never been extensions of me, of my history. Their names are Pascal and Henri, and they don't look like me. They have hair that's lighter in colour than mine, white skin, thick eyelashes. I did not experience the natural feelings of motherhood I'd expected when they were clamped onto my breasts at 3 a.m., in the middle of the night. The maternal instinct came to me much later, over the course of sleepless nights, dirty diapers, unexpected smiles, sudden delights.

Only then did I understand the love of the mother sitting across from me in the hold of our boat, the head of the baby in her arms covered with foul-smelling scabies. That image was before my eyes for days and maybe nights as well. The small bulb hanging from a wire attached to a rusty nail spread a feeble, unchanging light. Deep inside the boat there was no distinction between day and night. The constant illumination protected us from the vastness of the sea and the sky all around us. The people sitting on deck told us there was no boundary between the blue of the sky and the blue of the sea. No one knew if we were heading for the heavens or plunging into the water's depths. Heaven and hell embraced in the belly of our boat. Heaven promised a turning point in our lives, a new future, a new history. Hell, though, displayed our fears: fear of pirates, fear of starvation, fear of poisoning by biscuits soaked in motor oil, fear of running out of water, fear of being unable to stand up, fear of having to urinate in the red pot that was passed from hand to hand, fear that the scabies on the baby's head was contagious, fear of never again setting foot on solid ground, fear of never again seeing the faces of our parents, who were sitting in the darkness surrounded by two hundred people.

R U

—

B efore our boat had weighed anchor in the
middle of the night on the shores of Rach Gia,
most of the passengers had just one fear: fear of
the Communists, the reason for their flight. But as
soon as the vessel was surrounded, encircled by the
uniform blue horizon, fear was transformed into a
hundred-faced monster who sawed off our legs and
kept us from feeling the stiffness in our immobilized
muscles. We were frozen in fear, by fear. We no
longer closed our eyes when the scabious little boy's
pee sprayed us. We no longer pinched our noses
against our neighbours' vomit. We were numb,
imprisoned by the shoulders of some, the legs of
others, the fear of everyone. We were paralyzed.

The story of the little girl who was swallowed up
by the sea after she'd lost her footing while walking
along the edge spread through the foul-smelling
belly of the boat like an anaesthetic or laughing gas,
transforming the single bulb into a polar star and
the biscuits soaked in motor oil into butter cookies.
The taste of oil in our throats, on our tongues, in our
heads sent us to sleep to the rhythm of the lullaby
sung by the woman beside me.

My father had made plans, should our family be captured by Communists or pirates, to put us to sleep forever, like Sleeping Beauty, with cyanide pills. For a long time afterwards, I wanted to ask why he hadn't thought of letting us choose, why he would have taken away our possibility of survival.

I stopped asking myself that question when I became a mother, when Dr. Vinh, a highly regarded surgeon in Saigon, told me how he had put his five children, one after the other, from the boy of twelve to the little girl of five, alone, on five different boats, at five different times, to send them off to sea, far from the charges of the Communist authorities that hung over him. He was certain he would die in prison because he'd been accused of killing some Communist comrades by operating on them, even if they'd never set foot in his hospital. He hoped to save one, maybe two of his children by launching them in this fashion onto the sea. I met Dr. Vinh on the church steps, which he cleared of snow in the winter and swept in the summer to thank the priest who had acted as father to his children, bringing up all five, one after the other, until they were grown, until the doctor got out of prison.

I didn't cry out and I didn't weep when I was told that my son Henri was a prisoner in his own world, when it was confirmed that he is one of those children who don't hear us, don't speak to us, even though they're neither deaf nor mute. He is also one of those children we must love from a distance, neither touching, nor kissing, nor smiling at them because every one of their senses would be assaulted by the odour of our skin, by the intensity of our voices, the texture of our hair, the throbbing of our hearts. Probably he'll never call me *maman* lovingly, even if he can pronounce the word *poire* with all the roundness and sensuality of the *oi* sound. He will never understand why I cried when he smiled for the first time. He won't know that, thanks to him, every spark of joy has become a blessing and that I will keep waging war against autism, even if I know already that it's invincible.

Already, I am defeated, stripped bare, beaten down.

When I saw my first snowbanks through the porthole of the plane at Mirabel Airport, then too I felt naked, if not stripped bare. In spite of my short-sleeved orange pullover purchased at the refugee camp in Malaysia before we left for Canada, in spite of my loose-knit brown sweater made by Vietnamese women, I was naked. Several of us on the plane made a dash for the windows, our mouths agape, our expressions stunned. After such a long time in places without light, a landscape so white, so virginal could only dazzle us, blind us, intoxicate us.

I was as surprised by all the unfamiliar sounds that greeted us as by the size of the ice sculpture watching over a table covered with canapés, hors d'oeuvre, tasty morsels, each more colourful than the last. I recognized none of the dishes, yet I knew that this was a place of delights, an idyllic land. I was like my son Henri: unable to talk or to listen, even though I was neither deaf nor mute. I now had no points of reference, no tools to allow me to dream, to project myself into the future, to be able to experience the present, in the present.

My first teacher in Canada walked with us, the seven youngest in the group of Vietnamese, across the bridge that led to the present. She watched over our transplantation with all the sensitivity of a mother for her premature baby. We were hypnotized by the slow and reassuring swaying of her shapely hips, her round and generous behind. Like a mother duck, she walked ahead of us, asking us to follow her to the haven where we would be children again, simply children, surrounded by colours, drawings, trivia. I will be forever grateful to her for giving me my first desire as an immigrant: to be able to sway my bum the way she did. Not one of the Vietnamese in our group possessed such opulence, such generosity, such nonchalance in her curves. We were all angular, bony, hard. And so when she bent down to me, placing her hands on mine to tell me, "My name is Marie-France, what's yours?" I repeated each of her syllables without blinking, without needing to understand, because I was lulled by a cloud of coolness, of lightness, of sweet perfume. I hadn't understood a word she'd said, only the melody of her voice, but it was enough. More than enough.

When I got home, I repeated the same sequence of sounds to my parents: "My name is Marie-France, what's yours?" They asked me if I'd changed my name. It was at that split second that my present reality caught up to me, when the deafness and muteness of the moment erased my dreams and thus the power to look ahead, to look far ahead.

My parents, though they already spoke French, could not look far ahead either, for they'd been expelled from the Introduction to French course, that is, struck off the list of people who would receive an allowance of forty dollars a week. They were overqualified for the course but underqualified for everything else. Unable to look ahead of themselves, they looked ahead of us, for us, their children.

For us, they didn't see the blackboards they wiped clean, the school toilets they scrubbed, the imperial rolls they delivered. They saw only what lay ahead. And so to make progress my brothers and I followed where their eyes led us. I met parents whose gaze had been extinguished, some beneath the weight of a pirate's body, others during the all too many years of Communist re-education camps—not the war camps during the war, but the peacetime camps after the war.

As a child, I thought that war and peace were opposites. Yet I lived in peace when Vietnam was in flames and I didn't experience war until Vietnam had laid down its weapons. I believe that war and peace are actually friends, who mock us. They treat us like enemies when it suits them, with no concern for the definition or the role we give them. Perhaps, then, we shouldn't take too much stock in the appearance of one or the other to decide our views. I was lucky enough to have parents who were able to hold their gaze steady, no matter the mood of the moment. My mother often recited the proverb that was written on the blackboard of her eighth-grade class in Saigon: Đời là chiến trận, nếu buồn là thua. *Life is a struggle in which sorrow leads to defeat.*

M y mother waged her first battles later, without sorrow. She went to work for the first time at the age of thirty-four, first as a cleaning lady, then at jobs in plants, factories, restaurants. Before, in the life that she had lost, she was the eldest daughter of her prefect father. All she did was settle arguments between the French-food chef and the Vietnamese-food chef in the family courtyard. Or she assumed the role of judge in the secret love affairs between maids and menservants. Otherwise, she spent her afternoons doing her hair, applying her makeup, getting dressed to accompany my father to social events. Thanks to the extravagant life she lived, she could dream all the dreams she wanted, especially those she dreamed for us. She was preparing my brothers and me to become musicians, scientists, politicians, athletes, artists and polyglots, all at the same time.

However, far from us, blood still flowed and bombs still fell, so she taught us to get down on our knees like the servants. Every day, she made me wash four tiles on the floor and clean twenty sprouted beans by removing their roots one by one. She was preparing us for the collapse. She was right to do so, because very soon we no longer had a floor beneath our feet.

During our first nights as refugees in Malaysia, we slept right on the red earth, without a floor. The Red Cross had built refugee camps in the countries adjoining Vietnam to receive the boat people—those who had survived the sea journey. The others, those who'd gone down during the crossing, had no names. They died anonymously. We were among those who had been lucky enough to wash up on dry land. We felt blessed to be among the two thousand refugees in a camp that was intended to hold two hundred.

We built a cabin on piles in an out-of-the-way part of the camp, on the side of a hill. For weeks, twenty-five members of five families working together, in secret, felled some trees in the nearby woods, then planted them in the soft clay soil, attached them to six plywood panels to make a large floor, and covered the frame with a canvas of electric blue, plastic blue, toy blue. We had the good fortune to find enough burlap and nylon rice bags to surround the four sides of our cabin, as well as the three sides of our shared bathroom. Together, the two structures resembled a museum installation by a contemporary artist. At night, we slept pressed so close together that we were never cold, even without a blanket. During the day, the heat absorbed by the blue plastic made the air in our cabin suffocating. On rainy days and nights, the water came in through holes pierced by the leaves, twigs and stems that we'd added to cool it down.

If a choreographer had been underneath the plastic sheet on a rainy day or night, he would certainly have reproduced the scene: twenty-five people, short and tall, on their feet, each holding a tin can to collect the water that dripped off the roof, sometimes in torrents, sometimes drop by drop. If a musician had been there, he would have heard the orchestration of all that water striking the sides of the tins. If a filmmaker had been there, he would have captured the beauty of the silent and

spontaneous complicity between wretched people.
But there was only us, standing on a floor that
was slowly sinking into the clay. After three
months it tilted so severely to one side that we
all had to find new positions so sleeping women
and children wouldn't slip onto the plump bellies
of their neighbours.

I n spite of all those nights when our dreams spilled onto the sloping floor, my mother still had high hopes for our future. She'd found an accomplice. He was young and certainly naive because he dared to flaunt joy and light-heartedness in the midst of our dull and empty daily lives. Together, he and my mother started an English class. We spent whole mornings with him, repeating words we didn't understand. But we all showed up because he was able to raise the sky and give us a glimpse of a new horizon, far from the gaping holes filled with the excrement of the camp's two thousand people. Without his face, we could never have imagined a horizon without flies, worms and nauseating smells. Without his face, we couldn't have imagined that someday we would no longer eat rotting fish flung down late every afternoon when rations were handed out. Without his face, we would certainly have lost the desire to reach out our hands and catch our dreams.

U nfortunately, from all the mornings with this
impromptu English teacher, I remembered
only one sentence: *My boat number is KG0338.*
It turned out to be totally useless because I never
had a chance to say it, not even during the medical
examination by the Canadian delegation. The doctor
on call didn't speak a word to me. He tugged the
elastic of my pants to confirm my sex instead of
asking, *Boy or girl?* I also knew those two words.
The appearance of a ten-year-old boy and a
ten-year-old girl must have been much the same,
because of our scrawniness. And time was short:
there were so many of us on the other side of the
door. It was terribly hot in the small examining
room with its windows open onto a noisy alley where
hundreds of water buckets collided at the pump.
We were covered with scabies and lice and we all
looked lost, beyond our depth.

In any case, I spoke very little, sometimes not
at all. Throughout my early childhood, my cousin
Sao Mai always spoke on my behalf because I was her
shadow: the same age, the same class, the same sex,
but her face was on the bright side and mine on the
side of darkness, shadow, silence.

M y mother wanted me to talk, to learn French as fast as possible, English too, because my mother tongue had become not exactly insufficient, but useless. Starting in my second year in Quebec, she sent me to a military garrison of anglophone cadets. It was a way that I could learn English for free, she told me. But she was wrong, it wasn't free. I paid for it, dearly. There were around forty cadets, all of them tall, bursting with energy and, above all, teenagers. They took themselves seriously when inspecting in minute detail the fold of a collar, the angle of a beret, the shine of a boot. The oldest ones yelled at the youngest. They played at war, at the absurd, without understanding. And I didn't understand them.

Nor did I understand why the name of the cadet next to me was repeated in a loop by our superior. Maybe he wanted me to remember the name of that teenage boy who was twice my height. My first conversation in English started with me saying to him at the end of the session: "Bye, Asshole."

My mother often put me in situations of extreme shame. Once, she asked me to go and buy sugar at the grocery store just below our first apartment. I went but found no sugar. My mother sent me back and even locked the door behind me: "Don't come back without the sugar!" She had forgotten that I was a deaf-mute. I sat on the grocery store steps until it closed, until the grocer took me by the hand and led me to the bag of sugar. He had understood, even if to me the word *sugar* was bitter.

For a long time, I thought my mother enjoyed constantly pushing me right to the edge. When I had my own children, I finally understood that I should have seen her behind the locked door, eyes pressed against the peephole; I should have heard her talking on the phone to the grocer when I was sitting on the steps in tears. I also understood later that my mother certainly had dreams for me, but above all she'd given me tools so that I could put down roots, so that I could dream.

The town of Granby was the warm belly that
sheltered us during our first year in Canada.
The locals cosseted us one by one. The pupils in my
grade school lined up to invite us home for lunch so .
that each of our noon hours was reserved by a family.
And every time, we went back to school with nearly
empty stomachs because we didn't know how to use
a fork to eat rice that wasn't sticky. We didn't know
how to tell them that this food was strange to us,
that they really didn't have to go to every grocery
store in search of the last box of Minute Rice.
We could neither talk to nor understand them.
But that wasn't the main thing. There was generosity
and gratitude in every grain of the rice left on
our plates. To this day I still wonder whether
words might have tainted those moments of grace.
And whether feelings are sometimes understood
better in silence, like the one that existed between
Claudette and Monsieur Kiet. Their first moments
together were wordless, yet Monsieur Kiet agreed
to put his baby into Claudette's arms without
questioning: a baby, his baby, whom he'd found
on the shore after his boat had capsized in an
especially greedy wave. He had not found his wife,
only his son, who was experiencing a second birth
without his mother. Claudette stretched out her
arms to them and kept them with her for days,
for months, for years.

Johanne held out her hand to me in the same way.
She liked me even though I wore a tuque with a
McDonald's logo, even though I travelled hidden in
a cube van with fifty other Vietnamese to work in
fields around the Eastern Townships after school.
Johanne wanted me to go to a private secondary
school with her the following year. Yet she knew
that I waited every afternoon in the yard of that very
school for the farmers' trucks that would take us to
work illegally in the fields, earning a few dollars in
exchange for the sacks of beans we picked.

Johanne also took me to the movies, even though
I was wearing a shirt bought on sale for eighty-eight
cents, with a hole near one of the seams. After the
film *Fame* she taught me how to sing the theme
song in English, "I sing the body electric," although
I didn't understand the words, or her conversations
with her sister and her parents around their fireplace.
It was Johanne too who picked me up after my first
falls when we went ice skating, who applauded
and shouted my name in the crowd when Serge,
a classmate three times my size, took me in his arms
along with the football and scored a touchdown.

I wonder if I haven't invented her, that friend
of mine. I've met many people who believe in God,
but what I believe in is angels, and Johanne was an
angel. She was one of an army of them who'd been
parachuted into town to give us shock treatment.
By the dozen they showed up at our doors to give us

warm clothes, toys, invitations, dreams. I often
felt there wasn't enough space inside us to receive
everything we were offered, to catch all the smiles
that came our way. How could we visit the Granby
zoo more than twice each weekend? How could we
appreciate a camping trip to the countryside? How
to savour an omelette with maple syrup?

I have a photo of my father being embraced by
our sponsors, a family of volunteers to whom
we'd been assigned. They spent their Sundays taking
us to flea markets. They negotiated fiercely on our
behalf so we could buy mattresses, dishes, beds,
sofas—in short, the basics—with our three-hundred-
dollar government allowance meant to furnish our
first home in Quebec. One of the vendors threw in
a red cowl-necked sweater for my father. He wore
it proudly every day of our first spring in Quebec.
Today, his broad smile in the photo from that time
manages to make us forget that it was a woman's
sweater, nipped in at the waist. Sometimes it's best
not to know everything.

Of course, there were times when we'd have liked
to know more. To know, for instance, that in our old
mattresses there were fleas. But those details don't
matter because they don't show in the pictures. In any
case, we thought we were immunized against stings,
that no flea could pierce our skin bronzed by the
Malaysian sun. In fact, the cold winds and hot baths
had purified us, making the bites unbearable and the
itches bloody.

We threw out the mattresses without telling our
sponsors. We didn't want them to be disappointed,
because they'd given us their hearts, their time.
We appreciated their generosity, but not sufficiently:
we did not yet know the cost of time, its fair market
value, its tremendous scarcity.

For a whole year, Granby represented heaven
on earth. I couldn't imagine a better place in
the world, even if we were being eaten alive by flies,
just as in the refugee camp. A local botanist took
us children to swamps where cattails grew in the
thousands, to show us the insects. He didn't know
that we'd rubbed shoulders with flies in the refugee
camps for months. They clung to the branches of a
dead tree near the septic tanks, next to our cabin.
They positioned themselves around the branches like
the berries of a pepper plant or currants. They were
so numerous, so enormous, that they didn't need to
fly to be in front of our eyes, in our lives. We didn't
need to be silent to hear them. Now our botanist
guide whispered to us to listen to their droning,
to try to understand them.

I know the sound of flies by heart. I just have to
close my eyes to hear them buzzing around me
again, because for months I had to crouch down
above a gigantic pit filled to the brim with excrement,
in the blazing sun of Malaysia. I had to look at the
indescribable brown colour without blinking so that
I wouldn't slip on the two planks behind the door
of one of the sixteen cabins every time I set foot
there. I had to keep my balance, avoid fainting when
my stools or those from the next cabin splattered.
At those moments I escaped by listening to the
humming of flies. Once, I lost my slipper between
the planks after I'd moved my foot too quickly. It fell
into the cesspit without sinking, floating there like a
boat cast adrift.

I went barefoot for days, waiting for my mother to find an orphan slipper belonging to another child who'd also lost one. I walked directly on the clay soil where maggots had been crawling a week before. With every heavy rainfall they emerged from the cesspit in the hundreds of thousands, as if summoned by a messiah. They all headed for the side of our hill and climbed without ever tiring, without ever falling. They crawled up to our feet, all to the same rhythm, transforming the red clay soil into an undulating white carpet. There were so many that we gave up before we'd even started to fight. They became invincible, we became vulnerable. We let them extend their territory until the rains stopped, when they became vulnerable in turn.

W hen the Communists entered Saigon,
my family handed over half of our property
because we'd become vulnerable. A brick wall was
erected to establish two addresses: one for us and
RU

—
one for the local police station.

A year later, the authorities from the new
Communist administration arrived to clean out
our half of the house, to clean us out. Inspectors came
to our courtyard with no warning, no authorization,
no reason. They asked all those present to gather
in the living room. My parents were out, so the
inspectors waited for them, sitting on the edges of
art deco chairs, their backs straight, without once
touching the two white linen squares covered
with fine embroidery that adorned the armrests.
My mother was the first to appear behind the
wrought iron glass door. She had on her white
pleated miniskirt and her running shoes. Behind her,
my father was dragging tennis rackets, his face still
covered in sweat. The inspectors' surprise visit had
thrown us into the present while we were still
savouring the last moments of the past. All the
adults in the household were ordered to stay in
the living room while the inspectors started making
their inventory.

We children could follow them from floor to floor,
from room to room. They sealed chests of drawers,
wardrobes, dressing tables, safes. They even sealed the
big chests of drawers filled with the brassieres of my

grandmother and her six daughters, without describing the contents. It seemed to me then that the young inspector was embarrassed at the thought of all those round-breasted girls in the living room, dressed in fine lace imported from Paris. I also thought that he was leaving the paper blank, with no description of the wardrobe's contents, because he was too overwhelmed by desire to write without trembling. But I was wrong: he had no idea what brassieres were for. In his opinion they looked like his mother's coffee filters, made of cloth sewn around a metal ring, the twisted end of which served as a handle.

At the foot of the Long Biên Bridge that crosses the Red River in Hanoi, every night his mother would fill her coffee filter then dip it into her aluminum coffee pot to make a few cups that she'd sell to passersby. In the winter, she placed glasses containing barely three sips into a bowl filled with hot water to keep them warm during conversations between the men sitting on benches raised just a bit above the ground. Her customers spotted her by the flame of her tiny oil lamp sitting on the tiny work table, next to three cigarettes displayed on a plate. Every morning, the young inspector, still a child, woke up with the oft-mended brown cloth coffee filter, sometimes still wet and hanging from a nail above his head. I heard him talking with the other inspectors in a corner of the staircase. He didn't

understand why my family had so many coffee
filters filed away in drawers lined with tissue paper.
And why were they double? Was it because we
always drink coffee with a friend?

R U

—

The young inspector had been marching in the jungle since the age of twelve to free South Vietnam from the "hairy hands" of the Americans. He had slept in underground tunnels, spent days at a time in a pond, under a water lily, seen the bodies of comrades sacrificed to prevent cannons from sliding, lived through nights of malaria amidst the sound of helicopters and explosions. Aside from his mother's teeth lacquered jet black, he had forgotten his parents' faces. How could he have guessed, then, what a brassiere was for? In the jungle, boys and girls had exactly the same possessions: a green helmet, sandals made from strips of worn-out tires, a uniform, and a black and white checked scarf. An inventory of their belongings took three seconds, unlike ours, which lasted for a year. We had to share our space by taking ten of those girl and boy soldier-inspectors into our home. We gave them one floor of the house. Each of us lived in our own corner, avoiding contact except during the daily searches, when we were obliged to stand face to face with them. They needed to be sure that we had only the essentials, like them.

One day our ten roomers dragged us to their bathroom, accusing us of stealing a fish they'd been given for their evening meal. They pointed to the toilet bowl and explained to us that the fish had been there that morning, hale and hearty. What had become of it?

Thanks to that fish, we were able to establish communication. Later on, my father corrupted them by having them listen to music on the sly. I sat underneath the piano, in the shadows, watching tears roll down their cheeks, where the horrors of History, without hesitation, had carved grooves. After that, we no longer knew if they were enemies or victims, if we loved or hated them, if we feared or pitied them. And they no longer knew if they had freed us from the Americans or, on the contrary, if we had freed them from the jungle of Vietnam.

Very quickly, though, the music that had accorded them a kind of freedom found itself in a fire, on the rooftop terrace of the house. They had received an order to burn the books, songs, films—everything that betrayed the image of those men and women with muscular arms holding aloft their pitchforks, their hammers and their flag, red with a yellow star. Very quickly, they filled the sky with smoke, once more.

What became of those soldiers? Much has changed since the brick wall was put up between us and the Communists. I went back to Vietnam to work with those who had caused the wall to be built, who'd imagined it as a tool to break hundreds of thousands of lives, perhaps even millions. There had been reversals, of course, since the tanks first rolled down the street that ran past our house in 1975. Since then, I had even learned the Communist vocabulary of our former assailants because the Berlin Wall fell, because the Iron Curtain was raised, because I am still too young to be weighed down by the past. Only, there will never be a brick wall in my house. I still don't share the love for brick walls of the people around me. They claim that bricks make a room warm.

The day I started my job in Hanoi, I walked past a tiny room that opened onto the street. Inside, a man and a woman were arranging bricks into a low wall that divided the room in two. The wall got higher day by day, until it reached the ceiling. My secretary told me that it was because of two brothers who didn't want to live under the same roof. The mother had been helpless against this separation, perhaps because she herself had erected similar walls some thirty years earlier between victors and vanquished. She died during my three-year stay in Hanoi. By way of legacy, to the older child she left the fan without a switch, to the younger the switch without the fan.

I t's true that the brick wall between those two
brothers can't be compared to the one that existed
between my family and the Communist soldiers,
nor do these two walls carry the same history as do
old Québécois houses—each wall has its own story. It
is thanks to that distance that I've been able to
share meals with people who were the right arm
and the left arm of Ho Chi Minh without seeing the
rancour hovering, without seeing women on a train
holding old Guigoz powdered milk cans in their
hands as if they were jars of magic potion. For the
men shut away in re-education camps, it *was* a magic
potion, even if the cans held only browned meat
(*thịt chà bông*): a kilo of roasted pork shredded fibre
by fibre, dried all night over the embers, salted,
then salted again with nước mắm obtained after
two days of waiting in line, two days of hope and
despair. The women lavished devotion on those
filaments of pork, even if they weren't sure of finding
their children's father in the camp they were setting
off to visit, not knowing if he was dead or alive,
wounded or sick. In memory of those women,
I cook that browned meat for my sons now and
then, to preserve, to repeat, those gestures of love.

L ove, as my son Pascal knows it, is defined by
the number of hearts drawn on a card or
by how many stories about dragons are told by
flashlight under a down-filled comforter. I have to
wait a few more years till I can report to him that in
other times, other places, parents showed their love
by willingly abandoning their children, like the
parents of Tom Thumb. Similarly, the mother who
made me glide on the water with the help of her long
stick, surrounded by the high mountain peaks of
Hoa Lư, wanted to give up her daughter, pass her
to me. That mother wanted me to replace her.
She preferred to cry over her child's absence rather
than watch her running after tourists to sell them
the tablecloths she had embroidered. I was a young
girl then. In the midst of those rocky mountains,
I saw only a majestic landscape in place of that
mother's infinite love. There are nights when I run
along the long strips of earth next to the buffalo
to call her back, to take her daughter's hand in mine.

I am waiting till Pascal is a few years older before
I make the connection between the story of
the mother from Hoa Lư and Tom Thumb. In the
meantime, I tell him the story of the pig that travelled
in a coffin to get through the surveillance posts
between the countryside and the towns. He likes
to hear me imitate the crying women in the funeral
procession who threw themselves body and soul onto
the long wooden box, wailing, while the farmers,
dressed all in white with bands around their heads,
tried to hold them back, to console them in front
of the inspectors who were too accustomed to death.
Once they got back to town, behind the closed doors
of an ever-changing secret address, the farmers
turned the pig over to the butcher, who cut it into
pieces. The merchants would then tie those around
their legs and waists to transport them to the black
market, to families, to us.

I tell Pascal these stories to keep alive the memory
of a slice of history that will never be taught in
any school.

I remember some students in my high school who complained about the compulsory history classes. Young as we were, we didn't realize that the course was a privilege only countries at peace can afford. Elsewhere, people are too preoccupied by their day-to-day survival to take the time to write their collective history. If I hadn't lived in the majestic silence of great frozen lakes, in the humdrum everyday life of peace, where love is celebrated with balloons, confetti, chocolates, I would probably never have noticed the old woman who lived near my great-grandfather's grave in the Mekong Delta. She was very old, so old that the sweat ran down her wrinkles like a brook that traces a furrow in the earth. Her back was hunched, so hunched that she had to go down staircases backwards so as not to lose her balance and fall headfirst. How many grains of rice had she planted? How long had she spent with her feet in the mud? How many suns had she watched set over her rice fields? How many dreams had she set aside only to find herself bent in two, thirty years, forty years later?

We often forget about the existence of all those women who carried Vietnam on their backs while their husbands and sons carried weapons on theirs. We forget them because under their cone-shaped hats they did not look up at the sky. They waited only for the sun to set on them so they could faint instead of falling asleep. Had they taken the time to let sleep

come, they would have imagined their sons blown
into a thousand pieces or the bodies of their husbands
drifting along a river like flotsam. American slaves
were able to sing about their sorrow in the cotton
fields. Those women let their sadness grow in the
chambers of their hearts. They were so weighed
down by all their grief that they couldn't pull
themselves up, couldn't straighten their hunched
backs, bowed under the weight of their sorrow.
When the men emerged from the jungle and started
to walk again along the earthen dikes around their
rice fields, the women continued to bear the weight
of Vietnam's inaudible history on their backs.
Very often they passed away under that weight,
in silence.

One of those women, whom I knew, died when
she lost her footing in the toilet, perched above a pond
full of bullheads. Her plastic slippers slid. Anyone
watching her at that moment would have seen her
cone-shaped hat disappear behind the four panels
that barely hid her crouching body, surrounding her
without protecting her. She died in the family's septic
tank, her head plunging into a hole full of excrement
between two planks, behind her hut, surrounded by
smooth-skinned, yellow-fleshed bullheads, without
scales, without memory.

After the old lady died, I would go every Sunday to a lotus pond in a suburb of Hanoi where there were always two or three women with bent backs and trembling hands, sitting in a small round boat, using a stick to move across the water and drop tea leaves into open lotus blossoms. They would come back the next day to collect them one by one before the petals faded, after the captive tea leaves had absorbed the scent of the pistils during the night. They told me that every one of those tea leaves preserved the soul of the short-lived flowers.

P hotos could not preserve the soul of our first Christmas trees. Those branches gathered in the woods of suburban Montreal, stuck in the rim of a spare tire covered with a white sheet, seem bare and lacking in magic, but in reality they were much prettier than the eight-foot-tall spruce trees we have nowadays.

My parents often remind my brothers and me that they won't have any money for us to inherit, but I think they've already passed on to us the wealth of their memories, allowing us to grasp the beauty of a flowering wisteria, the delicacy of a word, the power of wonder. Even more, they've given us feet for walking to our dreams, to infinity. Which may be enough baggage to continue our journey on our own. Otherwise, we would pointlessly clutter our path with possessions to transport, to insure, to take care of.

A Vietnamese saying has it that "Only those with long hair are afraid, for no one can pull the hair of those who have none." And so I try as much as possible to acquire only those things that don't extend beyond the limits of my body.

I n any case, since our escape by boat, we learned
how to travel very light. The gentleman seated
next to my uncle in the hold had no luggage, not even
a small bag with warm clothes like us. He had on

everything he owned. Swimming trunks, shorts,
pants, T-shirt, shirt and sweater, and the rest was
·in his orifices: diamonds embedded in his molars,
gold on his teeth and American dollars stuffed in
his anus. Once we were at sea, we saw women open
their sanitary napkins to take out the American
dollars impeccably folded lengthwise in three.

As for me, I had an acrylic bracelet, pink like
the gums of the dental plate it had been made from,
filled with diamonds. My parents had also
put diamonds in the collars of my brothers' shirts.
But we had no gold in our teeth because it was
forbidden to touch the teeth of my mother's children.
She often told us that teeth and hair are the roots,
maybe even the fundamental source, of a person.
My mother wanted our teeth to be perfect.

That's why even in a refugee camp she was able
to find a pair of dental pliers to pull out our loose
baby teeth. She waved each extracted tooth in
front of us under the blazing Malaysian sun.
Those blood-stained teeth were proudly displayed
against the backdrop of a fine sandy beach and a
barbed-wire fence. My mother told me it would be
possible to enlarge my eyes and maybe even to fix
my ears, which stuck out too much. She couldn't

fix the other structural imperfections of my face, though, so at least I should have flawless teeth and above all not trade them for diamonds. She also knew that if our boat had been intercepted by Thai pirates, the gold teeth and those that were filled with diamonds would have been pulled out.

The police were ordered to allow all boats
carrying Vietnamese of Chinese background
to leave "in secret." The Chinese were capitalists,
hence anti-Communist, because of their ethnic
background and their accent. But the inspectors
were allowed to search them, to strip them of
everything they owned till the very last minute,
to the point of humiliation. My family and I became
Chinese. We called on the genes of my ancestors
so that we could leave with the tacit consent of
the police.

My maternal great-grandfather was Chinese. He arrived in Vietnam by chance at the age of eighteen, married a Vietnamese woman and had eight children. Four of them chose to be Vietnamese, the other four Chinese. The four Vietnamese, including my grandfather, became politicians and scientists. The four Chinese prospered in the rice business. Even though my grandfather became a prefect, he could not persuade his four Chinese siblings to send their children to a Vietnamese school. And the Vietnamese clan didn't speak a word of Szechuanese. The family was divided in two, as was the country: in the South, pro-American, in the North, Communist.

My uncle Chung, my mother's big brother, was the bridge between the two political camps. In fact, his name means *together*, but I call him Uncle Two because it is a South Vietnamese tradition to replace the names of brothers and sisters with their birth order, beginning with the number two.

Uncle Two, the eldest son in the family, was a member of parliament and leader of the opposition. He belonged to a political party made up of young intellectuals who situated themselves in a third camp, daring to stand between the two lines of fire. The pro-American government had permitted the birth of that party to appease the anger and turmoil of the young idealists. My uncle had achieved top billing in the mind of the public. On one hand, his political program appealed to the members of his team. On the other, thanks to his movie-star good looks, to his constituents he represented the hope for a semblance of democracy. A charismatic, happy-go-lucky young man, he had taken down the frontier between the Chinese and Vietnamese families. He was someone who could discuss with a cabinet minister the impact of a paper shortage on freedom of the press while at the same time wrapping his arm around the waist of the man's wife and leading her in a waltz—even though the Vietnamese didn't waltz.

All through my childhood, I had a secret wish: to be Uncle Two's daughter. Sao Mai was his princess, even if he sometimes forgot her existence for days at a time. Sao Mai was revered by her parents like a prima donna. Uncle Two had many parties at their house. And often, in the middle of the evening, he would stop all conversation to seat his daughter on the piano bench and introduce the little melody she was going to play. For him, during the two short minutes of "Au clair de la lune," nothing existed but the chubby-fingered doll tinkling away with the greatest of ease before an audience of adults. Every time, I sat under the staircase to memorize my uncle's kiss on Sao Mai's nose while his guests applauded. He gave her only two minutes of attention now and then, but it was enough to give my cousin an inner strength that I lacked. It didn't matter if her stomach was empty or full, Sao Mai never hesitated to boss around her big brothers and me.

M y cousin Sao Mai and I were brought up together. Either I was at her house or she was at mine. Sometimes at her place there wasn't even a grain of rice. When her parents were away, the maids disappeared too—often with the jar of rice. And her parents were often away. One day her big brother fed us some stale rice stuck to the bottom of a pan. He'd added a little oil and some green onion to make it into a meal. Five of us nibbled on that dried-up cake of rice. Other days we were buried under mountains of mangoes, longans, lychees, Lyon sausage, cream puffs.

My cousin's parents would base their choice of what to buy on the colour of a fruit or the perfume of a spice or simply according to the whim of the moment. The food they brought home was always surrounded by a festive aura, a sense of decadence and thrill. They didn't fret over the empty rice jar in the kitchen or the poems we were supposed to learn by heart. They just wanted us to stuff ourselves on mangoes, to bite into fruit and make the juice spurt, while spinning around and around like tops to the music of the Doors, Sylvie Vartan, Michel Sardou, the Beatles or Cat Stevens.

At my house, meals were always on time, the maids in attendance, homework supervised. Unlike Sao Mai's parents, my mother gave us only two mangoes to be shared by my two brothers and me, despite the dozens more that stayed in the basket. If we didn't agree about the portions, she took them back and deprived us of them until we'd reached a compromise to divide up the two mangoes among the three of us. Which is why I sometimes preferred to eat dry rice with my cousins.

I wanted to be very different from my mother, until the day I decided to have my two sons share a bedroom, even though there were empty rooms in the house. I wanted them to learn to stand by one another the way my brothers and I had done. Someone told me that bonds are forged with laughter but even more with sharing and the frustrations of sharing. It may be that the tears of one led to the tears of the other in the middle of the night, because my autistic son finally became aware of the presence of Pascal, a big brother he'd ignored during his first three or four years. Today, he takes palpable pleasure from curling up in Pascal's arms, hiding behind him in front of strangers. It may be that thanks to all that interrupted sleep, Pascal willingly puts on his left shoe before the right to accommodate his brother's obsessive rigidity. So that his brother can begin his day without irritation, without undue disruption.

My mother was probably right, then, not only to force me to share with my brothers but also to make us share with our cousins. I shared my mother with my cousin Sao Mai because she'd taken responsibility for her niece's education. We went to the same school, like twins, sitting on the same bench in the same class. Sometimes my cousin would replace our teacher when she was away, standing on her desk and brandishing a big ruler. She was five or six years old like the rest of us, but not in the least intimidated by the ruler since, unlike us, she had always been placed on a pedestal. I, on the other hand, would wet my pants because I didn't dare put my hand up, because I didn't dare walk to the door with all eyes focused on me. My cousin struck down anyone who copied my answers. She glared at anyone who made fun of my tears. She protected me because I was her shadow.

She dragged her shadow with her everywhere, but sometimes she made me run behind her like a dog, just for laughs.

When I was with Sao Mai—and I was always with Sao Mai—the waiters in what used to be the Cercle sportif de Saigon never offered me a lime soda after my tennis lessons because they'd already brought one to Sao Mai. Inside the big fences of this fashionable club were two very distinct categories of people: the elite and the servants, the infant kings in their immaculate white clothes and the barefoot youngsters who picked up the balls. I belonged to neither. I was just Sao Mai's shadow. I positioned myself behind her to eavesdrop on her father's conversations with his tennis partners at tea time. He talked about Proust while he ate madeleines, settled in his rattan armchair on the terrace of the Cercle sportif. We travelled with him through his memories of being a foreign student in Paris. He was as enthusiastic in his descriptions of the chairs in the Jardin du Luxembourg as he was about the cancan dancers' legs that went on forever. I listened to him from behind his chair, holding my breath, like a shadow, so that he wouldn't stop.

M y mother often got mad at me for being too self-effacing. She told me I had to step out of the shadows, work on my outstanding features so that the light could be reflected there. Every time she tried to take me out of the shadows, out of my shadow, I drowned myself in tears to the point of exhaustion, until she left me behind on the back seat of the car, asleep in the scorching heat of Saigon. I spent more time in people's driveways than in their sitting rooms. Sometimes I woke up to the sound of children innocently whirling around the car, sticking out their tongues and snickering. My mother thought that defending myself would strengthen my muscles. In time she was able to turn me into a woman, but never into a princess.

Today, my mother regrets not bringing me up
to be a princess, because she's not my queen in
the way that Uncle Two was a king to his children.
He maintained the royal status until his death, even
though he never signed a note for the teacher,
read a report card or washed his children's dirty
hands. Sometimes my cousin and I were lucky
enough to travel on my uncle's Vespa, my cousin
standing in front, me sitting behind. Sao Mai and
I waited for him many times under the tamarind
tree in front of our primary school, until the janitor
padlocked the doors behind us. Even the men who
sold pickled mangoes, guavas with spicy salt and
chilled jicama had already left the sidewalk in front
of the school when Mai and I, dazzled by the setting
sun, would see him coming in the distance, hair
windblown, wearing a fiery smile, incomparable.

He would take us in his arms and all at once not
only were we transformed into princesses, but we
were in his eyes also the prettiest, the most highly
prized. That moment of euphoria only lasted the
length of the journey: very soon he would have a
woman in his arms, rarely the same one, who became
in turn his princess of the moment. We would wait
for him in the sitting room until the new princess
stopped being a princess. Each of those women had
the satisfaction of thinking she was the chosen one,
even if she was well aware that she was only one
among many.

My parents were very critical of Uncle Two's
casual attitude. That was why, without
Uncle Two ever asking me, I never talked about
the long waits outside school or the evenings in the
sitting rooms of unknown women. If I'd exposed
him, he wouldn't have been allowed to pick us up.
I would have lost the chance of being a princess,
of seeing my kiss transformed into a flower on his
cheek. Thirty years later, my mother would like
me to place upon her cheeks those same kisses turned
into flowers. Maybe I did become a princess in her
eyes. But I'm just her daughter, only her daughter.

From Quebec, my mother sent money to Uncle Two's sons so they could get away by boat as we had done. After the first wave of boat people in the late 1970s, it no longer made sense to send girls to sea because encounters with pirates had become inevitable, a ritual of the journey, an inescapable injury. So only the two older boys set out on the fugitives' bus. They were arrested during the journey. Their father, my uncle, my king, had denounced them . . . Was it from fear they'd be lost at sea or from fear of reprisals against him, their father? When I think back on it, I remind myself that he couldn't tell them he'd never been their father, only their king. He must have feared being pointed to publicly as an anti-Communist. He was certainly afraid of appearing in public, where he'd have been at home a short time before. If I'd had a voice then, I'd have told him not to denounce them. I'd have told him that I never informed on him for being late or made mention of his escapades.

J eanne, our good fairy with a T-shirt and pink
tights and a flower in her hair, liberated my
voice without using words. She spoke to us—her nine
Vietnamese students at the Sainte-Famille elementary
school—with music, with her fingers, her shoulders.
She showed us how to occupy the space around us by
freeing our arms, by raising our chins, by breathing
deeply. She fluttered around us like a fairy, her eyes
stroking us one by one. Her neck stretched out to
form a continuous line with her shoulder, her arm,
all the way to her fingertips. Her legs made great
circular movements as if to sweep the walls, to stir
the air. It was thanks to Jeanne that I learned how
to free my voice from the folds of my body so it could
reach my lips.

I used my voice to read to Uncle Two just before he died, in the very heart of Saigon, some of the erotic passages from Houellebecq's *Particules élémentaires*. I no longer wanted to be his princess, I'd become his angel, reminding him how he had dipped my fingers into the whipped cream on café viennois while singing *Besame, besame mucho . . .*

His body, even once it was cold, even once it was rigid, was surrounded not only by his children, by his wives—the old one and the new—by his brothers and sisters, but also by people who didn't know him. They came in the thousands to mourn his death. Some were losing their lover, some their sports reporter, others their former member of parliament, their writer, their painter, their hand at poker.

Among all these people was a gentleman who was obviously destitute. He wore a shirt with a yellowed collar and wrinkled black pants held up by an old belt. He stood in the distance, in the shade of a royal poinciana laden with flame-red blossoms, next to a mud-stained Chinese bicycle. He had waited for hours to follow the funeral procession to the graveyard, which was in the outskirts of the city, enclosed within a Buddhist temple. There again he stood off to one side, silent and unmoving. One of my aunts went over and asked him why he'd pedalled all that distance. Did he know my uncle? He replied that he didn't know him but that it was thanks to my uncle's words that he was alive, that he got up every

morning. He had lost his idol. I hadn't. I'd lost neither
my idol nor my king, only a friend who told me
his stories about women, about politics, painting,
books; and mostly about frivolity, because he hadn't
grown old before he died. He had stopped time by
continuing to enjoy himself, to live until the end
with the lightness of a young man.

So perhaps my mother doesn't need to be my queen; simply being my mother is already a lot, even if the rare kisses I place on her cheeks aren't so majestic.

R U

—

M y mother envied my uncle's irresponsibility, or rather his capacity for it. In spite of herself, she was also jealous of her little brother and sisters' status as king and queens. Like their older brother, her sisters are idolized by their children for a variety of reasons, one because she's the most beautiful, another the most talented, yet another the smartest . . . In my cousins' eyes, their mother is always the best. For all of us, including my aunts and cousins, my mother was only frightening. When she was a young woman, she'd represented the highest authority figure. Zealously she imposed her role of older sister on her little sisters, because she wanted to break away from her big brother, who gobbled up every presence around him.

So my mother had taken on the duties of man of the house, Minister of Education, Mother Superior, chief executive of the clan. She made decisions, handed out punishments, put right delinquents, silenced protesters . . . My grandfather, as chairman of the board, didn't look after everyday tasks. My grandmother had her hands full raising her young children and recovering from repeated miscarriages. According to my mother, Uncle Two was the embodiment of selfishness and egocentricity. And so she became established as manager of the supreme authority. I remember one day when my grandmother didn't even dare ask her to unlock the bathroom door and release her little brother and

sisters who were being punished for going out
with Uncle Two without my mother's permission.
As she was only a young girl, she administered her
authority—naively—with an iron hand. Her revenge
against her older brother's nonchalance and the
way the children revered him was poorly planned,
because the youngsters went on playing in the
bathroom, and did it without her. All the fun of
childhood slipped between her fingers while, in
the name of propriety, she was forbidding her
sisters to dance.

O ver the past ten years, however, my mother
has discovered the joys of dancing. She let
her friends persuade her that the tango, the cha-cha
and the paso doble could replace physical exercise,
that there was nothing sensual or seductive or
intoxicating about them. Yet ever since she's been
going to her weekly dancing class, she says now
and then that she wishes she'd segued from her
days on the election campaign to the parties where
her brother, my father and dozens of other young
candidates amused themselves around a table.
Also, today she seeks my father's hand at a movie
and his kiss on her cheek when posing for photos.

My mother started to live, to let herself be carried
away, to reinvent herself at the age of fifty-five.

As for my father, he didn't have to reinvent himself. He is someone who lives in the moment, with no affection for the past. He savours every instant of the present as if it were still the best and only time, with no comparisons, no measurements. That's why he always inspired the greatest, most wonderful happiness, whether holding a mop on the steps of a hotel or sitting in a limousine en route to a strategic meeting with his minister.

From my father I inherited the permanent feeling of satisfaction. Where did he find it, though? Was it because he was the tenth child? Or because of the long wait for his kidnapped father's release? Before the French left Vietnam, before the Americans arrived, the Vietnamese countryside was terrorized by different factions of thugs introduced there by the French authorities to divide the country. It was common practice to sell wealthy families a nail to pay the ransom of someone who'd been kidnapped. If the nail wasn't bought, it was hammered into an earlobe—or elsewhere—on the kidnap victim. My grandfather's nail was bought by his family. When he came home, he sent his children to urban centres to live with cousins, thereby ensuring their safety and their access to education. Very early, my father learned how to live far away from his parents, to leave places, to love the present tense, to let go of any attachment to the past.

That is why he's never been curious to know
his real date of birth. The official date recorded
on his birth certificate at the city hall corresponds
to a day with no bombardment, no exploding mines,
no hostages taken. Parents may have thought that
their children's existence began on the first day that
life went back to normal, not at the moment of their
first breath.

Similarly, he has never felt the need to see Vietnam
again after his departure. Today, people from his
birthplace visit him on behalf of property developers,
suggesting he demand the deed to his father's house.
They say that ten families live there now. The last
time we saw it, it was being used as a barracks by
Communist soldiers recycled as firemen. Those
soldiers started their families in the big house.
Do they know that they live in a building put up
by a French engineer, a graduate of the prestigious
National School of Bridges and Roads? Do they
know that the house is a thank-you from my
great-uncle to my grandfather, his older brother,
who sent him to France for his education? Do they
know that ten children were brought up there but
now live in ten different cities because they were
ejected from their family circle? No, they know
nothing. They can't know: they were born after the
French withdrawal and before that part of the history
of Vietnam could be taught to them. They'd probably
never seen an American face up close, without

camouflage, until the first tourists came to their town some years ago. They only know that if my father takes back the house and sells it to a developer, they will receive a small fortune, a reward for confining my paternal grandparents to the tiniest room in their own house during the final months of their lives.

Some nights the firefighter-soldiers, drunk and lost, would fire through the curtains to silence my grandfather. But he'd stopped speaking after his stroke, which had happened before I was even born. I never heard his voice.

My paternal grandfather I never saw in any
position but horizontal, stretched out on an
enormous ebony daybed that stood on carved feet.
He was always dressed in immaculately white
pyjamas without a crease. My father's Sister Five,
who had turned her back on marriage to look
after her parents, kept watch obsessively over my
grandfather's cleanliness. She would not tolerate the
slightest spot or any sign of inattention. At mealtimes,
a servant would sit behind him to keep his back
straight, while my aunt fed him rice, a mouthful
at a time. His favourite meal was rice with roast
pork. The slices of pork were cut so finely they
seemed to be minced. But they weren't to be chopped,
only cut into small pieces two millimetres square.
She mixed them with steaming rice served in a blue
and white bowl with a silver ring around its rim to
prevent chipping. If the bowls were held up to the
sun, one could see translucent areas in the embossed
parts. Their quality was confirmed by the glimmers
that exposed the shades of blue in the patterns.
The bowls nestled gently in my aunt's hands at
every meal, every day, for many years. She would
hold one, delicate and warm, in her fingers and
add a few drops of soy sauce and a small piece of
Bretel butter that was imported from France in a
red tin with gold lettering. I was also entitled to
this rice now and then when we visited.

Today, my father prepares this dish for my sons when he's given some Bretel butter by friends coming home from France. My brothers make affectionate fun of my father because he uses the most outrageous superlatives to describe the tinned butter. I agree with him, though. I love the scent of that butter because it reminds me of my paternal grandfather, the one who died with the soldier-firemen.

I also like to use those blue bowls with the silver rims to serve ice cream to my sons. They are the only objects that I wanted from my aunt, the one who was driven out of her house after the death of my paternal grandparents. She became a Buddhist, living in a hut behind a plantation of palm trees, stripped of all material goods but a wooden bed without a mattress, a sandalwood fan and her father's four blue bowls. She hesitated briefly before complying with my request: the bowls symbolized her last attachment to any earthly concerns. She died shortly after my visit to her hut, surrounded by monks from a nearby temple.

I went back to Vietnam to work for three years,
but I never visited my father's birthplace some
two hundred and fifty kilometres from Saigon.
When I was a child, I would vomit the whole
way whenever I made that twelve-hour journey,
even though my mother put pillows on the floor of
the car to keep me still. The roads were riddled with
deep fissures. Communist rebels planted mines by
night and pro-American soldiers cleared them away
by day. Still, sometimes a mine exploded. Then we
had to wait hours for the soldiers to fill in the holes
and gather up the human remains. One day a woman
was torn to pieces, surrounded by yellow squash
blossoms, scattered, fragmented. She must have
been on her way to the market to sell her vegetables.
Maybe they also found the body of her baby by the
roadside. Or not. Maybe her husband had died in
the jungle. Maybe she was the woman who had
lost her lover outside the house of my maternal
grandfather, the prefect.

One day when we were deep inside the darkness
of a cube van on our way to pick strawberries
or beans, my mother told me about a woman, a day
labourer, who would wait for her employer across
from my maternal grandfather's place every morning.
And every morning my grandfather's gardener
brought her a portion of sticky rice wrapped in a
banana leaf. Every morning, standing in the truck
that was taking her to the rubber trees, she watched
the gardener move away in the middle of the
bougainvillea garden. One morning she didn't
see him cross the dirt road to bring her breakfast.
Then another morning . . . and another. One night
she gave my mother a sheet of paper darkened with
question marks, nothing else. My mother never saw
her again in the truck jam-packed with workers.
That young girl never went back to the plantations
or to the bougainvillea garden. She disappeared not
knowing that the gardener had asked his parents in
vain for permission to marry her. No one told her
that my grandfather had accepted the request of the
gardener's parents to send him to another town.
No one told her that the gardener, her own love,
had been forced to go away, unable to leave her
a letter because she was illiterate, because she
was a young woman travelling in the company
of men, because her skin had been burned too
dark by the sun.

Madame Girard had the same burned skin even though she didn't work in the strawberry fields or the plantations. Madame Girard had hired my mother to clean her house, not knowing that my mother had never held a broom in her hands before her first day on the job. Madame Girard was a platinum blonde like Marilyn Monroe, with blue, blue eyes, and Monsieur Girard, a tall, brown-haired man, was the proud owner of a sparkling antique car. They often invited us to their white house with its perfectly mown lawn and flowers lining the entrance and a carpet in every room. They were the personification of our American dream.

Their daughter invited me to her roller skating competitions. She passed on to me her dresses that had become too small, one of them a blue cotton sundress with tiny white flowers and two straps that tied on the shoulder. I wore it during the summer, but also in winter over a white turtleneck. During our first winters, we didn't know that every garment had its season, that we mustn't simply wear all the clothes we owned. When we were cold, without discriminating, without knowing the different categories, we would put one garment over another, layer by layer, like the homeless.

My father tracked down Monsieur Girard thirty years later. He no longer lived in the same house, his wife had left him and his daughter was on sabbatical, in search of a purpose, a life. When my father brought me this news, I almost felt guilty. I wondered if we hadn't unintentionally stolen Monsieur Girard's American dream from having wanted it too badly.

I also got back together with my first friend, Johanne, thirty years later. She didn't recognize me, neither on the phone nor in person, because she had known me as deaf and mute. We'd never spoken. She didn't really remember that she'd wanted to become a surgeon, even though I had always told my high school guidance counsellors that I was interested in surgery, like Johanne.

The guidance counsellors would call me into their offices every year because there was a glaring gap between my grades and the results of my IQ tests, which bordered on deficient. How could I not find the intruder in the series "syringe, scalpel, skull, drill" when I could recite by heart a passage about Jacques Cartier? I only mastered what had been specifically taught to me, passed on to me, offered to me. Which is why I understood the word *surgeon* but not *darling* or *tanning salon* or *horseback riding*. I could sing the national anthem but not "The Chicken Dance" or the birthday song. I accumulated knowledge at random, like my son Henri, who can pronounce *poire* but not *maman*, because the course of our learning was atypical, full of detours and snags, with no gradation, no logic. I shaped my dreams in the same way, through meetings, friends, other people.

For many immigrants, the American dream has come true. Some thirty years ago, in Washington, Quebec City, Boston, Rimouski or Toronto, we would pass through whole neighbourhoods strewn with rose gardens, hundred-year-old trees, stone houses, but the address we were looking for never appeared on one of those doors. Nowadays, my aunt Six and her husband, Step-uncle Six, live in one of those houses. They travel first class and have to stick a sign on the back of their seat so the hostesses will stop offering them chocolates and champagne. Thirty years ago, in our Malaysian refugee camp, the same Step-uncle Six crawled more slowly than his eight-month-old daughter because he was suffering from malnutrition. And the same Aunt Six used the one needle she had to sew clothes so she could buy milk for her daughter. Thirty years ago, we lived in the dark with them, with no electricity, no running water, no privacy. Today, we complain that their house is too big and our extended family too small to experience the same intensity of the festivities—which lasted until dawn—when we used to get together at my parents' place during our first years in North America.

There were twenty-five of us, sometimes thirty, arriving in Montreal from Fanwood, Montpelier, Springfield, Guelph, coming together in a small, three-bedroom apartment for the entire Christmas holiday. Anyone who wanted to sleep alone had to move into the bathtub. Inevitably, conversations, laughter and quarrels went on all night. Every gift we offered was a genuine gift, because it represented a sacrifice and it answered a need, a desire or a dream. We were well acquainted with the dreams of our nearest and dearest: those with whom we were packed in tightly for nights at a time. Back then, we all had the same dreams. For a long time, we were obliged to have the same one, the American dream.

When I turned fifteen, my aunt Six, who at the time was working in a chicken processing plant, gave me a square aluminum tin of tea that had images of Chinese spirits, cherry trees and clouds in red, gold and black. Aunt Six had written on each of ten pieces of paper, folded in two and placed in the tea, the name of a profession, an occupation, a dream that she had for me: journalist, cabinetmaker, diplomat, lawyer, fashion designer, flight attendant, writer, humanitarian worker, director, politician. It was thanks to that gift that I learned there were other professions than medicine, that I was allowed to dream my own dreams.

O nce it's achieved, though, the American dream
never leaves us, like a graft or an excrescence.
The first time I carried a briefcase, the first time
I went to a restaurant school for young adults in
Hanoi, wearing heels and a straight skirt, the waiter
for my table didn't understand why I was speaking
Vietnamese with him. At first I thought
that he couldn't understand my southern accent.
At the end of the meal, though, he explained
ingenuously that I was too fat to be Vietnamese.

I translated that remark to my employers, who
laugh about it to this day. I understood later that
he was talking not about my forty-five kilos but
about the American dream that had made me
more substantial, heavier, weightier. That
American dream had given confidence to my
voice, determination to my actions, precision
to my desires, speed to my gait and strength to
my gaze. That American dream made me believe
I could have everything, that I could go around in
a chauffeur-driven car while estimating the weight
of the squash being carried on a rusty bicycle by a
woman with eyes blurred by sweat; that I could dance
to the same rhythm as the girls who swayed their hips
at the bar to dazzle men whose thick billfolds were
swollen with American dollars; that I could live in the
grand villa of an expatriate and accompany barefoot
children to their school that sat right on the sidewalk,
where two streets intersected.

But the young waiter reminded me that I couldn't have everything, that I no longer had the right to declare I was Vietnamese because I no longer had their fragility, their uncertainty, their fears. And he was right to remind me.

Around that time, my employer, who was based in Quebec, clipped an article from a Montreal paper reiterating that the "Québécois nation" was Caucasian, that my slanting eyes automatically placed me in a separate category, even though Quebec had given me my American dream, even though it had cradled me for thirty years. Whom to like, then? No one or everyone? I chose to like the gentleman from Saint-Félicien who asked me in English to grant him a dance. "Follow the guy," he told me. I also like the rickshaw driver in Da Nang who asked me how much I was paid as an escort for my "white" husband. And I often think about the woman who sold cakes of tofu for five cents each, sitting on the ground in a hidden corner of the market in Hanoi, who told her neighbours that I was from Japan, that I was making good progress with my Vietnamese.

She was right. I had to relearn my mother tongue, which I'd given up too soon. In any case, I hadn't really mastered it completely because the country was divided in two when I was born. I come from the South, so I had never heard people from the North until I went back to Vietnam. Similarly, people in the North had never heard people from the South before reunification. Like Canada, Vietnam had its own two solitudes. The language of North Vietnam had developed in accordance with its political, social and economic situation at the time, with words to describe

how to shoot down an airplane with a machine gun
set up on a roof, how to use monosodium glutamate
to make blood clot more quickly, how to spot the
shelters when the sirens go off. Meanwhile, the
language of the South had created words to express
the sensation of Coca-Cola bubbles on the tongue,
terms for naming spies, rebels, Communist
sympathizers on the streets of the South, names
to designate the children born from wild nights
with GIs.

I t was thanks to the GIs that my step-uncle Six was able to buy his own passage and those of his wife, my aunt Six, and his very small daughter on the same boat as us. The parents of that step-uncle became very rich thanks to ice. American soldiers would buy entire blocks one metre long and twenty centimetres wide and thick to put under their beds. They needed to cool down after weeks of sweating with fear in the Vietnamese jungle. They needed human comfort, but without feeling the heat of their own bodies or of women rented by the hour. They needed the cool breezes of Vermont or Montana. They needed that coolness so they could stop suspecting, for a moment, that a grenade was hidden in the hands of every child who touched the hair on their arms. They needed that cold so as not to give way to all those full lips murmuring false words of love into their ears, to drive away the cries of their comrades with mutilated bodies. They needed to be cold to leave the women who were carrying their children without ever returning to see them again, without ever revealing their last names.

M ost of those children of GIs became orphans, homeless, ostracized not only because of their mothers' profession but also because of their fathers'. They were the hidden side of the war. Thirty years after the last GI had left, the United States went back to Vietnam in place of their soldiers to rehabilitate those damaged children. The government granted them a whole new identity to erase the one that had been tarnished. A number of those children now had, for the first time, an address, a residence, a full life. Some, though, were unable to adapt to such wealth.

Once, when I was working as an interpreter for the New York police, I met one of those children, now adult. She was illiterate, wandering the streets of the Bronx. She'd come to Manhattan on a bus from a place she couldn't name. She hoped that the bus would take her back to her bed made of cardboard boxes, just outside the post office in Saigon. She declared insistently that she was Vietnamese. Even though she had café au lait skin, thick wavy hair, African blood, deep scars, she was Vietnamese, only Vietnamese, she repeated incessantly. She begged me to translate for the policeman her desire to go back to her own jungle. But the policeman could only release her into the jungle of the Bronx. Had I been able to, I would have asked her to curl up against me. Had I been able to, I'd have erased every trace of dirty hands from her body. I was the same age as her. No, I don't

have the right to say that I was the same age as her:
her age was measured in the number of stars she
saw when she was being beaten and not in years,
months, days.

At times, the memory of that girl still haunts me. I wonder what her chances of survival were in the city of New York. Or if she is still there. Whether the policeman thinks about her as often as I do. Perhaps my step-uncle Six, who has a doctorate in statistics from Princeton, could calculate the number of risks and obstacles she has faced.

I often ask that step-uncle to do the calculation, even if he has never calculated the miles travelled every morning for one whole summer to take me to my English lessons, or the quantity of books he bought me or the number of dreams he and his wife have created for me. I allow myself to ask him many things. But I've never dared to ask if it was possible for him to calculate the probability of survival for Monsieur An.

Monsieur An arrived in Granby on the same bus as our family. In winter and summer alike, Monsieur An stood with his back against the wall, and one foot on the low railing, holding a cigarette. He was our next-door neighbour. For a long time, I thought he was mute. If I ran into him today, I would say that he's autistic. One day his foot slipped on the morning dew. And bang, he was spread out on his back. BANG! He cried out "BANG!" several times, then burst out laughing. I knelt down to help him get up. He leaned against me, holding my arms, but didn't get up. He was crying. He kept crying and crying, then stopped suddenly, and turned my face towards the sky. He asked me what colour I saw. Blue. Then he raised his thumb and pointed his index finger towards my temple, asking me again if the sky was still blue.

B efore Monsieur An's job was to clean the floor
of the rubber-boot plant in Granby, he'd been
a judge, a professor, graduate of an American
university, father and prisoner. Between the heat
in his Saigon courtroom and the smell of rubber,
for two years he had been accused of being a judge,
of sentencing Communist countrymen. In the
re-education camp, it was his turn to be judged,
to position himself in the ranks every morning
with hundreds of others who'd also been on the
losing side in the war.

That camp surrounded by jungle was a retreat for
the prisoners to assess and formulate self-criticisms,
depending on their status—counter-revolutionary;
traitor to the nation; collaborator with the
Americans—and to meditate on their redemption
while felling trees, planting corn, clearing fields
of mines.

The days followed one another like the links
of a chain—the first fastened around their necks,
the last to the centre of the earth. One morning,
Monsieur An felt his chain getting shorter when
the soldiers took him out of the ranks and made
him kneel in the mud before the fleeting, frightened,
empty gazes of his former colleagues, their bodies
barely covered with rags and skin. He told me that
when the hot metal of the pistol touched his temple,
in one last act of rebellion he raised his head to look
at the sky. For the first time, he could see shades of

blue, all equally intense. Together, they dazzled him
almost to the point of blindness. At the same time,
he could hear the click of the trigger drop into silence.
No sound, no explosion, no blood, only sweat.
That night, the shades of blue that he'd seen earlier
filed past his eyes like a film being screened over
and over.

He survived. The sky had cut his chain, had
saved him, freed him, while some of the others were
suffocated to death, dried up in containers without
having a chance to count the blues of the sky. Every
day, then, he set himself the task of listing those
colours—for the others.

M onsieur An taught me about nuance.
Monsieur Minh gave me the urge to write.
I met Monsieur Minh on a red vinyl bench in a
Chinese restaurant on Côte-des-Neiges where my
father worked as a delivery man. I did my homework
while I waited for the end of his shift. Monsieur Minh
made notes for him about one-way streets, private
addresses, clients to avoid. He was preparing to
become a delivery man just as seriously, just as
enthusiastically, as he'd studied French literature
at the Sorbonne. He was saved not by the sky but by
writing. He had written a number of books during
his time in the re-education camp—always on the
one piece of paper he possessed, page by page,
chapter by chapter, an unending story. Without
writing, he wouldn't have heard the snow melting
or leaves growing or clouds sailing through the sky.
Nor would he have seen the dead end of a thought,
the remains of a star or the texture of a comma.
Nights when he was in his kitchen painting wooden
ducks, Canada geese, loons, mallards, following
the colour scheme provided by his other employer,
he would recite for me the words in his personal
dictionary: nummular, moan, quadraphony, *in
extremis*, sacculina, logarithmic, hemorrhage—like
a mantra, like a march towards the void.

E ach of us had been saved in a different way during Vietnam's peacetime or postwar period. My own family was saved by Anh Phi.

It was Anh Phi, teenage son of a friend of my parents, who found the pack of gold taels my father had flung from our third-floor balcony during the night. The day before, my parents had told me to pull on the bit of rope that ran alongside the corridor if one of the ten soldiers living in our house should come up to our floor. My parents had spent hours in the bathroom clearing out the thin gold sheets and the diamonds hidden under the tiny pink and black tiles. Then they wrapped them carefully in several layers of brown paper bags before throwing them into the dark. The package had landed as expected in the debris of the demolished house that once belonged to the former neighbour across the way.

At that time, children had to plant trees as a sign of gratitude towards our spiritual leader, Ho Chi Minh, and they also had to retrieve undamaged bricks from demolition sites. My search through the debris for the package of gold therefore roused no suspicions. But I had to be careful, because one of the soldiers at our house was assigned to keep an eye on where we went and whom we were with. Knowing that I was being watched, I walked across the site too quickly and couldn't find the package, not even after a second try. My parents asked Anh Phi to take a look. After his search, he took off with a bag full of bricks.

The package of gold taels was returned to my parents a few days later. Subsequently, they gave it to the organizer of our sea-bound escape. All the taels were there. During this chaotic peacetime, it was the norm for hunger to replace reason, for uncertainty to usurp morality, but the reverse was rarely true. Anh Phi and his mother were the exception. They became our heroes.

To tell the truth, Anh Phi had been my hero long before he handed over the two and a half kilos of gold to my parents, because whenever I visited him, he would sit with me on his doorstep and make a candy appear from behind my ear instead of urging me to play with the other children.

My first journey on my own, without my parents, was to Texas, to see Anh Phi again and this time give him a candy. We were sitting side by side on the floor against his single bed in the university residence when I asked him why he'd given the package of gold back to my parents, when his widowed mother had to mix their rice with barley, sorghum and corn to feed him and his three brothers. Why that heroically honest deed? He told me, laughing and hitting me repeatedly with his pillow, that he wanted my parents to be able to pay for our passage because otherwise he wouldn't have a little girl to tease. He was still a hero, a true hero, because he couldn't help being one, because he is a hero without knowing it, without wanting to be.

I wanted to be a heroine to the young girl selling grilled pork outside the walls of the Buddhist temple across from the office in Hanoi. She spoke very little, was always working, absorbed in the slices of pork she was cutting then putting into the dozens of baguettes she'd already split down three-quarters of their length. It was hard to see her face once the coal had been kindled in the metal box blackened by grease accumulated over the years, because a cloud of smoke and ash enveloped her, suffocated her, made her eyes water. Her brother-in-law served the customers and washed the dishes in two pots of water set on the very edge of the sidewalk, beside an open sewer. She must have been fifteen or sixteen, and was stunningly beautiful despite her misty eyes and her cheeks smeared with ashes and soot.

One day her hair caught fire, burning part of her polyester shirt before her brother-in-law had time to pour the dirty dishwater over her head. She was covered with lettuce, slices of green papaya, hot peppers, fish sauce. I went to see her before lunch the next day to offer her work cleaning the office and to suggest that she sign up for a cooking class and English lessons. I was sure I would be granting her fondest dream. But she refused, refused all of it, by simply shaking her head. I left Hanoi, abandoning her to her bit of sidewalk, unable to make her turn her gaze towards a horizon without smoke, unable to become a hero like Anh Phi, like many people who have been identified, named and designated heroes in Vietnam.

P eace born from the mouths of cannon
inevitably gives birth to hundreds, to thousands
of anecdotes about the brave, about heroes. During
the first years after the Communist victory, there
weren't enough pages in the history books to fit in
all the heroes, so they were lodged in math books:
if Comrade Công downed two airplanes a day,
how many did he shoot down in a week?

We no longer learned to count with bananas and
pineapples. The classroom was turned into a huge
game of Risk, with calculations of dead, wounded or
imprisoned soldiers and patriotic victories, grandiose
and colourful. The colours, though, were illustrated
only with words. Pictures were monochromatic,
like the people, perhaps to stop us from forgetting
the dark side of reality. We all had to wear black
pants and dark shirts. If not, soldiers in khaki
uniforms would take us to the station for a session
of interrogation and re-education. They also arrested
girls who used blue eyeshadow. They thought
these girls had black eyes, that they were victims
of capitalist violence. Perhaps for that reason they
removed the sky blue from the first Vietnamese
Communist flag.

When my husband wore his red T-shirt with a yellow star in the streets of Montreal, the Vietnamese harassed him. Later my parents had him take it off and replaced it with an ill-fitting shirt of my father's. Even though I could never have worn such a thing myself, I hadn't told my husband not to buy it because I myself had once proudly tied a red scarf around my neck. I had made that symbol of Communist youth part of my wardrobe. I even envied friends who had the words *Cháu ngoan Bác Hồ* embroidered in yellow on the triangle that jutted out from the neckline. They were the "beloved children of the party," a status I could never attain because of my family background, even though I stood first in my class or had planted the most trees while thinking about the father of our peace. Every classroom, every office, every house was supposed to have at least one photo of Ho Chi Minh on the walls. His photo even displaced those of ancestors that no one had ever dared to touch before because they were sacred. The ancestors—though they may have been gamblers, incompetent or violent—all became respectable and untouchable once they were dead, once they'd been placed on the altar with incense, fruits, tea. The altars had to be high enough so that the ancestors looked down on us. All descendants had to carry their ancestors not in their hearts but above their heads.

J ust recently in Montreal, I saw a Vietnamese grandmother ask her one-year-old grandson: *"Thương Bà để đâu?"* I can't translate that phrase, which contains just four words, two of them verbs, *to love* and *to carry*. Literally, it means, "Love grandmother carry where?" The child touched his head with his hand. I had completely forgotten that gesture, which I'd performed a thousand times when I was small. I'd forgotten that love comes from the head and not the heart. Of the entire body, only the head matters. Merely touching the head of a Vietnamese person insults not just him but his entire family tree. That is why a shy Vietnamese eight-year-old turned into a raging tiger when his Québécois teammate rubbed the top of his head to congratulate him for catching his first football.

If a mark of affection can sometimes be taken for an insult, perhaps the gesture of love is not universal: it too must be translated from one language to another, must be learned. In the case of Vietnamese, it is possible to classify, to quantify the meaning of love through specific words: to love by taste (*thích*); to love without being in love (*thương*); to love passionately (*yêu*); to love ecstatically (*mê*); to love blindly (*mù quáng*); to love gratefully (*tình nghĩa*). It's impossible quite simply to love, to love without one's head.

I am lucky that I've learned to savour the pleasure of resting my head in a hand, and my parents are

lucky to be able to capture the love of my children
when the little ones drop kisses into their hair,
spontaneously, with no formality, during a session
of tickling in bed. I myself have touched my father's
head only once. He had ordered me to lean on it as
I stepped over the handrail of the boat.

We didn't know where we were. We had landed on the first terra firma. As we were making our way to the beach, an Asian man in light blue boxer shorts came running towards our boat. He told us in Vietnamese to disembark and destroy the boat. Was he Vietnamese? Were we back at our starting point after four days at sea? I don't think anyone asked, because we all jumped into the water as if we were an army being deployed. The man disappeared into this chaos, for good. I don't know why I've held on to such a clear image of that man running in the water, arms waving, fist punching the air with an urgent cry that the wind didn't carry to me. I remember that image with as much precision and clarity as the one of Bo Derek running out of the water in her flesh-coloured bathing suit. Yet I saw that man only once, for a fraction of a second, unlike the poster of Bo Derek, which I would come upon every day for months.

Everyone on deck saw him. But no one dared confirm it with certainty. He may have been one of the dead who had seen the local authorities drive the boats back to the sea. Or a ghost whose duty it was to save us, so he could gain his own access to paradise. He may have been a schizophrenic Malaysian. Or maybe a tourist from a Club Med who wanted to break the monotony of his vacation.

M ost likely he was a tourist, because we landed on a beach that was protected because of its turtle population, and it was close to the site of a Club Med. In fact, this beach had once been part of a Club Med, because their beachside bar still existed. We slept there every day against the backdrop of the bar's wall, which was inscribed with the names of Vietnamese people who'd stopped by, who had survived like us. If we'd waited fifteen minutes longer before berthing, our feet wouldn't have been wedged in the fine golden sand of this heavenly beach. Our boat was completely destroyed by the waves created by an ordinary rain that fell immediately after we disembarked. More than two hundred of us watched in silence, eyes misty from rain and astonishment. The wooden planks skipped one at a time on the crest of the waves, like a synchronized swimming routine. I'm positive that for one brief moment the sight made believers of us all. Except one man. He'd retraced his steps to fetch the gold taels he'd hidden in the boat's fuel tank. He never came back. Perhaps the taels made him sink, perhaps they were too heavy to carry. Or else the current swallowed him as punishment for looking back, or to remind us that we must never regret what we've left behind.

That memory definitely explains why I never leave a place with more than one suitcase. I take only books. Nothing else can become truly mine. I sleep just as well in a hotel room, a guest room or a stranger's bed as in my own. In fact, I'm always glad to move; it gives me a chance to lighten my belongings, to leave objects behind so that my memory can become truly selective, can remember only images that stay luminous behind my closed eyelids. I prefer to remember the flutters in my stomach, my light-headedness, my upheavals, my hesitations, my lapses . . . I prefer them because I can shape them according to the colour of time, whereas an object remains inflexible, frozen, unwieldy.

I love men in the same way, without wanting them to be mine. That way, I am one among others, without a role to play, without existing. I don't need their presence because I don't miss those who are absent. They're always replaced or replaceable. If they're not, my feelings for them are. For that reason, I prefer married men, their hands dressed in gold rings. I like those hands on my body, on my breasts. I like them because, despite the mixture of odours, despite the dampness of their skin on mine, despite the occasional euphoria, those ring fingers with their histories keep me remote, aloof, in the shadows.

I forget the details of how I felt during these encounters. I do remember fleeting gestures, such as Guillaume's finger brushing against my left baby toe to write his initial G; the drop of sweat from Mikhaïl's chin falling onto my first lumbar vertebra; the cavity at the bottom of Simon's breastbone, Simon who told me that if I murmured into the well of his *pectus excavatum*, my words would resonate all the way to his heart.

Over the years, I've collected a fluttering eyelash from one, a stray lock of hair from another, lessons from some, silences from several, an afternoon here, an idea there—to form just one lover, because I've neglected to memorize the face of each one. Together, these men taught me how to become a lover, how to be in love, how to long for an amorous state. It's my children, though, who have taught me the verb *to love*, who have defined it. If I had known what it meant to love, I wouldn't have had children, because once we love, we love forever, like Uncle Two's wife, Step-aunt Two, who can't stop loving her gambler son, the son who is burning up the family fortune like a pyromaniac.

When I was younger, I saw Step-aunt Two
prostrate herself before Buddha, before
Jesus, before her son, to plead with him not to go
away for months at a time, not to come back from
those months of absence escorted by men holding
a knife to his throat. Before I became a mother,
I couldn't understand how she, a businesswoman
with clenched fists, keen eyes, a sharp tongue,
could believe all the lying tales and promises of
her gambler son. During my recent visit to Saigon,
she told me she must have been a serious criminal
in her former life, if she was obliged, in this life,
to constantly believe the deceptions of her son.
She wanted to stop loving. She was tired of loving.

Because I had become a mother, I lied to her too by
remaining silent about the night her son took my
child's hand and wrapped it around his adolescent
penis, and about the night when he slipped inside
the mosquito net of Aunt Seven, the one who is
mentally retarded, defenceless. I shut my mouth
to keep my aging, worn-out step-aunt Two from
dying because she had loved so much.

Aunt Seven is my maternal grandmother's sixth child. Her number, seven, didn't bring the good luck it was supposed to. When I was a child, Aunt Seven sometimes waited for me at the door holding a wooden spatula, ready to hit me as hard as she could to drive out the heat that was stored in her body. She was always hot. She needed to cry out, to fling herself onto the floor, to let off steam by hitting. As soon as she started howling, all the servants ran through the house, leaving their bucket of water, their knife, their kettle, their dust cloth, their broom along the way, and came to hold her down. To this tumult were added the cries of my grandmother, my mother, my other aunts, their children and my own. We were a twenty-voice choir nearly hysterical, nearly mad. After a while we no longer knew why we were howling, because the original cry, Aunt Seven's, had been muffled by our own noise for so long. But everyone went on crying, taking advantage of the opportunity to do so.

Sometimes, instead of waiting for me at the door, Aunt Seven would open it after stealing the keys from my grandmother. She would open it so she could leave us and end up at large in the alleyways, where her handicap wasn't visible, or was at least ignored. Some ignored her handicap by accepting her twenty-four-carat-gold necklace in exchange for a piece of guava, or by having sex with her in exchange for a compliment. Some even hoped that she would become pregnant so they could make the baby the object of blackmail. At that time, my aunt and I were the same mental age, we were friends who told each other what scared us. We shared our stories. Today, my handicapped aunt thinks of me as an adult, so she doesn't tell me about her escapes or her old stories from the alleyways.

I too dreamed of being outside, playing hopscotch with the neighbourhood children. I envied them through the wrought iron grilles over our windows or from our balconies. Our house was surrounded by cement walls two metres high with shards of broken glass embedded in them to discourage intruders. From where I stood, it was hard to say if the wall existed to protect us or to remove our access to life.

The alleys were swarming with children skipping, with ropes braided out of hundreds of multicoloured rubber bands. My favourite toy wasn't a doll that said, "I love you." My dream toy was a small wooden chair with a built-in drawer where the street vendors kept their money, and also the two big baskets they carried at either end of a long bamboo pole balanced on their shoulders. These women sold all kinds of soups. They walked between the two weights: on one side, a large cauldron of broth and a coal fire to keep it hot; on the other, the bowls, chopsticks, rice noodles and condiments. Sometimes the vendor might even have a baby hanging from her back. Each merchant advertised her wares with a particular melody.

Years later, in Hanoi a French friend of mine would get up at five in the morning to record their songs. He told me that before long those sounds would no longer be heard on the streets, that those strolling merchants would give up their baskets for factory work. So he would safeguard their voices reverently and ask me to translate them along the way, then he would list them by category: merchants selling soup, selling cream of soya, buyers of glass for recycling, knife-grinders, masseurs for men, bread-sellers . . . We spent whole afternoons working on translations. With my friend, I learned that music comes from the voice, the rhythm and the heart of each person, and that the musicality of those unrecorded melodies could lift the curtain of fog, pass through windows and screens to waken us as gently as a morning lullaby.

He had to get up early to record them because the soups were sold mainly in the morning. Each soup had its own vermicelli: round ones with beef, small and flat with pork and shrimp, transparent with chicken . . . Each woman had her specialty and her route. When Marie-France, my teacher in Granby, asked me to describe my breakfast, I told her: soup, vermicelli, pork. She asked me again, more than once, miming waking up, rubbing her eyes and stretching. But my reply was the same, with a slight variation: rice instead of vermicelli. The other Vietnamese children gave similar descriptions. She called home then to check

the accuracy of our answers with our parents.
As time went on, we no longer started our day
with soup and rice. To this day, I haven't found
a substitute. So it's very rare that I have breakfast.

I went back to having soup for breakfast when
I was pregnant with my son Pascal, in Vietnam.
I didn't crave pickles or peanut butter, just a bowl
of soup with vermicelli purchased on a street corner.
Throughout my childhood, my grandmother forbade
us to eat those soups because the bowls were washed
in a tiny bucket of water. It was impossible for the
vendors to carry water on their shoulders as well as
the broth and the bowls. Whenever it was possible,
they would ask people for some clean water. As a
small child, I often waited for them at the fence near
the kitchen door with fresh water for their buckets.
I would have traded my blue-eyed doll for their
wooden chairs. I should have suggested it, because
today they've been replaced by plastic chairs, which
are lighter, don't have a built-in drawer, and don't
show the traces of fatigue and wear in their grain
as wooden benches do. The merchants stepped
into the modern era still carrying the weight of the
yoke on their shoulders.

The trace of the red and yellow stripes of a Pom sandwich-bread bag is burned into one side of our first toaster. Our sponsors in Granby had placed that small appliance at the top of the list of essentials to buy when we moved into our first apartment. For years we lugged that toaster from one place to the next without ever using it, because our breakfast was rice, soup, leftovers from the night before. Quietly, we started eating Rice Krispies, without milk. My brothers followed this with toast and jam. Every morning for twenty years, without exception, the youngest breakfasted on two slices of sandwich bread with butter and strawberry jam, no matter where he was posted—New York, New Delhi, Moscow or Saigon. His Vietnamese maid tried to make him change his habits by offering him steaming balls of sticky rice covered with freshly grated coconut, roasted sesame seeds and peanuts crushed in a mortar, or a piece of warm baguette with ham spread with homemade mayonnaise, or pâté de foie decorated with a sprig of coriander . . . He brushed them all aside and went back to his sandwich bread, which he kept in the freezer. During my latest visit to him I discovered that he keeps our old stained toaster in a cupboard. It's the only trinket he has carted with him from country to country as if it were an anchor, or the memory of dropping the first anchor.

I discovered my own anchor when I went to meet Guillaume at Hanoi airport. The scent of Bounce fabric softener on his T-shirt made me cry. For two weeks I slept with a piece of Guillaume's clothing on my pillow. Guillaume, for his part, was dazzled by the scent of jackfruit, kumquats, durians, carambola, of bitter melons, field crabs, dried shrimp, of lilies, lotus and herbs. Several times he went to the night market where vegetables, fruit and flowers were traded back and forth between the baskets of the vendors negotiating among themselves in a noisy but controlled chaos, as if they were on the floor of the Stock Exchange. I would go to this night market with Guillaume, always with one of his pullovers over my shirt because I'd discovered that my home could be summed up as an ordinary, simple odour from my daily North American life. I had no street address of my own, I lived in an office apartment in Hanoi. My books were stored at Aunt Eight's place, my diplomas at my parents' in Montreal, my photos at my brothers', my winter coats with my former roommate. I realized for the first time that Bounce, the smell of Bounce, had given me my first attack of homesickness.

During my early years in Quebec, my clothes smelled of damp or of food because after they were washed they were hung up in our bedrooms on lines strung from wall to wall. At night, every night, my last image was of colours suspended across the room like Tibetan prayer flags. For years I inhaled the scent of fabric softener on my classmates' clothes when the wind carried it to me. I happily breathed in the bags of used clothes we received. It was the only smell I wanted.

Guillaume left Hanoi after staying with me for two weeks. He had no clean clothes to leave me. Over the following months, I received in the mail now and then a tightly sealed plastic envelope with a freshly dried handkerchief inside, smelling of Bounce. The last package he sent me contained a plane ticket for Paris. When I arrived, he was waiting to take me to an appointment with a perfumer. He wanted me to smell a violet leaf, an iris, blue cypress, vanilla, lovage . . . and, most of all, everlasting, an aroma of which Napoleon said smelled of his country before he even set foot on it. Guillaume wanted me to find an aroma that would give me my country, my world.

I've never worn any other perfume than the one
that was created for me at Guillaume's request
during that trip to Paris. It replaced Bounce. It speaks
for me and reminds me that I exist. One of my
roommates spent several years studying theology
and archaeology in order to understand who our
creator is, who we are, why we exist. Every night,
she came back to the apartment not with answers but
with new questions. I never had any questions except
the one about the moment when I could die. I should
have chosen the moment before the arrival of my
children, for since then I've lost the option of dying.
The sharp smell of their sun-baked hair, the smell
of sweat on their backs when they wake from a
nightmare, the dusty smell of their hands when they
leave a classroom, meant that I have to live, to be
dazzled by the shadow of their eyelashes, moved by
a snowflake, bowled over by a tear on their cheek.
My children have given me the exclusive power
to blow on a wound to make the pain disappear, to
understand words unpronounced, to possess the
universal truth, to be a fairy. A fairy smitten with
the way they smell.

Wyatt was smitten with the *ao dài* because that outfit makes women's bodies look gorgeously delicate and tremendously romantic. One day he took me to a grand villa hidden behind rows of kiosks built on the ground where the garden had once stood. The villa was home to two aging sisters who were quietly selling off their furniture to collectors to ensure their day-to-day survival. Wyatt was their most faithful customer, so we were invited to recline on a big mahogany daybed like the one my paternal grandfather had, resting our heads on the ceramic cushions where opium smokers once lay. The owner brought us tea and slices of candied ginger. A slight breeze lifted the tails of her *ao dài* when she bent over to set the cups between Wyatt and me. Although she was sixty years old, the sensuality of her *ao dài* touched us. The one square centimetre of skin that was revealed mocked the ravages of time: it still made our hearts leap. Wyatt said that the diminutive space was his golden triangle, his isle of happiness, his own private Vietnam. Between sips of tea he whispered: "It stirs my soul."

When soldiers from the North arrived in Saigon, they too were stirred by that triangle of skin. They were troubled by the schoolgirls in white *ao dàis*, bursting out of their school like butterflies in spring. And so wearing the *ao dài* was soon forbidden. It was banned because it cast aspersions on the heroism of the women in green kepis who appeared on enormous billboards at every street corner, in khaki shirts with sleeves rolled up on their muscular arms. They were right to banish the outfit. It took three times as long to button it than to take it off. One brisk movement was enough to make the snap fasteners pop open. My grandmother took not three but ten times longer to put on the tunic, because after giving birth to ten children her body had to be sculpted, redrawn with a girdle that had thirty hooks and eyes, to respect the cut of that hypocritically modest and deceptively candid garment.

Today, my grandmother is a very old woman, but still beautiful, lavishly so, like a queen. When she was in her forties, sitting in her parlour in Saigon, she epitomized a whole era of an extreme kind of beauty, of opulence. Every morning a cohort of merchants waited at the door to present their finds to her. Most of them already knew her requirements. They brought new crockery, plastic flowers just arrived from Europe and, inevitably, brassieres for her six daughters. As the country was at war, and the market unstable, it was best to anticipate everything. Sometimes it was diamonds. All the Vietnamese women in our circle had a loupe for examining diamonds. I had learned very young to spot inclusions in diamonds, because it was a skill necessary for dealing with family finances. As the banking system was weak and transitory, women had to master the art of buying and selling gold and diamonds to manage their savings. My grandmother spent days at a time running errands without ever moving. In the midst of the sellers' visits, she also entertained friends or interviewed servants looking for work.

My grandmother's days were filled with these mundane tasks. And while she was a believer, she didn't have time to sit in front of Buddha. After the markets had been cleaned out of merchandise and merchants, after her Communist tenants had taken the contents of her safe and her

lace scarves, she learned to dress in the long
grey kimono worn by the faithful. Despite her
salt-and-pepper hair, which she quite simply
smoothed and tied into a bun just above the nape
of her neck, she was still stunningly beautiful.
She said her prayers at all hours of the day, in the
smoke of incense sticks, waiting for word from
her children who'd gone to sea. She'd let her two
youngest, a boy and a girl, leave with my mother
despite the uncertainty. My mother asked my
grandmother to choose between the risk of losing
her son at sea and that of finding him torn to
shreds in a minefield during his military service
in Cambodia. She had to choose secretly, without
hesitating, without trembling, without perspiring.
Perhaps it was to control her fear that she started to
pray. Perhaps it was to become intoxicated with the
incense smoke that she no longer left the altar.

In Hanoi, I had a neighbour across the street who also prayed every morning, at dawn, for hours. Unlike my grandmother's, though, her windows made of bamboo slats opened directly onto the street. Her mantra and her steady and incessant pounding on her block of wood intruded on the whole neighbourhood. At first I wanted to move, lodge a complaint, even steal her bell and smash it to bits. After a few weeks, though, I stopped cursing the woman because I was haunted by the image of my grandmother.

During the first years of immense upsets, my grandmother sometimes took refuge in temples. She wanted so badly to hide in them that she even allowed Aunt Seven to drive her. Aunt Seven didn't know how to drive a moped, because no one had shown her, and also because she wasn't supposed to leave the house. But the rules had been rewritten since the structural upheaval of her life and of life in general. For my handicapped aunt, that bursting of the family nucleus brought a kind of freedom, as well as an opportunity to grow up. The situation led her to start up the one moped that was left in the courtyard. My grandmother got on, and my aunt began to drive and drive, never changing speed, never stopping, even at red lights. She told me later that when she saw a traffic light she closed her eyes. As for my grandmother, she put her hands on her daughter's shoulders and prayed.

I would have liked Aunt Seven to tell me about how she had given birth while with the nuns. I don't know if she's aware that Aunt Four's adopted son is actually hers. I don't know how I knew. Maybe because the children listened through keyholes without the adults noticing. Or because adults aren't always aware that children are present. The parents didn't need to keep an eye on their children; they counted on the nannies to supervise them. But parents sometimes forgot that the nannies were young girls: they too had urges, they liked to attract the eyes of the chauffeur, the smile of the tailor, they liked to dream for a moment, as they looked at themselves in the mirror, that they too were part of the backdrop reflected there.

I always had nannies, but they sometimes forgot me. And I don't remember any of them, even if I often find them in a corner, out of focus, in the photos from my childhood.

My son Pascal also lost all memory of his nanny, Lek, very soon after we left Bangkok to come home to Montreal. Yet his Thai nanny had been with him seven days a week, twenty-four hours a day, for more than two years, except for a few days' holiday now and then. Lek loved Pascal from the very first moment. She showed him off in the neighbourhood as if he were hers, the most beautiful, the most magnificent. She loved him so much I was afraid she'd forget that inevitably they would separate, that someday we were going to leave her and, sadly, my son might not remember her at all.

Lek knew just a few words of English and I a few words of Thai, but all the same we managed to have long conversations about the residents of my building. The most cinematic image was that of the ninth-floor neighbour, an American in his thirties. One night he came home from work to find his apartment covered with feathers and moss. His pants had been cut in two lengthwise, his sofas ripped open, his tables lacerated by a knife, his curtains torn to shreds. All this damage was the work of the mistress he'd dismissed after three months of service. He shouldn't have exceeded the limit of one month, because the hope of a great love grew in her mind every day, even though she continued to be paid every Friday for her loving. To avoid a disappointment on that scale, perhaps he shouldn't have invited her to all those meals where she smiled without understanding anything,

where she was a decoration for the table, where she
swallowed vichyssoise while intensely craving a salad
of green papaya with bird chilies that tore your mouth
apart, that burned your lips, set fire to your heart.

I 've often asked strangers who came to Asia to
buy love on a one-time basis why, on the morning
after a wild night, they insisted on sharing their meal
with their Vietnamese or Thai mistress. The women
would have preferred to receive the cost of those
meals in cash, so they could buy a pair of shoes for
their mother or a new mattress for their father,
or to send their little brother for English lessons.
Why desire their presence outside of bed when
their vocabulary is limited to conversations that
go on behind closed doors? They told me I didn't
understand a thing. They needed those young girls
for a totally different reason—to restore their youth.
When they looked at those young girls, they saw
their own youth, filled with dreams and possibilities.
The girls gave them something: the illusion that they
hadn't made a mess of their lives, or, at the very least,
the strength and the urge to start over. Without them
they felt disillusioned, sad. Sad at having never
loved enough and having never been loved enough.
Disillusioned because money hadn't brought
them happiness, except in countries where
for five dollars they could obtain an hour of
happiness, or at least some affection, company,
attention. For five dollars they got a clumsily
made-up girl who came for a coffee or a beer
with them and roared with laughter because
the man had just said the Vietnamese word

urinate instead of *pepper*, two words differentiated only by an accent, a tone that is nearly imperceptible to the untrained ear. A single accent for a single moment of happiness.

One night, as I followed into a restaurant a man with a slashed earlobe like that of one of the Communist soldiers who'd lived in my family home in Saigon, I saw through the slit between two panels of a private room six girls lined up against the wall, teetering in their high heels, faces heavily made up, bodies frail, skin shivering, totally naked in the flickering light from the fluorescent tubes. Together, six men took aim at the girls, each with a tightly rolled American hundred-dollar bill, folded in half around a taut rubber band. The bills crossed the smoky room at the crazy speed of projectiles, finally landing on the girls' translucent skin.

D uring my first months in Vietnam, I was very
flattered when people thought I was my boss's
escort, in spite of my designer suit and my high heels,
because it meant that I was still young, slim, fragile.
But after witnessing the scene where the girls had to
bend down to pick up the hundred-dollar bills wadded
at their feet, I stopped feeling flattered out of respect
for them, because behind their dreamy bodies and their
youth, they carried all the invisible weight of Vietnam's
history, like the women with hunched backs.

Like some of the girls whose skin was too delicate,
who couldn't bear the weight, I left before the third
volley. I left the restaurant deafened not by the sound
of clinking glasses but by the imperceptible sound
of the shock of bills against their skin. I left the
restaurant, my head filled with the resonance of
the stoic silence of the girls who'd stayed behind,
who had the strength to strip the money of its power,
becoming untouchable, invincible.

When I meet young girls in Montreal
or elsewhere who injure their bodies
intentionally, deliberately, who want permanent
scars to be drawn on their skin, I can't help secretly
wishing they could meet other young girls whose
permanent scars are so deep they're invisible to the
naked eye. I would like to seat them face to face
and hear them make comparisons between a wanted
scar and an inflicted scar, one that's paid for, the other
that pays off, one visible, the other impenetrable, one
inordinately sensitive, the other unfathomable,
one drawn, the other misshapen.

Aunt Seven also has a scar, on her lower belly, the trace of one of her escapades in the maze of alleys where she inched her way between the vendors of ice and of slippers, between squabbling neighbours, angry women and men with erections. Which of these men was the father of her child? No one dared to question Aunt Seven because they'd had to lie to her during her pregnancy to protect her from her own belly by concealing it under the habit of the nuns at the Couvent des Oiseaux. The nuns called her Josette and showed her how to write her name in large dotted characters. Josette never knew why she was getting so fat or why she woke from a deep sleep to discover that she was thin. She only knew that Aunt Four's adopted son ran away, like her, as soon as he could. He criss-crossed the same alleys at the speed of light, holding his sandals so that his feet would feel the heat of the pavement, the texture of excrement, the sharpness of a piece of broken bottle. He ran all through his childhood. And all through his childhood we other children, young and old, ten, fifteen, even twenty of us, patrolled the neighbourhood every month. One day we all came home empty-handed, as did the servants and the neighbours. He left our lives along the same trail he'd arrived on, leaving as his only souvenir a scar above his mother's pubic area.

My son Henri runs away too. He runs to the St. Lawrence River on the other side of a highway, of a boulevard, a street, a park, another street. He runs to the water where the smooth rhythm and the constant movement of the waves hypnotize him, offer him calm and protection. I've learned to be a shadow in his shadow so I can follow him without upsetting him, without harassing him. Once, though, it took just one second of distraction and I saw him dash in front of the cars, excited and full of life as never before. I was staggered by the juxtaposition of his happiness, so rare, so unexpected, and my own anguish at the thought of his body thrown up in the air above a fender. Should I close my eyes and slow down to avoid witnessing the impact, to survive? Motherhood, my own, afflicted me with a love that vandalized my heart, puffed it up, deflated it and expelled it from my rib cage when I saw my older son, Pascal, show up out of the blue, and fling his brother onto the freshly cut grass of the boulevard median. Pascal landed on his brother like an angel, with chubby little thighs, candy-pink cheeks and a tiny thumb sticking up in the air.

I cried with joy as I took my two sons by the hand, but I cried as well because of the pain of that other Vietnamese mother who witnessed her son's execution. An hour before his death, that boy was running across the rice paddy with the wind in his hair, to deliver messages from one man to another, from one hand to another, from one hiding place to another, to prepare for the revolution, to do his part for the resistance, but also, sometimes, to help send a simple love note on its way.

That son was running with his childhood in his legs. He couldn't see the very real risk of being picked up by soldiers of the enemy camp. He was six years old, maybe seven. He couldn't read yet. All he knew was how to hold tightly in his hands the scrap of paper he'd been given. Once he was captured, though, standing in the midst of rifles pointed at him, he no longer remembered where he was running to, or the name of the person the note was addressed to, or his precise starting point. Panic muted him. Soldiers silenced him. His frail body collapsed on the ground and the soldiers left, chewing their gum. His mother ran across the rice paddy where traces of her son's footprints were still fresh. In spite of the sound of the bullet that had torn space open, the landscape stayed the same. The young rice shoots continued to be cradled by the wind, imperturbable in the face of the brutality of those oversized loves, of the pains too muted for tears to flow, for cries to escape from that mother who gathered up in her old mat the body of her son, half buried in the mud.

R U

—

I held back my cries so as not to distort the hypnotic
sound of the sewing machines standing one
behind the other in my parents' garage. Like my
brothers and me, my cousins sewed after school for
pocket money. With eyes focused on the regular,
rapid movement of the needles, we didn't see one
another, so that very often our conversations were
actually confessions. My cousins were only ten years
old, but they already had a past to recount because
they'd been born into an exhausted Saigon and
had grown up during Vietnam's darkest period.
They described to me, with mocking laughter,
how they had masturbated men in exchange for
a bowl of soup at two thousand dongs. Holding
nothing back, they described those sex acts naturally
and honestly, as people for whom prostitution is
merely a question of adults and money, a matter
that does not involve children six or seven years old
like them, who did it in exchange for a fifteen-cent
meal. I listened to them without turning around,
still sewing, without commenting, because I wanted
to protect the innocence in their words, not tarnish
their candour by my interpretation of the act.
It was certainly thanks to that innocence that
they became engineers after ten years of studies
in Montreal and Sherbrooke.

Coming home after leaving my cousins at the University of Sherbrooke, I was approached in a gas station by a Vietnamese man who had recognized my vaccination scar. One look at that scar took him back in time and let him see himself as a little boy walking to school along a dirt path with his slate under his arm. One look at that scar and he knew that our eyes had already seen the yellow blossoms on the branches of plum trees at the front door of every house at New Year's. One look at that scar brought back to him the delicious aroma of caramelized fish with pepper, simmering in an earthen pot that sat directly on the coals. One look at that scar and our ears heard again the sound produced by the stem of a young bamboo as it sliced the air then lacerated the skin of our backsides. One look at that scar and our tropical roots, transplanted onto land covered with snow, emerged again. In one second we had seen our own ambivalence, our hybrid state: half this, half that, nothing at all and everything at once. A single mark on the skin and our entire shared history was spread out between two gas pumps in a station by a highway exit. He had concealed his scar under a midnight blue dragon. I couldn't see it with my naked eye. He had only to run his finger over my immodestly exhibited scar, however, and take my finger in his other hand and run it over the back of his dragon and immediately we experienced a moment of complicity, of communion.

It was also a moment of communion when my large extended family got together in upstate New York to celebrate my grandmother's eighty-fifth birthday. There were thirty-eight of us, gossiping, giggling, getting on each other's nerves for two days. I noticed then for the first time that I had the same rounded thighs as Aunt Six and that the dress I had on was similar to Aunt Eight's.

Aunt Eight is my big sister, the one who shared with me the thrill of the word *goddess* that a man had whispered in her ear when she was sitting, out of my mother's sight, on the crossbar of his bicycle, encircled by his arms. She is also the one who showed me how to capture the pleasure of a passing desire, of an ephemeral flattery, of a stolen moment.

When my cousin Sao Mai sat behind me and embraced me for the cameras of her two sons, Uncle Nine smiled. Uncle Nine knows me better than I know myself because he bought me my first novel, my first theatre ticket, my first visit to a museum, my first journey.

S ao Mai became an important businesswoman, a public personality, a modern queen after she'd beaten dozens and dozens of eggs by hand—there were power failures five days out of seven in Saigon—to make birthday cakes that she sold to the new Communist leaders. Like an acrobat, she delivered her cakes by bicycle, zigzagging through other bicycles, avoiding the black smoke of motorcycles and the manholes with covers stolen. Today her cakes, and now also her ice cream, pastries, chocolate and coffee, are sold in every neighbourhood in the big cities, criss-crossing the country from south to north.

I am still the shadow of Sao Mai. But I like to be, because during my stay in Vietnam I was the shadow that danced around the bargaining tables to distract those with whom she was dealing while she deliberated. Because I was her shadow, she could confide in me her worries, her fears, her doubts, without compromising herself. Because I was her shadow, I was the only one who dared to enter her private life, which had been tightly sealed since the time when she sold "coffee" made from stale bread burned to a cinder then ground, on the sidewalk across from where she lived, ever since the windows of her house had been sold. Without asking permission, I relit the flames she thought had disappeared behind her now-massive facade. I cleared the way for frivolity by allowing her children to pelt each other with custard pies on my terrace, by putting them in a cardboard box full of confetti outside her room to wish her happy birthday when she woke up, by placing in her briefcase a red leather thong.

I like the red leather of the sofa in the cigar lounge where I dare to strip naked in front of friends and sometimes strangers, without their knowledge. I recount bits of my past as if they were anecdotes or comedy routines or amusing tales from far-off lands featuring exotic landscapes, odd sound effects and exaggerated characterizations. When I sit in that smoky lounge, I forget that I'm one of the Asians who lack the dehydrogenase enzyme for metabolizing alcohol, I forget that I'm marked with a blue spot on my backside, like the Inuit, like my sons, like all those with Asian blood. I forget the mongoloid spot that reveals the genetic memory because it vanished during the early years of childhood, and my emotional memory has been lost, dissolving, snarling with time.

That estrangement, that detachment, that distance allow me to buy, without any qualms and with full awareness of what I'm doing, a pair of shoes whose price in my native land would be enough to feed a family of five for one whole year. The salesperson just has to promise me, *You'll walk on air*, and I buy them. When we're able to float in the air, to separate ourselves from our roots—not only by crossing an ocean and two continents but by distancing ourselves from our condition as stateless refugees, from the empty space of an identity crisis—we can also laugh at whatever might have happened to my acrylic bracelet the colour of the gums on a dental plate, the bracelet my parents had turned into a survival kit by hiding all their diamonds in it. Who would have thought, after we avoided drowning, pirates, dysentery, that today the bracelet could be found perfectly intact, buried in a garbage dump? Who would have thought that burglars would steal from people living in an apartment as miserable as ours? Who would have imagined that thieves would saddle themselves with a ridiculous piece of jewellery made of pink plastic? All the members of my family are convinced that the burglars tossed it aside when they were sorting their haul. So maybe one day, millions of years from now, an archaeologist will wonder why diamonds were arranged in a circle and placed in

the ground. He may interpret it as a religious rite,
and the diamonds as a mysterious offering, like
all those gold taels discovered in amazing quantities
in the depths of the South China Sea.

A bsolutely no one will know the true story of the
pink bracelet once the acrylic has decomposed
into dust, once the years have accumulated in the
thousands, in hundreds of strata, because after
only thirty years I already recognize our old selves
only through fragments, through scars, through
glimmers of light.

In thirty years, Sao Mai resurfaced like a phoenix reborn from its ashes, like Vietnam from its iron curtain and my parents from the toilet bowls they had to scrub. Alone as much as together, all those individuals from my past have shaken the grime off their backs in order to spread their wings with plumage of red and gold, before thrusting themselves sharply towards the great blue space, decorating my children's sky, showing them that one horizon always hides another and it goes on like that to infinity, to the unspeakable beauty of renewal, to intangible rapture. As for me, it is true all the way to the possibility of this book, to the moment when my words glide across the curve of your lips, to the sheets of white paper that put up with my trail, or rather the trail of those who have walked before me, for me. I moved forward in the trace of their footsteps as in a waking dream where the scent of a newly blown poppy is no longer a perfume but a blossoming: where the deep red of a maple leaf in autumn is no longer a colour but a grace; where a country is no longer a place but a lullaby.

And also, where an outstretched hand is no longer a gesture but a moment of love, lasting until sleep, until waking, until everyday life.

A NOTE ABOUT THE TYPE

The body of *Ru* has been set in Granjon, a modern
recutting of a typeface derived from the classic
letterforms of Claude Garamond (1480-1561).
It is named in honour of Robert Granjon, a successful
sixteenth-century French publisher, punch cutter
and founder, and a contemporary of Garamond.

Display text and drop caps are set in Linotype Didot.